LEGACY
Les Cheneaux Islands

- A JILL TRAYNOR NOVEL -

D. ANN KELLEY
JAMES G. KELLEY

Lypton Publishing, Peoria, Illinois

Legacy

First Edition, May 2005
Copyright © 2005
Printed and bound in the United States of America.

Library of Congress Cataloging-in-Publication Data

Kelley, D. Ann & James G. Kelley
Legacy.
1. Fiction 2. Mystery 3. Great Lakes 4. Jill Traynor

ISBN 0-9752780-1-0
LCCN 2004195405
SAN 256-0143

10 9 8 7 6 5 4 3 2 1

Also by

D. Ann Kelley and James G. Kelley

Lighthouse Paradox

Dedicated to...

the greatest teacher that ever roamed the halls
of any campus

Angela Leonard

-JK

and

the professor who showed me a better way
to view the world

M. Heather Carver, Ph. D

-DK

WAYFARER'S MART
Johnswood Road
Drummond Island, Michigan

ARTWORK BY DOUG DIDIA

ACKNOWLEDGMENTS

Legacy was made substantially easier with the knowledge and assistance of several key individuals, whom we offer our sincere thanks.

Mrs. Shirley (Welsh) Howie was kind enough to detail her memories of her father's involvement as Sheriff of Sault Ste. Marie in 1934, when John Dillinger and John Hamilton visited there. Jim Howie, Sheriff Welsh's grandson, provided many hours of his personal research, and sifted through his grandfather's personal papers to provide us with an accurate portrayal of what really happened in 1934.

Josh Husted, of the Birmingham Police Department, and formally of the Kinross District Police Department, explained how the many law enforcement agencies of the eastern Upper Peninsula work together. Any deviances from actual protocol are entirely our responsibility, and carried forward for the purposes of cohesive story-telling.

Willard LaJoie, the Chairman and CEO of Central Savings Bank, as well as James North, the President of First National Bank of St. Ignace, both allowed us to use the real names and locations of the banks in our novel. Mr. LaJoie also informed us on banking practices, and the bank's role in a tourist community.

Linda Hudson, Supervisor of Clark Township and Marti Hart, Chairman of the Les Cheneaux Islands Antique Wooden

Boat Show & Festival of Arts, both provided their insight into Clark Township, the Boat Show, and Les Cheneaux Island culture.

John and Diana Grenier of Up North Studios created the jacket artwork and graphics. They answered many questions, and helped us connect with others in the Les Cheneaux area who were also instrumental. Brian White and MacKenzie Sand of the Quintek Group are responsible for the final jacket design.

Leigh Tye edited the novel.

The Bayliss Library Staff in Sault Ste. Marie were helpful during our research on John Dillinger's life. Paul Brewster connected us to several key individuals, and assisted our research on a number of levels.

Carol Martin allowed us unlimited access to the Wayfarer's Mart building and grounds.

Once again, Susan Kelley gifted us with unending patience, support, exceptional advice and unfailing encouragement. Without her presence in our lives and her contributions to our work, this book would not have been possible.

Last but never least, we deeply appreciate all those who have read or reviewed Lighthouse Paradox, sent us emails, called or stopped by North Haven and the Book Nook on Drummond Island, supported us at book signings, or shared their opinions and encouragement. Your words of thanks and commentary about our first novel, and excitement to see our second novel come to life, is the absolute motivation for us to continue writing, and we would be nowhere without you.

Prologue

Late April, 1964

Our Father who art in Heaven

Hallowed be thy name

Thy kingdom come, thy will be done

There was nothing distinguishing about the silver canister, except for the numbers scratched into its aluminum face. Inside, it held more than the answer to a question: it held the key to a riddle that would haunt the nation for decades, possibly eternity. It wouldn't fetch a five cent piece at a yard sale, but it was clenched in Frank's fist, carried close to his body, as if it held the weight of the world.

Thirty years hadn't changed the Wayfarer's Mart. The tall red painted walls were still graced by the same back porch. Time had treated the building kindly, evidenced by the barely touched surface, newly colored only by the growth of one hardwood tree, crawling up the crimson wall. Branches stretched outward toward the sun, as its leaves caressed the porch. Frank looked with longing at the place he first discovered as a teenager. Darkness cloaked the waterfront, with barely a sliver of the moon casting shadows on the ground. No sign of life blemished the façade of an idea ahead of its time, and certainly ahead of Drummond's. The Wayfarer's Mart was an upscale sporting goods store that catered to an elite clientele, and some claimed, that it was the largest store of its kind in the world. The sign in the window read CLOSED. Frank was unsure if it was closed for the season, or closed forever. Frank hesitated at the door—his journey almost completed.

On Earth, as it is in Heaven

With a deep breath, he opened the door, satisfied to hear it unlatch freely. Avoiding boards that once creaked, and making as little sound as possible, he searched the perimeter of the large, open room until his eyes located the voluminous, ink black safe. Like his first phone number, he never forgot the combination. Kneeling before it, he paused. Eyes driven to the tall ceiling. He searched for a God he abandoned decades ago. Frank waited, listening for the sign he knew would come.

A gust of wind rattled the building around him. His right hand grazed the cold silver knob, spinning the dial first to clear it. Carefully, he rotated the dial clockwise, found the number and spun the dial in reverse. He reached the next digit and slowly turned the dial to the right again, sensing the familiar tension before the final number. He barely heard the almost imperceptible *click*: perhaps the most beautiful sound imaginable.

Give us this day our daily bread

Frank grabbed the handle, pulled down, reveling in the feel of the round bars pulling back within the door, releasing the wall of steel to open. He set the canister on the ground as he ran his hands around the inside base of the safe. He felt each shelf to make sure it was as empty as it looked. One last time, he picked the canister up, felt more weight than existed as the sides of the aluminum seemed to scorch his palms. Gripping it in one hand, he traced the numbers with his finger: 231163, remembering when the old Italian etched it into the face. He allowed the canister to drop from his hands, and as it fell mere inches to the bottom of the safe, Frank clutched his chest, breathing as if for the first time in months. His lungs burned with hellfire stored in his body for the last thirty years, since he first chose the wrong path.

Is she still here? He closed the door, and spun the dial. With his back to the safe, he slid to the floor, tears falling freely from his eyes. *If I could go back and change things... if I had been strong enough to stay...* Sobs heaved through his body, as he longed for a way of life he never lived. What became of her? Shaking his head, grieving deeply, Frank knew he couldn't go back. He couldn't stay on Drummond, and he wouldn't visit anything from his past. In this safe, rests his atonement. This canister held answers that men would dedicate lifetimes to discover, and others would kill to destroy.

Forgive us our trespasses, as we forgive those who trespass against us

It may take years, but Frank knew that eventually the contents would find the light of day, and truth would be revealed. Knees to the ground, hands clenched together, Frank finished his prayer: the first of many.

Lead us not into temptation, but deliver us from evil.

Amen.

One

FUTURE

12:50PM, MONDAY, AUGUST 15TH, 2005
CEDARVILLE, MICHIGAN

"This is a hold up!" Tower boomed in a loud, clear, emotionless voice as he drew the nickel plated .38 caliber revolver from the front pocket of his grey hooded MSU sweatshirt. He pointed the barrel of the gun directly at the first teller, shoving the cold metal against her temple. Standing behind the counter of the First National Bank of St. Ignace, the woman trembled. Color drained from her face as her eyes darted over Tower, struggling to discern his features. She wouldn't be able to tell the police anything helpful. His head was covered with a dark green Michigan State ballcap. Shaggy blond hairs of a wig peaked out from under its edges. His eyes were covered with large reflective sunglasses, his upper lip disguised by a fake mustache.

Tower placed his backpack on the counter, as he drew back the hammer of the revolver. He waved his gun in the faces of the two customers. "On the floor, now! Get down, right now!" A woman, apparently in her late forties, turned her head to look at him fully, while bending hurriedly to the task. Tower slammed the bottom of his Nike tennis shoe into her rib cage, and pushed the gun barrel against her temple. "What are you looking at, bitch?" His voice was low, menacing. Satisfied when she began to whimper, a slow sardonic smile played across his face, as he tossed a plain canvas bag to the tellers. In his left hand, a small box with a blinking red light caught their attention. "Fill the bag, right now. Don't even consider putting the dye packs in. The bag on the counter holds a bomb. It can be detonated from several miles, so if either of you have screwed me, I will blow you to hell!" He rocked the detonator in his hand, capturing their attention. The tellers rushed to obey him, as they moved from the drawers at their desks to the opened safe behind them.

"Jan," Tower said, calling one of the tellers by name. "You have a beautiful daughter. If you don't move your ass a little faster, I can promise you the last thing she'll see before she dies is my face."

Terror overtook Jan as Tower recited her address, her daughter's name, and her husband's workplace. He continued with the other teller, as a cat toys with a mouse, terrifying them all. One of the customers shrieked as she huddled on the floor, urine pooling beneath her.

The synchronized digital watch on his wrist beeped from under the latex glove, and Tower punched the redial button on his cell phone. He retrieved the bags from the tellers, ordered them to kiss the floor, and rushed out the door, six seconds behind schedule.

Not bad.

"JUSTICE IS INCIDENTAL TO LAW AND ORDER."

J. EDGAR HOOVER

Two

Early April, 1934

J. Edgar Hoover sat squarely in his chair, with his back to his desk, gazing out the window. Several years of diligent, meticulous work brought him to this moment, but he knew the truth: this was his beginning. This case and this day would stamp the course of his future into the parchment of this nation, with absolute certainty. No one questioned his ambition or leadership. History would judge him by his decisions, his judgment. This was his time. Minutes from now, Hoover would leave his office, and cross the hall with rigid steps. With perfected pomp and forbearance, he would enter the large, open room from the right side, turn left and with five striding steps reach the podium.

He would give the reporters ample time to take pictures. They would record with their eyes and minds his bearing and unwavering solidity, his steeled face, with unblinking eyes. Cover photographs would capture his essence. He'd close his eyes for a moment, feeling out the pinnacle, and open them to the sight of pencils poised to scratch, frenzied, on to paper.

In cryptic shorthand, his words would be recorded. His first utterance would be tomorrow's headline. Speaking for precisely two minutes, he'd answer no questions and leave them as quickly and directly as he came. A man of his importance wouldn't be bothered with questions at a time like this. The message: John Dillinger *is* public enemy number one.

Wet snowflakes drifted toward the ground, dampening the spring day. Buds sprouted on trees, mocking the country's turmoil with calm and scenic nature. Gazing out the window, Hoover knew exactly what lay on the grounds by number, distance, and direction. He could recite the number of trees, shrubs, and landmarks visible as easily with his eyes closed as opened. He retained details such as the number of seams in a concrete sidewalk, how many cars were in the parking lot at any given time, and if pressed, he could supply their color, model, and make. His ability separated him from his peers. Without needing to, he pulled his pocket watch from his vest and rechecked the time. Ten seconds from now, Clyde Tolson would knock lightly on his door, and give him the nod. Standing, Hoover leaned over the corner of his desk, inhaling the scent from the vase of roses.

Following his carefully laid plan, he strutted to the podium with precise movements. When the metallic pings of the flashbulbs silenced, he closed his eyes and waited for pencils to cease. Clearly, loudly, and with absolute authority, Hoover spoke:

"I will not stand here today and give you yesterday's headlines. I will not talk about men and women that we, the Bureau of Investigation, have apprehended and imprisoned. I will not discuss those that have given their lives to bring these hardened criminals to justice.

What I will do, is answer the question that every American deserves to have answered." Hoover paused, slowly making eye contact with several key reporters. "I can't give you a date, but I can make a solemn promise. Soon, John Dillinger will be brought to justice. Today, here and now, I give you… America… my word!" His voice boomed across the room, fierce determination in his face, his body. "A leader without trust is nothing. I will step down if my word is not carried out.

I will have *law and order,*" Hoover's voice reverberated power. "America *needs* law and order."

Pencils moved at lightning speed, generating a low buzz in the room. Hoover knew the headline before the papers printed it: *Hoover to step down if Dillinger not collared soon!* If he didn't bring Dillinger in quickly, he would be searching for a new position. Fearless, he filled the reporters in on a few remaining details. He ingrained into the minds of the opinion leaders, and thus the nation, one irrevocable truth: America needed *him.* Need and opportunity beget power, and power was his for the taking. Who else would task 100 Bureau of Investigation agents to one end? He had been waiting for this opportunity, and the press had provided it. Dillinger had scored more headlines than any criminal in history, and Hoover would be the one to bring him down. Hoover paused again, allowing reporters a moment before continuing. "There is a $25,000 reward for knowledge that leads to Dillinger's arrest. This is the largest reward ever offered. Dillinger won't even be able to trust his friends. He will pay for his crimes as a highway man, bank robber, and murderer. America needs law and order." Silently, and just as clearly, Hoover conveyed another message: America needed *him.*

THREE

The final minutes of daylight faded fast, hopefully ending one of the last days of this cold, miserable winter. Another month and Anna Steve would sit on her porch in the early evening with just a sweater on, longing for the short respite of summer. Shivering a bit, she smiled as she placed an X through April 17th on her tannery calendar. She lived in a two story home, on a deeply sloped, wooded lot. Her home was located on Oak Bluff in the Algonquin district of Sault Sainte Marie, Michigan or "the Soo" as locals called it, one of the United States's oldest cities. In these uncertain times, Anna was glad for her home.

Sault Sainte Marie was founded in the sixteen hundreds, a crossroads for fur trade, and later on for lumber. It became renown because of the Soo Locks, which allowed ships to pass from Lake Superior to Lake Huron, and eventually became the hub for its survival. As the demand for iron ore grew, so did the Locks' importance, until it became one of the great shipping gateways of the world. The Soo would never grow to be a major city. Long winters and a below average cold climate would see to it. It would always be a comfortable small town, just the way Anna liked it. The easy nature of the people, and the familiarity that never changed made it home. The Soo, like all Upper Peninsula towns didn't have much to offer the next generation. To stay, its residents had to be willing to sacrifice.

Anna's family sacrificed in a different way, with one brother in prison and another brother's infamy on the rise. Although her notoriety as a celebrity's sister surrounded her, the town-folk gave her peace. Of course, as the right hand man of John "The Rabbit" Dillinger, the Sault Evening News mentioned her brother, John "Three Fingers" Hamilton on a daily basis. Anna said a quick prayer for her brother, knowing he must have very little peace. She prayed he would move to Canada, or somewhere that Hoover's men couldn't find him. Special marksmen on loan from the Army with orders to shoot to kill scavenged the outlaws' trail for clues. Anna rolled her head in a circular motion to relieve tension. Today's story about Hoover's dedication to hunting down Dillinger and her brother unsettled her.

Another shiver coursed through her body, and she almost missed the soft patterned knock at the back door that could only be Johnny's. She hadn't seen him in years, but she felt his presence.

Before she could reach the door, her brother opened it and walked through. Throwing her arms around his neck, she planted a kiss on her brother's weathered cheek. "Oh, Johnny!" Anna cried. "I don't believe my eyes."

"It's me, Sis." He hugged her fiercely, as if he might never have a chance to hug her again.

After a long moment, she pulled away from him. "For Heaven's sake, John. What are you doing here?" she asked.

"Visiting you," he replied, smiling.

Anna gazed over her brother's shoulder, realizing he was not alone. Another man stood in the doorway's shadow, and behind him, a young lady. John saw recognition in Anna's eyes, as she looked at Dillinger. He turned sideways so he could see them both. "Anna, this is..."

Before he could say another word, the man stepped forward and offered his hand with a wide smile. "My name is

John Dillinger, and I rob banks for a living." He paused for a moment, looking into Anna's eyes. "I'd understand if you didn't want me here, ma'am."

Anna had read and heard so much about the famous outlaw she felt she knew him already. She shook his hand, smiling graciously. "Any friend of my brother's is always welcome here, Mr. Dillinger."

Three Fingers shared a warm smile with his sister. "This is my sister, Anna. Anna, this is Patricia Cherrington, my girlfriend." Anna nodded her head at the young lady and welcomed Patricia into her home.

Emerging from a room at the back of the house, a young man hurried toward his uncle, hand outstretched. "Uncle Johnny!"

"Hey, Chuck." Three Fingers pulled his nephew into a hug. When separated, Charles offered his hand to Dillinger.

"Mr. Dillinger, it is an honor. I'm Charles, Anna's son."

"Well, I can surely see that." Dillinger grinned, shaking the outstretched hand.

Anna closed the door behind them. "You must be hungry. I'd be happy to fix you something for dinner."

Three Fingers nodded. "That'd be great, Anna," he said, following her into the kitchen.

Charles began to follow, but Dillinger headed him off. "Chuck, what are the neighbors like?"

"Nice enough." He thought about the question before adding, "Suppose they can be a little nosy at times. We should move your car into the garage."

"Come on." Dillinger led Charles out of the house, pointing to the car. "This is a brand new Ford V8. Uncle Johnny's going to give it to your mom."

Charles's face spread into a toothy grin. "Wow, Mom will love it."

"So will the young ladies," Dillinger encouraged, winking. Lowering his voice into a conspiratorial whisper,

They took more time than necessary to move the car into the garage and the second car around back. To avoid unwanted attention, they left the headlamps off. When finished, John leaned against the corner of the garage looking first north and slowly allowing his eyes to pivot to the south. The hardwoods were barren of leaves, allowing Dillinger to see deep into the shrouded still night. There wasn't as much as a wandering deer to mar the lifeless surroundings. If the neighbors were being nosy, they were doing so discreetly.

Charles walked up after exiting the garage through a side door. "Sure is nice, Mr. Dillinger."

The older man grinned, remembering a time when he was excited about cars. "It'll go eighty."

Amazed, Charles shook his head, wondering. "I've never gone so fast."

"Quite a ride."

Desperate to converse with the legend, Charles asked, "Is the Ford V8 your favorite car?"

"Nah, but it's a good one." Grabbing a pack of smokes from his jacket pocket, he caught Charles's grin. "Do you smoke?"

"Ma would skin me. I've been telling her there's nothing wrong with it, but hell."

John nodded, exhaling smoke rings. "Mind your ma. She's a good woman, probably knows best."

"What is your favorite car?"

"The Essex Terroplane is the finest car on the road. It's built by Hudson Motor Car Company and has a V8 that will do 90 plus." Smirking, voice lowered, he added, "It will outrun any cop car on the road."

"Is it that simple, Mr. Dillinger? All you need is a faster car?" Charles asked, worried if he had over-stepped his place.

Dillinger shook his head slowly. "No, there's more to it than that."

Charles urged him to go on with his eyes.

Hesitating, Dillinger considered whether or not to tell him more. "The Press calls it the T & T equation." John paused, taking a drag from his Camel. "T & T stands for Thompsons and Terraplanes. The Tommy gun was created to be used as a trench broom during the war. You know, Chuck, it can spit out eight hundred pieces of lead every minute." Dillinger grinned, then added, "But I can't afford the bullets."

"The Essex is the fastest car on the road." Dillinger stated. "Faster cars and more bullets give men like your Uncle and I an advantage."

Carefully absorbing every word, Charles tried to balance between looking foolish by asking too many questions and his desperate desire to learn more. The quest for understanding won out, and he asked, "What's a trench broom?"

Dillinger smiled at the younger man. "I asked that very question myself, once. If I understand correctly, the war was fought mainly in trenches in France by two equal powers. The struggle volleyed back and forth for some time. To break the deadlock, the Thompson submachine gun was invented. It was used to sweep the enemy from their trench. The Press gave it the name trench broom or Tommy gun." Dillinger took a final drag from his cigarette, flicked it to the ground.

Charles rubbed his chin, considering what Dillinger told him, still puzzled. "I don't understand why the law can't stop you. I would stop all terraplanes after a bank robbery until I found you. Before Dillinger could respond, Charles added, "It seems simple to me. No offense meant, Mr. Dillinger."

"It's quite alright, son. That kind of thinking would work

in some cases, but what if I didn't rob the bank? Different bandits have different methods." Dillinger explained.

Chuck looked at the ground, feeling foolish over his one dimensional thinking. He looked up again when he realized Dillinger wasn't going to make him feel stupid. The serious, thoughtful look on the celebrity's face showed that he was still considering how to explain his success to Charles.

There wasn't a single answer that Dillinger could easily give the boy. Often times, luck was simply on his side. "We use a three step system when we rob a bank. First, we drive a stolen car to and from the bank to do the robbery. The next step happens as soon as we get a chance. We change the plates, and drive that same car with clean plates to another location, where there's a fresh car with new plates waiting for us. The second car is always a good distance away from the robbery, so if we make it that far, we're usually home free."

Charles always hoped he would have the chance to meet Dillinger. Listening and loving every minute spent with his new friend and hero, he cleared his throat and took the opportunity to sell himself. "I'm a good shot, and a good driver. I'm looking for work, Sir. I'd love the chance to go with you and Uncle Johnny."

Dillinger looked the younger man over, taking his time to find the right words. "Look, Charles," he hesitated. "We're friends, right?"

Surprised, Charles nodded quickly.

Candidly, Dillinger leveled with him. "Do you want to live to be twenty?"

"Of course," Charles answered, surprised by the question.

"Your Uncle and I are hard a foot, son. Hoover and his G-men are on us like a pit bull. They have their teeth in our backsides and won't let go. I'm using all my tricks, and I'm not sure I'll be able to shake them." He met Charles's eyes.

"Your Uncle thinks his days are short. Hell, mine probably are too. It's why we came here. Three Fingers wanted the chance to come home once more. It's no life, Kid. Trust me on this." The hard edged life and stress could be seen, Dillinger's guard let down for a moment. He had aged a lifetime in the last few years, he thought.

Clarity washed over Charles, erasing bits of the naïveté that colored his youth. Times were hard, but they were harder on the path that Uncle Johnny and Dillinger chose. He took a moment to consider what Dillinger told him. "We're out here so Uncle Johnny can be alone with my mom, aren't we? He's saying goodbye."

Dillinger met his eyes. The hours Three Fingers had spent bragging about his sister's boy, were right on the mark. "Smart, too." Dillinger stomped out the end of his cigarette. "Use your head, and not a gun to get what you want. When you're sixty, you'll thank me."

They stood in silence for a few moments, before Charles pointed into the night sky. "Look, the Northern lights." The sky over Lake Superior was aglow. The light danced and blended colors beautifully. There'd be no more talk of gun slinging and bank robbing tonight.

FOUR

"Mama, do I have to do my homework now?" Shirley Welsh asked. "It's such a nice day. Can't I go outside and play?"

Pearl smiled down at her daughter. "Shirley, never you mind about the sun, and do as you're told." Pearl patted the top of her head. "I'm going upstairs to check on your brother. I want to see more of these math problems finished when I come back, okay?"

"Yes, Mama." Shirley bent her head to the task, scratching at the starched collar of her dress. Hearing footsteps in the kitchen she lifted her head, happy to have any reason to ignore the work. *It's probably Daddy*, she thought, tiptoeing to the arched door. Several men huddled in the kitchen, others walked quickly from the office through the kitchen and out the side door, carrying machine guns. Surprised to see so many, she backed up a step, peering out the window to see several cars pulled alongside the road. More men were outside, loading the machine guns into the cars. In awe, Shirley ran to the base of the stairs, just as her mom was coming back down.

"Shirley! What about your homework?"

"Mama, there are men with machine guns in the kitchen."

"Don't be silly. You wouldn't know what a machine gun looks like."

"Look, Mama," Shirley challenged, pointing toward the kitchen.

Pearl gestured toward the little girl's homework, but walked into the kitchen to investigate. She was surprised to see that her daughter was right. Bullets, coffee cups, and a hand drawn street map littered the kitchen table. Her husband, Sheriff Willard Welsh spoke quietly to suited men as he marked locations on the map. Noticing her right away, a look passed between the men, while Pearl waited patiently for her husband's explanation.

"We're ready, Sheriff," informed one of the G-Men.

"Go on outside. I'll be with you in just a moment."

The G-man nodded, "Ma'am," and joined the others outside.

Pearl waited until the men had left the house, before she asked, "He's here, isn't he?"

Sheriff Welsh leaned forward and said nothing, hoping that she understood why he couldn't.

Pearl leaned into her husband's embrace, feeling the heavy bullet-proof vest beneath his shirt. She remained stoic, but returned her husband's kiss. "Be careful," she whispered, as he grabbed a gun and joined the Bureau marksmen outside.

"See, Mama," Shirley said, as her mother joined her in the living room. "Machine guns."

"Do your homework, Shirley," Pearl reminded softly. What was going to happen to her husband? Why did Dillinger need to come *here* of all places, she wondered. *Oh God, keep my husband safe*, she prayed.

FIVE

After a reminiscent dinner filled with fond memories of growing up in the Soo, Anna filled her brother in on the whereabouts of family and old friends. Hamilton told Charles the story about losing his fingers in a sledding accident. By the time they'd finished, there wasn't much left of the pan fried whitefish, boiled potatoes, cole slaw and homemade bread Anna had provided. Claiming it was the best meal they had eaten in months, both men turned down her proffered whiskey. *They never drank.*

Noticing Dillinger's almost imperceptible glance at his watch, Hamilton stood and thanked Anna for the meal. His face was lined with regret, but he knew they couldn't stay any longer. "God, Sis. I'm fuller than I've been in years. Damned fine meal."

She recognized the line for what it was, and hated to see her brother leave. "Do you have to go tonight? I've got more than enough beds," Anna offered.

"It's just too risky, Anna. But thanks."

"When will I see you again?"

Hamilton wouldn't lie to his sister. "Purgatory?" he teased.

"Johnny…" Anna bit down on her lower lip, not wanting to make a scene, but desperate for his safety.

Hamilton shushed the question burning at her throat with a

gentle look. "I can't tell you where we're going. I don't want you to know anything that can get you in trouble. It's bad enough that we visited at all."

"You're always welcome, John."

"Don't worry about me. We're going somewhere safe, to lay low for a few days. We'll be just fine." He traced the tear sliding down her cheek with his fingertip. "Take care of Charles. Don't let him go down the road that Foye and I did. It's a road to a quick and deadly end." Face wet, she hugged him and said goodbye.

Death would come sooner than anyone realized.

SIX

Accompanied by two local officers and five agents from the Bureau of Investigation, Sheriff Willard Welsh knew exactly what they were up against. He personally read reports on dozens of accounts detailing Dillinger and Hamilton's exploits. Dillinger and his crew made crime look easy, while those left on the right side of the law looked foolish. He might be able to get away with such mayhem in the city, but not here in the north, where townsfolk were comprised of good people and word traveled fast.

The bulletproof vest hugged Welsh's chest tightly, rekindling the worry in his wife's gaze. He wasn't accustomed to keeping details from her, but he followed the rules. Since their home was attached to the jail, Pearl was a big part of the process. She cooked meals for those locked up and worked with the female prisoners who were often allowed to do chores. She suspected what he couldn't tell her, and she'd worry until she knew he was safe. Guilt gripped him, but one set of ears in the wrong place, and Dillinger would slip through their grasp again.

With just a little bit of luck, it would be over soon. He glanced over at the two local men, nodded. Besides the Bureau agents, Welsh enlisted the help of an officer from Brimley that was a crack shot, and an officer under him that was also deadly with a rifle. Both men served in the military during the Great War, and Sheriff Welsh knew they would stand firm and get the job done. Taking down two of the most wanted men in the nation sounded impossible, but the plan was relatively simple. Meticulously, Welsh and the G-men discussed every minute detail over the kitchen table in Sheriff Welsh's home.

The local men chosen by Welsh carried rifles, while Welsh and the agents held Thompson machine guns. If Dillinger and Hamilton didn't surrender quickly, they were authorized to shoot to kill. If anything even seemed odd, or remotely dangerous, they were allowed to open fire, and figure it out later.

Anna Steve's two-story home perched on an edge of Oak Bluff. On the sloped side, there was a single door with steps to the ground. Trees were well spaced with much open air between them, and April hadn't been kind enough to support leaves or undergrowth, which worked well for the agents. With the exception of the few trees, they had clear shots of the windows and doors from multiple directions. If Hamilton and Dillinger came out through the doorway, they would cut them down immediately. On the front side, there was also a door in the middle of the house, with a small porch. Two rocking chairs, placed outside a bit too early for the weather, were swaying with the breeze, to the right of the door. The garage and private driveway curled up from Fourteenth Street on the left side. Three G-men and Sheriff Welsh were positioned there. Two officers, one in each direction, were placed strategically along the ridge with rifles.

The local officers were offset to stay out of each other's shooting lane. One covered the back of the house and the other the front, each positioned a fair distance away, comprising a final line of defense that would only change if Dillinger and Hamilton headed directly for them.

After receiving signals that everyone was poised and ready, an agent lifted a mega-phone and demanded, "Come out with your hands up!"

NEWSPAPER ARTICLE:

HAMILTON VISITS SOO

APRIL 19TH, 1934

The 33 year old desperado, John "Three Fingers" Hamilton visited his sister, local resident, Anna Steve, April 17th. Wanted for auto banditry, harboring a fugitive, obstruction of justice, bank robbery, the murder of Sheriff Jesse Sarber of Lima, Ohio and for his work as a lieutenant of John "The Rabbit" Dillinger, Hamilton is on the 10 Most Wanted List of the Bureau of Investigation. According to Mrs. Steve's neighbors, Hamilton, Dillinger and an unidentified female, believed to be Hamilton's girlfriend visited with Mrs. Steve and her son, Charles, from 8:30 to about 11:00 pm. The Bureau of Investigation flew in five agents who worked closely with local Sheriff Willard Welsh.

Sheriff Welsh met the agents in St. Ignace then drove them to the Soo. With the help of other local officers the men developed the plan to encircle Mrs. Steve's home. Although the men carried Thompson Submachine guns, and high powered rifles, they were too late. Dillinger and crew were long gone by the time the agents carried out their plan on the 18th. For their troubles, the G-men were able to confiscate a V8 Ford Deluxe Sedan, found in Mrs. Steve's garage. The car is believed to have been a gift from Hamilton to his sister. Mrs. Steve was immediately arrested for harboring Dillinger, though she was not charged with harboring her brother.

Mrs. Steve and son Charles both claimed they have no knowledge of where the trio headed after leaving her home. Neighbors were also questioned, but knew nothing. Road blocks were set up on US2 and M-28, as well as at the St. Ignace car ferries, but thus far have failed to entrap them.

Agent Melvin Purvis, in charge of the Chicago Office and heading the hunt for Dillinger and Hamilton reported that the fugitive's "luck still holds, and once again the Rabbit is off and running." With a $25,000 bounty in place for Dillinger's capture, few people will be able to resist turning him in, and everyone is sure to recognize him with pictures headlining every newspaper.

Will the Bureau of Investigation really bring these men to Justice as they so often claim? Or is no bank safe from these hardened criminals that seem to always be one step ahead of the law? Where will John Dillinger's gang show up next? There seems to be no end in site to this latest run of banditry. Is Hoover out-matched by Dillinger's thugs? If you're wondering what move the criminals are going to make, just wait a day or two, and check out the newest headlines, because if I know one thing, they are going to strike again.

SEVEN

PRESENT DAY

AUGUST 12TH, 2005

"Will you check on Frank before you head home, Lisa?" Nancy asked, having just come in for her shift. The other nurse faced a stack of paperwork that she knew wouldn't get done unless she began attacking and sorting right away, while Lisa was still on duty.

Having worked on her feet for the last ten hours, save for a short lunch break, Lisa had spent the last two hours yearning for a good chair. She accepted Nancy's task, without complaining about her aching arches or sore back. Nancy hadn't been on the job for twenty minutes, Lisa thought, and she's got her shoes off and her butt in a chair.

Green Meadows was gifted with a generally jovial, qualified staff that "cares completely" about each and every resident. In the grand tradition of hospital-like environments, the two story retirement home failed to escape the medicinal white washed atmosphere that characterized care for the elderly. Lisa tugged at the hem of her bright pink scrub shirt and glanced over the paperwork for the patient/guest transferred into her wing today. Not that it really was her wing, she pondered with a glance thrown over her shoulder at the white board of the nursing station.

"Sure, I'll check on him." For Lisa, the patients felt like *her* patients, and that would have to suffice until she managed a wing of her own, she realized. She loved her work at Green Meadows, and relished the opportunity to spend time with people who had lived and seen so much more of life than she had.

According to the chart, Frank was moved into room 203 (a single) because his former roommate complained about Frank's incessant ramblings. Crazy talk, the roommate said. Chuckling at the thought of what "crazy talk," might be, Lisa closed the clip book and bustled to meet her new charge. "Good Evening," Lisa sing-songed.

"Hello there."

Well, he doesn't look crazy, Lisa thought, biting her tongue to quiet her laughter. After all, what does a crazy person look like? Shaking her head at herself, she smiled. "Welcome to the second floor, Frank. My name is Lisa Daye."

"Hello, Lisa. It's nice to meet you." His voice was calm and surprisingly strong for his pale coloring and gaunt face. His eyes were sharp and unclouded by pain killers.

Lisa beamed. "It's nice to meet you too. I hear we had a bit of a problem with your roommate, hey?"

"You'd think that man," Frank paused, silent for a long moment. "You'd think the man would have wanted to hear the word of God and his own country's history. There's nothing to a man that doesn't want to know the truth of life."

Lisa moved over to the window, sliding the blinds closed. Placating him, she asked, "And you know the truth of life?"

When he didn't respond right away, she gave him her full attention, aware of the color leaving his face and the grim set of his mouth.

"I know many truths." Lisa laid her hand on his arm, silently encouraging him to speak. "Unimaginable truths," he said, lifting his eyes to hers. "Please, Miss Daye. Sit and listen to an old man for a minute."

Lisa hesitated, frowning. Why did the crazies always have to tell her their stories? And, why today, when she was so exhausted she could barely stand?

"In small towns there are few secrets.

On islands there are none."

Joe Barber

EIGHT

Quinn gently nuzzled Jill's hair, pulling her body closer to his on the over-stuffed couch. The fire blazed and crackled, glowing embers reflected in Jill's gold flecked eyes. Romantic melody filled the air and Jill hummed softly along with it. She laid her head back against Quinn's body, allowing him to play with the thick, lustrous strands. He could lay here with her forever. Tonight, he would tell her he loved her.

Tap, tap, tap. Quinn groaned. *Go away, go away.* "Quinn! Quinn, wake-up!" The deckhand opened Quinn's door, and shook him.

"Huh?" Quinn forced his eyes open. The Drummond Islander IV was unloading. Damn, dreaming again, he thought.

"Hell, Quinn. I've been shaking you. You didn't hear me pound on your window?" The deckhand asked, dumbfounded. "Are you okay, man?"

Quinn rubbed the sleep from his face, still totally out of it. He nodded, sensing that was the thing to do.

The deckhand seemed to relax, his tone lightening. "Damn, I don't know where you hide her, but she must be one hell of a woman." Grinning, he leaned against Quinn's door. "You look like death. I bet you haven't slept in a week, right? But you had that lusty smile on your face, so you must be getting some. Does she have a sister?"

Wrinkling his nose, Quinn finally comprehended the other man was asking him questions. "What the hell are you talking about?"

"Shit, Quinn. Everyone on this ferry knows your plowing some off island babe. Towing this trailer back and forth doesn't fool anybody. Hell, you're off island three or four times a week, I'd say. If she has a sister, you just gotta hook me up, man. Share the love." The deckhand yelled over his shoulder, as he moved out of Quinn's ear shot, waving another car off the boat.

Quinn rolled his eyes, and shut his door. Alarmed that his overnight trips off island were being noticed, he resolved to tell Jill the truth. If the ferry crew thought he was seeing an off island woman, it wouldn't be long before Jill heard that rumor too. Starting up his Jeep, he steered his way off the ferry following M-134 to the left, joining in the chain of vehicles already headed in that direction. Quinn slugged on his warm Mountain Dew, fighting to stay awake.

Peering through the windshield into the sky, Quinn tried to estimate the time. The clock in the dashboard had been broken for months, and Quinn had no inclination to have it fixed. The sky probably held the answers, but not for Quinn. When he looked up, robin's egg blue was blanketed by layers of clouds puffy with rain.

Mindlessly continuing along M-134, he slowed his vehicle, gazing out at the new clearing and construction site. Dump trucks, an end loader, and a bulldozer with Black Bear Excavation and Redi-Mix emblazoned on their sides, littered the new development. Island gossip provided all sorts of notions about what was happening with the land. The only response the excavation company's owner gave was that the project was being funded through a law firm in Petoskey. Of course, no one believed that.

Quinn smirked, gazing out the window at the progress. *The bartender always knows.*

NINE

Drummond Island is a collection of vastly different ecological settings merged together to form a wilderness paradise. Jill remembered the words from an advertisement she had once read, believing them to be absolutely true. Flipping through photographs that glimpse the beauty and untouched nature of Drummond, she knew she hadn't really scraped the surface yet. Boxes piled upon boxes filled with prints, negatives, and snapshots stacked in her new office, recently moved out from the spare bedroom.

Over the last year, she discovered that the populated north shore was quiet, protected, and offered a view of smaller islands that are known for total solitude. The south shore, by comparison, viewed the open water that seemed to stretch forever. Huron pounded on the rocky southern coastline continually, and Jill knew she would choose to live on Cream City Point even if her grandparents hadn't left her their cozy, wood-framed house.

In the past year, with diligent effort and determination, Jill transformed the 960 square foot throwback from the 1960's, into something efficient and attractive: *home*.

Unsettled by the thought, she left the sorting project behind, absently running her hands through her dark brown hair. Her bare feet padded softly over the pavement and out the open garage door. *Home*. The word rolled over her body like a cresting wave curls over the rocky shore. When was the last time I felt home, she wondered, absently feeling the crescent shaped scar on her left forearm: the souvenir of the fatal car accident responsible for irrevocably changing Jill's life.

Stepping back, Jill gazed at the building before her, feeling for the first time that it belonged to her. Recently stained to match the new construction adjacent to it, the house she moved into fifteen months ago looked like a different place entirely. She added cosmetic differences like dark green shutters and updated window lathing that made all the difference to the home's aesthetic appeal. Fading sunlight warmed the side of the new garage, where Jill adeptly constructed more than merely a garage and storage area, but also a dark room and bunk house with bathroom: Space that she *always* wanted—yearned for, even.

Attached to her home via a breezeway that connected to the kitchen, the garage project also contained a brand new washer and dryer, which particularly thrilled Jill. The project and driveway extension, which stopped short of the house when Jill first moved to Drummond last spring, cost her nearly every cent of the forty thousand dollar inheritance left to her by her parents, as well as every extra bit she could spare from her paychecks. Her parents would be proud, she knew, even though she remembered little of them. Six years hadn't been enough time to learn the lessons they would teach, or the values they wanted to bestow on their only daughter, but Jill knew they loved her. Her grandparents never let her forget that she was *so* loved, and even though they did their best to raise her as their own, Jill had always been vaguely aware that she belonged somewhere else.

Home. She thought about what that meant to her. As much as her grandparents loved her, their house was never her own. Her grandfather became a home of sorts, always understanding her better than her grandmother did. Jill's keen sense of observation and attention to detail came from him.

This house, she thought, was not home when I moved here, but it is now.

When her parents were killed, Jill closed off emotionally to survive. When her grandfather passed away, she focused on caring for her grandmother to avoid reliving the pain of losing someone. Even as a child, she rarely sought out friends, because when she chose to love, she loved with her whole self. She never made a home, because that too, could be taken. Being left her grandparents' summer house, largely unused in their later years of life, was a window of escape. Once again, Jill focused on moving and changing, rather than living with the loss of almost everyone she ever loved. *And then she lost Joe.* With nowhere left to go, no direction to turn, Jill enfolded herself into Drummond Island, the way a bear hibernates in the winter, busying herself with expanding her portfolio, and building a space that she'd dreamed of having.

Almost magically, the space Jill craved for herself was finally available in a place she never intended on living for more than a summer. Cream City Point, with its winding curves and dense forest, became her own personal nirvana.

Surprised to realize her eyes were wet with tears, Jill smiled. Her garage didn't suddenly rise from the dust magically. She built it. With effort comes pride, and Jill beamed, knowing that with a few more strokes of her brush, the painting would be finished. Humming to herself, she climbed her wooden ladder and focused on all she had learned about construction in the last year. Pete Dombrowski, her employer and friend, had been good to her.

Leaning away from the ladder, she reached to touch the tip of her brush to the underside of the overhang. Even in a place few would ever see, Jill carefully painted even strokes. The sound of gravel crunching behind her made her smile. The sounds of the uneven gait, footsteps falling in a pattern dear to her, could only belong to Clark Eby, her late grandfather's best friend, and her neighbor.

"Looking good, Jilly," the gruff voice called.

Setting down her paint brush, Jill paused for a moment to visit, and met him on the ground, smiling to herself in anticipation of the banter that flowed so easily between them. "What have you got there?"

"The missus sent me over with ice tea for ya. She didn't want ya to get thirsty or something." Clark held out the glass, shaking his head.

"Thanks," Jill said, taking the cool glass from her friend. She appreciated his wide, wrinkled face, straying hair, and twinkling eye. Clark and Arlene were two of the last lifelong friends Jill had left. She waited for the good natured complaining that was sure to come. She didn't wait long.

"Truth is, I think she wanted me out of the house. She's been nagging at me about that damned yard sale she wants to have. She says all I've got is junk, and we should get rid of it. But dammit, Jilly. The stuff I've been keepin' is real valuable. I don't see why she doesn't understand that."

Clark and Cliff, Jill's grandfather, were collectors of monumental proportions. The two men first met at an auction haggling over the same object, and became fast friends. When the men introduced Clark's wife, Arlene to Jill's grandmother, Edna, the foursome began a lifelong friendship. Clark and Arlene loved each other with the same devotion that her grandparents once shared. With a pang that always accompanied familial thoughts, Jill listened, swallowing her smile to Clark's complaints with a sip of her sweetened tea. She'd hear the other side of the story from Arlene when she visited next. "Well, are you sure she wants you to sell *all of it*?" Jill asked.

Clark scuffed his foot against the ground, a bit sheepish. "No, no… but I don't see why I should have to part with any of it. We get along just fine with the space we have."

Jill raised an eyebrow, contemplating the two-car garage

next door, packed to the brim with stuff. The spare bedroom in
their house was in the same condition, and Arlene was fit to
be tied when Clark carried home a new pile from a flea
market downstate. The shed on Jill's property was still filled
with some of her grandfather's pieces, which she hadn't taken
the time to go through yet. Clark eyed her garage, eyes
gleaming. "Don't even think about it, Clark."

"What?"

"I built this garage, because I need this garage. And I am
not getting in the middle of this fight by letting you bring stuff
over here. Besides, I've still got all of Gramp's stuff to go
through eventually," Jill said, gesturing to the out building at
the edge of her property.

Grouching good naturedly, Clark gestured to the wide
berth of her building. "But, Jilly, look at all the space you
have. Surely, you're not going to need all of it. Heck, this
garage is bigger than your house."

"Yes, I really am. I am taking all my pictures and
negatives off of Dean's hands," she said, referring to her agent.
"Come on in, I'll show you."

Grumbling a bit, Clark followed her in. "Damn shame you
decided not to swing that six sided bit out front. Would be a
real nice addition to this place."

Jill nodded her head in agreement. "I'll probably regret
that I didn't just borrow the money and build it, but I hate to
go into debt for something I don't really need, you know? And
even though I'd like to have a six sided gallery for my prints
and pictures, there's always next year and the year after.
Right?"

"That's right. Probably smart, Jilly." Clark gazed around
him, letting a short whistle pierce the air. "I don't think I've
been in since you did the finish work. Damn, this is nice."

The building was divided into halves, with the half closest
to the house divided again. The darkroom in the back corner

of the building was preceded by desk space, with a drafting table and light table for viewing negatives along one wall. The desk was stacked with photographs from Jill's sorting project, with shelves running the full length of the wall above it. Colorful organizational bins were labeled, though empty thus far, above the desk. Running along the opposite wall from these workstations were built-in, locking drawers that were designed to store Jill's substantial and growing library of photographs.

"Who'd you get to make these cabinets for ya?" Clark asked, tapping the edge of a drawer unit.

"Pete and I did it."

"You made these?" Clark whistled again, astounded.

"Well… Gary Reed, one of the guys on the crew gave me some pointers. He used to work for that cabinet company, that I can never remember the name of, and Pete helped a couple evenings after that."

"Damned fine work, Jill. I had no idea you had set your teeth so hard in this carpentry business."

"I've been working with Dombrowski Construction for over a year, Clark. What did you think I was doing?" Jill asked.

"Errands?" Clark shrugged. "Sorry, darlin'. I guess I thought you were exaggeratin' a bit with this talk about being a carpenter. Always figured a young girl like yourself would be doin' something different. I shoulda known better. Ever since you were a little girl, once you got something in your craw, you went after it. Not like my grandkids and their fancy-shmancy lives. Damned shame the way my kids raised their young. But what can you do?" Clark shook his head a bit. "Cliff'd be damned proud of you, honey. You've done a real nice job with the place."

"Thank you."

"I still don't think you need all this space, though. You can handle thousands of pictures in here."

Jill shrugged. "I'm a bit trigger happy. And besides, room to grow."

"Funny that you've got locks on the drawers. Still got that city girl in ya, eh?"

"All my years in the city, I never had someone ransack my house until I moved here," Jill reminded, finishing the tea in her glass.

"Hogwash. It wasn't an islander that did that."

"No, it wasn't," Jill agreed, not wanting to go back there mentally right yet. "Come on, I'll show you the bunkroom."

Next to the photography processing area was a hallway with a bathroom, the breezeway connection to Jill's home, and a door that opened to the bunkroom. Inside the taupe carpeted bunkroom, plastic wrapped mattresses leaned against the wall.

"Need bed frames? I think I've got a bunk set in my garage. It might take a bit of work to find them…"

Jill held up her hand to stop his offer. "Actually, I'm going to try and make them this winter. Earlier, if I get a chance, but Pete's got me working so much, I barely have time to get photos taken, let alone make a bunk bed. It'll be nice to have some time off this week."

"Time off?"

"Carly arrives tonight."

"Oh, hell. We should go grab that bunk set then…"

"No, she can stay in my spare bedroom in the house." Jill said, musing over the last time she saw Carly, a smile lighting her face.

"It's empty too?"

Jill laughed. "Yes, and it's going to stay that way."

Frowning, Clark mumbled. "You know, it's been so long since anyone used our spare…" Clark's voice trailed off, as he caught Jill's smirk. Trying to change the subject from his guest bedroom back to hers, he said, "I can't see as how you need bunks. How much company do ya plan on having?"

"You never know when you're going to need another bedroom."

"Planning on marryin' or livin' with a fella, that I should know about? You haven't got a bun in the oven, do ya? Hell, I didn't even know you were datin' again."

"Oh, Clark. You're such a gossip. I'm not moving anyone in. And no, I am not dating again. I am definitely not pregnant. I can't even imagine having kids yet."

"It's about time you get around to datin, doll. You're quite a looker, with a head on your shoulders. I reckon you'd be able to find a real good match."

"That's it, Clark. I am not having this conversation, and the sun is drooping beneath the tree line. Get on home, before Arlene gets worried, and I'll finish my paint job."

"Alright. A man knows when he's not wanted." Clark grumbled.

Jill laughed at this, returning his glass before heading back to the ladder.

Over his shoulder, he yelled, "I'll ask around about young men for ya, Jilly. Don't you worry, I'll have you hooked up in no time."

Worried that he was as good as his threat, Jill continued painting with vigor, trying not to focus on her relationship, or lack thereof, with Quinn McCord. For the past four months, and probably longer if she really wanted to think about it, their relationship had been severely strained. Maybe Clark's suggestions wouldn't be all that bad.

TEN

Lisa couldn't bear to stay any longer today. The mint colored walls of Frank's antiseptic scented room were the bland, mirror images of every other room on the floor. No artwork of any kind broke the monotony. There was nothing to distract her from the medicinal, urine tinged scent that took residence in her nostrils everyday. Since Lisa had pulled the blinds closed moments before, any sense of life seemed to flicker out as if she flipped a switch. Pressing her hand to the small of her back, pain shot up through the arches of Lisa's feet, as if someone deliberately pounded stakes up into her legs. Ten hours standing on unbearable hard floors, with difficult, tedious work had taken their toll for the night.

With no reserve of energy left, Lisa simply couldn't bring herself to stay. And if Frank was blustering, then she definitely didn't want to hear it. "Frank, I'm just about to go home," Lisa said. "Can we talk tomorrow?" she asked, fiddling with the IV.

Rejected, Frank scowled. "You won't come back."

"I will come back," Lisa insisted. "It's my job." Lisa rolled her eyes at her own lame wording, but couldn't think of a more reasonable argument to give him.

"But you'll be busy," Frank grumbled. "I know all about the gangster John Dillinger and Three Fingers Hamilton. I met them on Drummond Island. There's a treasure buried there,

Miss Daye," offered Frank.

"Call me Lisa." She pivoted her head back sharply. Fatigue coursed through her body unchecked, but she couldn't have mistaken what he just said. Hesitating briefly, she asked, "Did you say Drummond Island?"

"Yes. You've heard of it? I used to live there."

"In Michigan, right?"

"That's right. We buried him there. John Dillinger and I buried him..."

"Buried who?" Lisa asked, but her pager chirped loudly.

Nancy rushed through the door at the same time. "Lisa, I need you. Room 217." Nancy tapped her wrist in a motion that Lisa recognized as their signal for "code blue."

Rushing out the door after Nancy, Lisa called over her shoulder, "I'll be back, Frank."

ELEVEN

"Get the hell off that ladder, girl!" Ball capped and grinning, Carly whistled in Jill's direction, jumping over the door of her red hot Mazda Miata convertible.

"Carly?! Hey!" Jill hurriedly climbed down the ladder and threw her arms around her friend.

Carly hugged her hard, pulling her off the ground a bit, as Jill squealed with laughter. "God, it's been a long time." She stepped back, looking her over. Jill's hair was even longer, and apparently thicker, though it was loosely pulled away from her deeply tanned face. The short sleeved red t-shirt hugged her small but strong frame, falling just above her blue jeans. "You're so skinny… haven't you been eating?" Carly pulled her cap off her head, and ran her fingers through her hair.

Jill ignored the question while rolling her eyes, and returned the appraisal. "You look amazing. And your hair is so short."

"Lance thought I'd be more intimidating with short hair." Carly "the firestorm" Folton was a firefighter by trade, and a kick-boxer by passion. "I don't know if it's working, but I haven't lost in a while." The black tank-top and shorts showed off her nearly 6'0" tall and solidly ripped figure, decorated with tattooed flames curling around her right bicep, and a nasty looking "firestorm" design on her shoulder.

"Just wait till the boys get a look at you," Jill teased.

"Not too close of a look," Carly countered. "I'm practically a kept woman."

At Jill's raised eyebrow, Carly shrugged the comment off. "We'll talk about that later. First, I gotta see your house. I mean, have you really been working hard enough to justify not visiting me at all this past year?" Carly popped her sunglasses off her face, and whistled. "Damn, girl. Look at this place. You designed this new part yourself, hey?"

"I had lots of help," Jill responded, shrugging off the compliment as she heaved one of Carly's bags out of the backseat. "Come on, I'll show you. This is all new," Jill explained, gesturing to the breezeway and garage. She left the door open behind them, and paused on the half-step. "Before the addition, my back door was right here where this arch is, so you'll get a sense of how small my house used to be. This is obviously my kitchen," Jill said, laughing. "And my dining room, and living room." Her kitchen was joined to her dining room and living room, separated by her butcher-block styled counter-top resting above homemade pine cabinets. Wood floors were covered with rag rugs; pine walls (darkened with age) throughout the home were decorated with various matted and framed scenic photographs. Last year, most of them showed pictures of trips out west, taken in her youth. They were slowly being replaced by scenes from Drummond. Her living room held an eclectic mix of slightly beat up furniture pieces, covered with throw blankets, and colorful pillows. The home's focal point, a split-hardhead fireplace, was surrounded by windows on both sides, and a French Door on its left, faced an even more engaging scene, as white caps slapped over the boulder littered landscape.

"Jill, I love it," Carly enthused. "I love the dark wood, and the coziness."

"Really?" Jill hadn't been sure how her friend would react.

"Oh, yeah. It's very down home. Just standing here makes

me itch to dig out some of the books I brought with me, and curl into one of those chairs."

Pleased, Jill nodded, understanding exactly what Carly meant. "I love this place."

"Your pictures are just amazing. I want to spend some more time looking at them, and you have to show me more."

"I will," Jill agreed. "How was your drive up?"

"Fast." Carly made a hissing noise and smiled. "I love my new car," she grinned. "I see you've got the Tracker still."

"Yeah. I've been spending too much money on my house to think about anything else," Jill explained.

"I hear ya. I feel like all my money goes to my damned trainer..." Carly's voice trailed off as she took in the small, but comfortable home. "What have you got going on here?" she asked, gesturing to the dining room table. It was covered with photographs and Jill's camera paraphernalia.

"New project." Jill set Carly's bag on the floor near the couch, and turned back toward the table.

Carly tossed her stuff in a pile on the floor and leaned down to examine the pictures. "These aren't yours, are they?" Her voice was matter-of-fact and gruff.

"No. Chase leant them to me from last year's boat show."

"Whose Chase? And what's a boat show?"

Jill clasped her hands together, gleeful. "I'm glad you're interested. I'd be delighted to not only tell you about it, but show it to you tomorrow."

"Aw... Jill! This is supposed to be a vacation," Carly whined. "You're not hauling me along on one of your damned work trips, are you? Please tell me that's not what you're doing. I swear I still have scars from..."

"Oh, get off it. That was a long time ago. Besides, you'll like the boat show," Jill stated. "Dean wants me to photograph from every possible angle. He's got several ideas in mind."

"Dean should get his head out of his ass, and encourage you to come shoot fights," Carly mumbled, the sound byte of an age old argument. "And who is this Chase? Are you avoiding the question on purpose?"

"Chase is an absolute doll."

"Mmhmm, go on. Cute?"

"It's not like that. But yeah, he's cute."

"Just cute? Or Hollywood cute?"

Jill ignored the question. "He's seventeen and way too innocent for you."

"Did I say I was interested? Before you go on, where's your can?" Laughing, Jill pointed toward the bathroom. "I'm still listening Jill, so keep talking."

"Do you remember me telling you about Quinn McCord?"

"Sexy bartender that you had the most intense kiss of your life with?" Carly called from the bathroom.

"I don't think I said that," Jill grumbled back. "But, anyway… yes. Chase is Quinn's little brother."

"I'll be damned. Maybe I'll have to see if he likes older women, hey?" Carly teased, her chuckle blending in with the sounds of the flushing toilet and running water. Carly paused to check out Jill's bedroom. "This view is amazing, Traynor."

Jill joined her friend, leaning her body against the doorframe. "Mmm," she voiced, appreciating the rolling waves.

Carly's survey of the room stopped on Jill's bedside table. A young, blond haired man grinned in front of a rusting truck. "Oh, Jill."

Hearing the concern, Jill looked up to see Carly holding Joe's picture. Her breath caught in her throat a bit, as she sat on the edge of her bed next to Carly. "Yeah, that's him."

"I wondered what he looked like," Carly studied the picture carefully. His eyes were gleaming with mirth and excitement, the crush of love, perhaps. "How is his family doing?" Carly's voice lost it's usual edge when she recognized the troubled look in Jill's eyes.

Jill shook her head. "As well, I guess, as anyone could expect. His sisters seem to be holding up... but his mom has trouble still. Joe was everything for her." Lost in memories, Jill's gaze blurred for a moment before she cleared her throat. "I can't believe it's been over a year, Car."

Carly anchored an arm around Jill, pulling her closer, waiting her out. Carly was the only person in the world, before Joe's death that Jill allowed to see her vulnerability.

"I mean, it's gone by so damned fast. Before, when my parents died... I found a way to pick up and move on. When Grandpa died, I focused on taking care of Grandma. When Grandma passed, I expected it. I just sort of found a way to busy myself through it."

"And aren't you doing the same thing now? Look around you, Jill." Carly said gently. "You've built a great garage, you're taking pictures. Hell, you're working construction full time. When you're not focused, you're absolutely exhausted. Admit it," she prodded.

"Yeah, but I *feel* it: his life, his death. I walk around in it." Jill brought her hands to her face, and shook her head slowly, searching for a way to explain her feelings. "When someone dies in a city, there isn't even a hiccup. But in a way..." Jill picked her head out of her hands, and met Carly's eyes. "Drummond Island stopped when Joe was killed. I mean... things continued, but you could see it in people's eyes. It was different. And I know, I only knew him a week, but I feel like I knew him my whole life. I see his parents at the store, I'm friends with his friends, I live in his world.

"For the first time, maybe ever, I've been forced to deal with loss. I can't shelve it, because everywhere I go, everyone knows that Joe died. The people deal with it in this nonverbal way, but together. At work, everybody misses him. But... it's healthy grief. I can feel myself healing, and not just with Joe.

But with my parents, and my grandparents. I find myself crying at the littlest things, and I know it's right." Jill noticed her arms folded tightly over her chest and she dropped them to her sides. With a deep breath, she wiped tears from her eyes, chuckling humorlessly. "See?"

"Wow," Carly whispered, moved. "Honestly, I never thought you would stay here. In the back of my mind, I kind of thought I'd talk you into coming back to the city with me this week." Carly hugged Jill tightly. "I haven't been here twenty minutes, and I can see that you've changed, Jill. I think this place just might be good for you, right for you."

Jill breathed deeply, touched that Carly understood and accepted. "Yeah."

"Enough of this emotional girly shit." Carly stood abruptly, holding her hand out to help Jill up. "Make me some coffee and tell me all about your love life!" Carly demanded.

"Ugh… *do I have to*?" Jill whined, accepting the help up.

"Absolutely," Carly said, grinning.

TWELVE

One flickering yellow colored light bulb hung three feet from the ceiling, barely lighting the contents of the dining room table, casting eerie shadows onto the rest of the cheap barn wood paneled apartment. Dark, heavy drapes covered the windows, blocking every trace of outside life from the room. The 85 degrees was amplified by the city's evening heat, but Tower liked it hot. He leaned back in the old red leather upholstered kitchen chair, balancing the chair on two legs, enjoying the way his sweat eased between his naked body and the leather, making him stick quite nicely. Tower traced his perfectly manicured fingernails over his taut abdomen muscles and smirked, while he looked over the directions he had read seventeen times before, knowing them by heart, but still meticulous about studying them again.

One end of the oval table supported a duffle bag brimming with new clothing, Tower detested. It might just be the worst aspect of the job ahead, he thought, grimacing. The center of the table held a lap top computer, cell phone, calculator, legal pad, two pens, a bottle of Blue Mountain water, and neatly stapled crisp white pages, type written and bulleted. Finally, on the side closest to Tower, two boxes stood: one was sealed, and one held a variety of items, chosen meticulously by his boss, Red.

Sweat beaded on Tower's tanned forehead unchecked. Silence enfolded him, as thoughts chased each other through his head. Solitude, soon to be disrupted, embraced him like a lover lost and he tipped his chair back a bit further, his back curving into the creases, his bare feet gripping the checkered linoleum. He closed his eyes and inhaled the scent of his unique odor, enjoying the anticipation of the week ahead. This was the best part, and with accomplishment, he had finally paired up with someone he could *learn* from. He would learn *everything* he possibly could, before disposing of his teacher. Like Junior, Red was a means to an end.

Junior, with all of his bumbling nonsense, would be here soon, and knowing Red's plans needed to be hidden from sight before then, Tower forced himself out of his reverie and finished the review. Thus far, the plan had succeeded perfectly. He had seduced and conquered the firefighter, orchestrated his elements of the plan with detail that would border psychological disorder. He recruited an expendable accessory, never once letting on the existence of a third party. This, of course, is where Tower would first part company with Red's plan. He would kill Junior, and take Junior's cut. He had devised a very believable story for Red, if it was a problem, but it shouldn't be. The plan didn't include a face to face meeting with the master.

His thoughts returned to Carly, and a knowing smirk filled his face. Developing the characteristics, personality and temperament of someone Carly found attractive was more than a mild challenge. The constant struggle for dominance between them had become a challenge of its own. Selecting just enough moments to let her win, and moments to maintain the "hard-ass" veneer that excited her was exhausting. The paycheck would be well worth the price.

Without looking at the clock, he knew he had one hour and ten minutes before Junior arrived, but he checked the time anyway. With renewed focus, he pulled on clear latex gloves, enjoying the way they nipped his circulation a bit at the wrist. Gingerly, he held the packet of nearly pristine white pages in his hands, lifted it to his nose and inhaled the scent of printed paper. Covered with a page merely labeled "The Plan," the document excited Tower. As clever and meticulous as Red designed the operation, in time Tower would exceed it. Flipping the first page over, he greedily anticipated the clever instructions he'd read so many times before.

THIRTEEN

"Aren't you tired? Do you want to nap or anything?" Jill offered, wanting to avoid the coming conversation. How would she explain the relationships in her life to Carly, when she barely understood them herself?

"Nap?" Carly scoffed. "We're going to visit and eat something," she decided. "Then we're going to the bar. I want to see what this island's got to offer."

"Oh, no. Remind me not to introduce you to Marci. You'll be fighting over the guys. Or maybe, they'll be fighting over you," Jill teased, preparing her coffee maker.

"Stop stalling, Traynor. I want to know what's going on with you. Who are you dating?" Carly plopped down on a kitchen chair, gazing up at her friend.

"I'm not dating anyone," Jill said, pulling coffee cups out of the cupboard.

"Seriously?" Carly raised an eyebrow.

"Seriously," Jill confirmed.

"Well, why the hell not?"

Jill joined her friend at the table, shrugged. "I'm kind of off the market to local guys."

"Off the market? Are you joining a convent?"

"Ha! Everyone thinks there's something going on with

Quinn and me, and even without Quinn in the picture, there's always the memory of Joe."

"If Quinn is in the picture, why aren't you dating him? I don't get it. You told me how close the two of you became after Joe was killed," Carly prodded, her voice gentle.

"Eh… it's kind of a long story. And honestly, Car, I'm not sure I'm ready to be dating anybody. I'm just trying to figure myself out at the moment, you know?"

"Bullshit. But if you don't want to talk about it right now, I'll let it go for the moment."

"Thank you." Carly could be such a stubborn mule with the rest of the world. With Jill however, Carly always seemed to know when to push and when to back off. "Besides, I want to hear about Tower."

"Mmm… swoon," Carly dramatized. "Tower is a bit of an ass most of the time, but such a charmer when he wants to be."

"What does he look like?"

"He's an inch or two shorter than I am, and thin, but really strong. I think he might be able to take me, even," Carly admitted, rising to fetch the coffee for them both.

"Really?" That Carly would admit anyone could better her, let alone someone she was dating, intrigued Jill. She held her cup steady while Carly poured.

"Yeah. Tower works out as much as I do. He's into martial arts and shit."

Jill hid her smile. Of course, Carly wouldn't pay attention to which kind of martial arts her boyfriend practiced. Carly believed in good old-fashioned sweat and weight lifting. Everything else was for amateurs, to Carly's way of thinking.

"He's really hot," Carly continued. "Kind of long-ish, dark hair. Big dark eyes. And he can level you with a look, when he wants to be intimidating."

Puzzled, Jill looked hard at her friend. Something in her friend's face didn't seem to correspond with her statement, but Jill couldn't place it.

"When we're fighting, sometimes he just looks threatening. He doesn't mean it or anything, but he can be quite intense." Carly hesitated, lost in her thoughts. "He's really smart. He should have done so much more in college than he did."

"What does he do for a living?" Jill asked.

Carly hesitated for a moment, before answering. "Ah… he's in sales."

It sounded more like a question, and Jill called her on it. "You don't know?"

"Well, I really don't know what he sells. He doesn't talk about it. He's kind of cheap. Ergh, he drives me insane sometimes. He claims to make decent money and he lives in this hell hole of an apartment. I refuse to go there, mostly. I make him come to my place."

"Well, come on. Can't you tell me something good?" Jill prodded, when Carly quieted for a moment. "How did you meet?"

"At a fight. He watched me take down this gorilla of a woman, and he *insisted* that I have a drink with him."

"What else?"

Carly smirked suggestively.

Jill held her hand up, stopping her friend from going further. "I really don't need to know *that*, Car. That's not the only reason you're with him, is it?"

"Of course not. He's uhm… I don't really know how to describe it, Jill. He's sort of bewitching. When I'm not right beside him, I want to be. There's this pull between us that's sexy as hell. Most guys don't even fight, they just roll over.

Tower's really tough, but smart, and in love with me, so he fights hard."

"What do you fight about?" Jill asked, sipping her coffee.

Carly expanded her arms toward the ceiling. "Everything. And it's not like we scream at each other. Tower fights with his eyes, his personality even. I have to be on my toes all the time around him. It's great."

Of course, Carly would think it's great, Jill mused. Carly loved conflict and competition, but how long could she continue with that kind of drama? Fighting was a great drain, even on Carly. Jill studied the vibrant energy exuded by her friend, and concluded that Carly could hold her own for a long time. Jill sipped coffee from her over-sized pottery mug and studied her friend. Lost in her thoughts, she welcomed the momentary silence.

One of the things Jill loved about Carly was her unique never-say-die personality. Before they met, Jill had lived a rather calm, though artistic life. When she was shoved into a dorm room with the larger-than-life woman, Jill learned lessons about living that she couldn't have realized from the sedate life with her grandparents. The vivacious kick-boxer never slowed down, never settled short of achieving every goal. She was a dynamic, powerful woman who thrived on challenge, but something in her eyes foreshadowed trouble. Deciding to pay closer attention and figure out what was going on with her friend; Jill forced a smile at the story tumbling forth. Carly's rambling took on an edge usually foreign to her tales. Her words seemed more carefully chosen, more devoid of emotion than her normal dramatics, and yet quite *anxious*.

Leaning forward, Jill focused on every detail: she heard the words as Carly chose them, the nonverbal gestures playing out in her friend's face, and the darkness lurking in her eyes. Gripping her own coffee cup too tightly in her hands, Jill sensed something was terribly wrong.

FOURTEEN

THE PLAN

The Bank Robberies will occur on August 15th, the Monday afternoon following the boat show.

1.   All materials and personal gear need to be inside the Jeep, by Sunday (August 14th) noon.

2.   Do not take any paperwork (credit cards, etc.) that can be identified as yours besides your driver's license.

3.   Check all fluids, tires, jack, all lights, and make sure gas is full before leaving. Do not fill north of Gaylord. Obey all traffic laws.

4.   Instruct Junior to take a cab to a public location, arriving by 9:15pm Pick him up by 9:30pm and follow the route marked on the map, north.

5.   Stop once during the trip (I suggest West Branch or Gaylord to refill gas) and go through a drive-thru to eat.

6.   Wear a ball cap at all times. Don't look anyone in the eyes and say as little as possible.

7.   Cross into the Upper Peninsula between 4:05 and 4:15am Use the "token only" line with the token provided.

8. Wear latex surgical gloves. Do not remove them from this point forward.

9. Have Junior steal plates from a car you choose (use the tool kit provided).

10. Steal a plain, four door, V8 car. Do not choose anything easily recognizable. Check gas, and tires.

11. Drive to the point shown on the map as the resting area off Chard Road. The Jeep should be faced out.

12. Use the bolt cutters and the padlock in the package (it matches the one at the gate now). Cut the lock, enter the gated area and relock. Put the old lock in the large canvas bag.

13. Stay inside the gated area. Stay by the cars and remain quiet. Test redial on cell phones. Go over plan one last time with Junior.

14. Give Junior the second watch, go over the plan with him *again*.

15. Leave the gated area at 12:34pm.

16. At 12:43pm drop Junior off across the road from the Central Savings Bank. Then call 911 and report a bus accident on M-123. Be frantic on the phone, hang up in the middle of your sentence. Tell them that many are hurt.

17. Begin robbing both banks at 12:50pm.

18. Stay only three minutes in the bank. It will help to make a violent (non fatal) example of someone early to ensure compliance. Junior will have five minutes, instruct him to collect fives and up. You should only concern yourself with twenties and up, and then tens if you have time. Note: It should be heavy due to deposit made every

Monday morning for the Hessel Casino plus the
boat show should make the banks loaded.

19. During your exit, Tower, hit redial on the
cell phone. This will be an audible two minute
warning for Junior to wrap up before you pick him
up in front of the bank.

20. Return to the Jeep's location. Try not to be
seen making the turn onto Three Mile Road or
Chard Road. Be sure that no one sees you enter
the gated area.

At this point, Tower smiled easily. He would split Junior's
take with Red as a sign of good faith, which he was sure
would smooth things over. Rubbing the tips of his fingers
together, enjoying the tight sensation of the gloves, Tower
continued to read. Days from now, he'd take another human's
life and quite possibly, more than one. His spine tingled as he
contemplated it: how would it feel to take a human life? Blood
rushed through his body, as he anticipated his victim's eyes
draining of vitality in the way his brother had described. It
may just be the best moment of his young life, and Tower
nearly itched with eagerness to fulfill this desire.

FIFTEEN

"Billy, it's not like you and Dee haven't talked about it," Quinn argued as he slid another glass of Pepsi across the bar to him. Billy had been in Quinn's face, discussing his numerous problems, which were all minor, for hours. Unfortunately for Quinn, this had become a habit, and although he was used to hearing complaints and stories from everyone, Billy's need for reassurance left Quinn exhausted. Of course, it didn't help that Quinn was running on very little sleep anyway.

Billy shrugged, accepting the pop. "I know."

Quinn's eyes perused the Northwood, taking in the nice mix of tourists and locals. "You even bought the ring. What's the hold up?" he asked.

"What if she says no, Quinn?" Billy raised his voice to accommodate Quinn's movements, continuing to talk as Quinn worked. "DeeDee is my whole world. I mean, what would I have done without her?"

Quinn stared at him hard. "Billy, Dee's been your saving grace for years. Hell, she should have left you a dozen times…" Quinn paused, realizing he's supposed to be building him up rather than tearing him down. "She wouldn't be with you if she didn't love you. She'll say yes, Billy. Just ask her."

"You think so, Quinn? Really, man? She'll say yes?" The

fact that Billy and Quinn had had this conversation a half a dozen times seemed to escape Billy. "Don't just tell me to make me feel better. She really loves me, right?" Like a dog begging for a bone, Billy waited for his friend's reply.

"She really loves you, Billy. She'll say yes." Quinn's voice was hard-edged and left no room for doubt. He knew, everyone in the bar knew, and everyone on Drummond pretty much knew DeeDee and Billy were a done deal. It was just taking Billy longer to realize it. "Go ask her."

Billy made a fist, grinning. "Yeah! I knew it!"

"Good, go." *Please*, go.

"Oh, no. You gotta help me plan it. It's got to be perfect."

Grimacing, Quinn shook his head. "Isn't there someone more qualified to help? I really don't know much about this marriage shit. What about Jill? Or Kate, better yet. Kate would love to help you." The door to the bar swung open quietly; DeeDee entered, bright red hair bouncing. For a fraction of a second, Quinn thought of warning Billy, but decided against it.

Slightly louder than necessary, Quinn blurted out, palms up as if in submission. "Okay, okay. I'll help you. Tell me again, Billy. How much does she mean to you? And how are you going to ask her?" Quinn's eyes met with DeeDee's over Billy's head, a silent warning stopped her from moving forward. Her eyes widened with surprise and Quinn knew she wouldn't come any farther.

"Man, that's a hard one. I guess…" Searching for the right words, Billy paused. "She's my life. I've loved her from the moment I first saw her and I've never stopped. She's seen me through my roughest times, and if she said yes, I would spend my whole life trying to make her happy."

"Well, then what?" Quinn prompted, catching a glimpse of DeeDee's eyes pooling with tears.

"What?"

"Practice. Show me exactly how you're going to ask her." Quinn dropped his voice an octave. "Have you got it with you?"

Billy nodded, thrilled with Quinn's new interest.

"Well, get it out."

Billy dug the ring box out of his pocket, showing it to him. He saved for months to buy her exactly what he hoped she would love.

"Come on, Billy."

"Okay, okay. You really want me to ask?" Billy looked doubtful.

"You have to get it right, man." Quinn stared at him, urging him to continue.

Soberly, Billy imagined DeeDee beside him, and with his whole heart asked, "Will you marry me, Dee?"

Screeching, DeeDee leaped onto Billy's back, dragging him to the floor. Pinning him down with her body flush against his, she covered his face in kisses. "Yes! Yes! Yes!"

The bar's occupants pounded their glasses on the table, hooting and hollering for the island couple. Walking in through the door at the exact moment, Carly raised her arms above her head, inadvertently blocking Jill's view. "Hell, yeah, I love this island. If you see a man and you want him, you just knock him down and take him! Hooya!"

"What's going on?" Jill asked, edging around Carly, shocked to see Dee tickling Billy to give up the ring, rolling end for end on the floor.

Holding his sides, laughing hysterically, Quinn waved to Jill. When he finally caught a breath of air, he yelled, "Billy asked DeeDee to marry him!"

"Yeah! Right on, Billy!" Jill yelled, joining in the commotion.

The blubbering redhead finally managed to see through her tears long enough to grasp the ring from Billy and started bawling anew. "Oh, Billy… it's so beautiful."

Overwhelmed, Billy's eyes teared up as well. "This is the happiest moment of my life, DeeDee. Do you really mean it? You're really gonna marry me?"

"Yes, Baby. I am so gonna marry you." She hugged him tightly, loving the sounds of their friends cheering. She picked herself up off the floor with him and took the requisite moments to ooh and ah with the girls about her ring.

While Billy was pounded on the back by various locals, Jill hugged DeeDee close, surprised at her own tears. "I'm so happy for you. You and Billy are going to be so awesome together."

"I'm not sure I'd still have him if it wasn't for you, Jill." DeeDee admitted, her voice low.

Jill smiled softly, knowing what DeeDee meant. In the last year, since Joe died, Billy's drinking escalated beyond control. It had taken Jill and DeeDee a lot of effort to get him to shape up. Jill argued and pleaded with Pete to get Billy's job back, and the young man began to grow up.

"Billy would've gotten it together eventually, Dee. He wouldn't have let himself lose you," Jill offered.

Dee smiled warmly, her gaze extending to Jill's friend.

"Oh, I'm sorry, but I don't think I introduced you to my friend, Carly."

Carly offered her hand, but Dee opened her arms and hugged her. "Any friend of Jill's is a friend of mine. You'll just have to come back for the wedding, Carly, since you were here for the engagement."

Laughing, Carly hugged her back. "I will definitely do that."

"Billy, honey. Come here and meet Jill's friend," Dee called.

Billy wrapped his arms around his new fiancé, and nuzzled the back of her neck. At Jill's grin, Billy let Dee go and hugged Jill hard. "Thanks, Jilly Bean."

Jill rolled her eyes at the nickname Chase had started. Introducing them, she was surprised when Carly initiated the hug with Billy. "I need to buy you both a drink, she offered. A round of tequila on me!"

Billy began to shake his head, but DeeDee beat him to the punch, winking broadly. "Carly, it's a lovely offer, but I have got to get this boy home."

Howling with laughter, Carly stepped back, watching the couple, with arms wrapped around each other, make their way out of the bar.

"What a way to start the night out! Damn, I love this place," Carly yelled, letting her eyes rove over the tall ceiling, wood paneled walls, and bar that stretched larger than life before her eyes.

"You should hear the stories about this place," Jill said.

Carly's sudden death grip on Jill's arm had Jill whirling toward her, wincing in pain. "Oh Lord, tell me that's not him," Carly demanded, staring at the bronzed alpha male behind the bar. "Are you sure you want him? You know, it wouldn't be that big of a deal for me to break up with Tower," Carly offered.

Jill's throaty laughter reached Quinn, as she eased her arm away from Carly. "No, you can't have him," Jill admonished quietly, waving at Quinn. "You've really got something going with Tower. Stop staring, for heaven's sake."

"I can surely look," Carly whispered back, not bothering to avert her eyes. "Jill, is there drool?" She touched the corners of her mouth, teasing Jill.

Jill rolled her eyes. "Pull yourself together, Folton. You're a kick boxer, show some reserve. He's not *that...*" Quinn looked curiously at Jill for a moment, before breaking the contact. He turned showing them a clear view of his thickly muscled arms. Jill gulped. "Promise to behave, and I'll introduce you."

"I'll behave," Carly mocked.

"Okay, then. Come on." Jill led the way to the bar, never taking her eyes from Quinn.

Carly edged herself in front of her friend, and thrust her hand forward past Quinn's to feel his upper arm, bare in the sleeveless t-shirt. "Wow."

Taken aback, Quinn snorted with laughter. "You must be Carly." There wasn't any question in his mind. The tall, angular, feisty woman oozed the dynamic personality Jill once described for him. He met Jill's eyes, happy to see her laughing too. It had been too long since he heard her laugh, he thought.

"Hell, yes." Carly removed her hand from his arm, and offered it to be shaken. "You are a knockout."

Quinn raised his eyebrows, shocked. His expression delighted Carly all the more, and she tossed a diva-like huff over her shoulder. "You've never told him he's God's gift to manhood? You're such an ass, Jill."

Carly still hadn't released Quinn's hand, when he carefully pulled away from her. "Uhm, I'm Quinn, by the way."

"I know," Carly said, settling on the nearest available barstool. She patted the top of the next one for Jill. Quinn used the momentary freedom to place a Corona on the bar in front of Jill, shoving a lime wedge through the neck, before handing it to her.

"Thank you, Quinn." Their hands touched briefly as Jill accepted the beer.

"What would you like to drink, Carly?"

"Tequila. I'm buying us all a round of tequila. You too, Quinn. And keep them coming," Carly winked.

Jill groaned, gripping the edge of the bar dramatically. "Oh, God. And I have to shoot tomorrow," she winced, just before she tipped back the first shot as the scent assailed her. She gulped it down, swallowing the urge to cough. "Wow! Am I going to live through this?"

"You're young, you'll be fine," Carly assured her.

Laughing, Quinn caught Carly's gesture to pour another round.

"I haven't seen you in a while, Quinn," Jill mentioned, watching her shot glass be refilled.

"You haven't been in the bar much," he countered.

But, you used to call me to hang out, or grab dinner or something, Jill thought. "Yeah, my garage is never ending. You'll have to come see it sometime," she offered, but Quinn was busily filling someone else's order, and Jill wasn't sure he heard the invitation.

Sixteen

Reading through the list, Tower flipped back and forth between the detailed instructions and the inventory. Surprisingly, he never actually checked to ascertain whether or not everything on the list was provided. Before going on with the instructions, he read through the list carefully, physically spotting each item.

2 cell phones

2 matching digital watches

2 empty canvas bags for the money

1 bridge token

1 Masterlock brand padlock

1 bolt cutters set

2 .38 caliber revolvers

2 bomb bags

2 switches with blinking lights

1 oversized plastic leaf bag

1 over-sized canvas bag, to bury items

1 toolkit

1 slim jim

four hundred dollars

Tower rose from his seat at the table, walked to a cabinet in the kitchen and removed a 9mm Beretta, 1 roll of paper towels, and one bottle of cleaning solution. Returning to the table, he added them to the items Red had provided.

Dialing the air down to 68 degrees, he noticed that the cooling system kicked in immediately. Tower took a few moments to shower, and dress in a t-shirt and lounge pants. He pulled back the drapes, further preparing for Junior's arrival. Picking up his cell phone, Tower dialed Carly's voicemail directly. The fight that had broken out when he told her he wasn't accompanying her to Drummond was legion. He affected the desired tone, the proper attitude before he spoke.

"Carly, it's me. I'm sorry about not being there with you. I bet you're having fun with your friend. I'm calling because I realized that you didn't give me the phone number up there. Call my cell, and leave it. I love you, Babe." Clicking End, he set the phone back down, picked up the instructions.

22. Stand in the center of the large leaf bag and remove your clothing (including your wig, mustache and sunglasses). Have Junior do the same.

Tower stopped, contemplating his additions to the plan. He knew he would take this step after he killed Junior, when he would use the paper towel and bottle of solution to clean his gun hand and arm. He would then dispose of the items in the plastic bag.

23. Make sure both guns are in the plastic bag. Once done, bundle the plastic bag inside the large canvas bag and place it in the back of the Jeep.

24. Open the sealed box and review contents at this time. Keep the backpack exactly as it is, and

place it on the seat behind you when you leave the gated road area.

25. On the last page of your instructions are notes and page numbers corresponding to the bird guide. Copy the notes in your own handwriting on the map, and in the margins of the bird guide book.

Who, but a master thought of details such as handwriting within an old bird book? Tower read the bird book as soon as he first received it, and several times since, spending the same amount of attention in familiarizing himself with every piece of the bag's contents. Thirty minutes after pulling a double bank robbery, and murdering Junior, Tower would be a tree hugger. With clean plates, he'd be free of anything that would tie him to the crimes, except for, of course, the money.

The clock flashed 7:17pm. He pressed and held the 3 on his cell phone. "Uncle Danny's," a cheerful voice called in his ear.

"My usual, please."

"Sure thing," the attendant responded, reading from her screen. "One medium pizza with green pepper, onions and cheese. Would you like breadsticks with that, Sir?"

"No, thank you."

"Thirty minutes."

Tower ended the phone call and eyed the steel cased switches. He would have just as soon carried real bombs into the banks, but the materials would look believable, especially to civilians. The threat of an explosive would be scary enough to ensure compliance. Dye packs, hidden in bundles of money, were usually triggered to impact at two hundred feet, Tower knew. If they detonated, the money would be covered in dye. All banks had them, but Tower was counting on being able to scare the tellers into leaving them out of the bags. The tellers, with Tower's help, would realize that giving up the money clear of the dye packs was smarter than risking their lives, and the building itself via explosion.

The last instruction on Red's list would be ignored.

26. Destroy this document.

Tower leaned back in his chair, pondering the divergence of his agenda from that of Red's. Tower's brother once told him that he should never work with a partner. Partners always have their own hidden agendas, their own selfish motives that never include the other's best interests. If you're going to work with a partner, Alec told him, take some measures of insurance. Insurance, Tower mused, was easier purchased than collected, but he followed his brother's advice.

Earlier in the week, Tower paid in full for 36 months advance rent on a safety deposit box from National Bank in Detroit. He listed his brother as a co-renter, and then tossed the key in a manila envelope and mailed it to his lawyer with instructions. Everything in Tower's will was provided for his older brother. Of course, since Tower didn't currently possess many assets, the will was something of a ruse to provide Alec with the key, should something go wrong. Another glance at the wall clock showed 7:58pm.

Tower looked at Red's last note, which was not part of the numbered list and existed on a separate, but attached piece of paper.

One last note: Once you are in the Jeep and leaving the gated road, you are tourists. Take a few moments to stop and clear your minds, before you continue. Make sure everything is as it should be, and that everything's been taken care of according to the plan. When you leave the driveway you have no knowledge of banks being robbed. If you see a car with lights flashing, do not assume they are looking for you. Pull over if they want to stop you, and assume that you have a broken taillight, or have been caught speeding. You cannot out run police officers in your Jeep, so you need to deal with them if the occasion arises. You're just tourists, nothing more. *Remember that.*

No matter what they were dressed like, allowing Junior to live would increase the likelihood of suspicion. Tower acknowledged the instruction for the value it held, before he moved on. With Junior out of the way, he knew he wouldn't have any trouble acting the part of a tourist.

Quickly, he moved the back pack and other items, along with The Plan, and put them in his closet. He slid the mirrored door closed just as the doorbell rang. Tower opened the front door to find Junior, precisely on time, holding the pizza box in his hand, as if he was serving it. With a smile he said, "Dinner."

"Sounds good, I'm hungry!" Tower enthused, opening the door wide, and gesturing Junior in. Junior wasn't such a bad kid, a little off, but usually willing to follow orders. Of course, he wouldn't live long enough to see a dollar of the take, but Junior bored Tower to tears with plans of jet-setting all over with fabulous women. Junior dreamed of a lifetime of thieving adventures that would result in little work and lots of play. It was Tower's job to keep Junior in line and following orders rather than thinking for himself.

"I'm getting so excited!" Junior rushed, slapping the box down on the table, and almost dropping it to the floor.

"Careful, asshole," Tower yelled, knocking Junior on his backside, pinning him down with his foot lodged on Junior's throat. Junior choked under the pressure. "How many times do I have to tell you? Keep your mind in the center. Can you imagine what would happen if you slammed the bomb bag on the counter? They'd know you were full of shit and we'd both be dead. Grow the hell up, and get serious. Do you hear me?"

Junior nodded, gasping for breath. Tower picked his foot up, and walked, calm as day, to the kitchen to fetch drinks.

SEVENTEEN

"No, no, no. It can't be morning yet."

"Get up, Carly."

Carly lifted her head up slightly, and groaned. "I am way hungover. Go without me." Carly pulled her pillow over her head.

"Not on your life. Get up!"

"You're hungover too!" She teased, pointing. "Ha, ha."

"Is that laughter I hear? It must mean you're awake," Jill said, leaving the room to finish putting her camera equipment together. Satisfied that everything was as it should be, Jill zipped up the camera bag. The phone rang. Surprised, Jill answered it, "Hello?"

"Hey, Jill." Quinn's rich voice sounded groggily in her ear.

"Hey. Why are you up so early?"

"Oh, hell. Is it morning already?" Jill could hear Quinn scratching his arm, imagined him running his hand over his head in the unconscious way he did in the morning, or when he was thinking.

"You must have closed the bar, hey?"

"Mm-hmm. Uhm, I just wanted to make sure you got out of bed okay. Today's your big shoot, right? Do you need help with anything?" Quinn was lying, and they both knew it. He wanted to hear her voice.

"Mmm, yeah it is." She enjoyed the lazy conversation filled with quiet moments when neither of them rushed to fill silence with words. They hadn't shared one in a while, but it was nice. "Carly's going with me, so if I need help with anything, I'll make her do it."

"Oh, right. Well... have fun, Jill."

"Thanks for calling, Quinn," she hesitated for the barest of moments before taking the plunge. "Hey, maybe we can get together later. Some time this week, and do something..."

"I'm so busy, Jill," Quinn returned quickly, wishing he could give her more time.

"Well, it's really not that big of a deal. I just thought I'd ask."

"No, Jill. *I want* to spend time with you," Quinn countered. "I'm just not sure when I'll be able to."

"Fine. See you later." Her words were as abrupt as her voice.

"Jill, don't be that way."

She sighed into the phone. "What way? I've gotta go. Bye, Quinn." Angry, she punched the talk button, ending the call. "Damn you." So, now he didn't want to date her? After all these months of flirting over the "friendship" line, she was finally ready and he wouldn't make time for her? Well, he could piss off, she thought, scowling.

"Damn who?" Carly questioned, draining the last bit of coffee from her cup, before refilling it for the road.

"Oh, nothing."

"Don't even try that with me. Who was on the phone?"

"Quinn."

"Is he hurting too?"

Jill picked her head up sharply, staring at her friend. *Were their relationship issues really that obvious?*

"He drank as much as we did last night. He must be." Carly slipped her feet into her tennis shoes.

"Uhm, I'm not sure." Jill looked at the phone, as if not recognizing its function. "Oh, boy. Wake up, Jill," she said, snapping herself out of it. *No more Tequila*, she silently vowed. "We need to go."

The drive to the ferry boat was quiet. Jill's was the third in a line of cars, with the others racing to the boat as well. They both pulled around the final corner to the ferry line, when Jill cursed as she saw the boat pulling away from the dock, with two cars before her. Jill eased her Tracker to the stop sign, surprised when the car in front of her pulled close to the gate.

"What's that girl doing?" Carly asked.

"That's Marci."

"Oooh… trampish Marci?" Carly questioned, having heard several stories the night before. "What is she doing?"

The bottled blond climbed on top of the roof of her Chevette, and ripped the shirt off her body, flashing the escaping ferry. "Come back!" She yelled.

The car ahead of them, filled with men, cranked up their music. Carly laughed aloud to hear Bad to the Bone, from the Terminator Soundtrack, fill the air.

"Take it all off, honey! Shake a little ass!" they hollered out the window.

Convulsing with laughter, the girls watched Marci do a little dance on her rooftop, and moon the ferry boat, shirt discarded on top of her car.

The ferry boat stopped in its normal rotation, and retreated back to the dock, lowering the gate to allow the vehicles on board. Carly threw her fist into the air and hollered. "Talk about girl power! She's so great."

"She's something. Great isn't the word that comes to my mind, but she's something," Jill mumbled.

"I have got to go meet this girl!" Carly exclaimed.

"Go right ahead," Jill said to the body flying out the door and up to Marci's car. "Wait until the guys hear about this," Jill murmured, thinking fondly of her crew members that shared a fetish for the voluptuous party machine.

As the deckhand lowered the gate to wave them on, he grinned. At least, Jill thought, it hadn't been Carly stripping. *Am I going to survive the week?* she wondered.

Eighteen

"Good morning, Frank," Lisa bubbled, bouncing into the room. Lisa's energy and enthusiasm endeared her to her patients. She wasn't supposed to be there yet, but she wanted to spend time with Frank.

"Oh, Lisa. Hello." The grey pallor of his face was worse today, and Lisa slid the blinds open, annoyed that no one else had done it yet. "I'm glad you've come."

"I told you I'd be back. You just need to believe me." Lisa's bright colored smock made the old man smile. She sat on the chair beside him, looking at him expectantly. "I've got some time on my hands, and I'm ready to listen. What about Drummond Island?"

Frank leaned back in his bed, looking at the young woman earnestly. His bright life-filled eyes belied the poor color in his age-pruned face. "It was late April, 1934…" Frank began, setting the scene, capturing Lisa's interest.

*   * 1934 *   *

Spearing the ground with his shovel, Frank heaved more dirt into the hole. When Lorraine asked him to help her friend, Frank never expected he would be helping John Dillinger bury a body. It was almost too much. It would have been too much for any man, but Lorraine looked at Frank with her big doe eyes and touched his face gently, encouraging him to say yes. So he did. Of course, he would help her in any way that he could. Didn't she know what she meant to him? Frank may have only been seventeen, but he knew the small framed, golden haired beauty had stolen his heart. He also knew Lorraine was star gazing when she thought of the outlaw, and dreaming when she said the two of them were going to be married someday. He counted on the infatuation subsiding when Dillinger road off into the night without her. Dillinger certainly wasn't going to fulfill her dreams by settling down and marrying her, Frank thought to himself, stealing another glance at the gangster. To his surprise, Dillinger's face was sunken with sadness, mouth set in a grim line as he shoveled dirt with strong, steady movements.

"He wanted to be buried here." Dillinger dug the tip of his shovel into the ground, leaning his weight against it for a moment. He stared past Frank, working through his inner demons. "Do you know why?"

Shaking his head, Frank mumbled, "No."

"Cause no one will find him here, that's why. No one will dig him up and slap his body on a wooden plank for townsfolk to take pictures of. Son of a bitch made me promise I'd bring him back when he passed." Lost in thought, Dillinger mimicked his late friend's voice. "No one will find me here, John. Drummond is the end of the earth." Dillinger's voice fell off, erased in his renewed energy to finish burying his friend.

"Why would someone put him on a slab of wood?" Frank asked, horrified.

"That's what they do with outlaws. They'd strip him down to his shorts and let people walk by and touch him. I've seen people stick their fingers in a man's bullet wounds before." Dillinger shuddered. "They leave the body out for days until it stinks to high heaven."

"He was right then," Frank agreed. "Drummond sure is the end of the world. Hell, I've seen ghost towns that get more action than this place does on the fourth of July!"

Dillinger nodded, smiled a bit.

Frank hesitated, curiosity winning out. "Why here? Why are you burying him at Wayfarer's? This is real public, you know?"

Dillinger stretched his arm toward the water in a grand gesture. "Look at that view. Have you ever in your young life seen a view so pretty as that? Cause I sure haven't. The sun rises right out there, and it'll warm him. Good folk will chatter within earshot, and he'll get to relax. There's even a great stone to use as his monument." Dillinger picked up his shovel and walked about six feet toward a good sized rock, with a large triangle shaped wedge on top, as if it was missing a piece of itself. "This will be his marker, Frank. This is his monument. Hamilton was a solid man, and I think this place will be around for a long time, filled with normal, good people. The kind of people that he'd want to be around. It's real fitting, ain't it?" Dillinger asked.

Frank nodded his head in agreement.

"And I'll know where to find him. I can come back and pay my respects."

"Are *you* worried about being put out on display?"

Dillinger shook his head. "Nah. I'm heading on down to Central America soon. I need to do a few more jobs, but then I'll be ready. Before I leave, I'll come back to collect what I've left here, but then I'll retire." Dillinger stared into the grave. His next shovel full of dirt obliterated the bed sheet wrapped body from view, and he matched Frank's pace once again. Moments passed in silence except for the sound of falling dirt, as the two men worked in unison, lost in private thoughts.

The location of the body suddenly made sense: Dillinger must have hid whatever he would come back for, with the body. He made up the fluff story of a good resting spot so I won't go looking, Frank thought. Worry gleamed through his eyes for a reason far different from the mere greed that underscored the gangster's life. If Dillinger planned on coming back, Lorraine might be silly enough to wait for him.

Nineteen

Jill and Carly followed the milling groups of people walking off of M-134, and down the hill into the heart of Hessel. Both State police officers and Mackinac County Officers directed traffic at the intersection. They passed the billboard that read "28th Annual Wooden Boat Show and Festival of Arts." Cars and trucks were parked on street sides, boasting **For Sale** signs. The cool morning temperature, brilliant blue sky, and light breeze made the walk immensely enjoyable.

As they walked into the heart of Hessel, Jill pointed out gift shops, a book store, and bars and restaurants along the road. Many of them were converted from multi-story homes that were fifty plus years old. The road led them due south, and with each step she took, Jill felt as if she walked into another time. Hessel was a time-forgotten community, with a quaint, cotton candy coloring that spoke of old values, and friendly residents.

The bottom of the hill was flush against the water, where the buildings and docks of the marina were home to the Boat Show. Jill pointed to the end of the line, and they joined the group together, waiting for their turn to pay.

"Look at the people. Seven bucks, right?" Carly questioned, looking through her wallet for the right bills. "How many people come to this thing?"

The lady behind the counter smiled. "We should have somewhere between eight and nine thousand this year."

"Unreal. Just to see some boats?" Carly mumbled over her shoulder at Jill.

"Beautiful boats, Carly. You've never seen boats so pretty. I should have showed you the pictures from last year," Jill said. "Put your money away. I'll pay for this," Jill insisted. "No arguments."

Carly raised an eyebrow, but nodded acceptance. "Thanks, Jill."

"Check out the tents over there," Jill pointed. "Those are filled with artisans."

Stepping forward, Carly let the woman at the entrance table place the band around her wrist. Aviator sunglasses of another era topped her nose, but looked appropriate on her strong, angular face.

Jill retrieved her change, and the pamphlets, while listening to the woman's instructions on where to vote for the people's choice award.

Moving through the opening, Jill gathered her camera, slinging the strap around her neck. "If you want to go shopping, I can go around and take pictures without you."

"Piss off, girl. I want to see the pretty boats," Carly exclaimed, inching her way through the strong and growing crowd.

"Carly, it looks like they're moving one of the Coast Guard boats. I'll be right back. I'm going to go over there for a few minutes."

"Sure," Carly responded.

The blue-green water provided a stunning contrast with antique wooden boats, that were really, in Carly's opinion, more works of art than vehicles in which to ride over the waves. Moving through the docks, at Jill's side, she became one of the throngs of admirers. She leaned over the roped railings to examine the attention to detail and craftsmanship. Many of them seemed *perfect*, often described in placards that told of the exact methods of restoration. Carly was less interested in the information, but enthralled by the vibrancy of the upholstery, the sheen of the varnish, and meticulous attention to details.

Jill, Carly observed, was in her element, her zone, her chi, or whatever the hell she wanted to call it. Forty-five minutes later, the camera carrying fiend allowed Carly to escape from her side. Carly shopped while Jill finished up on the must-have shots, and focused more on the artistic photography that she so loved.

Breezing Thru, a 1930, 26 foot Hackercraft was by far Jill's favorite. Others, like *Pretty Girl*, and *Sandbill* were stunners as well. She captured a quaint image of a little girl near a Chris Craft, called *Jezebel*. Several character shots, with blurred bodies, and swirling energy portrayed in dynamic colors of crystal blue-green water captured the essence of the Boat Show. Jill squatted near the water at the edge of a pier, carefully framing the *Gem of the Huron* in her viewfinder.

"Hey, there," a voice crooned, snapping her out of her zone. "Five dollars, please."

Jill's eyes met those of a seemingly affluent, yachtsman. From his perfectly pressed khakis to his polo shirt and sweater tied by the wrists over his shoulders, he was the stereotypical image of what a young wealthy boater should look like. Tall, he was much too handsome, with traces of Italian lineage evident in his dark tan skinned frame. Hair, darker than the color of his eyes by several shades, framed his face. "I'm teasing," he offered. "I'm Michael Marinello. Mike, actually. This is my yacht!" He gestured at the gleaming hull with pride. "You're welcome to take as many pictures as you like, but you're going to have to give me one." He offered her his hand to shake in greeting.

She shook his hand, balancing her camera in the other, while her camera bag was held firmly by the thick canvas strap anchored on her shoulder. "I'm Jill Traynor," Jill offered, a smile filling her face easily. "You'll get one, thanks. Your homeport's Drummond Island, right?" She pointed to the stern.

"Yes. As of right now it is, at any rate. I purchased the boat from a local. I have plans to live there for the rest of the summer. I haven't renamed it yet. The gentleman I purchased it from sold it to me on the condition that I enter it in the Show."

His voice was as smooth as his looks, and Jill felt the urge to speak more properly, suddenly worried that her relaxed behavior from working with the crew for the past year had corrupted her vocabulary. "Why Drummond?" Jill questioned.

"I'm doing some diving on a shipwreck over there for fun research."

"Isn't that an oxymoron? Fun research?" Jill quipped.

"For me, it's not. I'm a marine archaeologist, or rather, I'm going to be one. I'm attending school, but for the summer I'm taking quarters in my boat. She's moored at the Yacht Haven." He noticed the recognition in her eyes, and asked, "Have you ever been there?"

"I live on Drummond," Jill told him.

"It's a small world. Where? I mean, what part of the island do you live on?"

"Cream City Point."

"Sure, the south side. I'm familiar with the area because I've dived on the Russia."

Jill stared at him, blankly.

"It's a sunken ship out by Espanore Island."

When she continued to look curious, he shrugged. "It doesn't matter." Enthusiasm filled his voice. "I don't know anyone there. I don't make friends all that easily," he admitted, somewhat sheepishly. "Too shy, I guess."

"Why do I have a hard time believing that?" Jill countered, receiving a wide smile too perfect to be natural.

"That's quite the camera," Mike said, peering closer.

Jill smiled. "I'm a photographer."

"You're on an assignment?" His question was drowned out by the inward bounding Carly, who jumped between them with gusto usually saved for the very young.

"There you are, Jill!" Carly exclaimed, mindless of the conversation taking place. "You'll never believe some of the art. The food looks amazing, and I'm starved. Some of these artists have some really cool stuff." For the first time, Carly realized she interrupted something, and followed Jill's apologetic gaze until it rested on the tall Italian-American. "Oh, well, hello there," she gushed.

"Mike, this is my friend, Carly. Carly this is Michael Marinello."

"Are you from Drummond, too?" Mike asked, shaking her hand.

"No, I'm just visiting." Carly turned on her friend. "Why haven't you ever mentioned this guy? He's from the island?!"

Jill tried to bite back her laughter, but failed when Mike joined in. "I just met him, Carly."

"I was just about to ask Jill if she'd like to have dinner with me, but maybe the three of us can get together for drinks, instead," he suggested warmly.

"Hell, yes!" Carly enthused. "We'll be at the Northwood tonight. Maybe Chuck's after that, and you can meet us there. Come on, Jillian, we've got stuff to buy." Carly tugged on Jill's arm, dragging her along in a playful fashion.

Jill allowed herself to be pulled away, waving to Mike over her shoulder. Mildly irritated, Jill challenged her friend. "I can't believe you of all people just pulled me away from a guy, when you've been bugging me to be more flirtatious."

"Jilly!" Carly smirked. "I'm so proud of you. Flirting so openly, and wanting to go back. You're finally learning. There are two things you need to always remember. Are you listening?"

Rolling her eyes, Jill nodded.

"First, always keep the guy guessing. And second, there's only one thing more important than flirting: shopping."

"That may be true, but I'm starved." Jill said.

"There's a long line in front of the whitefish sandwich booth, but I'd like to try one of those." Carly glanced over, seeing Jill nod her head in agreement.

The women joined the line up. Laughing, Jill let Carly ramble on, while her thoughts returned to Quinn. If Quinn doesn't want to be with me, Jill considered, there's no reason why I shouldn't flirt with Mike. With her heart aching a bit, Jill pushed thoughts of Quinn away, and focused on Carly's conversation.

TWENTY

Ten more minutes, and then I'm giving up, Lisa decided. Of all people, Lisa knew better than to get caught up in Frank's crazy story. His eyes were unclouded by the creative glaze that she usually saw in people talking, just for the sake of talking. Through that, and her own solid ability to read people, Lisa believed him. Frank helped bury Hamilton on Drummond Island, and met the legendary John Dillinger. It was a spooky coincidence that another treasure hunt was wrapping itself around a place she first learned about only the year before, and it bothered her. Lisa didn't believe in coincidences, but she'd explore that later. For now, she would satisfy her nagging curiosity by delving through handfuls of websites on John Dillinger and Three Fingers Hamilton. So far, she'd only stumbled across the most boring of biographical information about Hamilton.

Aliases:	John Campbell, Three Fingers
Height:	5'8"
Weight:	Approx. 165 pounds (medium, stout build)
Hair:	Brown
Eyes:	Blue
Identifiers:	Long, irregular scar through the center of forehead; right index and middle fingers amputated; heart and banner tattoo with initials JH on left outer forearm

Lisa bit into her slice of cold, leftover pizza and continued searching. The website read: born in 1899 in Sault Sainte Marie, Michigan. That checked out with Frank's story, but she didn't find any mention of Drummond. Attempting a different channel, Lisa ran a search for the Island, quickly locating the Tourism Association link, which led her to a toll free phone number. Grabbing her cordless phone from the back of the desk, she dialed the number and waited.

"Drummond Island Tourism Association, how may I help you?" A pleasant voice filled Lisa's ear, and she couldn't help but smile.

"Hi, my name is Lisa Daye, and I have some questions."

"Hopefully I'll have some answers, go ahead."

"Is there a place there called Wayfarer's Mart?"

"Why, heavens yes. There's an antique store and a bed and breakfast there. Sam does luncheons and whatnot."

"Has it been around for a long time?" Lisa questioned.

"Forever, nearly." The woman laughed. "If legend is true, it was once the largest Sporting Goods store in the nation. It has changed hands several times, but Sam Sparrow's got it now and funny thing… looks almost exactly the same as it did way back when. Small things have changed, but it definitely carries a lot of Drummond's history with it. If you're interested in making a reservation there, I can give you the phone number," the woman offered.

"That'd be great, thanks. And Mr. Sparrow is the person I want to talk to?"

"Oh, dear, no. Sam is for Samantha. *Ms.* Sparrow."

"Okay, cool. One more question. Do you know if John Dillinger ever visited Drummond?"

"The gangster? Gee, I've never heard that, but it would have been before my time here."

Lisa thanked the woman for her help before hanging up

and dialed the Wayfarer's Mart, glad when the phone was picked up promptly.

Lisa began with a few warm-up questions about rates and the area before she narrowed her focus. "You know, I think I might have been there before, or seen pictures in my childhood or something. Does the building face the water?"

"Yes."

"I seem to remember large stones... or some sort of stone formation with a big rock with a funny triangle shape. Am I thinking of the right place?"

Sam laughed. "Yeah, you know what you're talking about. I have flowers out front by those rocks now."

"Well, I guess I'll need to start thinking about a return visit. One more thing... and this might sound strange, but have you ever heard of the gangster, John Dillinger visiting Drummond?"

Sam pondered it for a moment before answering. "It doesn't ring a bell, but Drummond has had a variety of unique visitors. It's the perfect place to get away from reality for a while, you know?"

Lisa chuckled softly, "I'm starting to sense that. Thanks for your help." She said her goodbyes, and hung up, eyes riveted to her computer screen. Frustrated, she flipped through Frank's file that she had snagged from work. The dates matched up for him to be on Drummond at seventeen, but anyone could have done the math correctly. He knew about the Wayfarer's Mart, but he was born in Christmas, Michigan. A quick search on the net, showed it to also be in the Upper Peninsula, so it was possible that he was familiar with the area from visiting. Or he could have even worked there, like he claimed, and merely added in the Dillinger bits. She backed up to the last site she browsed about Dillinger and Hamilton, and continued to look through it.

Stretching away from her computer, Lisa journeyed to the

kitchen to fetch another cold slice and a Coke. On the Formica counter were books she had grabbed from the library. As she nibbled on her pizza, she flipped through the first one. She browsed until she found pictures of something the caption reported was the body of John Hamilton. The body was covered in lye, and found in a gravel pit in northern Wisconsin. Frank was wrong then, Lisa concluded, but she picked up the next book anyway and looked through it, skimming for information on Hamilton. Returning to her computer, she ran a search for John Hamilton's death and location. Sifting through sites she had viewed before, she clicked on one that caught her eye. The website identified the burial site as Oswego, Illinois. Included in the attached files was a letter by John Edgar Hoover, signed by the man and stating that the Identification Order 1220 was cancelled, because John Hamilton was deceased. Lisa continued to scroll, finding another site that claimed Hamilton was buried near a sink hole. Another source claimed he was still alive, and attended the Hamilton family reunion in the 1950's.

Examining the picture in the book for herself, and reading more about it, she learned that the body's face and right hand were in pieces and barely distinguishable. Stranger yet, a horseshoe was found on top of the corpse. The FBI would not comment or release any further information or proof concerning John Hamilton's death, Lisa read. The conflicting reports of Hamilton's remains lent authenticity to Frank's story in her mind. If she searched longer, she might even be able to find more locations claiming Hamilton's body.

Amazed, Lisa pondered John Hamilton's story. Hamilton traveled to the Upper Peninsula because he knew he was going to die. Five days later, escaping a shoot out with Bureau of Investigation Agents, in Little Bohemia, Wisconsin, he was fatally wounded and dead within days. He had a keen sense that he would have no rest in death, so Hamilton demanded Dillinger to return him home. A shudder crawled up Lisa's spine, as she considered how right he was. When Dillinger was killed, he was put on public display, manhandled, photographed and dismembered.

Confounded, Lisa leaned back in her office chair and considered her choices. Hamilton was in the ground on Drummond because that's where he wanted to be. If she respected a fellow human's right to choose his own burial ground, she would leave it alone and pretend Frank had never told her the story.

If she ignored Frank's words however, Dillinger's loot would also remain in the ground, and how could she allow that? The truth would darken with night, and no one would be the wiser. Hamilton probably had relatives that would want to know where he was buried, perhaps give him a proper gravesite.

And, Lisa considered, *treasure was meant to be discovered*, but could she do her part for the survival of truth and discovery, and remain unaffected? If Hamilton really was buried on Drummond, his body had rested for many years. Finding him might bring answers, but it might also lead to more suffering.

TWENTY-ONE

After returning from the boat show, Carly went for a run and Jill went for a nap. Joining the Northwood crowd early on, Jill and Carly found a corner table and reviewed the day's highlights, while the bar filled around them. Careful to avoid Quinn, Jill allowed Carly to fetch drinks, or ordered from the waitress when she came to their table.

"Jill!" Chase called, skipping through the door with the unchecked energy of the young. Bounding beside him was the ever popular and present Golden Retriever, Ridge. All six plus feet of the seventeen year old Adonis stopped on a dime when he reached her table, and folded abruptly into the chair beside her. "Tell me it did not actually happen. I mean, I couldn't have missed it, right?"

"Hey, Chase. You haven't met Carly yet, have you?" Jill patted his arm to let him know she'd get back to the topic in a bit.

Carly got on all fours beside the pooch and rubbed his body down. "You're a beautiful dog, aren't you? Aren't you?" she cooed.

"No... but, I need to hear..." His voice trailed off, and his mouth opened to see the woman playing with his buddy.

"Carly, this is the infamous Chase McCord."

Chase whistled, taking a moment to appreciate Carly's

unique looks. "Damned glad to meet you, honey."

Bursting with laughter, Carly pulled Chase to her and kissed the hell out of him. When she finally pushed him back, he was breathless, and she was laughing. "You'll have to settle for that, doll. I'm taken, but you're cute."

"Oh wow…"

Jill groaned. "Carly, he's spellbound. Did you have to?"

"Of course, I did. Isn't it a beautiful woman's job to torment young men?" she laughed, tugging Jill's ponytail.

"But I'm the one that's going to have to put up with him, when you go home," Jill protested.

"Hey, ladies," Chase stumbled, regaining his composure. "No need for Carly to go home. Quinn and I've got plenty of room at the house."

Laughing, Carly hopped up from the table. "Another round, Jilly?"

"Bring it on."

"I'll take a bud," Chase offered.

"Not on my watch," Carly smirked. "Pepsi?"

Chase grinned. "Who told you?"

"You told me," Carly quipped, chuckling as she walked away from them.

"I never said how old…"

"She means your kiss, ninny. She was teasing," Jill explained.

Chase puffed up a bit. "Well," he said, feigning humility. "If she's never had the pleasure of someone with my youthful energy, she should experience the deluxe package. I am a true ladies man."

Snickering, Jill finished off her drink. "How is Noel?"

"I haven't talked to her in a couple days," Chase moped.

"In the dog house?" Jill teased.

"I took Cassie out."

"Chase!"

"Nevermind about my girls… is it true? Did Marci really strip and I missed it?"

"Awww, poor baby," Jill cooed. "I know how much you've been wanting to see her in action."

"It's true?" Chase's face drooped, his body sagging as he leaned his head on Jill's shoulder. "Hold me," he moaned.

Jill gave him a playful shrug, laughing. "You should have seen it."

"Hell yeah, I should have seen it! Details, Jill. I need details. How perfect are they, really? I mean I've heard that her knockers are even…"

"Hey!" Jill barked. "I am not discussing Marci's breasts with you."

Carly set the drinks on the table, joining in the laughter. "*I'll* tell you about them, darlin'."

"Ooh, there she is," Chase said, leaping to his feet to meet Marci at the door. "Marci honey! How could you let me miss the show?" Chase hollered.

Marci paused at the door. A quick survey of the bar had her frowning. Quinn was working. No real playing with the kid brother tonight, she thought. "Give me a hug, Gorgeous."

Chase wrapped Marci up in his lanky arms, grinning. He picked her up off the ground a few inches, making her hold tight and screech. "You've got to do it again, Marz."

"Maybe later, Cupcake. I need to go say hello to a friend." Marci twitched her backside at him, and winked, scouting the bar. She waved to Carly, saying nothing to Jill.

"You're killing me, here," Chase moaned as she walked away from him.

Billy chuckled from behind Chase. "Leave that one be, Chase. You don't want that. Trust me, you don't."

"Easy for you to say. You've got Dee. What is it about *older* women? Why don't the girls my age have that spark?"

Carly ruffled his hair, and tipped back one of the shots she brought to the table. "A woman grows into her body before she grows into her confidence, doll. That's what you're attracted to."

"Well said," Jill agreed.

"I can't believe Coop has Dinner here," Chase mumbled. "And so quiet."

"They don't feed people here?" Carly asked.

"Not Dinner," Billy chuckled.

"They only serve lunch here? Or breakfast too? Breakfast in a bar? Man, I love this place!" Carly hooted. "Eggs Benedict and a Bloody Mary. Hell, yeah."

The group chuckled.

"I've been saying he should have named that damned bird something else," Billy frowned.

"That ass is going to wreck it for me and Ridge," Chase grumbled, patting his dog's head.

More than confused, Carly tried paying attention. "Am I missing something?"

"Carly, look." Jill pointed, indicating the space underneath Cooper's table.

To Carly's shock a full grown turkey was laying at Cooper's feet, quietly eating popcorn out of his hand.

"What kind of a sick twist brings a turkey into a bar?"

Chase laughed easily. "The kind of guy that's a bud and a half short of a six pack."

"What's the story?" Carly asked, loving gossip.

Billy grabbed the seat next to Chase. "Everyone calls him Crazy Coop."

"He lives half a mile too far down a dirt road." Chase added.

Billy grinned, continuing. "He rents a room from Major. He loves that damned turkey."

"Why do you guys call it Dinner?"

"Coop named it Dinner," Chase explained. "Quinn must not have noticed it yet. He'll be pissed. What if the owners come in?"

"Quinn's too busy flirting with Big Chest," Carly sounded, gesturing toward the busty blond at the end of the bar. "Who the hell keeps a turkey in an apartment? And who's Major?"

Billy pointed toward the bar. "Guy on the end, playing Keno. He was in the war, but he's not really a Major."

"Nevermind about that, what else about this Coop guy?"

"Don't really know how he got so screwed up. He's always talking about how he's gonna get rich and shit." Billy explained.

"The car's in the driveway, but no one's home," Chase deadpanned.

Annoyed, Jill interjected, "I don't think any of us should be throwing stones. What has he done to hurt us?"

Properly chagrined, Billy nodded. "Yeah, I shouldn't be saying shit."

Of course, Jill had picked up on Cooper's presence as soon as she walked in. She didn't see Marci make her way to him, an unusual move for her. Marci loved attention, but she didn't normally solicit it from Cooper. She tipped back in her chair, to check out the scene for herself. Sure enough, Marci was leaning over the man, apparently talking. A casual glance toward the bar revealed that Quinn was flirting unabashedly with some nameless wonder. Quinn would see Marci, Jill thought. Quinn kept a tight watch on the island mattress's exploits while in the bar.

Jill allowed her attention to focus on the flirtatious drama playing out between the buxom woman and Quinn. Annoyed with him, and more than a little hurt, Jill beamed when she found a welcome distraction.

"I thought you were going to start at the Northwood and finish up at Chuck's, so I checked there first." Mike Marinello accused, while smiling. Ridge growled up at the stranger.

"You're okay, Ridge. Stop you're grumbling," Jill said. "We're headed there next, we just haven't made it that far yet."

Chase leaned down and whispered in his dog's ear, "Good boy, Ridge."

"Hello, Mike." Carly greeted.

Jill smiled. "Have a seat, and I'll grab you a drink so you can catch up a little before we change scenes." Casually patting her chair, she brushed past him with an uncharacteristically flirtatious toss of her hair. "What do you drink, Mike?"

"Manhattan, please."

She attempted to circumvent Quinn, by talking to the waitress, but Quinn was a step faster. "Hey, Quinn." Jill spoke softly, and tossed an exaggerated smile over her shoulder toward Mike.

"Jill," he welcomed. "What can I get for you?"

"A Corona for me, a Manhattan, and I think Carly wanted a… damn. Grab her a Corona, too."

Quinn raised his eyebrow. "A Manhattan, hey? Since when did you start drinking whiskey?" He asked, knowing the answer.

"It's for Mike."

"Ah."

"He's just a friend," Jill said, biting her tongue as soon as she said it. Quinn didn't say anything to that, so she continued. "Do you know that Coop has Dinner here?" Jill asked, trying to move the conversation away from her.

Quinn's eyes found Cooper, seated quietly near the window, and he scowled. "Here are your drinks, Jill."

Feeling Quinn's eyes on her as she returned to her table, she slapped the drinks into her friends' hands with less finesse than usual. "Let's drink these and get out of here."

"What's wrong?"

"Oh, nothing. I haven't been to Chuck's in a while, and Mike's right. We need to move along," Jill said, slugging a large swallow of her beer down.

Mike and Carly grinned at each other, hurrying to finish their drinks as well. When done, Carly stood up. "You kids run along. I'm going to use the little girls room. I'll meet you by the car."

Jill stood quickly, her vision blurring slightly. She staggered just a bit, tipsy from drink, but it was enough to have Mike using the age old excuse to wrap his arm around her and help her outside. They made their way to her Tracker, where Jill leaned against it for support.

Mike looked down at her, appreciating her understated beauty. Jill's mind raced with a dozen thoughts, which all seemed to vanish when Mike leaned in and kissed her. As he pulled back, Jill's eyes dashed to the well lit window of the bar. Leaning over Crazy Coop, stood Quinn: *staring right at her*.

Twenty-Two

Plunked in front of her television, Lisa couldn't bring herself to concentrate on the sit-com. Her mind continually returned to Frank's story. He sounded sure that Dillinger's motivation to bury Hamilton in an easily remembered place was about the gold, or cash, or whatever he had stashed there. If it was paper money, there was a good chance it'd be worthless, Lisa figured. If it was something else, like gold or silver, it would be worth much more than it was in 1934, and quite possibly a small fortune. Through Lisa's internet reading, she learned that Dillinger's gang was responsible for a variety of heists, so the stash could be literally anything.

Lisa disregarded anything that wouldn't survive seventy plus years in the earth and still increase in value. In all honesty, Lisa thought, she could be skipping past what the treasure was. She found three confirmed robberies of interest. Two of them included the theft of large quantities of quarters and half-dollars, along with some silver dollars. The face value of the coins at the time was $1,200.00, so today they'd be worth a great deal more. Interesting, but Lisa was more intrigued by the third search result.

In Daleville, Indiana, Dillinger made off with a coin collection owned by an officer of a bank, one J.N Barnard. Listed as "rare and valuable," Lisa wondered what kind of a coin collection, in the Depression Era, would be classified as rare and valuable, and what's more, what could it be worth today? If this collection was buried on Drummond with Hamilton's body, Frank's directions should make it an easy find.

Drummond Island nagged at her, carried her thoughts to the first time she heard of the place, when Beth went searching for her brother Richard. Lisa felt a pang in her heart, missing her friend. Discovering a hidden stash of something valuable was immensely appealing, but Lisa worried that she was following Richard's path: a quest resulting in a tragic death for a few rolls of 1943 steel pennies. Two blissful days off beckoned, and Lisa vowed to put the quest out of her mind for a while and rest.

Exhausted, Lisa headed for bed. The ringing phone woke her the next morning.

"Hello?" Lisa yawned into the phone.

"Hi, Lisa. It's Nancy. I'm sorry to call you so early on your day off."

Lisa winced at the early sunlight stabbing her eyes. "God, what time is it?"

Sheepish, Nancy said, "Quarter to seven."

Lisa groaned. 6:45am on her day off, she thought miserably. If it wasn't important she was going to take Nancy out back and beat her, she thought humorously, knowing she never would. "What do you need?"

"Frank has been badgering the nurses all night by asking for you. He's not doing very well, and normally I wouldn't even consider calling. You've spent so much time with him lately, that I thought you might want to know. He's asking me to grant a dying man's request."

Saddened, Lisa rolled out of bed. She stretched and yawned. "How bad is he?"

"Dr. Gentry gave him a day or two at the outside. His

body's just shutting down, Lisa. It'd be a miracle if he lived any longer."

"Did Dr. Gentry tell Frank?"

"Yes. Frank knows he's dying, and he says he has more to tell you. Will you come?"

"Yes, I'll be there." In her heart, Lisa believed him. Regardless if what he said was true, she believed that he believed it. She wasn't one to stand in the way of a dying wish to tell all. If it helped Frank to unburden his heart, she wouldn't deny him. "Tell him I'll get there as soon as I can."

TWENTY-THREE

Jill peered through the foggy fragments of a dream she could barely remember to stare at the alarm clock. She'd been waking up early every day for so long that she couldn't help but wake up this morning, even though she had every intention of sleeping in.

Guilt nibbling at her stomach, she rolled out of bed with a sound plan forming in her mind. She'll brush her hair and her teeth and drive over to Quinn's, to talk about this whole thing and get their feelings out in the open once and for all. She could bring a peace offering… Bear Claws. What will I say? She wondered, brushing her hair into her trademark ponytail. "I'm an ass, Quinn," she mumbled to herself in the mirror. "When Mike kissed me… I just went with it. I never expected you to see…" She started over. "Quinn," she practiced, "you're too real in my life… bleh. You're pathetic, Traynor." The fact is, Jill thought miserably, I am attracted to Mike… but he's not Quinn, and he'll never be Quinn, so I can't love him the same way. Love him? Jill thought, wincing. Who said anything about love? Shaking her head, she scraped the thought off her.

The drive to the main road is always the longest part, but it seemed to happen in seconds, as Jill found herself pulling into the Island Bakery & Deli. Moments later, she climbed back into her Tracker and seemingly even sooner, pulled into Quinn's driveway.

Quinn lived in a modest yellow vinyl-sided house with a separate two car garage on the side. His Jeep, as well as Chase's monster of a vehicle, were both in the drive. Amazingly, to Jill, many islanders had garages, but few of them seemed to actually park their cars inside them. Everyone's got a project kicking, or a garage full of off season toys and junk (treasure to them). It surprised her to hear noises coming from Quinn's garage.

According to Quinn, he never used it at all. She tried the side door but found it locked. Pounding on the door with her free hand, she waited, pleasantly admiring the patch of tomatoes that had been Chase's summer project.

The noise halted after Jill knocked again. Well, what the hell, she thought. *Either he doesn't hear me, or he's avoiding me.* Maybe it's Chase, with a girl inside, Jill mused. After all, Quinn routinely threatened to make him sleep out there, but Jill always assumed it was a joke. As she turned to leave, she heard the familiar squeak of the door open at the house.

"What the hell, Quinn! I'm up!" Chase greeted from the deck, clad only in boxers. "It's damned early for a Sunday, ain't it? Did whats-her-face leave? Oh, Jilly Bean!" He called as he realized the pounding fist belonged to Jill. Chase's bitching halted, as he leapt over the deck railing and approached Jill. Ridge hurried past Chase to nudge Jill's legs, barking and sniffing at the pastry bag, she now held well above his head.

Chase reached for the bag, but Jill backed up, holding them behind her. "Who is what's-her-face?" Quinn had someone over? *He was flirting with…what did Carly call her? Big Chest*, she remembered, but she didn't think he'd take her home. Alarmed, the back of her throat burned, but she controlled her expression.

"Come on, give me the bag!"

"Who'd Quinn bring home last night, Chase?"

"No one. Give it over."

The garage side door creaked open, and she relented with no desire for Quinn to hear her pestering his brother about his sex life.

"There is a God: A beautiful woman carrying a coffee and a donut." Chase looked into the bag and hooted. "Bear Claws, yummmmmy." Before she could stop him, not that she would have, he shoved a giant sized bite into his mouth and smacked his lips, before tossing a bite to Ridge.

Quinn opened the door just a crack, and actually shimmied out. To Jill's amazement, he padlocked the door behind him before even saying hello. "Good morning, Jill. Is that my donut, Chase?" His voice cracked a bit, and Jill noticed that he didn't quite meet her eyes. *He must have heard us talking. He must know that I know he had company.* Not that it matters, Jill argued with herself. He's free to be with whomever he pleases. She remained silent, glancing from Quinn to Chase.

With the decency to look sheepish, Chase frowned. "Ah, you don't mind, do ya big brother? I mean, a guy your age probably needs to watch what he eats anyway, right?"

Laughing uneasily, Jill handed Quinn her coffee, since Chase gulped down Quinn's with teenage enthusiasm. "You can have my coffee, but I'm eating my pastry. I'm starved." Jill waited till Quinn had taken a drink, then asked, "So, what are you doing in the garage?" *Is there a woman in there?* She thought, but didn't ask.

Quinn covered his mouth with a yawn. "Just puttering." She could almost see his nose growing, she mused. "What are you up to this morning?"

The casual answer should have eased her mind, but it didn't. Either Quinn was really hurt about last night, or he was hiding something. He avoided her eyes expertly, something that he never did. *Guilt?*

Chase's eyes darted from one to the other, and he backed off wordlessly.

Lost in her thoughts, her emotions played across her face like a movie screen, with Quinn watching patiently. "Uhm…"

"Listen," they both said at the same time.

"You first, Jill."

"Right." Jill pushed her hands into her pockets, rocking back on the heels of her feet. *He's obviously had someone over, and this was a colossal waste of time.* "I'm sorry for avoiding you last night," this part was true, though her intention was to say much, much more. "I don't know what came over me. I saw you with that other girl, and I… well, I was jealous. And I know," Jill held up her hand, urging him to let her finish. "I'm the one that stopped us from happening… well whatever might have happened. And, I just wanted to tell you that I'm glad you're seeing someone new."

He was shocked that Jill admitted being jealous. For months, he had been trying to get her to see that she's it for him. This "friendship" thing was ridiculous and it wasn't working. *Seeing someone new?* How'd she get that idea, he wondered, about to correct her when she continued on blithely.

"I guess we've both moved on," she said, pleased that she could keep a straight face. She hadn't moved on at all, and she desperately hoped her face didn't betray the truth. She gazed up at him, shielding nothing, with Quinn silent and somewhat dumbfounded.

Ah, Quinn realized. *She thinks she's moved on, and she's trying to make herself feel better for ditching me.* He shook his head, disgruntled. "Jill, you're moving on…" *but you love me*, he thought.

"That's right. And so are you," she cut him off again, attempting to try the 'friendship hat' back on, "So, what's her name anyway?"

"Her name?"

"Oh, come on. You can hold out on Chase, but you're not going to hold out on me," Jill teased, tension thickening her voice. *Deep breath, Jill.* Keep it together.

Damn Chase, Quinn thought. "It's really nothing, Jill. Who's the guy you're seeing?"

"I don't know if it's really going anywhere, but the guy I met is Mike. He's living on a boat," She added, rather lamely.

"What kind of guy lives on a boat?" Quinn retorted, frustrated and getting edgy. *When was the last time I really slept?* he wondered.

"Listen, Quinn. Maybe, I should go. After all, I interrupted whatever it is you were..."

"I wasn't doing anything!" he snapped more loudly then he intended. He sighed into his hands. He was hovering on the brink of... well, he needed to get back to work, though he hated to end his conversation with Jill. If he stayed out here, arguing with the defiant brunette, he might say something he didn't mean. Exhaustion had dulled his senses, and his focus. If he didn't walk away from her right now, he'd tell her just how much he loved her. He'd haul her into his arms and kiss her, just because she was frustrating him past the point of sanity. Since Quinn respected Jill more than that, since he had faith that eventually she'd come around, he needed to walk away from her *now*.

"What's wrong, Quinn?"

The concern in her voice reached past the cloud of emotions seemingly swirling over his head. "I... ah, I need to get back to work, Jill. I'll see you later?" he asked, starting to walk away from her.

Abandoned on the driveway, she shrugged. "Sure."

What the hell was going on with him? She stared after him, watching him retreat back into the garage, closing the door behind him. He never looked back; he never cast a glance in her direction.

With regret, Jill knew their chance for a relationship had passed. For the first time in her life, she lost someone dear to her because she made the wrong choices. Her own stupidity, her own fears, she realized, left her... *alone*. When people left Jill's life, it was by force, never by choice. Tears glistened in her eyes, as Jill's lower lip trembled. Like so many, she realized, she was just beginning to appreciate the depth of her connection with Quinn, now that he had chosen to walk away from her.

Humbled, and saddened more by this loss than she ever expected, Jill was assailed by something she'd never been willing to acknowledge. She loved him. Now that he was gone, she realized she loved him. The realization slammed into her like one of Carly's brick-like fists.

Tears streamed down her cheeks unchecked. From the house, Chase watched with dismay. Feeling like an absolute idiot to be left in Quinn's driveway, Jill turned and got into the Tracker.

TWENTY-FOUR

AUGUST 15TH, 4:13 AM

Pulling into the left lane, Tower was lulled by the hum of tires running over metal grates. With a start, Junior woke up beside him. "What the hell?" Junior rubbed his eyes, shaking the sleep from his body. "Tower, where are we?"

With his eyes on the road ahead, Tower considered ignoring the question. Junior would simply become more petulant. After all, this was part of Red's plan, and Tower hadn't deviated on the drive up at all. When he prepped Junior, he used the plans and streets correctly, but allowed Junior to believe they were headed for a rodeo town on the Dakota/Minnesota border. Red instructed that Junior was on a need to know basis, and simply didn't need to know the exact location.

"We're on the Mackinaw Bridge, heading into the U.P."

"Why are we taking the long way?" Junior groaned.

"We're not going west. The banks we're robbing are in a town about thirty miles from here."

"Why didn't you tell me?" Junior asked, confused.

"I'll carry out the plan as I see fit. The change in location is merely a shorter drive for you. You're not losing anything, Junior."

"You didn't trust me," Junior accused.

"No," Tower agreed. "Have you told anyone you were going out of town? Did you tell anyone about your get-rich-quick plan?" Tower steeled his eyes, hardened his voice. "Tell me the truth."

"Screw you. I told you I wouldn't tell anyone, and I didn't."

"Don't bullshit me," Tower warned, grabbing Junior's arm and squeezing, while his left arm maintained the steering wheel.

Junior squirmed. "I'm not." Tower eased his grip, finally let him go.

"If this works, we're going to play hard."

"Why wouldn't it work?" Junior asked, dubious.

"The unknown is our enemy. Stay with the plan, I'm confident we'll be fine," Tower responded. "Think about the women, sand beaches, and bottomless beer. This is just our beginning, Junior."

Junior grinned, allowing the fantasy to take hold. Tower leaned back, dropped the token in the funnel shaped receptacle and waited for the gate to rise, letting them into the Upper Peninsula.

4:17am. Right on time.

"Get ready. In a few minutes, you're going to hop out and steal a license plate. Grab the toolkit from the back," Tower instructed, driving into St. Ignace.

"Why are we stealing plates?" Junior asked.

"You dumb son of a bitch, how do you think you're getting back to Detroit?"

"Aren't we going together?"

"No. They're going to be looking for two men, so we're splitting up."

"Okay." Junior leaned over the seat, grabbing the kit.

"After that we'll steal a four door sedan. I want something with eight cylinders, that's a couple years old. Try to get something bland and unmemorable. You won't need the toolkit for the car, but you will need it for the plate. You should be able to find one up here, unlocked with the keys in it. Just take the slim jim," Tower instructed. "When you have the car, follow me. Stay about three hundred yards back until we turn left on Three Mile Road, then close up."

"You'll lead me to the hiding spot," Junior continued.

"That's right." Tower turned into a residential street, cut the lights and pulled over. "Go, now."

Junior took his kit from the bag, and quietly hopped out of the Jeep. He pulled the plates off the first car he saw quickly and quietly, before returning to the Jeep. Tower drove him several streets down, before letting him out to steal a car.

The first car that fit the bill was noticeably locked from Tower's vantage point. He watched Junior move across the street, obviously grinning even from this distance. Tower shook his head to himself, seeing the Cadillac. Junior slid into the driver's seat of the car and started the engine, Tower's cue to drive off, leading the second car back to I-75 North. They reached the M-134 exit which loomed faster than even Tower expected. In his rearview mirror, Junior's car followed at a good distance. At fifty-four miles per hour, it didn't take him too long to reach Three Mile. He turned left, then right on Chard Road. Minutes later, Tower snipped the padlock open with his bolt cutters, and pulled into the single track dirt road. Quickly and flawlessly executed, Tower considered as he waved Junior to pull in behind him.

Pointing the Jeep toward the exit, Tower hid it as best he could. Stretching out in the backseat of the Cadillac Deville, Tower rolled up his jacket for a pillow, and slipped one of the guns underneath his head. Junior wanted to chat, but Tower gave him one cold stare and the other man got the hint.

Clearing his mind, Tower set his digital watch to wake him at the appropriate time and dozed with one final thought. 5:43am. In seven hours, he'd be rich.

Twenty-Five

Lisa smiled, not quite managing to hide the sadness. She pulled the visitor's chair closer to the old man's bedside and sat down with him. "How are you feeling, Frank?"

Frank's skin had a dingy yellow pallor. "Lisa, there's so much to tell you," his voice was raspy and low. "Kennedy…" his voice broke into a fit of coughing. Lisa handed him his glass of water.

Worried, she stood next to him, wiping his forehead with a cloth. "Frank, you need to rest. I can come back later."

"No… no, I don't know how much time I have." He wheezed, taking several moments to regain his breath. "I need to tell you."

Lisa nodded, relenting. "Kennedy? Was that the name of someone you worked with?"

"President Kennedy, Lisa."

Lisa's head snapped back to him, pensive. Returning to her seat, she wondered if she should be listening, curious as to what he was going to reveal. Her stomach rolled, and she clutched her hands together, ready for his story.

"First, you have to realize that it was another time. Hoover built a career on catching men like Dillinger, running a tight ship, and in the 60s, it was all about communism and evicting the Red from America. After working on Drummond, I moved to Detroit. Eventually, I got involved with the teamsters. Unions were a different thing back then. I'm sure you've seen movies about Jimmy Hoffa."

Lisa nodded, knowing to stay quiet and wait him out.

"The films don't show the half of it. He was a bad one. I was an enforcer. By the time 1960 rolled around, I had been with the teamsters for years. Mostly I dealt with people who owed them money, or people who didn't want union members in their shops. I'm not proud of the work." Frank coughed, plunging the button to release more pain medication into his body.

"When Kennedy took office, everything was shady. Even the election results were seriously questioned in areas. Hoover let it happen, because he believed the dirt he had on Kennedy would be enough to blackmail and control him. When Jack appointed Bobby as Attorney General, the two brothers were one incredible force.

"Hoover's attempts to control Kennedy were ineffective. Bobby cracked down on the crime families, dirty deals, guns and drugs, the whole of it. He was cleaning house, while Hoover was generally looking the other way and ranting about communists. Immorality plagued America, according to Hoover, when a major portion of registered communists were members of the FBI! Electronic surveillance was becoming a thing of beauty, but it was strictly illegal. Hoover didn't follow the laws, and instead of turning all relevant crime information over to Bobby, he kept private files where all his taps funneled into." Frank sipped some water.

"Hoffa was in bed with a few crime families, but one in particular: the Marcello family down in Louisiana. Hoffa was pissed off, and stated publicly that Bobby would be killed, but Marcello had another idea. Kill Jack first, and replace him with someone that could be controlled. Johnson was in Hoover's pocket. Hell, he might have even been a part of it. Hoover was all for the idea 'cause Kennedy was going to force him to retire. Hoover knew Kennedy was going to be killed, and had electronic surveillance recordings of the plan. He did nothing. He didn't warn the Secret Service, turn over evidence, or alert the President. He simply looked the other way."

"You're telling me that the head of the FBI was part of the conspiracy to assassinate one of our presidents?"

"That's right."

"This family…"

"The Marcello family," Frank rasped, urging her to ask questions.

"The Marcello family worked with Hoffa to kill Kennedy?"

"That's right. And Hoover knew about it and chose to do nothing."

"How do you know all this, Frank?" Lisa's voice trembled. They weren't simply talking about murder, but a coup d'e-tat possibly involving the Vice President.

"Because I was one of the men that set up Oswald. I was a part of it, Lisa." Tears gathered in his old tired eyes, his body trembling.

"Oswald? You set up Lee Harvey Oswald?"

"That's right. I set him up under Marcello's orders in something called Lone Nut Theory."

"Oh God… Frank, this is a lot to take in. You're telling me," she whispered loudly and harshly. "You were a part of the group that assassinated Kennedy?"

Tears streamed from the man's eyes, and Lisa looked at him, as if seeing him for the first time. "Yes."

"And Johnson knew?"

"From a conversation I overheard, I believe so, yes."

"And this was done with a lone nut... a lone nut what?" Lisa questioned.

"Lone nut theory," Frank provided. "The idea is for the real killers to set a well-known crazy up in a location that could have provided the kill shot. To do that, you have to start preparing the crazy person with jobs, and build a level of confidence. That's what the Marcello family did with Lee Harvey Oswald. They brought him into their fold, then set him up to take the fall. Oswald was a very public Castro supporter, and Marxist. The man wanted to go back to the Soviet Union. He was definitely considered "nutty." The perfect guy to take the fall, really. He was very public about opposing Kennedy, and stupid enough, controllable enough to get him in the right place at the right time."

"Our government is set up so that's not supposed to happen... I can't believe it." Lisa paced the room in short, edgy steps. "How? Hoover knew and did nothing? How do you know this?"

"Lisa, it's linked."

"What's linked?" she questioned, holding the glass of water to his lips.

Frank sipped and calmed himself. "If Dillinger hadn't been so loved by the press, Hoover wouldn't have used his case to rise to fame. Hoover built his career and the very presence of the FBI, from that one criminal. If Hoover hadn't hunted Dillinger, he wouldn't have been running as hard from the law. He probably never would have come to Drummond, and he wouldn't have ruined my life.

"I left Drummond because of that man. Hoover became a great leader because of that man, and eventually helped Kennedy become president, only to let him be assassinated. What sort of country would we live in today, if Kennedy had lived?"

"Kennedy wasn't assassinated because you had something

to do with it, Frank," Lisa offered, softly, contemplating everything Frank told her. "If Hoover was that determined, he would have found a way. Kennedy would have been killed regardless..."

Frank shook his head. "Hoover didn't plan it. He just looked the other way, Lisa. The Marcello family pulled the strings. If I had come forward to the right people, I could have ended it." Frank started coughing again.

"I have proof, Lisa."

"Proof? What proof?"

"I have a canister with 16mm film, and a sound recording from a restaurant. It was insurance of sorts. In case Hoover turned on the Marcello family, they could use it against him. It was the trump card up their sleeves that they would never bring out unless they needed it. I stole it from them." Frank's voice became strangled as he struggled to say the words. "I'm the only one that knows where it is, and it can't die with me. It's in a safe..." Frank's next word was swallowed by a sudden spasm and cough. His face began turning a shade of blue, as he struggled to say the next word. Lisa hit the alarm for help.

"A safe place?" Lisa asked, as she and the others tried to help him. "Where? Where is the safe place?"

Frank shook his head, coughing and hacking. He struggled to speak, but his body wouldn't cooperate. His eyes bulged, as Nancy ran through the door, with a syringe in hand.

"It's okay, Frank. You'll tell me later." She held his wrinkled hand in her own, and encouraged Nancy to give him the medication.

Frank's eyes shut, as the drugs took affect.

"He's out, Lisa." Nancy checked the monitors. "He's still with us, but he's unconscious."

Lisa let out a long breath she didn't realize she was holding.

"Why don't you grab some air? Or hell, honey, go on home. He's out cold, and you should try and enjoy something of your days off," Nancy told her. "He'll be out for a while."

Slightly numb, Lisa nodded. "Call me if there's any change, or if he asks for me, Okay?"

"Sure thing," Nancy agreed.

Lisa headed to the parking lot. Frank revealed terrible truths, and she was determined to find his proof.

Twenty-Six

August 15th, 12:55pm

More money than Red expected, he was sure of it.

Tower wheeled the Deville into the parking lot of the Central Savings Bank, and with perfect timing, Junior backed out of the bank and dove into the backseat of the car. If Tower didn't know better, he would swear he was looking at his twin. The same exact outfit of Nike shoes, jeans, MSU sweatshirt and hat, blondish-brown hair sticking out, and mustache disguised the twenty pound weight difference between the two of them. An expert might notice the inch difference in height, but they weren't dealing with experts. Eye witness testimony was often the worse kind of evidence, Tower knew.

On cue, Junior yelled, "Go! Go! Go!"

Tower didn't need the order, and in seconds the Deville was on M-134 and heading west.

Twenty-Seven

August 15th, 2005

Cooper loaded the countertop with bags of pig skins, jerky, and strawberry flavored milk. When he traveled off island, he never failed to stop at the BP station, better known as the Cedar Pantry.

"Aren't you buying gas today, Cooper?"

Cooper gave the woman behind the counter a lopsided grin. "I'm going to pay at the pump," he explained.

Monica nodded her head, humming to the music in the background as she loaded a plastic bag with his purchases. He didn't reach for his wallet until everything was carefully inside the bag. When she gave him the price, he carefully pulled the neon orange Velcro wallet from his back pocket.

Finishing up his transaction, Cooper continued his ritualistic journey to the pay phone around the corner. No one answered his boss's phone, so Cooper assumed that there were no more off Island pick ups to be made. Walking back to his truck, he placed the bag of food inside and inserted his credit card into the gas pump reader, following the steps indicated.

His nerves calmed as the summer breeze ruffled his hair. Squeezing the pump's handle just so, he eased a few more pennies worth into the tank and finished the transaction. The receipt printed the time at 12:55pm. As he turned to re-enter his truck, he noticed the Central Savings Bank. A pale blue

Cadillac Deville entered the parking lot and pulled up to the doors, engine running.

Cooper froze in place as a college-aged man backed out of the main entrance, clad in a Michigan State sweatshirt and ballcap. He gripped a nickel plated wheel gun in his right hand. In his left hand, he gripped the handles of a large bag. In the mere flash of a moment, when Cooper was able to get a good look at the bank robber, he noticed that the man was jacked up, with erratic movements that could only come from some kind of a high. Probably adrenaline, Cooper thought, as he watched the man dive into the backseat of the Deville.

Someone is stealing my money, Cooper thought. Down deep, Cooper knew he was smarter than most people. Like sheep, people deposited their money into banks, where it just waited for Cooper to come take it. It was his plan, his lifelong idea, to collect the money left there for him. He was going to rob banks, he just hadn't done it yet. He'd heard the snickers. People looked at him, waiting until his back was turned to call him "Crazy Coop," or some of the other harsher nicknames. He rarely reacted, because he knew they'd see just how smart he was when he stole the money they placed in the banks for him. Anger seethed through his grinding teeth, as he realized these men were destroying his plan. How dare they, Cooper thought. *How dare these college assholes steal my money*, Cooper raged.

Jumping into his truck faster than ever before, he intended to steal back his money. The Deville zoomed out of the lot, heading west toward St. Ignace.

Cooper raced his truck around the store, only to be cut off momentarily by an SUV pulling a boat. Finally able to exit the parking lot, Cooper punched the old Ford through the gears as fast as it would gain speed. His hands began shaking when he still didn't see the Deville. He was about to give up, when he rounded a curve, spotting a glimpse of the car rounding another corner ahead.

"There you are!" Cooper cackled. Like a bloodhound, Cooper tracked the bag of money. He wouldn't let the Deville escape him.

Twenty-Eight

In the office at Federal Alarm, the desk employee covered her mouth as she yawned fully. The slow days bored her to tears. She sighed heavily when the First National Bank of St. Ignace (Cedarville Branch) alarm lit up her computer screen. Most alarms were accidentally set off by a teller. She would have to reset it as soon as she talked to the bank. She punched in their code on her direct access telephone line, and was shocked when a second alarm in the same town was triggered at the Central Savings Bank. Neither bank answered her call.

Following protocol, she notified St. Ignace State Police Dispatch. She was unaware that it received a call six minutes earlier, concerning an accident involving a tour bus. The bus was headed for Bay Mill's Casino on M-123, roughly three miles north of Trout Lake.

The 911 call delivered minutes earlier had captured the frantic voice of a man pinned inside the bus. The transmission was fuzzy, but it sounded as if the caller said a second car was involved and leaking fuel. The bus and car were somehow tangled in two big trees, and there was one hell of a mess. The line went dead, and the call went out across the air waves. When St. Ignace received the call from Federal Alarm, they knew they'd need further assistance and contacted Sault Ste. Marie's Central Dispatch. ER at War Memorial was notified to prepare for many injured arrivals. Ambulances, fire trucks, and police officers were tasked to the accident location immediately.

*   *   *

In a squad car heading north on M-129, Officer Paul Conkey smiled as he gazed out toward the Pickford Panthers' football field to his right. In two short weeks his son would hopefully be the starting quarterback. Mark was only a sophomore, but he was a smart kid with a good arm, and in Paul's opinion, more talented than the senior who normally played second string in the years before. Filled with underclassmen, Mark was an excellent choice for the betterment of future years, but Paul wouldn't blame the coach if he decided to give the senior the nod. He was jarred out of his trance when Dispatch began barking orders for vehicle call numbers to respond to the bus accident. Listening carefully, his vehicle number never sounded, and Paul continued his drive to the local diner for his late lunch.

He steered his car into the parking lot just as the dispatcher's voice filled his ears again. "Federal Alarm is reporting two possible R.A. scenarios in progress at two locations in Cedarville, Michigan: First National Bank of St. Ignace at 192 Meridian Street, and Central Savings Bank on M-134, just west of the light. Both silent alarms have been triggered with no callback response at either location. All units available, respond."

Sault Ste. Marie's Central Dispatch was connected to every law enforcement agent in the area that carried a gun, including the County Sheriff's Department, State Police, Sault Ste. Marie City Police, Tribal Police, and all DNR officers. If an R.A., which stood for robbery armed, (ass backwards to Paul's way of thinking) was in progress, they were going to need everyone they could get their hands on.

Officer Paul Conkey flipped on his sirens, slammed his foot down on the gas pedal, and raced out of town, heading in the direction of harm's way. It didn't get any more real than this, he thought grimly. *He'd earn his pay today.*

TWENTY-NINE

At the same moment, Tribal Police Officer Terra Cloudfoot snapped the steel cuffs around the drunk tourist's wrists and guided him toward the backseat of her SUV. The heavy drunk had been causing a serious spectacle while refusing to leave, so Terra was called to the rescue. Just another day in my exciting life, she thought with a scowl, longing to move to the city. After graduating with her Criminal Justice degree, the only job she was offered was with her tribe. She applied in bigger areas for jobs just outside her reach, hating to start at the bottom and work her way up. She ached to be a detective, actively pursuing real cases. Instead, she was stuck picking up drunk and disorderlies, and taking care of domestic disputes. Nudging the oaf handcuffed beside her, she rolled her eyes as he deliberately slowed their progress to the caged area in the back of Terra's SUV.

"Honey, why don't you join me in this cage 'ere, and I'll show ya how much fun we can have with these little babies," drunk man offered, leering at Terra, while fondling the hand-cuffs.

Annoyed, Terra gave him a little shove, attempting to push him right in, but the process took her longer than she hoped. Poking her head toward the open door, she prodded him along. If they continued at this speed, she was going to be standing outside the Casino all day long. The last thing she wanted was a complaint against her for force, so clocking the dumb SOB with the butt end of her gun wasn't an option. Smirking at the thought, she wrestled the man in the final distance, feeling satisfied.

"Baby, why don't you just let me go, and I'll be good. I can be *real* good to..."

"Hush!" Terra snapped.

"But I wasn't doin' anything wrong, Officer Cloudfoot," he argued, reading the name plate on her chest. "What kind of a name is Cloudfoot anyway? Have you got pretty feet? I bet you do. Why don't you show me your toes..."

Staring him down, she barely caught the beginning of a radio transmission. Scowling, she realized she'd turned her receiver down when she picked up the jerk, and she'd forgotten to turn it back up. The dispatcher's voice rang clearly into the car. Terra glared her passenger into silence as she listened to the dispatcher's words. "All cars: RA in Cedarville. Gun seen, not implied. Repeat: guns were seen. Suspects are two white males, mid-twenties, average height and build driving modestly new, light blue, four door Cadillac. Michigan plate believed to be Bravo, Tango, Three, balance unknown. Last seen, heading west on M-134."

Terra paid strict attention to where the robbers were last seen, and reversed her positioning with the drunk. "Come on, come out of there."

"You letting me go, Sugar?"

"No, I'm letting the guard deal with you." With a glance thrown over her shoulder, she realized the man had stepped away from his post. "Shit!"

"Huh?"

"Come on, get out of the car."

"I was just getting comfortable."

"Out! Now!" With more force than necessary, Terra hauled the man back out and walked him to the Casino doors. "Get your ass out, now!" She grabbed his hair and tugged, pulling him bodily out of the vehicle. She knew she shouldn't be walking the man back into the building, but she needed to catch the guard. *There's no way I'm going to baby sit a drunk when there's an armed robbery going down,* she thought. Glimpsing the edge of the guard's uniform as he rounded a corner, she yelled out. "Hey!"

Thankfully, the guard spun around, surprised to see her back in the building. "What's going on, Terra?"

"There's an RA in Cedarville. I need to go lend a hand. Dispatch is calling for all units. Can you take care of this guy?"

"Yeah, I will. Go ahead."

"Thanks," she yelled, sprinting back through the door.

This was her chance! If Terra could be instrumental in the take down, maybe even collar the assailants, she'd have one helluva resume item and a one way ticket out of the Upper Peninsula. Road block locations were being called out over the air, with various units responding. She cruised south on Three Mile Road, passing by Chard Road as she screamed toward M-134. Adding her voice to the radio chatter, she responded, "Tribal 419 moving south on Three Mile Road to join chase at M-134."

Blue! Light blue! Was the car she just passed light blue? As she passed Chard Road, she noticed a car stopped in the middle of the lane, from the corner of her eye. Its brake lights were on, and the car looked stationary, which is why Terra had disregarded it. She flashed back again, still speeding south. Slowing the image down in her mind, she could see one figure, leaning over the back seat of the car. Intuitively, she believed it was male, but she couldn't be sure. Robbers on Chard Road didn't make any sense, but Terra's lights and sirens were off. If it was the robbers, it was quite possible they hadn't noticed her. Without any more thought, she checked her rearview mirror, and spun the SUV around, kicking up gravel as she zoomed north on Three Mile Road. If she called it in, she'd have company in minutes, and if she was wrong, she'd hear snickers everywhere.

Chard Road didn't make any sense. If the suspects decided to take Three Mile, why didn't they just stay on it? If they were doing some strange loop, why didn't they wait and turn onto Rockview Road, which was about three quarters of a mile east of North Arrow Log Homes's log yard. They must be on Chard for a reason, or maybe, Terra thought, *I'm on a wild goose chase.* Either way, she would not be ridiculed or challenged for the collar, by calling the change of direction in.

That was merely her first mistake.

THIRTY

Officer Paul Conkey raced over the hill, slowing as he came to the corner of M-129 and M-134. In seconds, he'd be rushing at top speed west. According to the radio chatter, a Mackinac County Deputy Sheriff raced east a little over nine miles west of Cedarville, and about six west of Three Mile Road. The Tribal Officer drove in from the north on Three Mile Road. In the next several minutes, someone would spot the Cadillac. Paul listened to the radio, concentrating on driving as he heard the Sheriff's Department in St. Ignace send three more cars on the way. A roadblock was being set up at Nunn's Creek Road. Troopers were ready to start checking cars at the bridge, searching suspicious vehicles and persons. More cops were setting up at the corner of M-129 and M-48, two miles north of Pickford. The lone State Trooper in DeTour Village along with the DNR officer, who shared the office were on their way to a spot just east of Port Dolomite on M-134. They would set up another roadblock, building a careful net.

Four miles west of Cedarville, speeding at 90 miles per hour, he spotted the Mackinac County Sheriff as they passed each other. Conkey slammed on his breaks and wheeled the car into a U-turn, lowering his windows, as he pulled next to the other police car. The Deputy Sheriff's voice filled the radio. "Cadillac Deville is no longer heading west on M-134. I've just met up with Officer Conkey, and there is no blue car!"

Dispatch crackled out new orders. "Head back toward Cedarville, and canvas side roads." New roadblock locations filled the car, but Paul's thoughts raced backward. "US 2, west of St. Ignace. M-128 at Eckerman Corner. H-40 west of M-123." Conkey followed the dispatch's directive, thinking over the last few minutes when the answer dawned on him. "MSP213 to Dispatch. What is Tribal's call number?"

Responding at once, "MSP213, the call number is Tribal 419."

"Tribal 419, this is MSP213. Do you copy?" Conkey waited a moment, listening pensively to dead air. "Tribal 419, this is MSP213, please respond."

Long seconds passed, before the radio squawked in response. "Central Dispatch, this is MSP213. Can you give me the last location of Tribal 419?" he asked, even as alarm bells clanged in his head. He had driven from M-123 just north of Worth Road when the bus accident call came in. From Worth Road, through Trout Lake to Eckerman Corner, there were absolutely no signs of a bus accident. By now, the dispatcher would have known and retasked those cars. The dispatcher confirmed that Officer Terra Cloudfoot last reported heading south on Three Mile Road. The Deville hadn't been seen again since it was originally reported, and it couldn't have disappeared. If the robbers were smart enough to call in a diversion with the bus accident, they were smart enough to go to ground or change direction.

If Cloudfoot was heading south on Three Mile, perhaps she had seen something and went after the suspects. By why hadn't she called in? It was protocol to call in. Worried, Conkey reported his change of direction and headed for Three Mile.

Having driven up Three Mile at high speed till he reached the Casino, Paul Conkey learned from the Security Guard what his instincts already told him: Officer Cloudfoot was missing. Grabbing his radio, he placed the call. "Central

Dispatch this is MSP213."

"MSP213, go ahead."

"I've driven Three Mile Road north from M-134 to the Hessel Casino. Tribal 419 is not on this road, and has not returned to the Casino."

"Copy that. Additional help is on the way," the dispatcher didn't miss a beat. Paul sat at the edge of the driveway for a moment, unsure of what to do. He decided to backtrack much slower, and look more carefully at side roads to see if he'd missed something. Maybe he'd get really lucky and find someone sitting on a porch who could provide the answers he was looking for.

Paying careful attention to the cars he passed, he noticed a Casino bus, two cars filled with senior citizens (presumably headed for slot machines), a log truck, a white mini van, with a woman and child in it, and a red Jeep with oversized tires driven by one young male, all heading north. On the right side of the road, Paul found his first break and stopped his car, waving to a man cutting his grass.

Minutes later, he was back in. Sure enough, the grass cutter confirmed that a Tribal SUV drove by with one person inside it. Paul continued his mission. He passed Chard Road, a few private drives, and came to a lady sitting in a rocker on her porch. The same series of questions revealed no new knowledge. The woman couldn't confirm or deny whether the SUV passed, since she'd also been engaged in a lively conversation with her friend sitting just inside the house, through a screened door.

Standing on the painted porch, Paul's mind clicked through possibilities. To his way of thinking, there was only one possibility: Cloudfoot must have spotted the getaway car, or believed she had, and turned off Three Mile in pursuit. If she had seen something, why didn't she call it in? Paul wondered. It didn't make any sense to him, but he knew that seconds counted, he just wasn't sure where to spend them.

Thirty-One

"We did it man, we really did it! Just like you said we would," Junior hollered, caught up in the adrenaline rush. "It was so easy! I had so much time I took all the fives and even the banded ones." Junior laughed, replaying the scene in his mind, proud of his strict adherence to the plan. After chatter filled moments, Junior finally realized Tower still hadn't said anything, and raised his head to get a better view of Tower's face.

"Stay down!" Tower snapped.

Junior dropped back down, giddy and careless about Tower's tone of voice. *I'm rich*, he thought. Tower drove the car adeptly, checking his rearview mirror as he came upon Three Mile Road, glimpsing the sun's reflection on a windshield in the distance. He didn't have much farther to Chard Road, and they were nearly in the clear.

Seemingly, without a care in the world, Tower used his blinker and obeyed the speed limit, sure not to attract any unneeded attention to the Deville. As he wheeled onto Chard Road, he looked back over his shoulder, glimpsing a fifty dollar bill in Junior's hand. Tower just crested a hill across from a log mill yard, when he punched the brakes hard, causing Junior to lose his grip and slam into the back of the front seats. "Is that from the bank?"

From the corner of his eye, he noticed something blur in

the distance. When he blinked, nothing was there. He shook his head, to clear it. He rammed his opened hand against Junior's jugular, pinning his body to the back seat. He let him go just as quickly, allowing Junior to gasp for breath.

"Is that from the bank?" Tower asked, knowing that it was. "What else did you screw up? How many times did I tell you..." Taking a deep breath, Tower exhaled slowly.

Stuttering, Junior tried to respond but Tower was on him again, slapping him across the head. "Give that to me!" Tower pulled the fifty from his hand. "Do you have any more?" Before he could answer, Tower pointed his gun at him. "Don't lie to me, you little son of a bitch. Do you have any more?" he repeated.

"No, Tower," Junior's eyes bulged, fearful.

Tower glared at Junior. "Idiot."

"I just took one, Tower. Honest," Junior insisted. "I don't have any money and I didn't think one would hurt anything."

"You didn't think is right. I told you to follow the plan. Do not breathe if the plan doesn't tell you to! What else have you screwed up?"

Junior was shaking his head. "Nothing, I swear it."

Tower accepted the answer, shoving the bill in his shirt pocket. He turned around, and headed down Chard Road. Passing Fenlon Cemetery, he drove about another hundred yards, and pulled off and to the right, where they hid the Jeep the night before.

THIRTY-TWO

Cooper urged his Ranger forward, rounding the corner in time to see the Deville turn onto Three Mile Road. Following at a distance, Cooper realized the Deville didn't seem to be speeding. Easier yet! He thought, smirking. *Money, money, money...* would soon be all his.

Cooper hugged his side of the road as the Tribal SUV flew past him, southbound. The officer's head was craned toward Chard Road, but she continued. Having lost sight of the car, Cooper gazed down the side roads carefully. The Deville was just cresting over the first hill. He hit the brakes, slowed and turned around. He couldn't remember exactly, but thought the road was a dead end. If the robbers drove down it, they'd be coming back out, he figured. If he followed them, he'd be outnumbered and outgunned, since the bandits had at least one gun, and maybe more between them. Pulling into a wooded lot, near a green sign, #2968, Cooper wheeled his Ranger around and backed up to the edge of the tree line. With a clear view of the intersection, he hunkered down to wait.

THIRTY-THREE

A lifetime seemed to pass in the moments it took Terra to reach Chard Road, though it was bare minutes. Having grown up in the area, Terra knew these roads like the back of her hand. Although many roads were simply dead ends, Chard Road dumped onto Rockview. The smarter decision for the drivers would have been to stay on Three Mile, until they reached Rockview, rather than doing the jetty-jaunt they chose. Two answers came to mind: the suspects were changing cars, or going to ground.

Flying down Chard Road, with hopes to overtake the blue Deville, she passed the log yard, then the Fenlon Cemetery, driving as fast as the road allowed. The 90 degree corner curving left would mark the last mile or so before she came upon them. She spotted the back hoe, dump truck and bright orange county pick up trucks. She flashed her lights and pulled up close, motioning one of the men over. Terra leaned her head out the window and yelled. "How long have you been here?"

Puzzled, the vested man checked his watch. "Hour, maybe hour and a half."

"Has anyone passed through?" She demanded.

He pointed to the trench dug clear across the road.

Before he could give her a wise ass remark, she asked again. "Has anyone passed this point since you've been here?"

The man shook his head no, and Terra threw her vehicle in reverse, pitching the car in a total turn again. Seconds later, she was on her way back around the curve, slowing considerably. Angry with herself for wasting time, and for not following protocol, Terra canvassed the driveways from her car, searching for signs. She was just about to give up, when she spotted the gated road on the left. She knew she had never seen it open, and yet there were tire tracks leading up to the gate. Beyond the gate, the trail was composed of simple black earth. Tree limbs hung over the road, and the property was densely covered with forest. Pulling over, she followed her instincts, and hopped out of her SUV.

Upon closer examination, she found two sets of recent tire tracks. One set apparently made by some "normal" car, Terra concluded, wishing she was more knowledgeable about tracks. The other set, in Terra's mind, smacked of some type of SUV or Jeep. Pride tugged the corners of her mouth up as Terra knew she'd found them. Six months from now, she'd be able to work anywhere she wanted. Pulling the gun out of her holster, she jogged quietly down the path, using foliage as cover, hoping to surprise the bandits. She hadn't been here in years, but if memory served, a hunt camp sat four hundred feet on the left. Running every bit of information through her mind, Terra prepared herself. Searching the woods for the blue car, she culled the license plate information from her mind. Tango Bravo Three? No, Bravo Tango Three, she thought. She edged further into the woods, gun drawn and ready. *Should I call in for back-up?* She wondered. *No,* Terra decided. She could handle it, she was certain. She was sure she'd found them. In another few minutes, she'd be doing the police work that would score headlines.

She was mistaken.

THIRTY-FOUR

MINUTES EARLIER

Tower pulled the Deville to a stop, mere feet away from the Jeep's location, and quickly exited the car. Junior followed, unloading the bags of money. Working quickly, they hid the bags of money in the back of the Jeep, under a variety of vacation items. Tower tossed a screwdriver from the toolkit to Junior. "Grab the Deville plates," he ordered, quietly.

Junior nodded, and knelt down in front of the license plate. Tower stepped up, executing the next step in his addendum to the meticulously detailed plan. Gripping his .38 with two hands at an angle away from his body, he squeezed the trigger. The bullet tore through the center of Junior's neck, at the base of his head. Blood gushed onto the Deville, and Junior collapsed face first toward the back of the car, sliding as he twitched into a lifeless heap. Tower didn't hesitate to enjoy the kill or gloat, but merely moved to the next step of the plan.

Opening a large leaf bag on the ground, Tower stepped into its center and shed the clothing from his body into the bag. Completely naked, he stepped out of the bag and used the solution and paper towel from the kit to cleanse himself of any gun residue or blood. Satisfied, he pitched the cleaning materials and removed the plastic cap that had covered his real hair underneath the wig, now discarded. He tossed the cap into the leaf bag as well. The tree hugger clothing eased over his body, and Tower finished by placing the 9mm Beretta in the waste band of his khakis. He glanced at Junior's body.

The fifty dollar bill. Angry for forgetting it, Tower used a new glove to dig through the trash bag and find his sweatshirt. He shoved the bill in his pants pocket, and moved to Junior's body.

He heard a low rustle and snapping before he heard the words, "Freeze! This is the police!"

Thirty-Five

"Oh thank God. Ma'am, this man's shot and he needs help!" Tower spun around, desperation painted on his face. To his delight, her gun shook in her trembling hands. Tower raised his hands, moving backwards, and feigned falling onto the ground, as if panic stricken. As he reached his hands out to break the fall, his right hand slipped the Beretta from his waist band.

The cop's hesitation cost her, and Tower squeezed the trigger: two shots to the chest, one to her forehead, dead center.

Tower remembered an old saying of his brother's: if you can't talk your way out, shoot your way out. With no death penalty in Michigan, one life prison sentence was basically just as good as another. Tower stayed low to the ground, listening for noise. She must have been alone, he concluded. How did she find me? One rogue cop stumbling across their path? No way. Tower wasn't going to wait around to find out. He used the solution again and stripped the new shirt off his body, grabbing a new one from the Jeep. He looked over the scene pleased with the absolute feeling of power and satisfaction he felt. Tower sealed the trash bag, loaded it into the Jeep, leaving the bodies as they lay and moved on. *Seventeen minutes behind schedule.*

THIRTY-SIX

Coop chugged back the last of his second Strawberry Milk, and brushed the pig skin crumbs off his red plaid shirt. His fingers thumped against the dashboard, rhythmically keeping time. Bopping his head against the back window of his truck, he second guessed himself. *Too long, much too long,* he thought. Chard Road must have an outlet, but he couldn't be sure. One tribal cop, two state troopers running in opposite directions, maybe the same car turned around. The tribal cop hadn't come out yet. Why not? Why not, why not, why not? Bop, bop, bopped his head against the glass, pounding fists on the dashboard. *Log truck, white van, red Jeep. Man, woman and children, man. Log truck. White van held a woman. No woman could do this, he thought. It was definitely a man he saw outside the Bank. Jeep filled with vacation toys. Six shooter bumper sticker. Money, money, money.* Bop, bop, bop. Teeth gnashing together, Cooper put his truck in gear and rolled down Chard Road.

When he spotted the county trucks, he turned around. *No smiles, there. No money.* He investigated, when he saw the tribal SUV pulled off the side of the road. *Shiny new padlock. Footprints. Little footprints. Tire tracks.* His sneaker clad feet pushed against the trodden ground. *Bigger footprints.* A game bird's familiar call sounded like a smile to Cooper's grateful ears, and he calmed. Glass reflected sunlight beamed into his eyes, and he ducked back behind an old cedar tree at the road's edge. Advancing slowly, the same way he crept when he first spotted Dinner, he inched forward. *Fifteen steps. Twenty.*

He looked down and saw the blood soaked body at his feet. Gasping, Cooper retreated one step. Cooper whimpered low in his throat, almost missing a distant bird's *cluck, cluck, cluck. Deep breath in, out. Lady cop lay face up, forehead ripped open and blood soaked.* Fifteen feet from her body, lay the man Cooper recognized from the bank. *Red Jeep. Shit!.*

No money, no money, no money.

With one wailing cry, Cooper pounded his fists against his legs. Limbs shaking, he checked his plastic dinosaur watch. *Just enough time to make the 2:40 home.*

Thirty-Seven

Tower had followed the plans exactly, only having to detour when he ran into the Mackinaw County trucks putting the culverts in at Chard road. He backtracked to Three Mile, turned right onto Rockview. From there, he headed south on M-129, finally turning left at Swede Road. Only when the road was out of sight in his rearview mirror, did he begin to relax. Easing under the Port Dolomite Train Bridge, he followed the snaking trail, and Red's instructions, turning right on Thirty Mile Road. Approximately one hundred yards later, he recognized the orange ribbon marker Red spoke of, and pulled the Jeep over. About twenty feet from the road, exactly as Red promised, was a black, shrub covered, canvas tarp. The tarp concealed a decent sized hole in the ground, where four Goodyear tires (a bit smaller than the tires currently on the Jeep) and a Craftsman lift jack waited for him.

After changing all four tires, he rolled the others into the hole. Before he covered the area with the tarp, he also placed the bag filled with clothing, guns and evidence into the hole, and ditched his last pair of latex gloves. He stretched the tarp. Twenty yards south of the area, were two garbage bags hidden from view and filled with pine cones, needles, and ground items that he used to cover the tarp. Mother Nature couldn't have done a better job. The only incriminating evidence he still held were the bags of money, and the 9mm Beretta.

Returning to the Jeep, Tower opened the back hatch, and removed the two bags of money. He dumped the contents on the passenger seat, carefully separating 100s, from 50s and so on. When the bags were empty, he divided up the bundles tossing approximately equal bundles into each bag, not bothering to count out individual bills. Neither he nor Red cared about a few thousand dollars difference, as long as the amounts were close. It would be a long time before Tower knew exactly what the take was, but he knew it was more than they anticipated. After dividing the cash, he returned the bags to the back and inspected the area carefully from all angles.

Placing the backpack filled with nature paraphernalia in the passenger seat, Tower allowed his mind to fill with the sounds of birds in the distance. From this moment on, he was merely on vacation. He'd follow the route to Drummond with ease. Thirty Mile Road to M-48, then to South Caribou Lake. Finally, he'd roll into DeTour Village and from there, the Drummond Island Ferry Line, with no one the wiser.

THIRTY-EIGHT

"Well, hell's bells, Chase. Are you swinging that hammer or are you dancin'?" Bobby taunted. "If you were busy working rather than flapping your gums, you could at least be half as fast as I am. Now, I gotta start working on your side. Pete, you gotta give me somebody better to work with here," Bobby grumbled, enjoying the rib session.

Pete raised his head, taking in the scene, hiding a smirk. "Chase, if you can't work and talk at the same time, shut the hell up."

"So whose bringing what to my barbecue?" Jill asked, changing the subject.

Gary raised an eyebrow. "I have to bring something?"

"That's right."

"Do chips and dips count? Debbie don't cook too much," Gary mumbled.

"Sure. That'd be great."

Chase paused in what he was doing, to use his hands, imitating a large dish. "I'm going to bring a big dish of my manicotti recipe. I've got fresh tomatoes from the garden and…"

"I'll be sure to avoid that one," Bobby quipped.

"Leave Chase alone," Billy defended.

"What the hell are you stickin up for him for?" Bobby demanded. "You wouldn't even be here if it wasn't for Jill and Dee beating your ass out of the bar, and Jilly getting your job back for ya."

"There's nothing wrong with a man cooking, Bob." Billy rebuked, unaffected by the other man's perpetual running of the lips.

"I don't know," Bobby retorted. "If he didn't have so many girls chasing after him, I'd start to wonder. He gardens, he cooks…"

"Piss off, Bobby." Chase laughed. "I don't see your tactics getting you more girls."

"Hey, Jill. How'd the Boat Show shoot go?"

"Really great, Chase." Jill responded. "You should have been there."

"I was wanting to go myself, but plumb forgot on Sunday," Bobby mentioned. "I wanted to vote for my friend's boat for that People's Choice Award they've got. You don't know who won, do ya, Jill?"

"Actually, I brought the paper with me. I haven't had a chance to read it yet, but…"

"Read it aloud, Jill," Pete suggested. "I'd like to hear about it, but forgot my damn glasses at home."

"Okay," Jill grabbed the paper from her shoulder bag, and flipped to the boat show article. She cleared her throat, and began.

"1939 Custom Barrel Back Wins 2005 Boat Show

Island Jester, Best of Show, at Les Cheneaux by Jimmy Topuck

The twenty-three foot custom Runabout Barrelback Chris Craft received a boat load of awards, by the end of the day. Island Jester not only won *Best of Show*, but also the *People's*

Choice Award at the 28ᵗʰ Annual Les Cheneaux Antique
Wooden Boat Show and Festival of Arts. The awards didn't
stop there, as it also won first place in its class. Best of Show
is decided by a panel of judges and the People's Choice from
Boat Show spectators.

The owner of *Island Jester*, Mr. Young owns a summer
home on LaSalle Island and purchased the runabout from John
Pepper, in Lake Champlain, New York. Mr. Young then hired
Classic and Antique Wooden Boats of Hessel, to restore his
gem in the rough to its current state. "Every piece is original,"
says Mr. Young. "I've been looking for a Barrelback ever since
coming to the islands, four years ago. The crew at Classic &
Antique deserves the credit. It'd just be another boat if it
wasn't for their magic hands." When questioned about his
reasoning to name the boat *Island Jester*, he just smiled and
said the owner of Up North Studios told him it'd look good on
the transom."

Jill looked up from the paper to find all eyes on her. She
wasn't sure if she should continue reading, but Pete motioned
for her to go on.

"According to Boat Show Co-chairman, Molly Diamond,
attendance is up this year to over 9200. Great weather, and a
rebounding economy were cited as being reasons for the
uptick in spectators from last year. 167 boats were registered
for the show, with 144 showing.

The Boat Show in Hessel is Clark Township's biggest
event of the year, requiring up to 250 volunteers from as far
away as Traverse City to make sure everything runs smoothly.
The financial gain for the business community extends way
beyond this one weekend event. Not only does it bring over
nine thousand people to Hessel on the second Saturday in
August each year, it also creates year-round work. The buying
and selling, as well as storage, repair, restoration, lettering and
custom upholstery are just some of the services antique boat
enthusiasts have done in the area. Beyond the boating

community, the show allows a premiere location for over seventy local artisans to sell their hand-crafted items, and for local groups to raise money with food sales. Funds generated from the boat show are used to support two Les Cheneaux historical museums."

"No shit? They're not funded through taxes?" Bobby asked.

"I guess not," Jill responded.

"Bobby, shut up and let her finish." Pete growled.

"Sorry, Jill. Go ahead."

Jill cleared her throat and continued.

"In related news, the State of Michigan has a new cabinet level department called History of Arts and Libraries, and it is working with Travel Michigan to brand Michigan as the "Great Lakes Maritime Heritage" destination. One of their goals is to create an Upper Peninsula circle tour featuring the Great Lakes Shipwreck Museum, the Soo Locks, the St. Ignace Tall Ships Company, and a museum and hands-on learning center of national merit on Antique Wooden Boats in Clark Township. The circle tour would become the flagship route of the Great Lakes Heritage Destination. The state would assist with funding, cross promotions, and national press. Working with the E.U.P Nature Alliance, Clark Township is looked upon favorably by the state due largely to the continued success of the Les Cheneaux Antique Wooden Boat Show and its standing as one of the leading Antique Boat Shows in the country.

Please turn to page 16 for boat show results and pictures."

Jill cleared her throat again. "Do you guys want me to read any more of this?"

"Nah," Bob said. "Just skim through and tell me if *My Girl* is among the winners. I mean, did it get anything?"

"Ah…" Jill glanced through the captions. "I don't think so, Bob."

"Well, shit! If I'd been there, I know I could have rounded up some more…"

"Whoa, whoa. Quiet down." Pete moved to the radio, cranking up the volume.

"Leading the news this hour, there's been a dual bank robbery in Cedarville, Michigan. Both First National Bank of St. Ignace, and the Central Savings Bank were robbed simultaneously by two men, dressed in Michigan State athletic wear. Both are at large, armed and dangerous, driving a light blue Cadillac. Road blocks are being set up as this broadcasts, and if you see a light blue Cadillac, or these suspicious persons, please inform your local authorities. Do not approach these men. Thankfully, no one at either bank was seriously injured in the robberies."

"Whoa…" Pete breathed, sharing glances with the rest of the crew, as breaking news filled the room.

"That's bizarre."

"Who in hell'd want to rob Cedarville? There can't be all that much money there." Chase said, as the radio flipped to a new song.

Bobby and Billy nodded agreement, while Gary grabbed a carpenter's pencil and began scratching something down. Jill kept an eye on Gary, who paused and restarted with his scribbling every few moments. Twice, he stopped to draw a line through his last figure. "Okay, Gary. I'll bite. What are you doing?" Jill asked.

The rest of the crew quieted down to listen. "I've been doing the math on these bank robberies. I think there might have been a lot of cash in these banks."

"How much?" Jill asked.

"I might be off, but I'd say about $640,000.00."

"Your old ass," Bobby countered, incredulous. "Branch banks in Detroit don't even hold that much cash."

"Normally, you'd be right. Under these conditions, I think Cedarville was loaded," Gary refuted. "Jill, the Boat Show is seven bucks per person to get in, right?"

"Yep."

"What did the two of you buy, if you don't mind me asking?"

Jill paused, thinking back. "I bought a Boat Show poster and a sweatshirt. Carly bought a book, tank top, and metallic sun sculpture."

"I bet that was sweet," Chase commented.

Gary rolled his eyes. "How much did all that cost?"

"I spent a little over fifty bucks. Uhm, let me think. Carly spent about seventeen on the book, like thirteen on the tank, and maybe forty-five on the sun? I think that's right, Gary."

"About $125, total then?"

"Sounds right," Jill agreed.

"Did you eat lunch there?" He asked.

"Yes," her eyes sparkled. Gary was about to prove his point, she knew. "I think it was about 13 dollars for both of us."

"Anything else?"

"No. Oh, wait. I bought a five dollar raffle ticket."

"So, let's see. I'd say the two of you spent about $140.00, let's say, not including the tickets to get in. Why don't we be conservative, and assume that you and Carly are heavier than normal spenders. Let's say that the average dollars spent per person is only $45.00."

Jill's glance around the room confirmed that everyone was paying close attention.

"Seven bucks times 9200 people through the door, right?"

"Yeah, that's what the article said."

"That's $64,000.00, which is ninety percent cash. $45.00

times 9200, gives us $414,000." Gary said, checking his notes for confirmation. I'd be willing to bet it's at least seventy percent cash. That'd give us $290,000.00."

"See, there. Under 300, not over 600." Bobby piped in.

"Hold it. That's just the beginning. The banks close Friday night, preparing for the biggest weekend of the year. That's 4:30 Friday to 1:00pm Monday, when the banks were hit. That's almost seventy-two hours of cash build up from deposits made over the weekend from all area businesses and the boat show."

"Don't forget about the casino," Billy reminded.

"I was just about to get to that, Billy. The Hessel Casino deals in cash, as well. It's probably conservative, but I'd expect another $100,000.00 from the Casino alone. The rest of the area's businesses would probably rake in... maybe $700,000.00. Of course, only about fifteen percent of that would be cash. Another $105,000.00, let's say. Then there's the cash the banks would have on hand to cover this huge weekend. The banks would probably each have $40,000 extra, for a buffer. Add it up, boys." Gary smirked. "$640,000."

"How the hell do you know all that?" Bobby challenged.

"I pay attention and use some common sense. My sister owns a convenience store which is where I'm getting the fifteen percent ratio for cash transactions. I think I'm damned close. If anything, these numbers are conservative. I wouldn't be surprised if they took as much as $700,000."

"Well, hot damn." Bobby whistled convinced.

"Sounds like a lot of money to me." Kate sounded from the doorway.

"Katie!" Bobby hollered. A chorus of hellos met the petite blond, who waved in response.

Kate smiled richly at her husband, while standing on her tiptoes to kiss Pete's cheek.

Jill smiled at the couple, continually amazed by how well they fit together. Pete was a bald headed, stern speaking goliath of a man, with deeply tanned skin and forbearing presence. Kate, Jill mused, looked like a prom queen, even after having given birth to three children, the last of which arrived this year.

"Did you hear about the robberies, Kate?" Pete questioned.

"Yeah, I did. It's so terrible. I heard about it on the radio. All those poor people's money stolen," she shook her head sadly.

"Don't worry, Kate. The money's insured. What are you doing here, hon? And where are the munchkins?"

"Mom's got the kids. I made brownies for everyone, so I thought I'd stop by."

"Brownies!" Billy cheered. "The day just got a whole lot better. Where are they, Kate?" Billy and Chase both moved to rush past her, when she grabbed Billy.

"Not so fast, young man," Kate said sternly.

Alarmed, Billy stopped when Kate pulled him back. He turned to her, waiting.

"I can't believe I had to hear through the grapevine, that you asked DeeDee to marry you."

Chagrined, Billy nodded. "Sorry, Kate. It just kinda happened. I've been meaning to tell you."

Kate grinned, hugging him. "Congratulations, Billy. The two of you are gonna be together forever. I just know it."

Chase returned, with one brownie hanging out of his mouth and another in his hand, pushing the plate into Pete's grasp.

The crew had plunked all over the floor of the room, some of them perched on step stools or raw material stacks. Jill helped herself to a brownie, finding a place to sit near Kate, enjoying the impromptu break. No one seemed to mind, including Pete, who welcomed the distraction of his lovely wife.

"So, does your friend like Drummond so far, Jill?" Kate asked.

Turning to Kate, Jill smiled. "Yeah, she loves it. Taking a break from the constant training is really good for her."

"I bet," Kate agreed. "Here, honey," she said, offering Pete another brownie, after Gary handed the plate back to her. "How is Quinn doing, Jill?"

"I haven't seen much of him. Chase lives with him, you know."

"Of course, I know that," Kate said, looking to Chase.

"Quinn hasn't been in the house much at all. Or on the island much, for that matter."

"Really?" Jill questioned, hearing this for the first time.

"Yeah. I went to steal his ferry ticket the other day, and noticed that most of the punches were used. He bought that damned ticket last week."

"Did you ask him about it?" Jill inquired.

"No. He might realize I borrow it from time to time, and get pissy."

Kate grinned, pleased to know that Jill was still *very* interested. "So… how are the barbecue plans coming?"

"For God's sakes, don't encourage them Katie. We need to get this job done!" Pete grumbled, splitting a pointed look between Chase and Bobby, who were squabbling over the last brownie. "Better be heading off, Katie," Pete suggested. "If they slack off any more today, we're not gonna be able to buy Christmas presents for the kids."

"Oh, that was a low blow." Bobby winced. "Uncle Bobby isn't going to be responsible for no prezzies. Back to work!" He yelled, hauling Chase up by the forearm. "Come on, slacker." He echoed, laughing while he attacked the next job with gusto.

Thirty-Nine

At twenty-two miles per hour precisely, Cooper traveled down Ontario Street, carefully staying well under the speed limit. *Cops never smiled*, he thought. Two years ago, Cooper was given a ticket for going thirty through town, five miles over the limit. Careful not to make the same mistake again, he rolled into the ferry line, miserable to see the boat ramp being raised. *Red Jeep*. A red Jeep was parked on the right side of the boat. Diving out of his truck, Cooper ran to the gate and caught sight of the bumper sticker's words, just before the gate obliterated it from view.

Running back, and along the pier as the Drummond Islander IV pulled away, Cooper stared hard at the back of the man's head. A sly smile edged into his crazed face, when Cooper whispered, "I'll be your Huckleberry."

FORTY

Jill yawned fully as she made her way from her Tracker to the back door. Her thoughts were still mulling over, in no particular order, the upcoming party, the bank robberies, and Quinn's business off the island.

She walked through the door, puzzled at the grunting noise emanating from the living room. Stepping closer, she peered over the edge of the high-backed couch. Shrieking, Jill leapt backward as if burned, hand on heart, slamming into the dining room table at the sight of Carly's naked sweat covered body, cavorting atop some man on her living room floor. Just as quickly as she came in, Jill turned around, and called out, "Take your time. I'll be back in a few hours," before escaping through the back door.

Oh my, she thought, finally noticing the book propped against the door frame, momentarily transported back to her college experiences of walking in on Carly with a variety of individuals. Unable to suppress her laughter, she giggled all the way back to her Tracker. After the first three times when the unsuspecting and quite naïve Jill walked in on Carly, they developed a system. If either of the girls needed privacy, they'd prop a copy of some old book at the base of the doorframe. The challenge came when Jill needed to occupy her time creatively when propped books became a regularity. Quickly, she learned to leave some camera equipment in her car at all times.

Several minutes passed with Jill going around bikers, and waving to passing cars. Without realizing, Jill found herself pulling into Quinn's driveway. Thankfully, no one was home, she realized as she parked near the house. Like a mouse sneaking through a house for a savory bit of cheese, she eased her way over to the garage.

The door was locked with a padlock system that seemed laughable on Drummond Island. The garage door refused to budge, even when she heaved with all her strength. Covered with opaque plastic, the windows revealed nothing. Walking around the perimeter of the building, she noticed that every window was *perfectly* covered, even those surrounded by trees at the very back of the garage.

Barking and bounding toward her, Ridge leapt up onto Jill. "Shit," Jill whispered, rubbing Ridge's big beautiful golden head, realizing she'd been caught. "Hey, Ridge."

"What the hell are you doing?" Chase barked, much like his lovable Golden Retriever, all noise and no bite. His puzzled expression slowly darkened. "Oh, oh, oh. I get it… you're in on whatever this is that's going on with Quinn, eh? Pretending like you don't know what's going on at work…"

Jill continued to pat the dog's head. "Chase, I'm snooping."

After a moment of silence, Chase's face filled with admiration. "Really? Wow." He thought about it for a long moment. "So, you really don't know what's going on either?"

"I haven't got a clue. I'm sorry I'm sneaking around, but…" Jill followed Chase from behind the building.

"Hell, I love ya for it," Chase said, turning to look at her, eyes twinkling.

"You don't know where Quinn keeps the key?" She settled beside him on the deck's stairs leading up to the house. Ridge laid near her feet with his head comfortably resting on Jill's foot.

"I have looked everywhere." Chase yawned, talking through it. "He must have the damn key on his body or something."

"Have you tried just asking Quinn what he's doing out here?"

"Yeah, it never works. He always has a stupid answer."

"And you haven't pressed him?" Jill urged.

"You know how Quinn gets. He can be downright shitty, if he doesn't want to talk about something."

Jill nodded, accepting. "Do you think it's a woman?" she blurted before she could stop herself, instantly regretting it.

"You can't mean he keeps a woman locked up in the garage, do you?" Chase contemplated it for a moment. "Whatever is going on with him, Jill, it has to do with this building." He crooked his head toward the wall.

Jill accepted this, but still couldn't scrape the thought of Quinn with another woman from her mind.

"What about all the trips off the island?" Chase countered.

"Maybe the woman lives off island."

"Then why is he so shady about the garage?"

Puzzled, Jill shook her head. "I can't come up with anything."

"Jill, I'm really worried about him," Chase confided. "He's really tired, all the time. He's working less at the bar, but I don't see him at all. He's going off island quite frequently, and never mentions it. And he looks like hell."

"I've noticed an attitude, and the odd behavior... but I haven't picked up on all the little details. What could it be? What else have you noticed?"

"He's kind of cheap lately. And he seems really stressed," Chase began, pausing to weigh something in his mind before he chuckled. "Okay, this is going to sound weird."

"What?"

"He smells funny."

"*What?*"

"He smells really strange sometimes."

"Like a woman's perfume?" Jill asked.

"Jill! Would you get women off the brain! He smells funny when he comes in from the garage. Most of the time, he goes straight to the shower. I almost think he's covering something up. Drugs, maybe?"

"Oh, no. Quinn can't be into drugs, Chase."

"The moodiness? The trips off island? The locked up garage? What if it is drugs?" Chase argued, not really believing it.

"It can't be drugs. Quinn's not stupid. He wouldn't risk it." Jill stated.

"Whatever it is, it can't be good. If it was okay, he'd tell us about it, wouldn't he?"

"He's pretty private," Jill shrugged, patting Ridge absently. "Is it possible that we're just overreacting? Maybe we're looking at it from the wrong angle," Jill suggested.

"Then how do you want to look at it?"

"What's been going on around here that Quinn might be a part of?"

"Bank robberies," Chase blurted.

Shocked, Jill leaned away from him, staring. "Chase, you can't for a second believe that Quinn had anything to do with the bank robberies."

"I think he went off the island this morning."

"Chase, I heard two people were murdered."

"Yeah, you're right. No way. Quinn can't be involved," Chase agreed, feeling like a dumb ass to have even considered the idea. "What about some sort of moon-lighting that he doesn't want anyone to know about?"

"Quinn loves the Northwood," Jill replied.

"Shit, I'm out of ideas."

"Yeah, me too. Keep your eyes open though, okay?" Jill prompted.

"You too," Chase encouraged. They sat beside each other in comfortable silence for a moment, before Chase asked, "So what's going on with that Mike guy?"

A spark rippled through Jill's spine, when she thought of the tall Italian being interested in her. She smiled involuntarily.

Seeing the expression, Chase groaned. "Quinn is in love with you."

Jill raised her eyebrows. She had formed a unique friendship with Chase but he had never been so specific and earnest about his brother's feelings before. "I used to think so, Chase. I'm not so sure anymore. I mean, who is that blonde woman I keep seeing him with?"

Grinning, Chase nudged her playfully. "So, you have been paying attention."

Ignoring the smug look on his face, she nudged him back. "Do you know who she is?"

"Brenda something," Chase shrugged.

"Are they dating?"

"I wouldn't worry about…"

"Chase! Tell me."

He relented. "I've seen her car here a few times in the early morning. Once at night, but I never stick around to figure if she's stayed over, or what's going on. I asked Quinn about her, but he told me she was just a friend. He refuses to talk about her, Jill."

"Damn. It's over, isn't it? I guess, Quinn and I are just meant to be friends."

"Oh, please. You'll get him back. It's just like me and Noel." Chase hesitated, before adding, "Or me and Rachel, or Kim, or Tiffany. And speaking of women, do you think Carly goes for the younger, better looking suave type?" He asked, breaking the serious tone.

Laughing, Jill stood up, giving Ridge a little nudge off her foot. "What are you doing tonight?"

"Bonfire at Big Shoal."

"Don't let Cole catch you," Jill said, referring to the Deputy Sheriff.

"Okay, Ma." Chase teased.

FORTY-ONE

"There she is! Hi!" Carly called, glancing up from the stove as Jill walked into the house. She pulled Jill's too small robe closed, smiling. "Sorry about earlier, Jill. I left the book but…"

"There wasn't an extra car in the drive, so I wasn't paying attention."

"He parked next door."

"Oh, okay. Whose the guy? Is he still here?" Jill asked, dropping her voice low, amused to see Carly look so cuddly in the thick cream colored terry cloth ensemble.

"Tower decided to surprise me. Isn't he great? He's such a hound dog. I feel totally worn out. He's taking a shower."

"Oh, wow." Jill breathed, relieved. "Carly, that's great. I was worried you picked someone up at the bar or something." Jill inhaled the air, "You're making chili, aren't you?"

"Mm-hmm. And cornbread."

Jill chuckled. Carly was crazy about cornbread. Jill sat down on the dining room chair, feet propped on the tabletop's edge. "The most unusual thing happened today…"

"The bank robberies in Cedarville?"

Jill's eyes widened. "How'd you hear about it?"

"I heard it on the radio, but then Marci filled me in with what she's heard."

A sharp, odd sounding whistle pierced her thoughts. "Carly, you failed to tell me our hostess is exquisite." Tower said, his voice dead calm. Cold eyes swept shrewdly over Jill, blatantly evaluating her body.

It didn't sound like a compliment, but Jill figured it was meant to be one, and gave him the benefit of the doubt. Jill crossed her arms in front of her, realizing abruptly what she was doing and stretched her hand toward the man, welcoming him. Tower's hand was cool and damp from an apparently cold shower. "Thanks."

Oblivious to any tension, Carly smiled. "Jill this is Tower. Tower, Jill."

"It's nice to meet you, Tower."

"I'm sure it is," Tower replied, as he held Jill's hand longer than necessary, giving her a light squeeze.

"Oh, Tower." Carly groaned. "Don't start teasing Jill, too."

Jill returned to her seat, saying nothing, vaguely uncomfortable. She gestured for Tower to sit down. She couldn't help staring at him for an extra moment. His dark hair was combed straight back, dripping onto his moss green, long sleeved Henley shirt. Hazel eyes, bushy eyebrows, and a once broken nose formed a unique composite of facial features. "I don't know why, but you look really familiar to me." Jill looked up at Carly, then back at Tower. "Have I ever met you before?"

Tower leaned back on the kitchen chair, silent. He shook his head from side to side slowly. Done with his appraisal, he turned his attention to Carly. "What are you wearing?" he asked, disgusted.

Carly laughed at the robe. "I found it in Jill's closet."

"Please change."

Carly grimaced. "Okay. Stir the chili for me?"

He nodded, grabbed her before she passed, and kissed her soundly.

Confused by Tower's personality, and her reaction to him, Jill shook her head as if to clear it. She grasped for something to say. "Did you have a nice drive up, Tower?"

"What exactly is a nice drive?" he questioned, looking for clarification without sounding totally unpleasant.

So much for small talk, Jill decided. "A drive without incident," she defined.

With his back to her, stirring the chili, Tower smirked, contemplating the definition. Would stealing cars, robbing banks, and killing people qualify as *incident*? *Nah.* "Yes, then. It was a nice drive."

"You must have seen the roadblocks, hey?"

"Roadblocks?"

"Yeah, a couple of banks were robbed off island today."

"I must have come through earlier, Jill. I didn't see anything."

Carly returned to the kitchen in a tank top and shorts, and grabbed long necks for the three of them from the fridge. "Not to change the subject, but what do you all want to do with the rest of the week?"

"Are you still thinking of going to Mackinac Island?" Jill questioned, accepting the beer.

Carly shot a questioning look to Tower.

"Count me out. I used most of my money to get here," Tower said somberly.

"Yeah, I think I'd rather hang here too," Carly agreed easily, wrapping her arms around Tower and tickling him. "Do you want help with any of your house projects? My stud here is mad ripped strong. I mean… I could take him, but together, we're a helluva team."

"You could not take me," Tower admonished, spinning her around and gathering her hands behind her back.

She didn't fight him, but from Jill's vantage point, it looked like Tower may indeed be right. Carly giggled and he let her go, kissing her nose. The kick-boxer leaned against the table, smiling pleasantly. "We should go to the bar tonight. I want Tower to meet Marci."

"Now that's something a person doesn't hear everyday," Jill joked.

"I ran into her at the store today. She was microwaving a sandwich at Wazz's, so I joined her. Oodles of gossip just spilled out of that girl. Is she always like that?"

"I don't know her too well," Jill responded.

"Hmm. You should hear her theories on those bank robberies."

"Oh?" Jill asked, perking up.

"She thinks there's this weird local guy that knows something, or is involved... what the hell is his name?" Carly considered it for a moment, then shrugged. "Anyway, she's got somebody fingered for being a part of it."

Tower raised an eyebrow, his back again turned to the women. Gossip or real knowledge? he wondered. Perhaps he'd have a chance to ferret out information from the girl, he thought.

"Local as in *Drummond Island* local?" Jill asked.

Carly shrugged again. "I think so, but hell. I was trying to get the low down on your new man."

"Oh, no. Don't tell me she's had sex with Mike. And please don't tell me that you mentioned I'm interested in him, because she'll twist it all around and sleep with him just to spite me." Jill pulled the hair tie from her hair, absently working the kinks out of it as she chatted.

"I didn't say a word, but she didn't know much about him. She's been seeing someone pretty regularly this summer."

"You're kidding me? Like the same guy regularly?"

"So she says."

"Who?"

"I don't have a clue." Carly laughed. "We should go to the bar and see if we can find out."

"I think we should go to the bar, Carly. Good idea," Tower agreed.

FORTY-TWO

The only fact that eased Lisa's mind as the day passed quietly into night, was Nancy's promise to call her if Frank's condition changed. Since her telephone never rang during the evening, Lisa knew Frank was still with them. Although off today, she decided to start the day with a visit to Frank. With luck, he'd tell her where the film was located and what, after all these years, he wanted her to do with it.

After a quick shower, and a few moments to slip into her wildly patterned muumuu, Lisa hopped into her Oldsmobile and headed for Green Meadows. She would only stay an hour or so, and then she'd be off, taking care of errands that were impossible to do during her work week. The short drive wasn't long enough for Lisa to organize any of her thoughts, or even fully wake-up. Her refrigerator was void of Coke, and as Lisa ambled her full body out of her car and into her work place, her first stop was at the lobby's Coke machine. She plunked quarters in, listened to the sweet sound of the plastic bottle thud into the opening, and twisted the cap off.

"Ahhh… " She laughed enjoying the fizzy refreshment, and hopped on the elevator before her work buddies noticed her and pulled her into conversation. Frank's room was located close to the elevator, so Lisa didn't bother stopping by the nurse's station before she swung around the door frame.

Entering Frank's room, Lisa saw a stocky grey-haired man

dressed in black, kneeling next to an empty bed, looking through drawers of the bed stand. Frank was nowhere to be seen. Alarmed, Lisa cleared her throat.

The man turned, showing his priest's collar to a surprised Lisa. "Hello. What can I do for you?"

Suddenly remembering that she wasn't wearing her work uniform, she stepped forward to introduce herself. "Hi, Father. I'm Lisa Daye."

The priest smiled and shook her hand. "I'm Paul Lawrence."

"I'm one of Frank's nurses," Lisa said, explaining her presence. She smiled apologetically over her appearance. "It's my day off. Did they move Frank to another room?" Lisa asked.

"Monsignor Beretti passed away yesterday evening," Father Lawrence told her.

Lisa exhaled, relieved. "I'm sorry for your loss, Father, but my patient wasn't a priest."

Father Lawrence crooked his head to the side, studying the nurse. "You said you were looking for Frank, didn't you?"

"Yes," Lisa began, confused. *Beretti*. It wasn't possible, was it? She wondered, as realization struck her. "Frank was a priest?"

Father Lawrence nodded his head. "Yes, he was."

She took a seat in the visitor's chair to catch her breath.

"My Child, I can see you were close to him." Father Lawrence waited until Lisa looked up. "I take it that he never told you?"

Lisa shook her head. "No. In fact, he told me stories from his life that he couldn't possibly... things he couldn't have known as a priest."

"Monsignor Beretti was called to the priesthood late in

life, but by all means, he was devout in his duties. If he'd started earlier, I'm of no doubt that he would've become a Bishop." Father Lawrence's voice trailed off, as his thoughts deepened. "Actually, I started out as his confessor, and later on, he became mine."

Lisa's eyes widened as she observed the naked grief pass through Father Lawrence's eyes.

Puzzled, Father Lawrence spoke, "I'm surprised he didn't tell you. You said that he shared stories with you, from his life before?"

Lisa leaned against the wall, beleaguered. "Yes."

Father Lawrence shook his head, surprised. "He never spoke of his life before…" He returned to the bedside table, pulling a thick black book from the drawer, before he closed it. "We received word yesterday. Typically, our priests have the option of living in a retirement home when they grow older, if they need assistance or special care. Frank didn't want that. I got here as soon as I could." Father Lawrence made the sign of the cross. "He's with God now."

"Just yesterday… I talked to him just yesterday. I promised him I'd be back. I had both yesterday and today off work, but I told the nurse to call me if there was a change in his condition. She must have forgotten." Lisa swiped tears from her cheeks with the back of her hand. "He was telling me a story."

Father Lawrence smiled softly. "Would you like to pray?"

"I haven't been to church in a while, Father."

Picking up the worn black leather bible from the bed, Father Lawrence asked, "When did you leave the church, Miss Daye?"

"How did you know I'm Catholic?" She asked.

"You called me *father*. Only a Catholic would have done that." Frank ran his fingers over the book's tired edges. "You know, Frank didn't have any family to speak of, Lisa. You cared for him in his last days, and I know you were close to him, to come in on your day off."

Wondering where he was going with this, Lisa waited respectfully.

"I think you should have this," the priest held the bible to her opened hands.

"Oh, Father, I couldn't."

"Please, go ahead and take it." His eyes twinkled sadly. "Maybe it will bring you back to the church."

Lisa nodded, swallowing her tears. "Thank you, Father."

"I need to go see to some details. It was very nice to meet you, Lisa."

"Thank you," Lisa offered, bringing the heavy black book to her chest. The priest left her alone in the room. She sat down on the visitor's chair. She should have stayed with him yesterday, she thought. Flipping the bible open, she found a single piece of paper amidst prayer cards and margins filled with notations. Unfolding the weathered page, she read a quotation from John F. Kennedy.

Inhaling deeply, Lisa prayed for direction. If only Frank had lived long enough to tell her where to find the secrets he spoke of, she thought, and more importantly, what to do with them.

"Let the word go forth from this time and place, to friend and foe alike, that the torch has been passed to a new generation of Americans, born in this century, tempered by war, disciplined by a hard and bitter peace, proud of our ancient heritage, and unwilling to witness or permit the slow undoing of those human rights to which this nation has always been committed, today at home and around the world.

"Let every nation know, whether it wishes us well or ill, that we shall pay any price, bear any burden, meet any hardship, support any friend, oppose any foe to assure the survival and success of liberty."

JOHN F. KENNEDY

FORTY-THREE

Carly watched sweat bead on Tower's naked back, as he finished up and handed the roller to her. They were just finishing applying water seal to Jill's front deck. Monday night at Chuck's was a bust, even though the beers were good. Everyone had a different theory about the robberies, and they all wanted to share them, particularly with Jill. She'd been here a little over a year, and her opinion was already valued, Carly realized. She smiled to herself as she washed the paint brushes and rollers with the soapy water mixture Jill provided.

"What are you thinking about?" Jill asked, noticing Carly's smile.

"Hmm. I was just thinking about how weird you were when we first moved in together and how you've grown since. The people here really like you, Jill."

"I was weird?!" Jill joked. "You were the one with the pink hair and the crazy music that scared my grandpa half to death."

"He wanted to wheel you right around and take you back home. Remember?" Carly asked, reminiscing.

"No, that's not entirely true," Jill corrected. "He wanted me to go antiquing with him at the time. He couldn't imagine why I would trade four weeks in a camper with him and Grandma, for starting college early," Jill shook her head.

"You were so quiet and tiny looking. When you told me

you were going to be working with police officers, I thought you'd fall over dead with your first assignment."

Tower looked up, wary. "You wanted to be a cop, Jill?"

"No. I worked for a couple semesters taking pictures to help out a local department during school. No big deal." Jill shrugged, turning back to Carly. "The first time I met you, you told me you were going to be a mortician."

"Scared you, didn't I? Can you imagine that?"

"Scary sense of humor, period. You gave me nightmares, until I figured you out." Jill admitted. "And I was so worried when you laughed at my college plans."

Carly chuckled, filling Tower in. "The first time we met, Jill told me she had no intention of graduating in anything. Here I was, this crazy party queen... thrilled that I had a book worm of a roommate. I was hoping she'd rub off on me, and the first thing out of her mouth is that she's not declaring a major, and further, she has no intention of graduating."

"Why'd you go to school then?" Tower asked. "To find a man?"

"I went to school to study photography, but they didn't have a major program. After I took all the classes I wanted to in college, Carly and I got an apartment together and I went to photography specific schools. Most of them are just a few weeks at a time. I needed a home base." Jill set her brush down, smiling at the accomplishment.

"You've found one now, Jillian."

"You sound surprised that I fit in somewhere," Jill accused.

"No, not at all. I'm just surprised how quickly you've got local people asking you your opinion on stuff like the robberies. I mean... no offense, but what could you possibly know about the robberies?" Carly asked.

Jill raised an eyebrow, but said nothing.

Carly noticed Jill's reserved expression, and wondered if Jill was offended. "I didn't mean that in a bad way, Jill."

Jill recalled her role in finding Joe's killer – but she let it go, knowing Carly didn't mean to insult her.

"What are we having for lunch?" Tower asked.

"Leftovers, or we need to go to town. Actually, I need to go to the store anyway." Jill voiced.

"I'll come with you, but I need a shower," Carly said.

"Take all the time you need. I need to flip the laundry over, and make a phone call." Following the couple into her house, Jill picked up the phone and headed to her breezeway, dialing Dean's number as she walked. Crouching in front of the dryer, she unloaded Carly's clothing into an empty laundry basket.

Dean's phone rang once in her ear, before his voice replaced the sound. "Hey, Jill."

"How'd you know it was me?" Jill asked.

"Caller ID says *Unknown*. You're the only person I know that lives in a place that can't be traced through Caller ID. How'd the shoot go?"

"Good. I haven't had a chance to develop anything yet, but I think I got some good stuff," Jill responded.

"Actually, you're never going to believe this, but I've already sold your pictures. So, let's hope you've got some good stuff."

"You're kidding me."

"No, not at all. I didn't realize it, but the Hessel Boat Show in the world of wooden boats is pretty much the big dog. The woman at the magazine talked my ear off. Cedarville has one of the largest remaining fresh water marsh systems in the world. I guess, according to this magazine woman, you can see it if you're standing on the moon. It's like the Great

Wall of China of marsh systems. She says those islands are chuck ass full of really old money, Jill. They've got lots of readers in that area. She is so juiced about your shots. I think I made her damn day."

Grinning, Jill enjoyed his excitement, even if she didn't care for his rambling.

"In fact, if you have the right shot, your work can make the cover of a national boating magazine. Like a $2500 payday for the cover alone. Are you hearing me? This is big! There's a writer doing an upscale piece on a few of the larger boat shows. When I told him you were shooting the Les Cheneaux Antique Wooden Boat Show, he jumped at it. This could be really big for you, Jill. I hope you've got a really great picture for them to use," Dean finished.

"I think I might have several." Her voice strained, as she leaned into the dryer to grab a sock she missed and was surprised to find a fifty dollar bill crumpled near the back. She slid the bill into her pocket and tossed the sock into the basket.

"Good. That's what I wanted to hear. Get them done and send them down."

"I will, but…" Jill could hear a soft thudding noise in the background, as she pictured Dean at his desk with his feet up, tossing something into the air and catching it. "Carly's visiting."

"Ah, the fire goddess." Dean sighed, reflecting on his crush for Jill's friend and the last time he made a fool of himself in front of her.

Jill laughed. "That's the one."

"No problem. Just do it as soon as possible."

"Okay. Take care, Dean."

"You too." Dean hung up the phone, leaving Jill to listen to dead air, until she could set the basket down and turn the phone off.

Dripping wet, dressed in crops and a tye-dyed Hog's Head Saloon t-shirt, from a spring break trip to the Keys, Carly raced into the dining area, nearly knocking Jill over. "Are you ready to go?"

"Quick shower," Jill commented. "We need to fold the laundry."

"Tower will want to iron them anyway, leave it be. Let's go." Carly tugged Jill's arm, leading her out the door. "I'll drive," Carly called, swinging a leg over the Convertible's door.

"Oh, Car. I've got fifty bucks of yours. I found it in your laundry. Here," Jill said.

"It's not mine."

"I know it's not mine," Jill countered.

"Must be Tower's." Carly hesitated, wondering what to do with the bill. "That ass hasn't purchased a thing since he got here." Carly squinted at the bill, and without another thought shoved it in her pocket. "We'll spend it on the beer."

"I thought you were going to tone down the drinking."

"Changed my mind. Besides, I'm going to be drinking at your barbecue tomorrow night. No sense in stopping cold turkey, just to start up again at your party. After all, a vacation isn't really a vacation without alcohol."

"Isn't it amazing how we can justify anything?" Jill asked, laughing as she moved on.

"If you only knew," she mumbled.

FORTY-FOUR

Beth's sand colored walls were filled with Native American art. For the ninth time this week, she appreciated her find in subleasing a furnished duplex just a few blocks from War Memorial Hospital. Overflowing boxes still lined her walls, the trademark signature of her last year of moving around, but hopefully she'd be settled for a while now. Living in the Upper Penisula of Michigan was quite different from upstate New York, but the trees were still gloriously green, and the people friendly. It had been a hard decision to come here, but when Richard was transferred from a prison in Jackson to one in Kinross, Beth felt it would be remiss in her duties as a sister not to be near him. For the first time in her life, she had more family than she knew what to do with. Although she wasn't setting any speed records in meeting the rest of the clan, her relationship with her new grandfather was becoming stronger every week. *New grandfather*, Beth thought, smiling at the irony of the words. She'd known Cal was her grandfather for over a year now, but she hadn't yet become accustomed to it.

It had taken some extreme circumstances, for fate to work itself out and introduce Beth to a family she never knew existed. For so long, the only family she knew were her mother's, a tight-lipped group who spent very little time together. Cal was a man with many layers, troubled still with his grandson, Joe's death, and Richard's responsibility for the murder, but Beth agreed to help him struggle through it.

Smiling, she corrected herself; they struggled together.

Stretching her legs out on the sofa, Beth smiled sleepily as her tea kettle's piercing whistle had her wrapping the summer quilt tightly around her body, snuggling into her cushy slippers and padding to the stove. As she touched the handle, memories and feelings of her father coursed through her. Her "feelings," as she called them were becoming clearer, and more focused since she began consciously trying to understand them. Unfortunately, her paranormal experiences influenced her work. When she touched or listened to a patient, she was sometimes overwhelmed by the patient's emotions. She began accepting her feelings as a natural part of her being, but worked to control them. Beth dearly loved being a nurse, and didn't want to lose confidence in her abilities because she was overwhelmed by the emotions coursing through her patients.

Pouring hot water from her father's blue speckled tea kettle, she dipped the chamomile bag into the water and inhaled. When she was settled back on the sofa, she flipped open her brand new cell phone and dialed Lisa's number. It had been an odd couple of days, to say the very least, and Beth could use her friend's ear. Lisa answered after the first ring.

"H'llo?"

"Li, it's me."

Lisa exhaled, relaxed into her Lazy-boy. Beth always knew what to do. "Bethy, thank goodness. How are you?"

"Tired. What's going on?" Beth asked, recognizing the troubled tone in Lisa's voice.

"Well, one of my patients died."

"Aw, Li, I'm sorry."

"It's part of the job, but this one… God, it's a long story."

"I'm listening."

Lisa filled Beth in on the details of Frank's confessions. Beth said very little, until Lisa finished. "Do you think you'd be interested in doing a little snooping on Drummond?"

Beth hesitated, mulling it over. She had relatives on Drummond, but her connection with them was tenuous at best. Cal was just beginning to repair his relationship with his daughter, and Beth didn't want to complicate things.

Sensing Beth's reluctance, Lisa continued. "I wouldn't even ask, but Frank insisted there's a body buried there, and the authorities should know about it. Let alone the fact that there might be treasure there."

"Lisa, I just can't get involved with anything like this right now. I'll give you Jill's email address though. She'll tell the right people, and if there's something there, she'll know how to find it," Beth said. "I don't think I'd tell her about Kennedy though, Lisa. Especially since you don't know where the proof is. He didn't give you any clues, at all?"

Lisa frowned, unsettled that Beth didn't want to help her, but more worried about her friend's exhaustion riddled voice than her reticence. "He was about to tell me. He said it was in a safe place, but that could be anywhere."

"On Drummond though?" Beth inquired.

Lisa considered it, running her conversations with Frank through her mind. "Honestly, I don't know. I got the impression, but he had a spell. He died before he could tell me."

"Email Jill, Lisa. She'll know about these places Frank mentioned."

"On another note, when exactly are you going to be passing through Cleveland? Have you gotten the time off yet?" asked Lisa.

"My boss told me I could take the time, but I'm not sure which days yet. I'll call you and let you know as soon as I do, but I know I'll be there in like… two weeks."

Lisa grinned. "I'm so excited to see you." After finishing the conversation, Lisa contemplated the email she needed to write, unsure of how to begin.

FORTY-FIVE

Quinn ran his hand over his head, annoyed with the length of his hair. He hadn't even had enough time get his hair cut. Gazing into the mirror behind the bar, his bloodshot eyes stared back at him. Like beebees rattling around in a runaway boxcar, Quinn's head ached from too little sleep and the effort to make some hard decisions. Heavy down the path of being burned out, Quinn considered his options, attempting to ignore Brenda's plan. There were only so many more days in which he could keep up with this frenzied pace he was meeting.

Too many trips off the island, long nights labored away in the garage, and Jill always on the cusp of hearing the rumors which would irrevocably damage their relationship, eroded Quinn's sanity. Maybe, it was already too late. When Quinn saw Jill kissing that other man, he was filled with the urge to pull the head off the bastard, snap his neck, and pummel his body like a punching bag. Catching the violence lurking under his skin, he attempted to laugh at himself. He didn't know Jill's new man, and he couldn't blame him for trying to steal her. He knew enough: Mike was a suave, well-dressed, educated, trust fund baby, with big open eyes on Jill. Why wouldn't she be interested? He certainly had more to offer her than *Quinn, the bartender*, did at this point. In the midst of his restocking, a high pitched voice scraped against his thoughts, demanding his attention.

"Seen a Jeep?" Cooper asked.

Quinn raised his eyebrows. "Well, hell yeah. I drive one, Cooper."

"A red Jeep?"

"There's probably a dozen of them on the island. Why are you looking for a red one?" Quinn waved to Marci coming through the door. Her blond hair softly framed her face, and Quinn welcomed the distraction. Her breasts spilled over her scooped neck, rose colored shirt. Her long legs were accentuated by her short skirt and her three inch platform shoes. She batted her eyelashes at him the way she always did, and for the first time in years, the bartender was exhausted enough to be tempted.

"Do you want pretzels, Coop?"

"I'm looking for a Jeep! My money is in it." He moved on, leaning over a table of locals.

For once, Marci wasn't in the mood to agitate Cooper. She leaned over the bar provocatively, tapping the end of her menthol cigarette for Quinn to light. "What's up with Cooper?" she whispered.

Quinn shrugged, bringing life to Marci's cigarette with the flick of a flame. "Hell, if I know."

"He didn't go to work this morning," Marci informed.

"Is there anything you don't know, Marci?" Cooper never missed work, and everyone knew it. The man was jacked up on medication most of the time, but he never missed work. *Never.*

She nodded. "Major told me this morning that Cooper was off island yesterday."

"When did you see Major?"

"I woke up next to him," she purred.

"I should have known better than to ask."

"Damn straight." Marci laughed softly. "I think Cooper might be involved."

"With the robberies? No way. He's not smart enough, Marz."

Marci's full eyelashes fluttered over mischievous eyes. "Something's going on, Quinn. I can smell it."

Quinn finished pouring her Long Island Ice Tea, and slid it to her. "You're smelling something alright, but I don't think it's these robberies."

Offering him a luscious wink, Marci swiveled around on the bar stool, and prowled the bar with her eyes. Quinn stared at the back of her head absently for a moment, before returning to his restocking tasks. The problem with making life altering decisions, Quinn thought, was giving something up. Rubbing his hand against the dark wood stained counter top, Quinn knew giving up the Northwood would be a mistake. I love this place, he thought. *I love watching sports with the locals, and listening to the island gossip, and talking to the tourists. I love Marci's antics, and visiting with the guys, and seeing nightly drama unfold.* On Drummond Island, there was no greater source of entertainment. And if he gave it up, what excuse would he have to see Jill?

The sumptuous brunette never left his thoughts for more than a moment, and now that she was beginning to date someone else, it would be even more difficult to see her. Brenda's offer, to Quinn's utter distaste, was beginning to look more appealing.

FORTY-SIX

WEDNESDAY

"How many people are going to be at this shindig of yours tonight?" Carly asked, a reluctant participant in Jill's last minute shopping.

"Oh, boy," Jill muttered. "Well, it really depends on how many people decide to come."

"Didn't they rsvp?"

Jill shook her head. "This is Drummond, Carly. A backyard barbecue doesn't entail written invitations or rsvps."

"How many did you invite?"

"About thirty people," Jill said.

"Jill! Thirty? And all you've got in the cart is beans, chicken and hamburger. You can't even make macaroni! We're doomed!" Carly sounded exasperated.

"No, no, no, that's where you're wrong. A year ago, I could barely cook mac and cheese. I've learned a thing or two."

"Where? How?" Carly asked, unconvinced.

"Kate's showed me some things."

"Kate is Pete's wife, right? How did she make you sit through cooking lessons?"

Jill continued on as if uninterrupted. "Kate was pregnant, so I helped out. When the woman gets nervous or worries, she cooks."

"Even if you're this great chef extraordinaire…"

"I never said that!" Jill exclaimed.

"How do you expect to feed thirty people on meat and beans?"

Jill rounded the end capped aisle and steered her cart toward the pickles. "Everyone brings a dish, Car."

"Oh. What if they all bring the same thing?"

"You're kind of over worried about this, aren't you?"

"I don't want to be stuck cooking at the last minute," Carly complained. "And you haven't been talking about this that much. I just figured it was a small handful of people. If you're having thirty over, I'd have thought you'd be talking about it a bit more than you have been."

Jill shrugged. "Thirty is a small handful on Drummond." She turned her cart around, and headed toward the check out. Over her shoulder, she called, "Come on, Carly. We've got quite a bit to do."

Surprised by her friend's confidence in feeding thirty people, Carly wondered if Jill had any idea what she was getting herself into. "We're gonna need more beans," Carly decided, as she grabbed the third jar that Jill had left behind, and made her way to the register. It wasn't boring here, that's for sure, Carly mused.

FORTY-SEVEN

Leaning back on Jill's office chair, Tower listened to the computer connecting to the internet. He flipped through the emails in her inbox. A new message filled the screen from someone named Lisa Daye, subject: urgent.

Opening the message, Tower leaned forward.

Dear Jill,

I'm a friend of Beth DeForge's, and this might seem strange for me to be emailing you, but I've heard a lot of really nice things about you from Beth. She felt you would know what to do with what I'm about to tell you. A few days ago, one of my patients told me a story that has to do with Drummond Island. His name was Frank Beretti, and he claimed to have lived on Drummond during the spring and summer of 1934. Actually, I'm sure he lived there longer, but that's when he talked about working there. During that time he said the gangster, John Dillinger visited the island. Frank helped Dillinger bury the body of another gangster, John Hamilton, at the Wayfarer's Mart. Honestly, Jill, this might be a wild goose chase, but I believed him. Frank passed away a few days ago, so I'm sorry that I'm the only source to answer questions. He did tell me that the body is buried about six feet from a large group of stones. One of the stones has a large triangle wedge at the top. The large rocks are between the mart and the water, on the left if you're facing the water.

Not only is there a body there, but Frank believed there's gold, or money, or something really valuable, also buried with the body. He's not sure what it could be, because Dillinger didn't tell him. Dillinger robbed many banks, as well as other things, so I really don't have a clue. I'm telling you all this, because Beth says you're a good person, and you'll take this seriously. I wouldn't email you unless I believed Frank's story. Beth couldn't go investigate because she's still unpacking from her recent move. She spends quite a bit of time visiting Richard. Please email me, and tell me what you think, and what you find out.

Thanks,   Lisa Daye

Since childhood, Tower studied the great criminals intensely. Dillinger, as one of the most infamous criminals to score American history, served as a pin-up model for Tower's life. Tower located the Drummond Island tourism magazine of Jill's. The Wayfarer's Mart was clearly marked. Why would Dillinger visit Drummond Island? he wondered. Pacing Jill's small living room, Tower thought back to the books he'd read on Dillinger's life when it hit him: Three Fingers Hamilton was originally from the Upper Peninsula. Hamilton could have even been born on Drummond, Tower considered. Anyway, he thought, if he was from the area, it made sense that he'd want to be buried somewhere close.

Contemplating his options, Tower barely contained the energy pouring through his veins. I could at least go check the area out, he thought. I can do that with a low profile. Red's instructions sounded like a siren blasting through his head: *no reckless movements.* Screw it, he decided, grabbing his keys. Before he closed Jill's email down, he printed a copy, and then deleted the message from Lisa.

Slipping his gun from the hiding place in his Jeep, he tucked it into the waistband of his pants, and hopped in. He felt opportunity knocking once again. With a larger than expected take at the bank, and now this, Tower would walk away a rich man. Red's instructions be damned, Tower thought. If there's something to take, *it will be all mine.*

It was worth the risk.

FORTY-EIGHT

"Come on, McKenzie. Make a decision," Kate urged, gently.

August's surprising heat had driven Kate and her children to the Drummond Island Tee Pee for a treat. McKenzie was getting to that age where she appreciated making her own decisions.

"I'll have a cone. No, a flurry."

"What kind?" the woman behind the glass asked.

"No, a cone," McKenzie volleyed, twisting the bright blond hair she inherited from her mother on a finger. "A medium twisted cone, dipped in chocolate."

"Honey, are you sure you want a medium? You usually get a small." Kate advised, jostling Joey in her arms to keep him entertained. The baby dropped his bunny rattle on the ground. Balancing him carefully, Kate squatted down to pick it up.

"Medium, Mom. I'm hungry." McKenzie decided, her voice firm like her father's.

Kate stood back up. "Okay, but we're gonna have lots of good food at Jill's."

"Medium," McKenzie insisted.

Kate nodded to the woman behind the glass, patting her daughter with her free hand. "A medium it is."

Cooper tapped on Kate's arm, staring down at McKenzie. "I need to get ice cream."

"McKenzie, here. Take Joey, and I'll grab your ice cream. I'm waiting for my flurry anyway." Protectively, Kate urged her children away from Cooper.

"Chocolate, please!" Cooper said.

"Okay, Coop." The woman behind the glass smiled.

"Hi, Mrs. D."

"Hi, Cooper."

"Seen a Jeep?"

"A Jeep?" Kate asked, puzzled, her eyes scanning the parking lot across the street. "There are two right over there." Her voice was smooth and kind, as she received the ice cream cones through the sliding window.

Cooper turned to look over the vehicles she referred to. As he turned back, shaking his head, he stopped mid-stride, staring at a red jeep that crested the hill.

"There's another one," Kate smiled. "Bye now, Cooper."

"I'll be your huckleberry," Cooper whispered.

"What?" Kate asked, thinking he still might be talking to her. Cooper didn't turn to look at her again, but stared up the road.

"Coop, your ice cream's ready."

Ignoring the woman, Cooper ran back to his truck, jumped in and peeled out of the driveway. Kate shared a look of bewilderment with the woman holding the chocolate ice cream dish.

"I wonder what a huckleberry is. That Coop's a little strange, isn't he?" the woman said.

Kate smiled with a shrug, paid the woman and joined her children.

FORTY-NINE

"You're here early, beautiful," Carly called, as Chase filled the doorway, his arms loaded up with stacked glass casserole dishes.

"I thought I'd drop by a little early and help Jilly out." Chase winked, setting the dishes down. "She here?"

"Yeah. She's outside, lining up the grills."

"Grills, plural?"

"She borrowed one from the Eby's and one from the Dombrowski's," Carly explained.

"That's kind of over the top, isn't it? There's one in the back of her Tracker."

"That's what I thought. The one in the back of her car is from the Dombrowski's."

"I'll go see if I can help."

"Not so fast. What is all of this?" She gestured to the stacked dishes.

"Manicotti stuffed with my famous basil tomato sauce and ricotta cheese." Chase puffed up a bit, seeing her eyes gloss over with appreciation. "I also brought some fresh baked bread. And this," Chase lowered his voice to a conspiratorial whisper. "is filled with cream cheese blintzes. This is just for you and Jill, so you'll want to hide them."

Carly stared at him, duly impressed. "You made this stuff?"

"Sure did."

"I'm impressed!"

"I'm a man of many talents." He winked broadly, emphasizing the word *man* and opened the glass door.

"Darlin, you are too adorable." Carly murmured, more to herself than anyone, as Chase was well out of ear shot.

Pulling the third grill behind him, he whistled to Jill, who was busy examining the gas tank of one of the cookers.

"Hey, Chase." Her face lit up with her thousand watt smile. "Thanks for hauling that over here."

"No problem. Have you got an empty tank?"

"Yeah, I think so."

Chase crouched down, examining the tank for himself. After shaking it, he nodded, unhooking it from the grill. "I'll run it in for you." He lifted the lids, wincing. "Do you have a grill brush? I can clean these up for you." He offered.

"I can get them. You don't have to spend your afternoon helping me. In fact, why aren't you working?"

"Dentist appointment this morning, so I got the day off. No big deal for me."

"I appreciate it," Jill said.

"Well, when we don't have family, I like to think we get to choose family." The sides of Chase's mouth turned up softly.

Arching an eyebrow, Jill looked at him. "What do you mean?"

"Oh, you know, how Quinn and I are adopted and you don't have any family left. I like to think that we're kind of orphans together," Chase said, shrugging it off. When Jill remained speechless, Chase looked at her, realization dawning. "He's never told you?"

"No, he never said a thing. When? How? You guys look alike... how..."

"Quinn and I are real brothers, Jill. He was about eight, and I was just one year old, when we were given up. We've never met our father... well, I've never met him. Quinn knew him when he was a kid, but he doesn't talk about him. I can't believe he's never told you."

"In all these months..."

"Well, you haven't seen him much in the last four or five," Chase corrected.

"We spent every waking moment together for weeks after Joe died. I think I've told him every story there is to tell about my life, and he never said a word. He told me about you, and stories of his teen years. Innocuous stuff, now that I'm thinking about it." Jill's legs folded underneath her, and she plopped to the ground, Indian style. Chase sat down beside her, picking a black eyed susan from the earth. "Talk about being a terrible friend. I don't even know him, do I? Why didn't I ever put that together?"

"Jill, you're too hard on yourself. Honestly, I'm sorry that I said anything, but you're like... you're like a sister to me. I can really talk to you, and you listen."

Jill studied him. His nose bridged with freckles, eyes lighter than Quinn's, but just as filled with character. Summer hued blond hair brushed away, from his broad forehead, above a face not quite as angular as his brothers, a body just as tall, nearly as strong. Dressed in falling apart sneakers, a football jersey and jean shorts, he was every bit the young American sweetheart that high school girls swooned over. The boy drowning in his sea blue eyes, was troubled.

"What's wrong?" Her calm tone stopped his fingers from twirling the flower.

Chase began to shake his head, but paused, looking into her deep green eyes. "I am *really worried* about him. He's been changing for months, and I used to think it was you. Quinn was hung up on you and acting out, I thought. But lately... he's impossible. He never talks to me. He doesn't even hang and watch movies with me anymore. Nothing. I see him more at the bar before he chases my ass out of there, than I do at home. Quinn is all I really have... if he's into something, I don't know what..." His voice cracked a bit as his words trailed off.

She knew all too well what it was like not to have anybody to lean on. "Chase, we'll figure it out. We'll sit down with Quinn, and make him tell us what's going on. We'll do it together. Okay?"

Chase nodded his head. "You're really going to confront him with me?"

"Yeah, I am. Not tonight, not here. But soon."

"Okay." Chase exhaled deeply, hopping to his feet in the next moment. "I'm gonna take that tank in, and get it filled at Johnson's. I'll be back."

"Thanks, Chase."

"No problem."

Jill watched as the young man hoisted the tank over his shoulder, and disappeared from sight. *Yes, she would find out what Quinn was up to*, she vowed silently.

FIFTY

Adopted. Of all things, Quinn never told her he was adopted. Jill checked the pot of beans bubbling in her oven, while Carly paced the floor ranting about Tower's absence. *Adopted.* Eight years old and given up, but why? Chase didn't tell her, and she couldn't ask him. Embarrassed, Jill stared into the oven, listening to the bacon sizzle from the top of the baked bean concoction. Who was his mother? Did he still talk to his real mother, or did he argue often with his adoptive mother? Why didn't he tell me? she wondered. She spared a glance toward Carly, tuning in for a moment, to listen to her friend blather on about Tower.

"…and he just disappeared for hours. What could he possibly be doing? He knew I wanted him to stick around and help out. It's just like that time a few weeks ago when…"

Jill knew Carly wasn't talking to her but merely ranting, so she didn't feel bad for not paying closer attention. Chase and Noel were busily setting up chairs outside, and Jill was glad Chase brought the girl with him.

"Hi, Aunt Jill! Your building looks nice." McKenzie chorused, following after her brother, holding a whaling Joey in her arms.

Jill extended her arms to take the fussing baby from McKenzie. Kate followed, her arms laden with a giant bowl of homemade potato salad.

"Look at that," Kate whispered, amazed. "He's been crying for twenty minutes, and the moment Jill picks him up, he's fine. Pete's out in your garage, checking out the..." Kate shrugged. "Honestly, I wasn't paying attention to what he's checking out."

Strolling through the door, Tower grabbed Carly from behind and kissed her exposed shoulders.

"Where have you been?" she hissed.

"Kate, this is Tower. Tower, Kate," Jill said silencing Carly with a look, "and these are her beautiful children. McKenzie, Kyle, and Joey."

Introductions made all around, Jill appreciated Kate's brimming green bowl. "This potato salad looks awesome. Check out my beans, Kate," Jill encouraged, backing into the screen door, running smack into Bobby's chest.

"Well, honey, hot damn!" Bob teased. "Wanted to tell ya, I'm here. I'm going straight out to the grills to work on the corn."

"You're grilling corn?" Carly questioned, batting Tower's hands away from her body.

"Hell, yeah. Haven't you ever tasted grilled corn on the cob? Come along, and I'll show you how it's done." Bob invited, ignoring Tower, while scooping Carly along with him.

"Jill!" Gary called from the doorway. "Debbie needs help with the chips. Hey, Boss." Gary said, nodding to Kate.

"Why can't you help Debbie?" Kate called out. "What can she possibly need help with? Opening the bag? Putting them in a bowl?" Kate muttered.

Gary popped his head back in the door quickly. "Pete's tearing something up in Jill's garage and needs help."

Jill's mouth dropped open. "I'm gonna go check on Pete. Here's your baby back," Jill pushed Joey back into Kate's arms, chagrined to hear Kate laughing merrily at her husband's antics. "Tower, will you see if you can help Debbie?" Jill asked, happy to see him nod before she ran through the breezeway.

Surprised to find the entire Dombrowski crew in the garage, it took her a few seconds to realize they had been waiting for her. Set up along a workbench near the back of the garage was a brand new DeWalt Miter Saw, and a new tan colored leather carpentry belt, filled with all the tools that she needed for her work. "Surprise!" Bobby called from the back, causing the guys to laugh.

"What did you guys do?" Jill asked, rushing over to the bench, joy filling her voice. "This is so awesome!"

"No self-respecting finish carpenter can live without one of these," Gary said, gruffly, looking at her new toy with her.

"I wanted to get you something girly, Jill, but Pete wouldn't hear of it." Kate called.

"It's a garage warming gift! How can a garage warming gift be girly?" Bobby grumbled.

"We all chipped in," Chase announced.

"Pete and Kate put in the big bones," Billy added.

Touched beyond words, Jill took turns hugging each of them.

"And check out the tape measure, Jill. It's got one of those kick-ass laser level things in it." Chase said, pointing it out.

"Too cool," Jill agreed, admiring her new toys.

Kate laughed. Carly and Tower stood in the doorway, watching Jill play with her toys, chatting with the guys about special features. The arrival of the Barbers nudged Bobby and Chase back toward the grills.

"Hey, hold on a minute, Bobby," Mary Barber called out, rummaging through the basket of goodies she brought for the get together. She pulled out two bottles of barbecue sauce and handed them over. "Use that on the chicken. Chase, take this basket in for Jill, would you?"

"Yes, ma'am." Bobby nodded, as Chase accepted the basket.

Making her way through the dispersing group, Jill hugged Mary warmly. "Thanks for coming, Mrs. Barber."

"How are you doing, dear?" Mary asked, walking through Jill's breezeway into her home. "Well, you must be busy," Mary answered, gesturing to Jill's garage. "This is beautiful." She dropped her voice low, as she and Jill walked the long way back to Jill's kitchen, arm in arm.

Stepping into her kitchen, Jill was shocked to see her counters neatly arranged and jam packed with dishes. "Wow, look at the food." Chase walked in behind her, angling toward the stove to check his warming manicotti.

"Where's Noel, Chase? You didn't abandon her somewhere, did you?" Jill questioned.

"Carly is giving her kickboxing lessons out front," Chase said, groaning. "I shouldn't have told Noel that Carly's a fighter. I shouldn't have even introduced them. Now, I'm gonna have to get some lessons to keep up with her," he complained, good natured, for all his belly-aching.

Jill shared a smile with DeeDee, listening to Chase whine as they added serving spoons to the salads. "Have you heard I'm getting married, Mary?" DeeDee asked, holding up her ring finger.

"Oh, DeeDee. That's so wonderful! I've always known you two were gonna be together." Mary chuckled, gazing at the ring. "Billy's always been sweet on you, honey. It's about time he asked you to marry him."

"Well, if it hadn't been for Jill, I don't think I would have married him, Mary." DeeDee admitted. "It wasn't until Kate and Jill talked Pete into giving him his job back that Billy really got his shit together."

"That's what friends are for." Mary added, gazing from DeeDee to Jill.

"Have you set a date?" Kate asked.

Attempting to hide a frown, DeeDee leaned against Jill's sink. "We're going to just have a Justice of the Peace do it, I think."

"What?!" Kate gasped. "Why?"

"Billy and I don't have much money, and neither do my parents. If we spend the year saving for a big wedding, we'll never move out of that place we rent. I really want to buy a place, you know?" DeeDee shrugged. "I'd like to own something before we have babies, and I wouldn't mind having a dozen baby Billy's running around. It's just one day, right? No big deal to just have it done in a courthouse." Despite her efforts, her voice fell flat.

Shaking her head, Kate stared the girl down. "Absolutely not. Your wedding day is the most important day of your life. You and Billy are both Drummond Island kids. There's no way that I'm going to allow the two of you to get married without a wedding party."

Mary nodded just as vehemently. "We'll get the town hall, and Kate and I will cook. Won't we, Kate?"

"That's right." Kate agreed.

"I'm helping," Chase volunteered.

"What are you helping with?" Quinn asked, slipping in from the breezeway. "Sorry I'm late, Jill."

"Right on time," Jill countered, her eyes gently studying him. She pointed to a cooler on the floor, as Mary piped in with more ideas. Quinn took his place by Jill's side and cracked open a Corona. They talked about the wedding plans for several minutes, with everyone volunteering to help with the various tasks, before being interrupted by Bobby's yelling.

"Chase, your girl's learning to kick ass out here!" Bobby

laughed, from the open doorway. "The chicken and burgers are done."

Relaxing against the counter, Quinn's chest swelled with love for the feisty brunette who had become such a part of this place. "Where can I fill a plate? I'm starving."

Sliding an arm between Mary and Kate, Jill handed him a plastic plate. "Food is on, people. Fill a plate in the kitchen, then grab your chicken or burger and corn from the grills. Keep drinking, cause there are coolers all over." Jill instructed.

As Billy entered through the door, DeeDee jumped into his arms. "Baby, we're gonna have a real wedding."

Confused, Billy patted her head, trying to find the reason for tears. "What's wrong, Dee?"

"They're... gonna... a real wedding!"

Through her blubbering, Billy was even more confused than before. "You said you were okay with a judge. You know we can't afford..." Billy's eyes swiveled to Jill's, slowly taking in the dozen or so eyes staring at him. "What's going on?"

Mary smiled, stepping forward to explain, just as her husband and the rest of the gang filed into the house. "Billy, we're going to help you with your wedding. Kate, Chase and I are going to cook. Quinn's mixing drinks. The Ebys' son is going to give us a real good discount on the flowers. Bobby's going to roast a pig. Jill's going to show Chase how to take pictures. Quinn's going to get the DJ."

Billy stepped back from Dee, gazing into her joyful face. He looked up at Mary, then Kate. "Really?"

"The kids want to have a place, Pete. There's no reason why we can't help with the wedding." Kate grinned across the room at her husband.

"I'm all for that, hon." Pete said. "Though, I don't see why this oaf deserves it." He teased, elbowing Billy gently in the ribs.

"A real wedding!" DeeDee said, still amazed. "An island wedding, with paper plates and home cooking? We can invite everybody, right?"

Billy wrapped his arms around his fiancé, grinning from ear to ear. "I thought you said you were okay with a judge."

Dee looked at the ground before she met Billy's eyes. "I lied," which sent Kate and Mary into gales of laughter.

Quinn kissed the top of Jill's head, sharing in the energetic, love filled aura of the group. "Move aside people, I'm hungry. Did you make this pasta, Chase?" He asked, scooping a ladle full onto his plate.

"Sure did."

"Looks good," Quinn complimented, considering his brother for a moment. The teen had sprouted more than an inch in the last few months, Quinn thought. The best part of Drummond's summer was evaporating under his nose, and he was missing it.

Jill grabbed a piece of barbecued chicken and corn, choosing to sit on the floor of the deck, leaving the chairs for her guests. Bobby joined her on the porch, hauling a heaping plate, two beers clenched under his arm. She smiled widely, her first barbecue was well underway.

FIFTY-ONE

"Ohmygod, what is this stuff?" Bobby groaned, from his lawn chair. "Mmmm."

"Heaven," Chase mumbled, smacking his lips.

"If I died right now, I'd die a happy man." Billy said, smiling at his fiancé. "This barbecue sauce is intense. Where the hell'd you find this stuff, Jill?"

To everyone's amusement, Chase licked the barbecue sauce off of a piece of a chicken, rather than eat the chicken. "What?" he asked, innocently, when Jill laughed at him.

"I found it in a little store in Mackinaw City. It's called Three Bobs, or something." Mary said.

"Bobs?" Chase quirked.

"Bobbers," Tom Barber corrected. "I'm the one who found it, Mary. Three Bobbers Over Land Barbecue Sauce. It's really hard to find. First time I saw it was in Petoskey. Apparently, they've got it in Mackinaw now."

"What the hell's in it?" Chase wondered. "Quinn, you tastin' this shit, man?"

"Really good." Quinn agreed, between bites.

"Well, damn. I should have had the chicken." Carly grumbled, "Is there any left, Bobby?"

Bob hopped up, peering under the lid. He shoved the last

piece into his mouth, and with his mouth full said, "Naw, Carly. None left."

"Ass," she hissed, tossing an ice cube at him.

"H'llo!" Sheriff Cole called, waving to the crowd.

"Hey, Sheriff!" Jill hopped up from her seat, following him inside.

Making himself at home, Cole filled a plate. "How're you doing, Jill?"

"I'm real well. How are you? I can see you're on duty, hey?" Jill asked, taking note of his uniform. "No beer for you. Can I get you a soda?"

"Yeah, anything regular," Cole responded, heaping his plate with food. He accepted the soda from her with thanks and followed her outside.

"Know anything new about those robberies?" Bobby questioned.

"Not too much, Bob. I'm not involved with the investigation at all. Drummond doesn't really have anything to do with it, you know?"

Bobby nodded.

"It's a real shame that a cop was killed," Pete piped in.

"She was a native officer. Young, too. So was the man that was killed. We don't know who he was yet, but damn young," Cole shook his head, sadly. "Ballistics aren't back yet for specifics, but I think the cop probably surprised them, clipped one, and was killed before she could get the other." Cole shrugged. "Listen. I hate to eat and run, but I have got to go. I'll be back later, if I can. Make sure no one drives home drunk, Jill."

"No problem, Cole."

"And Jill…" Cole began, before leaving.

"Yeah?"

He lowered his voice, for her ears only. "Keep your eyes open. You see or hear anything funny, you let me know."

"Will do," Jill agreed, meeting his eyes. Troubled by the worry laced in Cole's stare, something nagged her thoughts, barely out of reach. What was that about? She wondered. Jill shook the thought off her, knowing she'd consider it later. She caught Quinn's eyes on her, and smiled back. Maybe it's not too late yet, she thought.

"Auntie Jill!" Kate called, in a childlike voice, thrusting baby Joey into Jill's open arms. Quinn took the baby from her before she could voice an argument, and tossed him playfully into the air before catching him again.

"Jill?!" A voice called, distantly.

As Jill rose to her feet, she heard Carly whisper, "oops." Without time to check on Carly's problem, Jill made her way back through the house, surprised to see Mike Marinello filling a plate in her kitchen.

"Good evening, Bella." Mike said, appraising Jill with his eyes. He leaned toward her, planting a light kiss on her lips. "I hope it's okay that I came here tonight. Carly told me about your event, and it was too big of a temptation not to come."

"I'm sorry that I didn't invite you, Mike. I didn't figure you'd want to hang with a group of people you didn't know," Jill excused, lamely. "Actually, I'm not sure…"

"What you feel about me?" Mike questioned, expectantly.

Sheepish, Jill nodded, noticing that his eyes were centered in the hollow of her throat. "What?" She asked, when his eyes widened slightly.

"What is…that?" he choked out, leaning down near her throat.

Jill felt her neck, looking down to see where Mike's interest lay. Her fingers closed around the necklace. "My grandma's locket?" she asked, smiling. She opened it for him, showing pictures enclosed of her parents.

Running his fingers over the intricate design, his eyes danced with interest. "It's beautiful. Do you know how she got it?"

"Not really, no. I know my grandpa gave it to her, but I'm not sure where he got it." She caressed the gold lovingly. "I've had it since I was little."

"What was your grandmother's name, Jill?"

"Edna Kinney," Jill responded, but raised her eyebrows. "Why are you interested?"

"Oh, no reason really. Sorry. I have a bit of a fondness for old jewelry. It comes from doing so much research on shipwrecks. It's handy to have some knowledge." Mike shrugged. He pushed a dark brown lock of hair from his forehead. He cleared his throat, before he spoke again. "Listen, don't worry about the other, Jill. I didn't mean to rush you or anything, and honestly I'm not sure about you either," he teased. "If you want me to go, I will."

"Don't be silly. There's lots of food, and Carly can introduce you around. I'm gonna go check the fridge in my garage, and see if there's more beer. It seems like we're going through it a bit faster than I expected." Jill said, sliding past him.

"Okay."

On the deck, the baby began squirming in Quinn's arms. "I think he's getting tired, Kate."

"I should lay him down on Jill's bed." Kate responded.

"I'll take him," Quinn offered.

"Yeah, you know right where Jill's bed is," Bobby joked, just quietly enough that Quinn didn't hear him.

Pete slugged him lightly, giving him a warning look. "Don't go there, Bobby."

Quinn scowled after seeing the "Mike" character that seemed to be dating Jill, readying a plate in the kitchen. Annoyed with himself for getting his hopes up again, Quinn nodded to the other man, before putting Joey in Jill's bedroom. Rocking Joey in his arms, Quinn was lost in a memory of seeing his brother for the first time. Smiling softly, he laid the baby down in the middle of Jill's bed. He rubbed the baby's back, soothing him until the little tyke settled down. He moved pillows on either side of Joey, to stop the baby from rolling off the bed. His eyes roamed around Jill's bedroom, surprised to see a picture of himself amongst a collection on her dresser. His visual journey ended on the framed snapshot of Joe Barber on Jill's bedside table. Adjusting it, so it faced the baby, Quinn whispered, "Watch over him, Joe."

Tower walked back into Jill's house, just as the phone started ringing. Mike's hands were quicker, answering the phone as if he belonged there. "Hello?"

From her duplex in the Soo, Beth DeForge, inhaled sharply. Rubbing her hand over the back of her neck, she spoke. "Is Jill there?"

"Jill? Yes. Please wait a moment, and I'll let her know she has a call." Mike set the phone down.

"Is the phone for Jill?" Quinn asked the guys.

"Yeah." Tower responded, while Mike nodded.

"Quinn, we're gonna play some volleyball. You in?" Chase asked, his face falling as he noticed Mike. "Oh, hi, Mike."

"I'll play," Mike volunteered.

"Check the garage, would you please?" Mike asked. "I'll see if she's outside."

"Sure," Quinn responded. "Hey, Jill. Phone call," he called out.

Quinn took one look at Mike edging through the door, into

his group of friends, and decided against it. Tower followed him. Quinn shared a look with his brother, who was still waiting inside the door. "Actually, I've gotta go, Chase. Let Jill know I said thanks, okay?"

Chase frowned at his brother. Jill slid past Quinn, who waved good-bye as she picked up the phone. Kyle hollered and jumped on Jill's couch with abandon, playing some space jumping game that Jill hadn't figured out yet, while McKenzie tried to get him to stop.

"Hello?" Jill asked, cradling the receiver. Hearing nothing beyond the kids' noises, she covered an ear and spoke again. "Hello?"

"Jill…" Beth breathed heavily. "It's…Beth."

Alarmed to hear her friend's voice strained, Jill pressed the phone tighter against her ear. "Beth, what's wrong?"

"My neck," Beth gulped, recognizant of Jill's background noise for the first time. "What's going on there?"

"I'm having a party."

"Jill! Volleyball, honey! You're on my team!" Bobby hollered.

Jill waved him off, holding up her hand to signify she'd be with him in a minute. "Beth, what's wrong?"

"The man who answered your phone. He's dangerous, Jill."

"What? I'm sorry, Beth. I can barely hear you."

"Don't be alone with him. Stay away from him, Jill. I have strong feelings from that man. He's not safe, Jill," Beth insisted. "I'll call you back tomorrow. I just called to check on Lisa's email."

"Lisa?"

"Lisa Daye, my friend, e-mailed you. Did you get it?"

"I haven't checked my messages in a couple days, Beth."

Concerned, Jill moved away from the children, annoyed to hear her phone fill with static. When Beth had a feeling, Jill knew to listen.

"I'll call you tomorrow."

"Beth, are you…"

"Jill! Hang up the phone! We've got a game." Bobby yelled, impatient.

"Don't be alone with him, Jill. Promise me."

"Beth, I don't understand…" *Why would Beth think Quinn was dangerous?* Jill thought, perplexed.

"The man who answered the phone is dangerous, Jill. Do not allow yourself to be alone with him. Promise me."

"Beth…"

"Promise me," Beth demanded.

"I promise," Jill agreed, confused.

"Okay." Relief eased into Beth's shoulder blades, knowing her friend would keep her word. "I'll call you tomorrow."

FIFTY-TWO

"14, 8. Game point." Chase called out, serving the volleyball over the net. Jill had opted out of the games a while ago, and was instead taking candid shots of her friends at play. Several hours of chatting, gaming, and general fun, convinced her that her first party had been a success.

"No way, pipsqueak!" Bobby retorted, bopping the ball back over the net. "It's more like our score is fourteen, and your team might be at ten."

No one knew how many points the teams had earned, and none of them cared too much. Chase decided to make up points as he went along. Tower seemed annoyed that they weren't keeping score well enough, but he had quit playing a while ago anyway.

"I need another beer!" Pete yelled, after missing the ball by less than a foot and catching Chase's affected scowl. "Jill, got any more? This cooler's empty."

Jill grimaced, tipsy. "We might be out, Pete." She hadn't anticipated the group staying as late as they had, and had drank enough herself to know she was in no condition to go get more.

"Tower, hon. Will you go get some more?" Carly whined, sticking out her lower lip. "Pleeeeeease," she begged.

Considering it for a moment, Tower agreed. "Sure. What does everyone want?"

"I want some wine coolers. I need to check on the baby, Pete, so give Tower some money, kay?" Kate called over her shoulder, as she slid past him into the house.

"I don't need any money, guys. I can get the drinks," Tower said, refusing their outstretched bills.

"Hey, grab the plate of cookies, would ya, Katie?" Bobby called just before Kate stepped out of ear shot.

"No problem." Kate yelled back.

"Tower, you wanta get some donuts for morning?" Carly suggested.

"Donuts! I made cheese blintzes for you and Jill!" Chase complained.

"Blintzes?" Bob yelled. "Are you serious? Damn, you'd make a good wife."

"Would you like to come with me?" Tower asked Carly, knowing she'd say no.

"Do I have to?" Carly questioned as he walked away from her.

Tower smirked. "No, I'll take care of it. Later."

"Thanks, Tower." Jill said.

"You know, I don't think I ever hauled in our beer. Debbie, did you bring it in?" Gary questioned.

"No, I thought you grabbed it." Debbie responded.

"I'll go get it," Chase offered, pulling Noel along with him.

"Kids," Pete chuckled. "Cole didn't stay long, eh? Hell, I barely saw him."

Jill shook her head. "No."

"Do you think Cole knows more than he's letting on?" Bobby asked. "I mean that tribal cop, and all? Seems damned fishy to me."

"The cop was tribal?" Billy questioned. "I didn't know that. What the hell would a tribal cop be doing with bank robbers? I thought they just policed tribal issues."

"When something that big goes down, they call on everybody to pitch in," Pete informed. "I believe Cole does know more than he's letting on. This is the biggest crime to hit the EUP in a long time. I bet every law enforcement agent around is in on this."

Bobby nodded. They were all left wondering: *What did Cole know?*

FIFTY-THREE

Pulling bills from Carly's wallet, Tower slipped them into his pocket and made his way into Jill's garage. Already bracketed on one wall, were a couple different sized shovels. He grabbed them, unsure of what he would need, and continued through the parked cars to find his Jeep. Surprised to see the back hatch open, Tower peered around the edge. *Easy*, he thought, gripping his Beretta behind his back. "What are you looking for?" he asked, assuming it was someone from the party.

Cooper backed up from the open Jeep. "You've got my money from the banks."

As Tower glimpsed the other man's face, he realized he'd never seen him before. He whipped his gun from his waistband to hold it with both hands, chest height. "What the hell are you doing?"

"I was going to rob those banks, and you took it from me," Cooper told him.

"Who are you?" Tower questioned, his gun held tightly with both hands, leveled at the strange man's chest.

"Cooper," the rambling man continued, building up speed as he lanced Tower with accusations. "I saw you. I saw you in the stolen car. I was at the gas station across the street. You turned onto Chard Road, and you killed a lady cop. And your partner. I saw their bodies, and now I see you."

Tower scanned the area for anyone who might be witness to the confrontation. "How did you follow me to Drummond? I never saw you," he countered, replaying the scenes in his racing mind, as he tried to decide what to do about this crazy fool.

"I didn't follow you. I went home, and saw you in the line up. I saw your Jeep. *I'll be your huckleberry*. It's on your bumper sticker."

Tower's mind replayed Red's words. *Do nothing to stand out*. His Jeep was a popular color, with the most popular brand of Goodyear tires. The bumper sticker was a clear identifier, and why the hell hadn't he removed it before he headed north? Carly bought it for him, and stuck the sticker on his Jeep. Removing it would have caused an awkward confrontation, but he should have done it anyway. *Shit*! He could strangle the bitch with his bare hands for leading him to this colossal screw up.

"You've got my money. It's right there." Cooper pointed toward the back of the Jeep. "I can feel bundles of money in there. I was gonna rob those banks, and you did it first. It's my money in there."

Tower looked over the surrounding scenery again, checking once more for anyone who may be watching or listening. When satisfied that they were truly alone, he relaxed his arms, dropping his gun to his side, and allowed Cooper to relax. "Listen, I'm not greedy," he began, "I'll split this with you, but you've got to help me with something."

Cooper's eyes darted back and forth. I'm gonna get my money, he thought. "What?"

"I've just learned about a buried treasure on Drummond, and I need help getting it." Tower explained, observing the darting eyes of the other man. *Free labor*, Tower thought. His trigger finger itched over the cold metal in his hand.

"Buried treasure?" Cooper asked. "Here?"

"Here on Drummond, yeah." Tower reached into his pocket, pulling out the folded email from earlier. "An old gangster from the thirties buried a man with treasure here. If you help me find it, I'll give you some of my money and half of the treasure."

"It's my money. I had the idea first," Cooper insisted.

"You're a cocky bastard for a man facing a gun." Tower's deadened eyes stared at the man. He leveled the gun, aiming it at Cooper's chest. "Either help me with the treasure, and I'll split the take, or I can put a bullet in your chest, and find somebody else to spend your money."

Cooper considered it for a long moment. He rocked from side to side, evaluating Tower. "I'll help."

"Fine. Get in on the driver's side."

Cooper complied, backing the red Jeep carefully out of Jill's driveway. Tower checked for curious eyes, turning 360 degrees, peering out the windows. Cooper attempted to ask Tower questions along the way, but was met with stony silence.

"Do you know where the Wayfarer's Mart is?" Tower asked.

"Everyone does. Did the gangster own it?" Cooper asked, trying to understand.

Sizing Cooper up, Tower realized the other man would be easy to handle. "No. He was a guest with a dead friend."

"How much money will I get?" Cooper questioned.

"Stop talking, and drive." Anticipation building, Tower kept the gun ready in his hand, and considered the treasure that could be waiting for him. *What did Dillinger leave me*? He wondered, as he leaned his head back against the seat, steeling himself for the drive across the island.

Using Lisa's directions verbatim, Tower examined the stones, taking several minutes to decide which one was the marker the email referred to. Finally deciding, he paced off the six feet from the triangle wedged stone, and dug his shovel into the ground. Cooper joined him, and together, the two men relocated piles of earth, working around the ever present stones, cursing quietly at some of the more difficult ones.

Tower looked the other man over. Cooper's long face was distorted idiotically while he dug his shovel into the ground. Digging took longer than Tower anticipated, but when Cooper's spade turned up a remnant of tattered and largely decayed cloth, Tower knew they were nearing the end. He gingerly edged around the object, pulling up bones.

"Is that the treasure?" Cooper asked.

"Silence," Tower hissed. Below the layer of bones, he moved aside the cloth pieces, feeling into the ground with his hands. They continued to dig, lengthening and deepening the hole past the point that still made sense. It could have been paper money, long decayed in the earth. Perhaps someone else had learned of the treasure years ago, and removed it. More realistically, Tower thought, it never existed. An old man's story became a bit juicier, so the nurse would listen. Furious, Tower asked. "Is there anything on your side?"

"Nothing."

"Ah, here. I see something. Gold. Shit," Tower said. He dug his fingers into the ground. "Cooper, I can't get it." Tower stepped out of the hole. "You try."

Cooper moved greedily into Tower's place.

Tower pointed to the ground. Cooper couldn't see what Tower pointed to, so he lowered himself to his hands and knees, with his head mere inches from the ground.

"Do you see it?" Tower asked, not waiting to hear the answer as he swung his shovel up over his head, bringing it smack against the back of Cooper's skull. The crack rang in Tower's ears. He quickly shoved Cooper's lifeless body into the hole. Satisfied with the kill, even though there was no treasure, Tower quickly covered the old bones and the new body.

Once the hole was filled, Tower recovered it with the grass patches they'd been careful to move when they began. Using his feet and shovel, he leveled the ground as best he could. When he checked the sight out earlier, he made a mental note on the location of a garden hose. Now using it, he sprayed the ground, encouraging the grass to take hold. He didn't want Coop's body found anytime soon, and with luck, no one would investigate the differences in the surface.

As he drove from the Mart, he realized hours had elapsed since he left the party. Another thought, more troubling than the first, occurred to him: Did Cooper tell anyone about his Jeep? Did he let anyone in on the fact that he witnessed the bank robberies and knew about the parties responsible? There were many Jeeps in the north, but he couldn't believe his stupidity in leaving the bumper sticker, a rare identifier, on his vehicle. He needed to leave Drummond, and yet Red's words filled his mind like a mantra: Follow the plan.

FIFTY- FOUR

"It's just like you thought. Carly's dead to the world, Jill," Chase said. After the last guests left, save for Chase, Carly curled up in the spare room and passed out. Jill made a deal with Chase that he could only drink alcohol if he stayed the night on her sofa. "Where do you think her boyfriend went? I can never remember his name."

"Tower. Uhm," Jill tossed empty cans into a paper bag. "I don't know."

"What do you think of him? Kind of odd, isn't he?" Chase questioned.

Jill shrugged, agreeing with Chase's assessment one hundred percent. "I'm trying to give him the benefit of the doubt."

"Yeah, sorry. I shouldn't be talking about him. Hell, I don't even know the guy. I think it's just that I didn't like the way he was looking at Noel." Chase folded up excess lawn chairs on the deck, leaning them against the side of Jill's house. "That Mike guy left pretty early, didn't he? I thought he was going to play volleyball with us, but he left right after he ate."

"He left without saying goodbye." Jill nodded, distracted. Her phone call with Beth kept replaying through her mind. "So did Quinn."

"Yeah," Chase agreed, scowling. He waited a beat, seeing

her crestfallen face. "It was a really good party, Jill. You're probably tired, hey?"

Jill paused, considering. "No, actually, I'm not." She sounded surprised. "I don't know where I got my second wind from, but I'm not tired in the least."

"Me either," Chase said, continuing to pick party remnants off the grounds. "When should we talk to Quinn, Jill? Sooner the better, right?"

"How about tomorrow?"

"After work?"

"Well, I wasn't supposed to work at all tomorrow, but I told Pete that I'd come in and finish up the molding. I was supposed to have the whole week off, but working means more money for me, so I'm not complaining. Uhm, anyway, what was the question? Sorry, I feel really scattered at the moment." Jill finished her task, and leaned against her deck railing.

"Too much beer," Chase chuckled. "Do you want to talk to Quinn after work?"

"Yeah, that sounds good. I'd like to spend some time with Tower and Carly tomorrow afternoon, since they're leaving on Saturday. I'll come over after you get off work. Is Quinn going to be there?" Jill questioned.

"I haven't got a clue. If Carly's leaving, we can wait till after she goes, Jill."

"No, I don't want to wait. We'll give it a try. If it doesn't work tomorrow, we'll stake him out. Eventually, he has to come home," Jill said. "We'll get to the bottom of it, Chase. If Quinn's in trouble, three heads are better than one, right?"

Chase nodded. "Hey, do you want to play checkers?"

"Checkers?"

"I saw the game in the spare room when I was looking in on Carly. Do you play?"

"Do you?" Jill countered.

"I'm wicked with checkers. I've been wanting to learn how to play chess, but I haven't had the chance yet."

"I would have pictured you for more of a video game type," Jill commented.

"Well, hell yeah. I've got computer games to rival the notches in Marci's hi heels."

Amused, Jill walked back into her garage, rolled down the door, and finished tidying the area. With one last loving look at her garage, she flipped the light switch off, plunging her addition into darkness. She enjoyed silence, which she attributed to growing up in a home without other children. In absolute quiet, her bare feet padded against the concrete, her mind retracing the day in the way she always did before going to sleep.

"You're more beautiful in the dark."

Gasping with shock, Jill's hand flew to her chest. "What?"

Tower stepped closer. "Isn't the darkness more appealing?" He traced his pinky finger from her forehead, following the curve of her nose. "Humanity is revealed in the absence of light. You are a fascinating woman, Jillian. I wonder if there could be something between..."

Shuddering against his touch, Jill stepped back. "What are you doing in here?"

"I used the shower." He spoke slowly, drawing out each syllable until there was no remnant of life left within the words.

To compensate, Jill spoke faster. Why am I so freaked out? She thought. *It's not like Carly hasn't dated weird guys before.* "Why didn't you use the one in the house?"

"I didn't want to talk to anyone, or wake anyone for that matter. I needed some time alone. I'm not good with people. I'm sure you understand, Jillian. Don't you?" He brushed his fingers against her arm, causing her to back up again. "Now that we're alone, we have a chance to get to know each other. Don't we, Jillian?"

The way Tower used her name had Jill's skin crawling. With one side stepping movement, she hurried past him, making her way back into the house. "Carly's asleep in the guest room. Do you need anything before you go to sleep?" she asked, not bothering to look over her shoulder, as she walked back into the house. A thought occurred to her, she spun around before she reached the breezeway. "Where'd you put the beer? And what took you so long?"

"I stopped by at the Northwood and played pool for a while. I forgot to bring more beer, but by the time I left, I realized your party would have to be nearly over."

"Oh." Jill said.

"Your island is a unique place. I think it must be filled with secrets."

"Why would you say that?" she asked, staring into his cold, dark eyes. She shivered as her question was met with stony silence.

"Jill, are we gonna play checkers or…" Chase's voice trailed off, spotting Tower. "Tower. You're back."

"Good evening," Tower greeted, "and night. You're right, Jill. It's time for me to sleep." Tower's eyes touched once more upon Jill's, before he silently retreated into the bedroom.

After Tower closed the door behind him, Chase looked hard at Jill. "Jill, you're pale. What's wrong?"

Jill pulled a kitchen chair from her table and sat down. "How much did I drink tonight?" she asked, more to herself than her friend.

Chase shrugged. "I don't have a clue."

She leaned her head against her dining table.

"Jill, are you okay?" Chase asked, concerned.

Taking a few deep breaths, Jill lifted her head, wishing she were talking to the older McCord brother, who would know just what to say. Quinn would pull her into his arms and comfort her. Ha! Jill thought. Quinn would simply confront the weirdo. Jill was pleased to have Chase there just the same. "I think I'm just tired."

"Did Tower do something?"

"Don't worry, Chase." Jill quelled Chase's concern with an affected smile. "You should get some sleep."

FIFTY-FIVE

THURSDAY

"Jill, where do you keep your lunch pail?" Chase called out, rubbing his wet hair with a towel.

"Check the cupboard next to the stove," Jill replied. She scooped her wet hair into a pony tail. She pulled on blue socks that matched her t-shirt, and work shoes over those. Her jeans were stained with paint and remnant materials from the job, but she liked them.

"Ah. Got it! Thanks." Without thinking, he picked up Jill's ringing phone. "Traynor's," he greeted.

"Hi, is Jill there?" Beth raised an eyebrow, glancing at the clock. She knew they both worked during the day, but she wasn't sure when Jill woke up.

Jill stepped into the living room, ready for the phone.

"Yeah, one sec." Chase tossed it into her cupped hands, and returned to his cereal.

"Hi," Jill said.

"Good morning. It's Beth. Is it too early to call?"

"Hi. Of course, not. I'm just getting ready for work." Jill walked back into her bedroom, closing the door behind her. "You know, Beth, ever since we talked yesterday, I've been thinking about what you said. I just can't believe that Quinn would want to hurt me."

"Quinn?" Beth asked, startled. "Quinn answered the phone?"

"Yeah, and we've been having our differences lately, but I know he would never hurt me," Jill insisted. "I trust your feelings, Beth. I just can't make any sense of it. I mean, why would Quinn want to hurt me?"

"I don't know, Jill." Beth voiced, troubled. "Are you sure Quinn answered the phone?"

"Yeah... well, no. Actually Beth, I didn't see him answer the phone. He's the one who told me I had a phone call, so I assumed it was him. When I picked it up, the room was empty except for a couple of kids. God, I wonder if it was... no, I'm not even going to think about that."

"When I called you, and the man said hello, the feelings I picked up were overwhelming. I can tell you this, when he spoke to me, he must have been thinking about hurting you, or something violent related to you at that exact moment," Beth explained.

"I can't imagine Quinn would be thinking violently about me," Jill returned.

"I can't explain it, Jill. I know you trust Quinn, but whoever answered the phone is *not* your friend. You're scared, Jill. I can sense that. I am so sorry to worry you."

"It's more than the phone call, Beth. It's more than I can get into now though," Jill spoke softly, aware of Carly and Tower sleeping in the next room.

Beth changed the subject. "Did you get a chance to check out Lisa's email?"

"I checked my email this morning, and didn't find a letter from your friend. Did Lisa have the right address?"

"You're still using the one I send you messages at, right?"

"Yep, same one. And I know it's working because I got a message from Uncle Dave this morning," Jill told her. "What's the message about, Beth?"

"I would have rather you heard it directly from Lisa, but I'll try to explain it to you. Have you ever heard of John Dillinger?"

"Gangster from the twenties?"

"Thirties, yep. Lisa had a patient that said he helped Dillinger bury a body on Drummond. The patient thought there was treasure there, and Lisa thought we should do something about it. I asked her to email you the story."

"Do you know where on Drummond, Beth?"

"No. I don't remember what Lisa told me, but she knows. I'll call her and ask her to resend the message, maybe she typed it in wrong," Beth suggested. "She's pretty detail oriented, so I can't imagine her screwing it up, but who knows."

"I'd be happy to help though."

"Great. I'll let her know. You coming to the Soo anytime soon? It'd be great to get together for lunch, hey?" Beth invited.

"My friends from downstate are up at the moment, but yes. I would love to spend some time with you."

Jill glanced at the clock. "Tell your friend to email me again, and tell her I'm definitely willing to help."

"Thanks, Jill." Beth waited a beat. "Take care of yourself."

"I will. Thanks, Beth."

Jill clicked the phone off. Returning to the kitchen, she beamed when she saw Chase making them both fried egg sandwiches for work. A cheese blintz and cup of coffee was waiting for her on the dining room table. "Chase, you're such a sweetheart."

"I know it. One of the many reasons why the ladies love me," he joked, placing the wrapped sandwiches in Jill's pail.

"Your pail is sharing some space with me, okay?"

"That's fine."

"Cool." Chase finished eating his Lucky Charms and placed the empty bowl and spoon in the sink along with the frying pan. "Hey, do you think we should call Quinn and tell him we want to talk to him?"

Jill considered it for a moment. "It's not a bad idea."

Chase nodded, picked up the phone and dialed his home number. He wasn't surprised when the answering machine picked up. He left the message, his mind consumed with worry for his brother and the approaching conversation this afternoon.

FIFTY-SIX

Jill pulled into her driveway after spending half the day finishing up Pete's work list. She was pleased to see the note scribbled in Carly's nearly impossible hand-writing: "Kayaking to Whitney Bay. Be back at dinner time! Pizza sounds really good. Luv, Carly." Along the wall above the dining room table, a framed print of Drummond Island hung. Jill had purchased it at an Arts and Crafts show the year before, from a local artist. Tracing her finger from Cream City Point west along the shore, she estimated that they'd be gone for a while, and come back tired. Hopefully, they'd have an early night. Jill was exhausted from night after night of bar hopping, and last night's party. She enjoyed the bar and drinking as much as the next person, but she rarely drank when she had to work the next day. She loved Carly to pieces, but the girl was a lot of work, Jill thought with a grin.

Chuckling, Jill tossed the note in the garbage and busied herself with emptying the dishwasher, and refilling it with dirty dishes. Neither Carly or Tower thought to clean up after themselves, which reminded Jill of the old Jefferson saying: 'Company is like garbage, after three days, it all stinks.'

Laughing to herself, pleased for a bit of solitude, she plunged into cleaning mode, windexed windows and swept down hardwood floors. She cranked the radio on as she dusted, jamming along, attempting to empty her mind of the last few days' worries.

Walking into her garage, she couldn't help shivering as she contemplated the creepy moment with Tower the night before. With a pad of paper and pen in hand, she looked over her workbench and peg-board wall, where brackets were attached to the wall holding household things, that Jill was beginning to amass. It was her goal to computerize a list of things she needed and wanted, so whenever she came into a bit of extra money from her photography, she could spend it wisely.

The possibility of a $2500 bonus from selling a cover photograph was burning a hole in her pocket. Where her workbench ended, her tall or bulkier tools were stored. A coil of garden hose was neatly wrapped and hanging next to a pick, shovels, and finally, a garden rake and brooms. Stepping next to the shovels, she looked closely at the wall. With an attention to detail that nagged Jill constantly, she took another look at her shovels. Dirt had fallen from one of the tools onto the concrete floor. Closer examination revealed that they'd both definitely been used, Jill concluded. Clark had keys to her house and garage, and often let himself in to borrow a tool. Jill never minded, but she couldn't imagine why he would borrow her shovels.

Setting aside the puzzle, Jill scribbled some notes about better storage for her cans of paint. She had remnants from the construction that she wanted to keep for touch-ups, but she'd have to put them somewhere else. She also wanted new countertops for her kitchen, but that would come later. She set her notepad and pen in her new office, and locked up her garage.

Pizza, she thought. Changing out of her work clothes, Jill grabbed her shoulder bag and headed out the door. Jill loved driving to PINS. She always drove the long way around, unless she was stopping at Quinn's house, located on the Maxton cut across. Rolling down her window, she slowed down to enjoy every moment of the hardwood trees leaning out over the road, interlacing leaves to create a canopy of brilliant green life.

Jill walked into the bowling alley-restaurant combination at 3:40 to find it sparsely filled. She waved to Noel, who was busy with a customer. Sheriff Cole sat at one of the long tables with Detective Bishop, and others she didn't know. She nodded to Cole, pleased to see him gesture her over.

"Hey, Jill." After introducing her to the other group members, Cole finished by asking, "You remember Bishop, right?"

"Of course," Jill said, shaking the detective's hand. "What brings you to Drummond?"

Bishop shuffled in his chair. "Oh, routine stuff, Jill. I heard you had a nice barbecue last night, eh? Cole was making us so hungry talking about it, that we had to come get some grub."

"It was a lot of fun," Jill agreed, curious about the blow-off answer. "I'll let you guys get back to your talk. I need to place my order."

"Nice seeing you, Jill," Bishop said.

Jill smiled, meeting Noel at the counter.

"Are you placing an order?" Noel asked.

"Yes. Although, I have no idea what to get us, now that I think about it."

"Pepperoni and cheese is pretty classic," Noel suggested.

"Sounds good. Make it a large, and I'd like some breadsticks too." Jill gave her a sheepish smile. "Actually, I really like the cheese sauce better than the marinara. Is there any way you can give me two cheese dips and not the red sauce?"

"Sure," Noel agreed. "Would you like a Coke while you wait?"

"That'd be great, thanks."

After fetching Jill a soda, Noel stepped back around the counter, chatting with the cook about the order and another customer's special requests. Jill found herself looking up at the posters of peppers at the top of the wall behind the open kitchen, with ceilings forever tall.

Cole tapped her on the shoulder. "Sorry about Bishop's song and dance, Jill."

"What's really going on?" Jill asked.

Cole lowered his voice. "Money from the Cedarville bank robberies has turned up on Drummond."

Alarmed, Jill's eyes widened. "The robbers are here?"

"Well, some of the money is, anyway. The feds think the robbers are long gone, but I think it's damned strange." Cole admitted.

"Where? How?"

"We're not sure where from yet, but we've narrowed it down. One bill showed up in the Credit Union, and was traced right back to the Central Savings Bank in Cedarville. It's the only one anyone has caught so far. It could have only come from one of a couple places. It was deposited at the Credit Union on Tuesday night." Nonchalantly, Cole looked back toward his table, checking to see that Bishop and the others were still seated.

"Was it a fifty?" Jill blurted.

Cole narrowed his eyes at her. "Yes. How do you know that?"

"Just a guess," she replied.

Cole searched her face. "Are you and Bishop related?"

"Huh?"

"I can stare at your face all day, but I'm not going to learn anything from it," Cole derided.

Jill smiled. "Sorry, Cole. I'm not trying to blow you off."

Yes, you are, Cole thought, but gave up. "Something else that's bizarre. Cooper is missing."

Jill's eyes widened. "He is?"

"Yeah. Major banged on my door this morning, royally pissed. Apparently, that turkey of Cooper's was pecking on Major's door. Major went to yell at Cooper, and discovered that he wasn't there. He asked me to go looking for him, but I haven't had a chance what with Bishop and the others coming in to investigate the lead."

"Do you think he could have had something to do with it, Sheriff?" Jill questioned, doubting it, but wanting to hear Cole's thoughts.

"I've been thinking about that all day, but I don't think so. It's not that I put it past him, I just don't think he has the chops for it. Major called my cell phone and let me know that he spent the morning driving around looking for Cooper's truck. Apparently, he found it about a half mile from your house, Jill."

"You're kidding me? He went looking for Coop's truck and found it on Cream City Point?" Jill asked. "Doesn't that seem a bit strange to you? Drummond's huge. If Major realized that Coop was missing this morning, how could he have found it that fast?"

Cole shrugged broadly. "Nothing about Major or Cooper surprises me anymore." He considered it for a moment. "He wasn't at your barbecue last night, was he?"

"No, not at all. I barely know the guy."

"Word got out that Cooper's missing. My answering machine is filling up with messages. I keep checking it from my cell phone. Actually, now that I'm thinking about it, I need to do that again." Cole said, pulling the cell phone from his chest pocket. "It doesn't work for me," he said, waiting for his machine to click in. "Whoever planned and carried out these robberies was meticulous, and in my opinion, brilliant."

"What makes you say that?"

"This is just between you and I, right?"

"Sure," Jill agreed.

"Two robbers hit the banks simultaneously. They were both dressed exactly alike. They dumped a car and had a secondary car in the wings for escape. The second robber was executed by the first, with the cop somehow killed just afterward or just before." Cole looked into the air before him for an answer, replaying the scenario in his mind. "Most likely, after. I'm sure we don't even know the half of it yet, but there aren't clues."

"What do you mean, there aren't clues?"

Cole held up his hand, silencing Jill. "Four messages, no make that five. Oh, what's this?" he muttered, more to himself than Jill, scratching notes on a small pad of paper. "Someone at the TeePee says she saw him yesterday afternoon." Cole shook his head, scratching notes on a pad of paper he retrieved, from his chest pocket. "If I find Cooper on some crazy hike through the woods to find a new pet, I'm gonna shake him."

Bothered, Jill leaned against the counter. Small details came together. The fifty dollar bill floating through her dryer had to be a coincidence, she thought. *Could Carly really be involved with a murderer?* "No clues, Cole?"

"The stolen car was clean. Two dead bodies, tire tracks. Now a fifty. That's it." Cole informed, struck by Jill's expression. "Jill, I don't like the look on your face. Do you know something you're not telling me?" Cole questioned. "If you're playing in my sand box Jill, it's rude not to share your toys."

Jill swallowed air, leveled her eyes with his. "No, Cole. Nothing, really. It's just been a long couple of days, and I'm having a hard time thinking that anyone from Drummond could be mixed up in this. But why would robbers just come here, if they weren't from here? It seems silly to lock yourself onto a place with no clear escape route, when people are looking for you."

"Then again, Jill, it might be the brightest thing a robber could do. Think about it. Who in their right minds would entrap themselves on an island? I think it's damned intelligent. No one would look here. Even when they slapped up all those damned road blocks, they never thought to check the ferry."

"Didn't they block M-134?"

"Yeah, but do you have any idea how many back roads there are around here? This is a good spot to lay low. It was damned smart, until the idiot spent some of the money. That's what I can't figure. How can you be smart enough to pull off a dual bank robbery, then dumb enough to spend some of the money a few days after you pull the heist? It doesn't figure. Especially, in a small area like Drummond."

Jill darted her eyes toward the dining tables. Cole quieted down, recognizing the signal. Sure enough, Bishop and the others walked toward them.

"Ready to go?" Bishop asked.

Cole nodded. "Yep. I was just waiting to settle up with Noel, here. Go on out to the car, I'll be right behind you." They both said goodbye to Jill again, and took Cole's suggestion. Cole gestured Noel over, and paid the bill. When he left, Noel frowned.

"Did he tell you about Crazy Coop missing?" Noel asked.

Jill nodded. "Yeah."

"Major eats in here quite a bit. He complains about Cooper, but I think he's really worried. Coop's pretty habitual," Noel commented.

"I don't know too much about him," Jill returned. "I've seen him at the bar, and Quinn has complained about him a little, but I'm not sure I've ever spoken to him."

"He keeps to himself mostly," Noel shrugged, suddenly

smiling. "Thanks for letting me come to your party, Jill."

"Don't be silly. You're always welcome," Jill invited.

"Chase is pretty hot," Noel blushed. "I meant to say, he's pretty cool. Yikes."

"It's okay," Jill laughed. "He is."

"He's different from the guys around here. Maybe, you don't notice the difference since you're not from here, hey?" Noel asked.

"I think you might see Chase as different, just because you didn't grow up with him. It's hard to have a crush on someone you knew in diapers." Jill smiled, "Drummond has a lot of great guys."

Noel wrinkled up her nose. "Not ones that are my age, Jill. You just don't know what it's like. Chase is new."

"Small town blues," Jill teased. "I know what you mean."

FIFTY-SEVEN

4:28pm, Jill took note of the time, as she glanced at her dashboard clock. She cruised around the corners, trying to decide what to do. If she ran the pizza home and then returned to Quinn's house, she'd be late. Carly and Tower could wait, she decided. She'd be a bit early, but with a wide smile, she looked away from the road, for a brief moment to confirm her camera bag's presence in the backseat. If Ridge was home, she could get some pictures of him, she thought. Pulling into the driveway, she smiled, seeing the Golden Retriever's tail wag near the window. She was just about to grab her camera when Chase's booming age-old Bronco, pulled into the driveway behind her. On second thought, she left the gear in the car and shut her door.

"You just get here?" Chase asked, as he jumped out of his vehicle.

"Yeah. How'd the rest of the day go?"

"Good. Pete said we'll actually get the job done in time," Chase enthused.

"I saw Noel."

"Oh, yeah? Did you buy pizza?"

"Carly asked me to buy some for dinner. Do you think it'll be okay if I leave it in the car while we talk to Quinn?"

"Yeah, it'll be fine. Come on in," Chase gestured, leading her into the house.

Jill followed him, saying hello to Ridge on her way in. She had always loved Quinn's house, bachelor pad that it was. The front door opened into the living room, featuring over-sized, brown toned matching furniture. Quinn owned the kind of couch one could curl up and die on, Jill thought. She kicked off her shoes, and nestled herself in one of its corners, leaning her head back against a well worn blanket. A variety of green plants decorated the home. One began at the top of an enormous entertainment center, and cascaded down the side, almost touching the floor.

Chase patted his dog's head, before moving on. "I'm gonna rinse off real quick, Jill. Quinn should be here any minute."

"Okay."

Chase was as quick as he claimed, popping out of the shower, in fresh clothes. He nudged Jill awake. "Come on, Jill. Wake up. Quinn's pulling in."

"I'm not sleeping. I'm just resting for a moment," Jill said, groggily.

"Liar," Chase teased.

Quinn's weary feet scuffed across the deck, and Jill sat up straighter. He opened the door, surprised to see Jill and Chase looking at him expectantly. "Hi, Jill. This is a surprise."

"Didn't you get my message this morning?" Chase asked.

"Yes, but you didn't say Jill was going to be here too."

"Didn't I? Oops," Chase voiced. "We need to talk, Quinn."

Jill remained quiet for the moment, studying Quinn's features. He looked, unquestionably exhausted. Her heart broke for him. "Will you sit down and talk to us, Quinn?" she asked, softly.

Quinn met her eyes, then his brother's and sighed. "Okay." He sat down on the chair adjacent to the couch. "What's up?" he asked.

"That's what we want to ask you," Chase said, his tone absolutely serious. "Lately, you've been... well, absent." Chase chose his words carefully, looking to Jill for help.

"We are worried about you," Jill added.

"And you've teamed up against me?" Quinn asked.

"We've teamed up for you," Jill corrected.

"Something is going on with you, Quinn. We want to help. Whatever it is, you can tell us," Chase insisted. "You're not around, at all. You're off the island all the time, and up at strange hours doing funny things in the garage, that you won't tell me about. Whatever your secret is, we can help you." Chase hesitated. "Is it drugs? Or, maybe you're having a liaison with an off island women? Or God, maybe an affair with a married lady?" Chase cast an apologetic glance to Jill, rushing into his next question. "Why aren't you sleeping?"

"One sec, guys." Quinn hopped up from the couch. He opened the refrigerator and pulled out three beers. He twisted the tops off, and handed one each to Jill and Chase. Quinn had never given his brother alcohol before. The gesture shook Chase.

"What the hell?" Chase mumbled.

Quinn sat down, taking a long pull from his beer before he began speaking. "I want you both to know that I never intended to keep some big secret from you. I'm not on drugs. I'm not a closet alcoholic, or doing strange illegal things. I'm not seeing anyone," he said, as his eyes caught and held Jill's for a long moment. "I haven't been interested in another woman for a long time."

Jill drank from her beer, finally returning her eyes to his.

"I am an intensely private person. I don't like being the center of attention, and I don't like discussing my life with anyone. I have a hard time talking about myself. Our mother," Quinn hesitated. "God, there's so much about my life I should have told you, Jill. I'm sorry."

Jill shook her head. "Don't apologize."

"I don't even know how to tell you about my childhood..."

"Chase told me that you were both adopted, Quinn." Her voice was barely a whisper, but she startled Quinn.

She must have felt sick to hear that from someone else, Quinn thought. They both knew how much Jill had revealed to him, sharing her very soul with him. He repaid her by keeping his life a secret. To his disgust, his eyes mirrored hers, as he felt he betrayed her.

"Quinn, it's okay." Jill said. She reached across the edge of the couch and gripped his hand in hers. "We'll talk about us later. Right now, we need to talk about you."

Chase looked on expectantly, waiting for his brother to continue.

"Our real mother," he began again, "talked incessantly about everyone's problems. She drove our father away, Chase. I'm sure there was much more to it than that. I remember our father being so angry with her about things she would say about him, to the neighbors. When we were taken in, I loved the way our new parents interacted. Mom and I," he said, speaking of their adoptive mother, "have our differences, but she taught me another way. I never really intended to keep this from you. When I began, I just figured it would be a hobby."

"What is it, exactly?" Chase asked, trying to mask his impatience.

"Do you remember the chicken from Jill's party?"

"What?" Chase shook his head, suddenly sidetracked.

"Three Bobbers Barbecue Sauce," Quinn responded, grinning.

"What about it?" Chase asked, dumbfounded.

"I created that sauce. I own Three Bobbers Over Land. Well, for the time being anyway."

"What?! Back up, I'm missing something! That's your secret?" Chase exclaimed, trying to make sense of it. "You created it?"

"Yeah."

"It's the best damned sauce I've ever had, Quinn. I didn't even know that you cooked still... what the hell!" Chase looked at Jill, sensing her equally shocked reaction and relief.

"What do you mean, for the time being?" Jill asked.

"I'm selling it."

"Wait a minute, shithead!" Chase railed at his brother, a mixture of relief and anger allowed the sudden outburst to escape unchecked. "Back up. Start from the beginning and tell the whole of it," Chase demanded, chugging down the rest of his beer.

Quinn chuckled. "I started experimenting over three years ago."

"Three years?" Chase asked, amazed. "Three flipping years?!"

"Actually, closer to four. Not quite four," Quinn shrugged.

"You just decided to start making barbecue sauce for fun?" Chase asked.

"No, no. I make marinade rubs, and meat seasonings, and all kinds of stuff. It's just the barbecue sauce is the product taking me to the next level."

"So, let me understand this. You make this sauce in the garage, and then what? Did you just start selling it to area businesses?"

Quinn laughed. "That's how I began, yeah. It's way bigger than that now." His brow furrowed, as he thought about it. "All I do on Drummond anymore is mix the spices together.

There's a second company that bottles the products, and mixes in the other ingredients. It's being carried by a good sized grocery chain and specialty stores, in seven or eight states now. Once I got into the grocery stores, I could make deals for shelf space. If you're in the system, it's much easier to get them to take other products," Quinn explained. "I just need to create the item that everyone clamors for. The barbecue sauce is my big dog. That's why I've been so exhausted. I need a factory, and I've bought the land to build one here, but I simply don't have the money to put it together."

"Land?" Chase choked. "Where?"

"You know that big piece on M-134 that's being cleared out right now? That's mine. I have plans for Admiral Sheet Metal, Inc. to build me a steel sheeted building. For starters, I need it to be 60 by 140 feet, 16 feet tall. I'll have a 20 by 60 ft area with two stories, for offices, and a creation kitchen."

Quinn grabbed a pen and pad of paper, from the end table. He quickly sketched a crude drawing to show them what he had in mind. "It'll have three loading bays that can handle 18-wheelers. This thing is gonna cost some money though. The way I figure it, I need $658,000.00 as a bare minimum to really get this going. I've got orders backed up that I can't meet, because I just don't have the space. There's even more money to be made in some of these rubs and marinades, but I'll lose the money by outsourcing the labor. And *I am not*," Quinn emphasized, "trusting anyone else with my recipes. I've got about $113,000.00 of what I need. I can swing a loan for $265,000.00, but I can't talk the Credit Union into giving me any more than that. They have rules, and I don't have any real credit history off of Drummond. I don't have any assets to cover it, and my age works against me. I'm 280k short." Swigging down another swallow of his beer, Quinn shook his head.

"Where the hell'd you get 113 thousand?" Chase asked.

Smiling for the first time, Quinn answered his brother's question. "I've saved every extra cent from selling this stuff that I've made, and I came into my trust fund. You haven't yet," Quinn mentioned.

Jill leaned back, overwhelmed. "You never said a word."

"Well," Quinn shrugged. "No, I didn't. I've handled it pretty well, up until the last six months or so. Somehow, it got into the right hands, and the orders started coming out of the wood work. I have no time to experiment with new products, because I'm working on mixing, and delivering, which I shouldn't have to do. It's too big for me to handle, and to do anything serious with it, I need this building."

"A factory that size is going to need some serious employees to run it," Chase observed.

"Yep, it will. But, it's not my problem anymore. I'm selling it."

"No way! You can't sell it. I can help."

Quinn smiled sadly. "It's way bigger than that. Besides, the American Food Company wants to take it national. They're trying to buy me out. That woman, Brenda Elliot keeps popping in with a new proposal. I know you've seen her around, Chase. Anyway, it kills me to have to sell it. I love Three Bobbers, especially, when I'm creating new recipes. I don't even have time to care for the tomatoes anymore," Quinn said, disgruntled.

"You started the tomato garden that I've been laboring over all summer?" Chase deduced.

"How do you think it got there?"

"I just figured it came with the house."

Quinn chuckled. "You know that glassed in lean-to, on the side of the garage?"

Chase nodded.

"In the beginning, I used that area to experiment with tomato seedlings."

Chase's inner cook couldn't help but ask. "What kind of tomatoes do you use in the barbecue?"

"Hydroponics: Expensive little jewels, but they're the best."

"Unreal," Chase ran his fingers through his hair. "Ambitious son of a bitch, aren't you?"

Quinn grinned. "If it had worked, yeah. It won't be such a bad deal to sell it," Quinn tried to make it sound as if he wasn't selling his baby. "I'll get to spend more time with you guys, and more time working at the bar."

Jill squeezed his hand. "Quinn, you obviously love it. There has to be a way to keep it."

"How much are the other guys offering you?" Chase asked.

"Eight hundred thousand," Quinn answered.

"No shit! Wow, eight hundred..." Chase's eyes bugged out a bit. "Quinn, you can't sell it! If they're offering you 800 thousand, it must be worth millions. This is something to make your stamp on the world with," Chase enthused, gathering speed. "Why don't you use my trust fund?"

Quinn shook his head. "You're not old enough, for one. Mom will never agree to it. And second, absolutely not. That money is for your future."

"I can talk her into it, Quinn. There's no reason why I can't give it to you," Chase argued. "I could be your partner. You could sell me shares for my money. That would help my future."

"You're going to college."

"Culinary school," Chase corrected. "Cooking is the only thing I really love doing, and you know it."

Quinn raised an eyebrow. "Even if you did use your

money, which I'm not allowing, it wouldn't be nearly enough. I need $280,000.00, and if miraculously, there was some way to come up with that kind of money, it would be just enough to get me started. We're talking about milk crates to sit on, no sign out front, and loading trucks by hand. There's no way, Chase. I've been over the numbers so many times I could puke. Besides that, Brenda has given me a deadline."

"How much time do you have, Quinn?" Jill asked.

"I have to fax the signed agreement on Wednesday," he responded. "They know I have a cash problem. The timeline is short, because they're trying to force my hand."

"Wow," Jill exhaled deeply. *Thank God*, she thought. She was worried for Quinn, but in a good way, she decided. She and Chase had been so far off the mark. Never once, did either of them consider that he could be spending his time building something. Relief surged through her. Quinn was just fine, albeit exhausted, but fine. Besides that, something in the way he looked at her, told her he still cared.

"I feel like celebrating, or crying. I can't get over this, Quinn. I moved up here to spend more time with you, and it's like I never figured it out." Chase shook his head. "I can work with you. I'll quit my job with Pete, and I'll work for free."

"I can't let you do that." Quinn shook his head.

"Well, you don't have a choice. I have to go to school in a few weeks anyway. Football practice starts in a couple days, but I can work around it. Why do I need money anyway? Just give me like forty bucks a week for gas and playing a bit, and we'll make this work. I know we can."

Quinn was touched. "You know, this is just the first part of my plan."

"What else are you hiding up your sleeve?" Chase asked.

"Eventually, I want to build a second factory in a rich tomato growing area. In time, I want to build a Yooper themed restaurant, called Three Bobbers. I have menu ideas and floor plans sketched out, but no money."

Chase groaned, but he was grinning. "You've got a menu?!"

"Road Kill Stew, Freezer Burned Ribs, Venison Chili. The restaurant would look like a really old 1950s trailer with a tar paper lean to addition on the outside."

"You mean, animated. As if Disney did it?"

"Exactly!"

"You're killing me, Quinn. Do you know how great that would be? Oh, man! Promise me, you won't sign until you talk to me again."

"Chase, there's no way…"

"Promise me, Quinn." Chase nearly begged. He couldn't allow his brother to give up on his dreams when he was so close.

"Okay."

Chase's words reminded Jill of her phone call with Beth. Since Quinn started talking, she hadn't thought about her own problems, or worried about the bank robberies. Like dominoes, one thought and concern slid into her mind after another. At least, Quinn wasn't sick or in trouble. Or in love with another woman, Jill thought, gazing down at their interlaced fingers. Big Chest from the bar was the woman trying to buy Quinn's company. Jill tried to make sense of the thoughts swirling through her mind. But, how could Beth be wrong? She hadn't bothered to pull her hand away. Her hand fit so well in his, and she'd wasted so much time trying to do the right thing, that she missed out on being with Quinn, she thought. Of course, Quinn didn't have much time for her either, lately. She looked up, surprised to see Quinn studying her face.

"Quinn, what did you say to Beth DeForge yesterday?" she asked, suddenly changing the subject.

"What?" he asked, thrown off guard. "Beth? Is she here? I haven't seen her."

"No, when you spoke to her on the phone. At my house yesterday, she called and you answered the phone. What did you say to her?"

"I didn't answer your phone," Quinn shook his head.

"You didn't? Are you sure?"

"Yeah. I was laying Joey down on your bed, when the phone rang."

"Who answered it?"

"Hmmm. Tower, I think." Thoughts crossed through Quinn's eyes, and Jill could see he was really pondering the question. "It could have been that Mike guy, though. I'm not sure. Why?" Quinn asked, glancing down at their hands. Jill's had gone cool.

Jill shrugged. *Tower*, she thought. It had to be Tower.

"Jill, what is it?" Quinn asked.

"Do you have to work tonight?" she inquired.

"Not at the bar, but I need to mix some pails of ingredients together. Why?" Quinn asked.

"I can help with that," Chase interrupted. "It's time to take the locks off the doors."

Quinn nodded his head, pulled a set of keys from his pocket and tossed them to his brother.

"I was just wondering if you guys wanted to come over for pizza," Jill hedged. I don't want to be alone with Tower, she thought, but didn't say it. "Did you hear about Cooper?"

"What about him?" Chase asked.

"He's missing. I saw Cole at PINS. I guess Major's really worried," Jill informed them.

"Coop's been acting strange lately."

"Doesn't he always?" Chase mumbled.

"He was asking around about a red Jeep."

"A red Jeep?" Jill asked.

"Yeah," Quinn knew her face so well. He shook himself out of it, concentrating. "Why?"

I can't tell him, Jill thought. Chase went to answer the phone, diving off the couch on his way to the kitchen. He walked the cordless phone into his room.

"Why don't you stay here, and I'll cook you dinner," offered Quinn.

Jill melted, wishing she could. "There's a pizza in my car. Carly's expecting it."

"Okay, pizza's fine then."

Chase returned. "Sorry, guys. I need to bail. There's a big party going on tonight." He tossed the phone on the counter. Took one look at his brother, and made the extra effort to place it back in the charger. "Are you going to Jill's?"

"Yeah," Quinn replied. "I hate to drive over there by myself though."

Jill retrieved the pizza from her Tracker. "I'll leave my car here, and go with you. We'll get it later," Jill resolved, standing up, as she pulled her hand away from Quinn's.

FIFTY-EIGHT

Pulling into Jill's driveway, Quinn observed two red vehicles, one Convertible and one Jeep. He pointed toward the Jeep, as he angled around it. "Is that…"

"Not now, Quinn." Jill sat in the passenger side of his Jeep, pensively gripping the pizza box. She led the way to the house, by passing her usual garage entrance, for the back door. Carly and Tower weren't back yet. "Thank you," she whispered toward the ceiling.

Quinn caught the gesture. "Do you want to just leave the pizza and go back to my place? We need to talk, Jill."

"Is it really bad to want to get away from your guests?" she asked, embarrassed. "I can't bear the thought of spending another night down the hall from him."

"Stay with me," he offered. Quinn moved toward Jill's front door, squinting through the window at the horizon. The afternoon sun reflected off the water. He held up his hand, creating a shield over his eyes. "I can see them off the coast, Jill. It's time to make a decision."

"Let's go," she decided, scrawling a note: "'I'm staying at Quinn's. Don't wait up.' Oh, wait. Let me grab Chase's pictures, real quick." She jogged into her office and found the envelope from earlier. "Okay, I'm ready now."

Unable to stop himself, his face broke into a wide smile.

Once they were inside the Jeep and headed out the driveway, Jill looked in the rearview mirror. Her gasp filled the car.

Quinn slammed on the brakes. "What's wrong?"

Through the mirror, as clear as day, on Tower's bumper was a white sticker. Jill craned her head around to get a clear view. Reading the words aloud this time, her face drained of color. "I'll be your huckleberry," she whispered, her breath uneven.

"What are you talking about?"

"Drive."

"What's wrong?"

"Quinn, drive! Now!"

Without further argument, Quinn peeled out of the driveway, rounding the corners more quickly than usual. When they reached the main road, she turned to him. "Quinn, he did it. Tower robbed those banks."

"What? What the hell has been going on? What have you been keeping from me?"

"You're one to talk, Quinn. Everyone has secrets." Jill's hands shook. "I'm sorry. That was uncalled for."

"No, I had that coming. No more secrets?"

Jill smiled. "No more."

"Then start talking."

"I don't even know where to start."

Quinn kept his eyes on the road, but anger filled him. How could he have let himself become so focused on his own problems, that he missed what was going on right in front of his nose? "Jill… talk to me."

"I didn't want to believe it." Jill inhaled deeply, as she concentrated on calming herself down. "Carly has always dated really strange guys, but never anything like this one. The first day I met him, he was looking me over, as if I were a piece of meat, and Carly seemed aware."

"Did you say anything to her? Or him, for that matter?"

"I thought I was overreacting," Jill admitted. "Carly has changed, Quinn. There have been a couple of times since she came here, that I've been defensive. Hell, look how I just snapped at you. She's rougher, and she doesn't seem to see it. Tower is blatantly hostile, and she excuses his behavior with a wave of her hand. It's as if he has this bizarre control over her, which is so unlike Carly."

"Go on," Quinn encouraged.

"When I moved up north, over a year ago, she was just as obstinate and opinionated, but she listened to reason. She held value for some amount of normalcy. Before Tower arrived, she seemed pretty typical for Carly. Tower was never supposed to come."

"He arrived after Carly, right?"

"He arrived on Monday."

"On the day of the robberies?"

"Yes, I came home from work to find them together in my living room," Jill explained.

"Together?"

"Yeah," Jill responded. "I didn't want to see any more of that, so I went to your house."

"My house?" Quinn questioned, thinking back to Monday. "I didn't see you Monday, are you sure?"

"Yeah." Jill looked down, before admitting, "I was snooping."

"You were?"

Jill found a smile. "Chase caught me. We were both so worried about you, that we had a big talk, trying to figure out what was wrong with you. Anyway, I went home after I figured they had enough time to finish up and get some clothes on."

"Was this the first time you met Tower?"

"Yeah. He was creepy, Quinn." Jill shook her head, trying not to focus on how Tower made her feel.

"And you didn't say anything to Carly?" Quinn asked, doubtful. If Jill was anything, it wasn't meek.

Jill hesitated. "Carly is kind of sensitive. I mean, she's not sensitive in the traditional sense. She doesn't tear up when she's insulted, but she gets defensive. Carly and I have gotten into it over guys before. She thinks that I don't understand her life, or the way she lives. I think, that she thinks…"

"What?" Quinn asked when Jill paused.

"Well, maybe she thinks I don't approve." Jill shrugged, pausing to consider what she said. "I guess in a small way, she's right. I don't care how she lives, as long as she's happy and healthy. She isn't the same girl I lived with, even though she was still such a firecracker back then." She shook her head, thinking about it. "She's different now."

"How has she changed?"

"She's always fighting. She fights fires, women, and friends. She spends her whole life fighting. I can't believe that's a good thing," Jill whispered. "I don't think she's happy. The last thing Carly wants to think about is if she's happy or not, and honestly, if I question her lifestyle—well, who am I to talk about happiness? I'm not an authority on the subject, by any stretch. We both know it. Before this week, I hadn't seen her in over a year. I wasn't about to start an argument, but there's something bizarre about their relationship. He's kind of scary and rough with her one moment, and casual the next." Jill shuddered, contemplating. "It's like he's playing a part. He's on display, as if he's not the real Tower. Though I have no idea what the real Tower is like."

"So, Carly's boyfriend creeps you out from moment one, and you didn't say anything because you didn't want to upset her?" Quinn asked, trying to understand.

Jill sighed. "Yep, that's pretty much it."

"That doesn't prove he robbed a bank, Jill."

"I know. Sorry, I got sidetracked." Jill took a moment to collect her thoughts as Quinn pulled into his driveway. As she thought back over the days, she remembered something that had bothered her. "When I met Tower, I felt like I knew him from somewhere."

"You've met him?"

Jill shook her head. "No, I don't think so, Quinn. I usually remember when and where I've met someone. I can't place it. I just feel like I've seen him somewhere, which doesn't really have any bearing on any of this, it's just weird." She let the thought go, following Quinn back into his house.

She took a seat on a bar stool, propping her elbows on the tall counter's overhang. Quinn offered her something with kick, but she declined and settled for juice. He poured her a large glass of apple juice, setting it in front of her. He encouraged her to continue as he pulled ingredients from his cupboards.

"Okay… where was I?" Jill asked.

"You remember Tower from somewhere," he prompted.

"Right, I did some laundry. Tower was being cranky, and Carly doesn't do domestic chores unless she has to, but Carly put their laundry in my basket, so I did theirs too."

"Okay," Quinn responded, wondering where she was going with this.

"On Tuesday, I found a fifty dollar bill in my dryer."

"That's a lot of money to leave in your pocket, isn't it?" Quinn asked.

"Exactly," Jill agreed. "Carly's always leaving money in her pockets, but this wasn't hers."

"Tower's really cheap. Actually, I don't get the sense that he's cheap. I get the feeling that he's a taker." It was the first time she allowed herself to communicate honestly about her concerns.

"Okay, it's still a long way from proving he robbed the banks," Quinn said.

"It gets worse." Jill sipped her juice, watching Quinn mix a variety of unlabeled ingredients into a sauce pan. "He told Carly he used all of his money to drive up."

"So, he's a liar?"

"Carly and I spent the money at Wazz's that evening. This afternoon, Cole told me a fifty dollar bill from the bank robbery turned up on Drummond Island. Bishop and a federal agent are here, today, investigating."

"Coincidence," Quinn said, playing devil's advocate.

"Last night, Tower left the barbecue, and didn't return for nearly four hours," Jill said, gathering steam. "He was supposed to run for more drinks, but when he returned he didn't have anything with him."

Quinn looked unconvinced.

"Quinn, he was gone for hours. And he was weird," Jill shuddered. "I think he wanted to sleep with me."

Quinn faced her, giving her his full attention. "What makes you think that?"

"I was in the garage, tidying up. Your brother was a big help, by the way, and I shut the lights off, before I crossed through. The jerk didn't say anything until we were in the dark, and I think…" Jill's voice trailed off as she concentrated on what took place. "I think he was lying. He must have been."

"About what?"

"He told me he was in the garage to use the shower. I never heard him."

"How long were you in the garage?"

"Not very long," Jill admitted.

"Keep going. What happened next?"

"He touched me."

"Where?" Quinn demanded.

"In the garage."

"No," Quinn rolled his eyes. "Where did he touch you?"

"Oh, just my nose. He touched my arm too, but his voice was so unsettling. I got away from him, but if Chase hadn't been there, I'm not sure what would have happened."

"Where was Carly?"

"Passed out in the bedroom."

"That bastard…" Quinn vented.

"Anyway," Jill hurried forward, cutting off Quinn's thoughts.

"No, wait a minute. Why didn't you say anything to Tower?"

"I was a bit drunk." Jill excused.

"Jill, you know damned well that your instincts are rarely wrong. If you felt creepy, you should have said something."

"Will you let me tell it?" She asked. "Besides, he didn't say anything that could be nailed down. It's not like he said something specific that I could challenge him on. I walked into the house before it hit me. I asked him where the beer was, and he told me that he didn't buy any. He stopped at the Northwood, and got carried away playing pool."

"That's a lie," Quinn stated.

"I think so too," Jill agreed.

"No, it really is, Jill. The pool table's been broken for the last couple days. I called the guy to repair it, myself. It's not getting fixed till tomorrow."

"He was lying." Jill felt vindicated. "I knew it."

"Okay, so Tower disappeared last night. Even if he lied, what does that have to do with the robberies?" Quinn challenged.

"Cooper," Jill stated, as if that cleared up the confusion.

"Huh?"

"Cooper, according to you," Jill said pointedly, "specifically mentioned that he was looking for a red Jeep."

"And he's been talking about money, but that doesn't link them up, Jill."

"When I was at PINS today, Cole came up and talked to me. While he was next to me, he phoned his answering machine and checked messages. On his notepad, he wrote the word "huckleberry," with a question mark. He was mumbling as he wrote notes, so I know that the huckleberry connection had something to do with Cooper's disappearance. Cooper's truck was found about a half mile from my house."

"You think Cooper was part of this," Quinn concluded.

"If he was involved in the bank robberies, why was he looking for Tower's Jeep?" It didn't make sense, Jill thought, as thoughts volleyed back and forth. "On the other hand, yes. I think, somehow, Cooper is involved and they must have met up together before he went missing."

"Cooper's not too bright, Jill. Do you really think he had something to do with this? Besides, I thought there were only two bank robbers. We know that one of them was murdered. Where does Coop fit into all this?"

Frowning, Jill shook her head, frustrated. "I'm not sure.

That's just the problem. There are more clues and questions, than I have answers for." Shaking her head, she voiced, "There's something missing." She thought about it for a minute, popping off her stool to pace. "If Cooper was involved, why would he be connected to Tower's Jeep? If Cole heard a message relating Cooper to Tower, he would have reacted. I even asked Cole if he thought Cooper was tied to the robberies. Cole wasn't leaning in that direction."

"The timing of his disappearance is awfully convenient," Quinn inserted.

"He didn't take Dinner with him."

"How do you know?"

"Major saw Dinner outside his door this morning, which spurred his hunt for Cooper."

"Then he didn't leave. He wouldn't have left that turkey behind, Jill. He must be here somewhere," Quinn said, as he stirred pasta noodles in his pan. "Back up for a minute. What about the phone call with Beth? What's up with that?"

"She was calling to ask me if I received an email from her friend," Jill explained. "Do you remember me telling you about Beth's paranormal feelings?"

"Vaguely."

"Well, she gets these sensations from other people and objects, I guess. When someone answered my phone, she sort of received the feeling that he wanted to harm me." Jill explained, unsure of her understanding of Beth's feeling. "I know. It sounds odd, and it's not something I would normally put a lot of stake in—but she's usually right. Actually, I've never known her to be wrong."

"Harm you, personally?"

"Yes," Jill answered. "Apparently, Tower must have been thinking about me when he answered the phone."

"I'm not sure he did, Jill. Mike and Tower were both

standing near the phone."

"It had to be Tower," Jill decided. "Why would Mike want to hurt me? Tower's a creep. After last night, it doesn't surprise me."

"You thought I answered the phone, didn't you?" Quinn remained motionless.

"It was you who told me I had a phone call. No one else was in the living room but the kids when I picked it up." Jill shrugged. "I didn't believe it, Quinn." Jill looked at Quinn directly. "I never believed that you'd want to hurt me."

"You were worried about me. It crossed your mind that I could be into drugs or worse. Why didn't you think I'd hurt you?" Quinn challenged.

"It's like you said, Quinn. I followed my instincts." When he remained unsure, she paused. "I'm here now, aren't I?"

"Yeah, you are." he agreed. "Why are Beth's friends emailing you?"

"I'm not sure. I never received the message, which reminds me. Beth is supposed to check into that. There's a body buried somewhere here that she wants me to look into. Hmm, I guess I'll just talk to her tomorrow."

"A body?"

"And treasure, yeah."

"No shit. This is getting a little weird, don't you think? How the hell is Beth connected to this? I mean does shit just seem to find this girl or what? How does she know about it?"

"Well, I haven't gotten the email yet. Beth told me it has something to do with a patient."

"Her friend is a nurse too?"

"I guess so," Jill responded. "Beth gave her my email address, and her friend sent me the email, but I didn't get it."

"Odd," Quinn sounded.

About to respond, Jill lost her train of thought as the aroma of Quinn's dish reached her. "That smells amazing, Quinn."

Quinn winked. "I've wanted to cook for you, for a long time."

Jill's voice softened as she asked, "Why didn't you tell me?"

He hesitated, knowing that she referred to Three Bobbers. "It never seemed like the right timing. I was going to tell you."

"When?"

"The night you told me we needed to stop seeing each other. I was going to cook for you and tell you then, but…"

"I ruined it," Jill finished.

"I guess it wasn't the right time."

"It is now, isn't it, Quinn?"

Quinn studied her. She was talking about more than revealing secrets, and he knew it. "I think so."

"What are we going to do?"

With the change in tone, Quinn recognized she was talking about Tower again and rolled with her. "We should talk to Cole."

"What if we're wrong?" She stepped closer to him, leaning against him, staring at the bubbling concoction he brewed.

Quinn wrapped his arms around her, tilting her face up with his hands. He couldn't help enjoying the way "we" sounded. "We know something's wrong. We know enough that we should be talking to Cole." Dipping his wooden spoon into the pasta sauce, he blew on it to cool it down and offered her a taste.

Smiling, she accepted. As the spoon touched her mouth, she moaned.

Chuckling, Quinn pulled the spoon back. "Like it?"

"*Love* it."

FIFTY-NINE

Soft, yellow morning rays of light crawled in through the heavy living room drapes, touching down on Jill's face, before they slipped down the couch and across the shag carpeted floor. Quinn leaned against the arch of the hallway, leading to the bedrooms, and watched her sleep for several moments. He hadn't even tried talking her into taking his bed, or sleeping beside him, or anything else for that matter. Their relationship was just getting back on its feet, and he wasn't about to tremble the ground with too much pressure. Leaving her alone last night, either made him the last of the good guys, or a complete idiot. It was probably the latter, but the girl was plainly in love with his couch, a hand-me-down gift from his mother, so Quinn tried not to beat himself up too badly.

Her eyelids fluttered open, as if sensing Quinn's presence. Jill was one of the few people he knew, besides himself, that could wake-up completely awake. Chase always stumbled around the house, grumpy as a bear, for an hour, before he had anything decent to say.

"Good morning," Jill said on a breath, stretching her arms back.

"Feel like breakfast?" He asked, scooching her legs to sit beside her.

She smiled up at him, brushing the hair back from her face. "I might still be full from dinner… but, are you cooking?"

Quinn chuckled softly. "I thought I'd take you out to the Bear Track. A change of venue might be good for our deductive reasoning," he teased.

Jill lowered her hands back to her sides, setting her left hand beside his. "Okay, I could go for that. Did Chase come home last night? I didn't hear him."

"Yeah, he did. He's already gone to work again." Quinn picked her hand up, absently playing with her fingers.

"What time is it?"

"Time to get up and go to breakfast with a really hot bartender," he encouraged.

"You've been spending too much time around Carly," she squeezed his hand in hers, bringing his hand to her lips, where she kissed him. Her face tightened, as her thoughts returned to her friend. She lowered Quinn's hand, but kept it in her grasp. "That's the thing I'm having a hard time with."

"If she's involved with this?" Quinn questioned.

Jill nodded. "I don't want to think that. I shouldn't be thinking that, but I can't help but wondering. Carly's different…"

"You know, Jill, you keep saying that. But what if you're different?"

Jill paused, considering. "It's possible." After a moment, she shook her head. "No, it's not possible. I've changed and grown and whatnot, but the Carly I knew never would have been involved in killing someone."

"She beats people up for part of her living," Quinn reminded.

"I know, but that's competitive." Jill excused.

"It's a pretty fine line, Jill." Quinn disagreed. It wasn't that he didn't like Carly, but he felt like he needed to counterbalance Jill's willingness to believe her. "Come on, let's go to breakfast."

"Okay, okay. Do I have time for a shower?"

Quinn shook his head, but said, "Yes. Do you want some coffee?"

"No. Five minutes, and I'll be ready to go."

She dashed off to the shower leaving Quinn to sit and ponder last night's events. He loved cooking for her, especially since she was a pretty dismal cook herself. It was good to have Jill near him, and it was such a relief to have shared his ambitions with her. By telling his story, and his plans, he felt light enough to walk on air.

Jill stepped out of the bathroom, towel drying her hair. She finished off, dumped the towel in Quinn's laundry basket at the foot of his bed, and reappeared to slide her sandals on. "Are you ready?"

"Am I ever," Quinn sounded, following her to the door.

Jill paused at the door, spinning around to face him. "Can I use your phone?"

"Yeah. Why?"

"I'm gonna call Beth. She should still be home, getting ready for work." Jill peered past him to the stove top clock. "I want to see if she talked to her friend, because I didn't get a chance to check my email last night," Jill explained, picking up Quinn's phone, and dialing the number from memory.

Beth answered on the second ring. "Good morning."

"Hi, Beth."

"Jill, hi. I just tried calling you, with no answer, so I left you a message on your answering machine."

"What did you say?"

"I talked to Lisa, and she tells me that she received one of those return receipts. She can prove that the email was opened, Jill. She re-sent it, but her email program can absolutely confirm that it was opened. Is there a ghost at your house?" Beth asked, half-kidding.

"Worse," Jill confirmed, contemplating the possibilities.

"Oh?" Beth hesitated, glancing at her clock. "Did you get the new one?"

"I haven't been home to check it."

"Why don't I give you Lisa's number, Jill? You can call her, and she'll talk to you about the email. Does that work?"

"Yes, that works." Jill agreed.

Beth gave her the number, and Jill stored it in her mind, making small talk before she hung up the phone. Jill punched in Lisa's number, which clicked into her voicemail automatically. Jill left a message with her number, before she followed Quinn out the door.

"What's going on?" Quinn asked, as he hopped in his Jeep.

"Beth's friend received an electronic return receipt for the email she sent me, that I never got." Jill sighed. "Do you think Tower got into my email?"

"Tower or Carly, right? Someone must have opened it, and then deleted it." Quinn surmised, as they lapsed into comfortable silence. Several minutes passed before Quinn pulled into the parking lot of the Bear Track, pleased to see Sheriff Cole's SUV parked off to the side. Two birds, one stone, he thought. "It's decision time, Jill."

"Yeah, I see that," Jill agreed, as she stepped down to the ground. She led him through the doors, picking a table in the back, near the window.

The waitress held up the menus. "Do you need these?"

"No, I know what I want," Jill said, looking to Quinn.

"Me too. I'll take a coffee, and three slices of French Toast and a side of bacon."

"I'll have the same thing, but just two slices," Jill echoed.

"Great," the waitress replied as she spun around, passing Cole on the way.

"Mind if I join you?" Cole asked, receiving a nod before he pulled a chair out from the round table, sitting near Jill and Quinn. "Jill, I've got some questions for you."

"Hold on. Is there any word on Cooper?" Quinn asked.

"No, he hasn't turned up yet. I'm really getting worried about this. Bishop's having scent dogs brought down tomorrow."

Jill leaned forward. "You have questions for me, Cole?"

Sheriff Cole propped his hand on the butt of his holstered gun, in the unconscious telling motion that meant he was serious. "Remember me telling you about the fifty dollar bill, that turned up from the bank robbery?" he asked.

"Yes, of course," Jill replied.

"Well, your friend Carly spent one of the bills in question. We can't tell if it's the exact bill, but we pulled the surveillance from Wazz's, and you're large as life, caught on video tape, standing right next to her." Cole paused, giving Jill a stern look. "Now, when we were at PINS, you asked me if it was a fifty, so imagine my shock when I see you spending one on the day in question." Cole said, his voice stern with authority. "What are you not telling me, Jill? What is going on?"

Jill took a breath, pausing as the waitress delivered their coffees, before revealing the whole story. She didn't cast any suspicion on her friend, but merely reported the facts as they had learned them to Cole. When she reached the huckleberry reference, he stopped her.

"How did you know about the phone message about Cooper?"

"You were talking about Cooper, and wrote huckleberry in your note pad."

"And you read my notes?" he asked, looking none too thrilled as he clenched his cup a bit tighter.

"It's not like you were trying to shield them," she defended, quieting once again, while the waitress handed out plates of food.

Cole let her continue, connecting Cooper to the red Jeep, owned by Tower with the bumper sticker. She poured syrup over her thick slices of French Toast. Jill finished discussing the buried body and treasure, and missing email when Cole stopped them again.

"You're telling me that there's a body buried somewhere on this island and you want me to find it? I don't have time for a wild goose chase, Jill." Cole informed.

"I'm just telling you that it's possible Tower went looking for it," Jill explained.

"All of this is pretty circumstantial," Cole admitted. "It won't be enough to arrest him."

"Would it be enough to look through his Jeep?" Jill asked.

"Not without a warrant."

"Would it be enough to get a search warrant?" Jill persisted.

Cole shook his head. "I don't think so, but I could run it by Bishop."

Jill shook her head. "Is Bishop here?" Jill asked.

"No, he's back in the Soo." Cole rubbed his chin, thinking. "I don't think I'll talk to Tower without him here though. If he's really the bank robber, he murdered two people, and one a cop. It's not a stretch to think he'd kill anyone in his way." Cole sipped his coffee, lost in thought, when a clear notion came to him. If Tower was responsible for the robberies and murders, it was possible he was also involved in Cooper's disappearance. After all, Cooper's truck was located just a half-mile down from Jill's home, where Tower was staying.

"Do you really think Tower is responsible for the robberies, Jill?"

Jill met his eyes. "Yes, I do."

"Do you think your friend is involved?"

Hesitating, Jill examined her conscious. "No, I don't."

"Why not?" Cole questioned quickly.

One fact spiraled through Jill's mind, saving her friend. "It was her decision to spend the fifty, Cole."

"Is that right?" Cole asked.

"Yes. She thought it was Tower's, and spent it on purpose. Besides, she was with me on the morning of the bank robberies, and she drove up separately. I really don't believe she had anything to do with this."

"Okay. I'll call Bishop, and get him to come down. I need to clear up the others with fifty dollar bills anyway. It's a bit of a turkey shoot, since some of the places in the mix don't have surveillance, but with everything you've told me, that won't matter quite so much." Cole swallowed another drink of his coffee. "Alright then, I'm off to call Bishop. I'm going to look into some of these other possibilities, then we'll come over and question Tower. When are they leaving?"

"They are both planning on leaving tomorrow," Jill informed.

"Alright, but dammit Jill, you could have mentioned your concerns yesterday, when I saw you at PINS."

"It was just a bad feeling yesterday, Cole. I really didn't know until I saw the bumper sticker."

Cole stood up from the table. "Alright, then. Don't put yourself in danger. Keep Quinn or somebody with you, Jill. I don't want you to be alone with him. Do me a favor—don't do anything to tip them off, and dammit, keep me informed!" Cole instructed, making his way out of the restaurant.

Quinn watched Cole leave before turning back to Jill, who popped her last bite of breakfast into her mouth. "So, what's next?"

"Let's go back to your house, and try calling Lisa again."

"You know, just because Cole can't snoop in Tower's Jeep doesn't mean we can't." Jill suggested.

"No way." Quinn shook his head decisively, knowing that was a bad move.

"But Quinn…"

"Are you crazy? He's a killer, Jill. We're not doing anything to Tower's Jeep, without Cole with us every step of the way. Tower has no reason to hurt you, if you don't give him one." Quinn advised.

"Alright," Jill agreed, albeit reluctantly.

SIXTY

"'Lo?" Lisa greeted, breathless.

"Is this Lisa Daye?" Jill asked.

"Yes, who is this?"

"My name is Jill Traynor. I'm a friend of…"

"Beth DeForge," Lisa supplied. "I just got your voicemail. Beth told me you didn't receive my email."

"That's right. I think someone looked at it and deleted it, but it wasn't me." Jill explained, sighing involuntarily. "It's a long story, but Beth told me you sent it again. I'm not in a place where I can check it, so I was hoping you could just tell me where the body is buried."

"Sure," Lisa agreed. "It's out in front of a place called the Wayfarer's Mart. If you're facing the building, on the water's side, it's on the right, near a big pile of rocks. Specifically, it's six feet out front from one with a triangular wedge on the top."

"Who is it?" Jill asked.

"A gangster named John Hamilton. The famous bank robber, John Dillinger and a patient of mine buried him there in 1934. My patient Frank, believed there was treasure buried with the body."

"And you said all this in the email?" Jill asked, concerned.

"Yes. Are you going to tell the authorities, Jill?"

"Yes, I am."

"Can you let me know, if you find anything?" Lisa asked, thinking about Frank.

"Of course," Jill responded. "I'll give you a call as soon as I know anything."

"Thanks, Jill."

Jill hung up the phone, feeling unsettled. As quickly as she set it down, she picked it back up, dialing another number.

"Who are you calling?" Quinn asked.

"Clark." Jill responded quickly.

"Why the hell…"

She held up her finger, as the phone started ringing in her ear. Quinn closed his mouth, taking a seat at the counter. He opened a white envelope that Jill had brought with her last night. Flipping through photos absently, he realized they must be from the boat show.

"Good Morning," Arlene's voice filled the phone.

"Hi, Arlene."

"Oh, Jill! I haven't gotten a chance to tell you how much fun I had with all the young people at your barbecue."

"Arlene…" Jill began, only to be cut off.

"It's not everyday that I get to visit with you kids. For that matter, you don't visit me enough either," Arlene scolded. "Clark tells me how you and he visit all the time, and I feel so bad that I don't get a chance to talk to you as much. Although, I know he just wanders over. That man is such a bother…" Arlene continued.

"Arlene…"

"He just putters around all day long, and he never gets anything done that I ask him to. Heavens, I asked him to clean out that hall closet, and do you think he could do that? No. So, that's what I'm doing with my morning...."

"Arlene!" Jill called, more abruptly than she wanted to.

"Oh, I'm sorry, dear. I'm just going on and on, and not giving you a chance to say anything, aren't I? I should learn to shut my mouth, and give you a chance to talk. It was just yesterday, that my grandson Tommy called me, and when I hung up the phone I realized I really hadn't learned anything new about the boy. Gee whiz, golly gumpers, I just miss y'all so much, I can't help but talk your ears off. And you're right next door, Jilly. It's such a shame that we don't talk more than we do. I miss your grandma so much. We'd just sit for hours talking about our husbands, and our kids... such a good woman, that Edna. She was the best friend I ever had, and since she passed there just isn't anyone to talk to... it is so sweet of you to call. You're a sweet girl, Jill, just like your granny."

Guilt filling her to the brim, Jill hated to ask for Clark. "Arlene, I'm so sorry, but I need to talk to Clark."

"Oh." Arlene's voice drooped, making Jill feel even worse. "Clark!" She yelled. "Clark, Jilly's on the phone for ya!" She yelled, holding the phone away from her mouth, well within Jill's earshot, she mumbled, "Shoulda known better. Jill wouldn't be calling for me."

"What ya mutterin' about, hon?" Clark asked, taking the phone from his wife.

"Don't mind me," Arlene muttered.

"Jill?" Clark said, by way of greeting.

"Hi, Clark. Did you borrow my shovels in the last couple days?"

"Shovels?" Clark furrowed his brow. "No, Jill. I've got my own shovels. I haven't borrowed anything in a long while. Are shovels missing from your garage?"

Damn, she thought. "No, no. It's nothing to worry about, Clark. I just thought I'd ask. I need to get going though…"

"Okay, darlin'. You need anything, you let me know."

"I will. Thanks, Clark." Feeling badly that she cut Arlene off so abruptly, she added, "Tell Arlene I'll be over to visit her as soon as my company goes home." Jill hung up the phone, perplexed. "I think that son of a bitch used my shovels to dig up the treasure."

"Back up," Quinn prompted, still absently gazing into a photograph. "Where did Lisa say the treasure is?"

"Buried with a gangster, John Hamilton, out in front of Wayfarer's." Jill paced Quinn's kitchen, contemplative.

"These are some nice snaps of the boat show." Quinn complimented, moving on. "I didn't think you had developed them yet. You know, the Mart makes sense, actually. That place has been around forever. Now, what about the shovels?"

"After my party, I went into my garage to put away the new things the guys bought me, and I noticed there was something off about my shovels."

"Off?"

"They were dirty. Someone put them back after using them, but slightly skewed."

Quinn's eyes popped widely. "Isn't that when Tower touched you?"

"Yeah, you're right. He was in the garage." Jill said. "We need to tell Cole."

"Different style than normal," Quinn mumbled, as he focused on one photo, frowning. "You never told me that Tower went with you."

"With us where?" Jill stopped pacing, to stare Quinn down.

"The boat show," Quinn supplied.

"He didn't."

"I beg to differ." Quinn corrected, holding up a photo.

"Quinn, those are Chase's pictures, not mine. He loaned them to me so I could get a feel for the Boat Show. He took those last year."

"Well, unless I'm on crack, that's Tower." Quinn said, holding one of them up.

Jill grabbed the picture from his hand, studying it. Sure enough, Chase's picture focused on a boat, but Tower was clearly caught leaning against the railing of a dock, slightly blurred, but easily recognizable. "Well, well… this dates him in Cedarville last year. He was probably casing the damned area," Jill surmised. "I knew I recognized him from somewhere. Unreal!"

"Isn't that Carly next to him?" Jill looked at where Quinn was pointing, to the very edge of the picture.

The picture only showed a sliver of a woman, red fabric stopping with a flair at the knee, implying the figure wore a dress. An expanse of the woman's arm was captured in the image, before it was obscured behind Tower's back. "Carly doesn't wear dresses." Jill examined it closely. "It could be anyone."

"Call Cole, Jill."

"Right." Jill picked the phone back up, dialing Cole's cell number. When he answered, she filled him in on their new knowledge of the burial site, as well as the picture.

Cole listened carefully, allowing a moment to pass before he spoke. "Jill, I've got my hands full at the moment. I'll call Bishop and let him know about the picture."

"Do you mind if I go out there, and see if I can find anything?" Jill asked.

Cole considered it. "Okay. Go out to the Mart. Take pictures of everything before you touch anything. Get permission from Sam, Jill. Don't touch anything without permission. Keep me informed. And Jill…"

"Yeah?"

"We never had this conversation. You decided to go digging on your own, okay?" Cole pressed.

Jill smiled. "What conversation?" she asked, before she hung up the phone.

"Are we going for a road trip?" Quinn asked.

"How do you feel about doing a little treasure hunting?"

SIXTY-ONE

Jill and Quinn walked into the lobby of the Wayfarer's Mart, behind Sam Sparrow, the owner. Since Quinn knew her, Jill decided it would be best for him to do the talking. He was about to start when Sam's attention was diverted by the ringing phone. She encouraged them to shop, while she excused herself.

Antsy to begin, Jill was surprised to find a selection of antiques that looked like they belonged in her home. She juggled her camera bag to her left shoulder, so she could better reach items from shelves. There were several wooden planks running along one wall, loaded down with a heavy variety of impossibly grouped items. Everything from old records, to stacks of old magazines and papers, seated next to boxes of miscellaneous items, seemed to continue all the way down the substantial length of the room, on multiple levels of shelves. Her eyes danced away from the collection, riveted by the architecture, and tall ceilings.

"Jill, get a load of this," Quinn called out.

She made her way back to him, laughing at his awestruck expression, as he caressed an antique faded black behemoth safe. "Oh, Quinn. Is it even for sale?" She couldn't help snickering at his face.

"There's no tag, but isn't it awesome?"

"There must be some kind of psychological clue about a

man that likes big safes," Jill teased. "I'll have to dust off my old textbooks and figure it out."

"Shaddup," he retorted. "This is just too neat. If there was a way to keep... you know..."

Three Bobbers, of course she knew, Jill thought. "You'd buy it?"

"Yeah. This is just the kind of thing my place would need." Quinn decided, casting his glance toward Sam, as she returned to them. "How much is this going for?" Quinn asked.

"It's not for sale. The safe was here when I bought the place. I don't even know what the combination is, and neither did the people who sold Wayfarer's to me," Sam admitted. "They thought it was empty, but I haven't been inclined to hire a locksmith to open it. Actually, I might be willing to sell it." Sam considered it for a long moment. "Say, five hundred dollars?"

Quinn shook his head slowly. He hadn't spent five hundred dollars on anything frivolous in a *long* time. "I'll have to think about that one, but thanks."

"You said before, that you needed a favor?" Sam inquired.

Quinn hesitated, contemplating the best way to ask. "We'd like to look at your grounds."

"Actually," Jill corrected. "We might want to dig a hole out front."

Sam listened to the strange request. "You want to dig up my property?"

"Well, we believe there might be a body buried there. It's possible there might be treasure there as well." Jill explained. When Sam remained unconvinced, Jill told her the story of Lisa's patient, and Dillinger's burial of Hamilton. She omitted any connection to the bank robberies, since she couldn't prove it, and didn't want to add speculation.

"Yes, of course you can look. And if you want to dig, go

right ahead, as long as you try to make it look nice again when you're done. I have my garden shovels leaning against the house out front, if you need to use them. Make yourself at home, but if you find treasure, I want a cut." She laughed, pointing out the window. "The rock wall you're talking about is right out there."

"Thanks, Sam," Quinn said, giving her a broad wink. "We'll see that you're taken care of."

"Your welcome."

With Sam's blessing, they walked down the sloped hill, with Quinn making a bee line for the rock pile. Jill, on the other hand, stared at the ground. Crouching down, she deliberated for a long moment.

"Jill, here it is."

"Quinn…"

"This is the rock, so it must be…"

"Right here," Jill finished for him. Patches of the grass were askew, and even though whoever replaced them, had done a good job of it, a closer inspection revealed the truth. "We were right. This has been dug up."

Quinn spun around, looking for himself. "Shit! Well, if this isn't proof, I don't know what is."

"Even if Tower dug this up, it doesn't prove he had anything to do with the banks," Jill corrected. "It's merely our theory, that the same person is responsible for both." Jill pulled her camera from her bag, taking pictures from every possible angle before they began, while Quinn grabbed the shovels.

The ground eased onto their shovels, until Quinn hit something a bit more solid than dirt. Jill kneeled down next to the ground, carefully brushing away the loose bits until she uncovered part of an arm. "Oh my God!" Gasping, she backed up. "Quinn, that's not a 70 year old body."

Quinn jumped back, as if the body could somehow hurt him. He took several moments to breathe, calming from the shock before he leaned forward. He reached forward, to investigate further when Jill stopped him.

"Don't touch it, Quinn. This is a crime scene," Jill advised.

Quinn backed up a step, squinting down at the wrist. Large as life, the plastic Jurassic Park yellow and black watch, advertised the owner. "It's Cooper," Quinn stated, still quite breathless. "I'd know that watch anywhere."

How many dead bodies did she need to see in her lifetime? Jill wondered, as the reality of Cooper's dirt covered corpse assailed her. "Tower did this, Quinn. Tower killed him."

"Yeah," Quinn exhaled, unable to conjure any other words as he stared at the lifeless arm, looking for answers that wouldn't come.

Finally, Jill spoke, her voice trembling. "We need to call Cole." Carefully, Jill used her established foot path and backed out of the area, instructing Quinn to do the same. They let Sam know what they found, and used her phone to call Cole. When Cole picked up the phone, Jill wasted no time, and skipped to the punch line.

"We're at Wayfarer's, Cole. We found Cooper. He's dead," Jill rushed. "Tower must have killed him. He must have discovered my email, then connected with Cooper somehow, and buried him here."

Cole said nothing for a moment, taking a deep breath. "Don't touch anything, Jill."

"I know."

"Stay where you are. I'm on my way. I'll call Bishop and have him bring down investigators. Don't let anyone near the site."

"I won't," Jill responded.

"I'm on my way."

Jill set the phone down, walked back to where Quinn sat with Sam. "Have you noticed anyone here, or heard any strange noises?" she asked.

Sam shook her head, sadly. "I was down state for a couple days. I just got back this morning. The police are coming?" Sam questioned.

Jill nodded. "Cole will be here in a few minutes, but they'll send a team down from the Soo. I'm sorry about this," Jill offered.

"I'm sorry for Cooper," Sam responded.

SIXTY-TWO

Even though Alec shared stories and tales with his younger brother, Tower never fully understood, how deeply taking another human's life would effect him. He'd planned on how to kill Junior, and anticipated enjoying it. Anticipation wasn't anything like the kill. Planning hadn't prepared him for the rush of adrenaline. Unadulterated joy seemed to burst somewhere inside him and pour through his body in much the same way that blood had poured from Junior's wounds.

The cop was a momentary thrill, but he couldn't take the time to revel in the feeling. He killed Cooper out of necessity, but replaying the eerily loud crack of the shovel smacking the back of the idiot's head, was still enjoyable. Sitting on the edge of Jill's bed, he imagined what it would be like to suck the breath from her lungs, steal the life from her body. And that is what I am, Tower thought: a thief.

Watching Carly through Jill's bedroom window, he realized that she didn't move with the same natural fluidity that seemed to emanate from Jill. Whether she was laughing, fighting, or hauling kayaks from the water to the ground as she did now, the liquid femininity present in most women seemed to elude the fighter. It had never occurred to Tower to kill her.

When he met Jill, her intelligence shined through her vivid green eyes, portraying her emotions as clearly as movie screens in a theater. Tower held his breath for a moment, imagining those eyes filled with fear. Shivering with pleasure, he picked up Jill's pillow, bringing it to his face. Inhaling her rich scent, Tower relaxed, setting the pillow back down. She didn't sleep there last night, he thought.

Moving through her bedroom, into the main body of the house, he located the answering machine. A quick glance out the window, confirmed that Carly was in no hurry to come in. He pressed the play button.

"One new message," the mechanized voice began. "Hi, Jill. This is Beth. I am calling to let you know that I talked to Lisa. She told me that she received a return receipt when the email was opened, confirming that you opened it. I asked her to resend it, so if it disappears again, let me know. I know you'll want to go check it out. There must be a ghost living in your house, hey? Hopefully, it's not the guy with the treasure." The sound of Beth chuckling on the recording, filled the room. "Call me whenever you get a chance to. I want to know you're okay."

The answering machine clicked off, leaving Tower motionless. He couldn't stick around, deleting Jill's emails forever. Eventually, she would suspect him for the missing email. In a small place like this, it wouldn't be long before Cooper's disappearance became an issue. If Jill followed the email's clues to Wayfarer's, she'd find Cooper. It had been an unfortunate mistake, to check her email in the first place, an even bigger mistake to actually go looking for treasure.

Red's words haunted him: Don't do anything to draw attention to yourself.

He needed to leave, *now*.

As Carly walked closer to the house, Tower brought the phone to his ear, developing a plan. As she climbed the short steps up the deck, he turned his back on her, and started talking.

"I know the Kastburgh account is mine, but can't you do it without me this once?" Tower asked, tensing his muscles as Carly came through the front door. "Yeah... yes, I understand..." Tower turned, scowling for Carly's benefit. "Fine. I'll be there." He clicked the phone off, with a hiss.

"What's wrong?" Carly asked.

"Babe, I have to leave."

"Now?" Carly inquired. "We're not supposed to leave till tomorrow."

"I know," Tower agreed. "I'm sorry. Phil needs me to pitch... never mind, I know how my work bores you."

"Do you want me to come? We could still caravan," she suggested.

Tower hesitated, as if considering it. "No, Carly. You should stay. You'll have a little more time with Jill before you have to get back to work."

Carly nodded, frowning. "Do you need gas money?"

"If you don't mind," he said, hiding a smirk in the palm of his hand, as he turned away from her. Tower kissed the girl farewell, grabbed the bags he'd hastened to pack, and left her behind.

Leaving was really for the best, he thought, climbing into his Jeep. If he stayed close to Jill any longer, he might have to act on some of his more *primal* urges.

SIXTY-THREE

Jill, Quinn and Cole stood on the sidelines while the investigating team carefully removed the dirt surrounding Cooper's body, collecting bits of evidence here and there. Over two hours had passed, since Jill and Quinn first arrived at Wayfarer's, but they barely noticed. Jill repeated the story from beginning to end twice with Detective Bishop, going over and over the finer points of everything she'd learned about her houseguest: his arrival timing, bizarre behavior, the fifty dollar bill, the huckleberry bumper sticker, the missing email and resulting treasure hunt, lies concerning his whereabouts during the barbecue, the dirty shovels, their discovery of his presence at the boat show a year earlier, and the location of Cooper's truck in connection to Tower's presence at Jill's house preceding Cooper's murder. Again and again, Bishop challenged Carly's possible role in the bank robberies and murders.

According to Jill, only two people had unrestricted access to her computer: Tower and Carly. Jill was emphatic that Carly had nothing to do with the crimes. Cole supported her, but Bishop was relentless, hammering away at Jill's story. Jill reiterated the points that saved Carly: it was Carly's idea to spend the fifty dollar bill from the robberies, and Jill could personally vouch for Carly's whereabouts during the robberies as well as during the night of the barbecue, when Cooper was obviously murdered. Quinn added information in whenever he could, but Bishop focused on Jill's observations from her proximity to the suspect.

Bishop used his cell phone, attempting to garner a search warrant from a judge. When he convinced the judge, he made another phone call, instructing an officer to bring it down. As Bishop cleared details with the officer, Cole's phone rang. He moved away from the group to take the call. When he returned, his face was grave.

Jill's eyes met his, curious.

"There's been an accident at Pike Bay Road and M-134," Cole stated, his voice solemn.

"What happened, Cole?" Quinn asked.

"I don't know. But, Jill... there's a red Jeep on fire."

SIXTY-FOUR

John Wheeler drove an empty log truck heading east on M-134, away from the ferry, at a speed *consistent with the speed limit*, as one man in a red Jeep, drove straight onto M-134 from Pike Bay Road, without stopping. One second's worth of distraction was all they needed: the insulated coffee cup from home provided it for John, as it slipped out of his grasp, just as he rounded the first corner of the Pigeon Cove nightmare.

The coffee spilled onto his leg, burning his inner thigh, leading to a yelp, a distracted movement to grab his pant leg away from his skin, with his truck barreling on. The sound of a car careening around the corner, and the pull of air as a car passed him, heading in the opposite direction brought Wheeler's attention back to the road.

The fire engine red Jeep, never stood a chance. Wheeler's truck plowed into the Jeep broadside, pushing it sideways off the road. The side panel caved in under the pressure, as the passenger's side tires lost their seal, popping as Wheeler slammed on his breaks.

The driver's side of the log truck's front wheel blew. The Jeep, still moving from the momentum of the truck's force, rolled onto the passenger's side, and continued to roll down the short incline. Stopping just short of the tree line, it burst into flames, severing the guide wire to the electrical pole, stationed a few feet away.

By the time Cole and Bishop arrived at the scene, the fire truck had finished foaming down the area. A few small trees were scorched, but everything was handled now. Cars drove by slowly, heads angling toward the vehicles, parked along the road's edge.

As Quinn and Jill neared the scene, her eyes swept over the details as she tried to make sense of what happened. The ambulance was parked on the side of the road, but it was evident that no one from the Jeep would need their services. One of the EMT's spoke to a man she didn't recognize, apparently the truck driver, who sat on the ground, elbows resting over his bent knees, looking shaken. Cole and Bishop made their way out to the Jeep. Cole was already getting details from the Fire Captain. The Jeep was absolutely demolished, and burned to boot, making it nearly impossible for Jill to recognize if it was even Tower's vehicle. Intuition told her that it was, but she waited, looking on from the road's edge. Impatient, she moved toward the truck driver, taking a seat next to him.

"Are you okay?" she asked.

He nodded his head, coughing into his hand. "The Jeep just appeared out of nowhere," he began. "I took my eyes off the road for just a second, and wham… there was no time. I had no time…" His voice shook, leaving Jill the impression that it took every shred of his control, to stop himself from breaking down. "That poor man," he muttered.

Jill nodded sadly, waiting. Minutes that seemed to last for hours inched by, before Cole finally started back toward the road. Quinn helped Jill to her feet before Cole reached them.

Cole struggled with his choice of words. Finally, he decided on the direct approach. "There's just one man in the Jeep, Jill. I'm sure it's Tower, but he's burned a bit. He probably died on impact," Cole conjectured, shaking his head.

"We're going to wait for the forensics team to get here. I'm not allowing anyone to touch anything in the Jeep until then."

"You're sure Carly wasn't in there with him?" Quinn asked, as he wrapped his arm around Jill's shaking shoulders.

"I'm sure." Cole nodded gravely. "Bishop just placed a call. The investigators should be here in just a little while. They'll be able to go through the vehicle. I'm going to take the driver's statement."

"I need to tell Carly," Jill told him.

"Would you wait for me?" Cole requested. "I'd like to go with you. I have questions that need to be answered, and Carly may now be the only person capable."

"Do you want me to just wait here?" Jill asked, feeling a bit like a fish out of water, with nothing to do but watch from the sidelines.

"I'd appreciate it," Cole responded, already walking away from her.

Jill leaned against Quinn. "How could this possibly happen now? We were on our way to confront him and he...died. It doesn't make any sense."

"Fate just happens, Jill." Quinn shrugged. "Thank God, Carly wasn't with him."

"I wonder where he was going. He couldn't have been going to town." Jill rubbed her temples with her fingertips, attempting to ease her mounting headache.

"Maybe he was leaving the island," Quinn suggested.

"A day early?" Jill asked, doubtful. She bent her knees, folding her body toward the ground, where she sat Indian style. Quinn found a seat beside her, as he watched Cole and Bishop take turns asking the driver questions. Bishop, they both knew, hated coincidences. He'd be looking for some hidden motive or purpose behind the driver's actions.

More quickly than anyone expected, the forensics team arrived. The Jeep, surprisingly enough, had finally landed right-side up. After evaluating the scene for himself, and talking to the driver, Cole pieced together what happened. Tower must have looked to his left first, then right, where a car sped by capturing Tower's vision. Rather than look to his left again, Tower followed the car out, finding himself directly in the truck's line of fire, with nowhere to go. Of course, it was merely Cole's hypothesis, but he guessed the forensics team would probably agree with him. It might have been as simple as Tower not looking in either direction, and just as deadly.

"Cole! You're gonna want to see this!" Bishop yelled, holding something small between his gloved hands.

Cole excused himself and rushed toward the scene. The forensics team had carefully removed Tower's body from the vehicle. Cole watched as they carefully zipped the black bag around the burned corpse. Pressing forward, he reached Bishop's side in a moment. Laying in Bishop's gloved hands was the scorched edge of a one hundred dollar bill. Peering into the back of the Jeep, Cole could make out a few other bills from the largely burned debris.

"Oh, look what we have here…" one of the investigators murmured, pulling out a 9mm Beretta, with a pair of evidence tongs.

"Wasn't it a 9mm that killed the cop in…" Bishop began, his voice trailing out as the forensics agent nodded. "Son of a bitch, the girl was right," Bishop mumbled, gesturing his head toward Jill. "We've got our scumbag, Cole. And the money burned up… unreal. Of course, we'll have to wait for the lab to tell us that, but this has got to be our guy."

Cole nodded. "We should go ask the girlfriend some questions," he prompted.

Bishop shook his head, over the site. He handed the bill in

his hand to an investigator and cuffed Cole's upper arm lightly, lowering his voice to a whisper. "Now that's how a nasty case like this should end… no long trials, just a burned up bad guy." Bishop handed out a few more directions, before they made their way back toward the road. "What's the girlfriend's name again?"

"Carly… ah… Folton," Cole supplied.

"Do you believe Jill?" Bishop asked, eating up the ground with his long stride.

"About Carly being innocent in all this?" Cole clarified. "Jill thinks so, yes."

Bishop nodded, silencing again as they came upon the young couple. "Time to go talk to Carly," Bishop informed.

Jill raised her eyebrows, waiting.

"We found the money, Jill. Most of it totally burned up, but there are a few bills left. I'd bet anything that they're from the banks," Cole said, receiving a hard-edged look from Bishop. "We need to ask your friend some questions."

Jill nodded slowly. It was one thing to believe Tower was involved, it was another to *know* it. Jill's thoughts lingered on the picture showing Tower at the boat show the year before. Jill had argued with Bishop passionately, refuting every explanation he offered for Carly's involvement, with her own sense of loyalty driven logic. Everyone, including Quinn, was convinced that Jill believed Carly was innocent. As they drove back to Jill's house, one question plagued Jill's mind: *Could Carly be involved?*

SIXTY-FIVE

"Jill, long time no see, girl…" Carly's voice trailed off as she watched Quinn, Sheriff Cole, and a suited man follow her friend in. Carly's eyes widened for a moment, before they settled on Jill. She stood up from her perch on the couch, searching her friend's face. "What's wrong?"

The guys waited while Jill moved forward. Taking a deep breath, Jill leveled her eyes with Carly's. "Carly, there's been an accident."

Surprise darted across Carly's face, but she waited, well aware of the three men closely observing her.

Direct, Jill thought. If someone had to give me bad news, I'd want to know directly. "Tower's dead."

"What? No! That can't be… he left the island, Jill. His boss needed him back at work, and he left. It must be someone else." Carly searched Jill's face for doubt, but none came. She brought her hands to her mouth, choking out the words, "You're sure?"

"Yes, I'm sure," Jill confirmed, before quietly explaining what happened.

Carly crumbled back to the couch as if she'd been hit. Her breath was shallow, her face pale as she comprehended what Jill was saying. An accident…a truck, she blocked out the words for a moment, and focused on breathing. "Oh, God."

Quinn poured a glass of water from the tap, and handed it to Carly.

Carly accepted the glass, sipping slowly. Her eyes were dry, but her face was pale. Jill studied her friend closely. "Carly, Sheriff Cole and Detective Bishop have to ask you some difficult questions."

"*Difficult* questions? About Tower?" She suddenly seemed to remember there were more people in the room, and her eyes narrowed suspiciously.

Bishop stepped forward, gesturing toward Jill's table and chairs.

Absently, Carly joined them at the table, looking to Jill for reassurance.

Quinn remained standing so the rest could sit. He leaned against Jill's counter, watching.

"Can you tell us *how* you met Tower, Carly?" Bishop questioned.

Carly leaned back in her chair, rubbing her hands roughly against her face. "I met him at a fight. He bought me a drink, which led to another and… we were together for hours, talking and drinking before he asked me out again. We've been together ever since."

"When did you first meet?" Cole questioned.

"I don't understand. What does this have to do with a car accident?"

"Please answer the question, Carly," Cole urged.

Puzzled, Carly relented. "It was about six months ago, or something like that." Carly shrugged sadly. "Dates have never been my strong suit."

"Have you visited Tower's residence?"

"Yeah. I've been there a few times."

Cole took his small pad of paper from his pocket and slid

it and a pen to Carly. "We'll need the address."

Carly scratched the address down. "What is this about?" she asked.

Bishop met her question with one of his. "Did Tower ever mention family members or friends… did he live with anyone?"

"He lived alone. I never met any of his family or friends, but I know he has a brother," Carly informed him.

"How long in advance were the two of you planning on visiting Jill?" Bishop continued.

"Tower wasn't planning on coming. I've been talking about it since Jill moved here, last year," Carly said.

"Originally, Tower must have wanted to come, Carly," Jill interjected. "I remember you telling me that the two of you were going to come together."

Carly thought about it for a moment before she nodded. "Yeah, you're right. Sorry. Uhm… I told Tower about Jill right in the beginning. The first day I met him… she just came up in conversation. It was that same week that I invited Tower to come with me, I guess. The only time he could get off work was this week, so I got the week off too. Of course, then his boss changed plans, which caused Tower to stay behind."

"Why did you drive separate vehicles?" Bishop asked.

"I just told you," Carly sounded irritated. "He wasn't coming."

"But he did come," Bishop pushed.

"Yes, he surprised me."

"And you didn't know he was coming?" Bishop pressed.

"I just told you that." Carly stared at him. "What is this about?" she demanded, her voice raised.

"Carly, what do you know about the bank robberies in Cedarville?" Cole inquired.

Frustrated, Carly blew out a short breath. "Just that two banks were robbed on Monday. Nothing else, really."

"So, for the record, you're saying you had no prior knowledge of the robberies?"

"Why would you think I would know anything about the bank robberies?" she asked, aghast.

Bishop and Cole shared a look before Cole began. "Carly, we have reason to believe that Tower was involved in the dual bank robbery that took place in Cedarville."

Carly's eyes widened. "Oh. And you think I knew about it, or…had something to do with it?" she questioned.

Jill shook her head. "I don't think you knew, Carly."

Bishop and Cole shared another meaningful look before continuing their line of questioning. "Your boyfriend robbed the two banks in Cedarville, Ms. Folton," Bishop stated matter of factly, deliberately watching Carly's eyes for her reaction. When she showed no real sign of surprise, Cole shook his head, perplexed.

Cole spoke first. "You don't seem all that surprised that Tower had anything to…"

"Listen, guys." Carly clutched her bottom lip, interrupting them. "I don't really know how to say this. Tower is…" Carly paused, looking at Jill. "Was, rather, a bizarre, manipulative person. He was a leech, and I've been coming to my own breaking point with his damned antics, all week. He'd go just far enough that I'd want to get him in a choke hold, and then he'd ease up and be so damned attractive that I forgot why I was pissed off at him. This trip here," Carly waved her arms to encompass the area. Her voice was shaky, but she continued. "This trip was the first time I had spent several days with him, twenty-four hours a day. I really didn't know him that well."

"You dated for six months, didn't you?" Bishop pressed.

"Yes, but between rotating shifts at the fire house, and

intense training… I don't have a lot of free time. It goes to show that it took me over a year to come visit Jill, doesn't it?" Carly retorted.

"You never noticed that he was a bit strange before this week?" Bishop challenged.

"Of course, but when it's eccentric, it's part of the appeal. When it's weirdness, it's creepy. I found him eccentric, not weird." Carly explained, as if her definitions cleared everything up.

Bishop looked confounded by Carly's answers. "Are men capable of murder attractive, Carly?"

"Murder?"

"We recovered a 9mm Beretta from Tower's Jeep. I believe we'll discover that it's the same gun used to kill a police officer," Bishop explained.

"Murder?!" Carly gasped, color draining from her face. Carly took another sip of her water. Jill could tell that the connection hadn't occurred to her friend. Her unique angular face dropped into her rough, working hands with a thud. She collected herself, before she looked up, meeting Bishop's eyes evenly. "I didn't know anything about this. You're not suggesting that I had anything to do with this?" Carly's eyes sought Jill's. "I didn't… I couldn't…" She sputtered. "I'm not a part of this. Jill, you have to believe me."

"I do, Carly," Jill reassured her. "It'll be alright."

The connection was broken by Bishop's surly announcement. "Carly, we're going to need to take you in for further questioning."

"Am I being charged with something?" Carly demanded.

"No," Bishop responded. "But we need to ask more questions, and I'd rather do it at the station. I would like you to volunteer. If you don't, I can bring you without your consent."

Carly hesitated, as if struggling with her thoughts. "Fine, I'll come."

"Do you need me to get you a lawyer?" Jill offered.

"If I'm charged, I'll get a phone call, won't I?" Carly asked.

"Yes," Cole answered. "Carly, it's your legal right to have representation with you during your questioning."

Carly shook her head, her expressions numbed. "I have nothing to hide."

Jill glanced at Bishop. "Does she have time to pack her things?"

Bishop nodded, as he stood from the table. He looked Carly over. "Are you going to drive up? Or would you like me to drive you?"

"I'll drive, Detective. I'm already packed, Jill. I thought I'd leave tonight, or early tomorrow morning anyway." Carly stood up, clenched her shaking hands together.

Bishop nodded to Jill, heading out the door. He paused before he left, which drew Jill's eyes toward him. "I'm going to need those shovels, Jill."

"Quinn, could you get them for him?" Jill asked.

"Yeah." Quinn pointed toward the garage. Bishop and Cole followed him, allowing the women a moment of privacy.

"Carly, I can come with you," Jill offered.

"No. I'm a big girl, Jill." To Jill's astonishment, tears pooled in Carly's eyes. "How could I have been with someone so evil? He killed those people, didn't he?" Carly asked, not expecting an answer.

Jill cried, wrapping her arms around her friend in comfort. "I'm so sorry this happened, Carly. Are you sure you don't want me to come?"

After a long hug, Carly pulled away and wiped the tears

from her eyes with the back of her hand. "I'll be alright. If I need a lawyer, I'll call my dad. He always knows what to do," Carly paused. "There's something else isn't there? I can see something in your eyes, but…"

Jill swallowed. She couldn't tell Carly about Cooper. She agreed that she wouldn't reveal anything to Carly without Cole's presence, and she stood by that. "I'm sorry about Tower…" Even if Tower was a thief and a murderer, Carly had cared about him and Jill recognized that.

Carly bit her lip to stop further tears. "You suspected him, didn't you? When you didn't come home last night, I wondered if he'd said something to you. He did, didn't he? He hit on you. Why didn't you talk to me about it?" Carly asked.

Jill couldn't raise her eyes for a long moment. Tracing her fingers absently across her jaw, she finally looked at Carly, and realized she didn't have to explain it. *Carly remembered.*

Carly nodded, holding up her hand to stop Jill from speaking further. Tears poured freely from her eyes, and she pulled Jill into her arms and hugged her tightly. "I'm so sorry, Jill. I'm sorry for not believing you before, when we were in college. You're right, you know…" Softly, Carly continued, "If you told me, I probably wouldn't have believed you now, either. Somewhere, I would have known it was true… but I'm so damned stubborn. What is it with me and men?"

Jill smiled. Every great friendship bore its share of skeletons, and theirs was no different. She watched her friend gather her bags, hugged her again before she left. Cole told her they'd be in touch, and followed Bishop. After they left, Quinn took one look at Jill's stricken face and left her alone for a while.

When he returned, he found her wrapped in her grandma's quilt, shivering in the unusually cool evening. He sat next to her on the steps she built with Joe, and waited. Jill leaned against him, but said nothing for several moments, as her fingertips traced her jaw line again.

"She broke this once," Jill whispered, tapping the left side of her face.

Quinn's eyes widened with astonishment, but he let her continue.

"About a year after we met, her boyfriend harassed me. He used to hit on me all the time, before he started dating Carly. I was never interested in him," Jill shuddered. "Carly was. She thought he was the great love of her life. She walked into our apartment, and Keith was kissing me. I was trying to get away from him, but... when Carly saw us together, she went a little crazy. She shoved me against a wall and punched me. I was yelling for her to stop, but she beat Keith up, pretty badly."

"And you remained her friend, after that?" Quinn asked, incredulous.

"Yeah. It took me a while to forgive her... a long while, but I did. She just... reacted. I understood, I guess. Sometimes, when you want something so badly, you don't want to hear the truth, you can't see the truth."

Quinn considered that for a moment. "What did Carly want?"

Jill sighed. "Happiness, I guess. She always thought I had a thing for her man, and when she saw me betraying her... she went nuts. She didn't even believe me for a while. Keith eventually admitted the truth, and then she apologized."

"She hit you so hard she broke your jaw and you forgave her?" Quinn asked. "Wow. I don't think I could've done that."

"She was the only friend I had. Of course, I forgave her." Jill sipped her coffee. "I haven't forgotten, Quinn. I never think about it, but that's why I didn't tell her about my creepy conversation with Tower. She wouldn't have believed me."

"Why would Carly think you would stand in her way of happiness?"

Jill deliberated before she answered. "In Carly's mind, if one isn't happy—then it's his or her job to make everyone else miserable too. Nature of the beast, so to speak."

"That's kind of twisted," Quinn muttered.

"She gets it from her mother. Let's not think about it, okay? I need to just separate myself from all of this for a while." Jill burrowed closer to Quinn, inhaling his spicy scent. After a moment, she stood, helping Quinn stand beside her. "I'm going to take a shower, and then maybe we can go get some dinner or something, hey?"

"I have to work at the bar tonight." Quinn consulted his watch. "Actually, I should get going, but you're going to need your car. I can run you back to my house first. Or if you're up for it, I could come get you after work, but I close tonight. If you didn't want to go anywhere tonight, I could grab you in the morning," Quinn suggested.

"No, let's go now," Jill decided.

Jill closed and locked the French Door behind them, dropping the quilt on her couch. Quinn noticed the answering machine blinking.

"Jill, you've got messages."

"Press play," she called over her shoulder, as she stepped into her bedroom for a second.

They listened to the message from Beth, before Mary's voice filled the room.

"Jill, it's Mary Barber. Please call me as soon as you can… I just can't believe this letter… you must be so shocked…call me, Jill." Mary's voice was overflowing with emotions and confusion.

Jill rounded the corner, squinting at Quinn, before Kate's voice filled the room.

"Hey Jill, it's me. Listen, Mary's been calling around trying to find you. I know you weren't working today, but give her a call when you can, okay? Thanks."

"I wonder what that's about..."

"Give her a call," Quinn encouraged. "We've got time."

Jill followed his advice, picked up the phone and dialed the number. A busy signal beeped in Jill's ear. "I'll call her later. Let's go." Jill locked her back door behind her, but she couldn't shake Mary's concerned voice from her mind. Troubled, Jill couldn't help but wonder: *what now?*

SIXTY-SIX

Jill angled her head as she slid her key into the back door lock, clicking it open. She tossed her mail onto her kitchen table, kicked her shoes off haphazardly, and walked into her garage. Her body felt emotionally water-logged, heavy and burdensome. If she could separate herself from this past week, just snip it out with some shears and tie the ends back together, she would. It was different to make the wrong choices and regret them, but Jill hadn't. Carly may have, Jill considered, pursing her lips together in thought. She shook her head, attempting to clear it, and found a seat on her office chair. Her *To Do* list was growing monumentally, but she couldn't find the release her dark room normally provided.

Frustrated, she stepped into her new and barely used bathroom, intending to splash water on her face. The shower curtain was pulled open, dirt remnants obvious along the drain. Evidence, she thought, grimly. Tower was indeed taking a shower out here, probably to remove dirt gathered from the crime scene. Leaving it untouched, Jill stumbled through the house with no real destination. Her home felt dirty, though her tables were dust free, her floors vacant of Carly's trademark litter. An unfortunate aura, most likely only present in Jill's mind, hovered over her home: A murderer walked through these rooms, she thought, glancing into the messy spare bedroom. Of course, not for the first time, she realized. With a deep, heaving sigh, she walked outside, sat on a rock and allowed Huron to wash over her toes.

Pulling her hair from the band it was caught in, she allowed the wind to carry it, tangle it, do whatever it wanted, unchecked. Her bare feet relaxed against the rocks. Slowly, Jill quieted her mind and allowed herself to relax. She concentrated on inhaling the pure Great Lakes air, and exhaled her fears and worries. With every breath, she calmed considerably. Bringing her knees to her chest, she perched her feet on the boulder and reconnected with her centermost values and beliefs. Loyalty was as much her weakness, as it was her strength. Even if Carly was involved with Tower's crimes, Jill couldn't turn her back on her.

Friendships, Jill thought, arose from the damnedest situations. When she moved to Drummond, her most cherished relationships had all but ended. Uncle Dave and Carly were the only two left, but then something bizarre happened. Jill hadn't wanted to experience the pain of losing someone she loved again, so she started over. Sooner than she ever dreamed, she found herself opening up like a flower unfolding its petals before the sun, and her life seemed to brim with people she cared about, new friends she formed lasting bonds with. As Carly was among the first, she would be among the last. Jill's heart broke for her.

Slowly, Jill rose from the rocks, reached her arms out from her sides and appreciated the sun's last fingers of light. She made her way back to the house, slipping through the French Doors, and to the kitchen where she tossed the old coffee filter, and set a new pot to percolate. She sat down on a dining chair, and flipped through her mail: an HWI sale flyer from the hardware, a JCPenney sale catalog, a credit card statement, and an eggshell white, thick envelope, with her name and address typed neatly on the front. A glance to the return address read, Baker and Baker, Attorneys at Law, with a New York address. Wrinkling her nose a bit, she ripped the envelope open, and carefully pulled the papers out.

The phone rang. "Hello?"

"Oh, Jill! Thank God, you're home. Did you get the letter?" Mary asked.

"I'm just beginning to go through my mail now," Jill began. "Which letter do you mean?"

"It's from a law firm in New York. Uhm… Baker and Baker." Mary supplied.

"It's right here," Jill answered, picking the letter up.

"Set the phone down, Jill. Read the letter, but don't hang up, okay?"

"Uhm… sure." Jill responded, confused. She did as she was asked, and set the phone down.

Ms. Traynor,

Elizabeth DeForge has retained this office with regard to the legal aspect of a monetary division resulting from a Treasury procured finders fee. During June, 2004, in her family's residence in Batavia, New York, one hundred and thirty eight 1943 copper pennies were discovered in the kitchen sink's drain pipe. Ms. DeForge relinquished the pennies to the Department of Treasury, where they were sold over a period of eight months to museums, and private coin collections in the United States and abroad. Remaining pennies were auctioned, resulting in the Treasury's gross return of $3,726,000.00. Auction and brokerage fees comprised $558,900.00, resulting in $3,167,100.00. The Treasury paid Ms. DeForge a finder's fee of ten percent, $316,710.00.

Rather than collect the full fee herself, Ms. DeForge requested that the money be divided in three equal shares. She will be the recipient of one third, where the funds will be allocated directly for her brother's care and defense; one third will be given to Thomas and Mary Barber; and the final third is to be given to you. From Ms. DeForge's third, she has deposited $12,500.00 at a 4% return to yield $500.00 per year, which has been set up to fund a memorial scholarship with DeTour Area Schools. This scholarship will be given annually to a worthy student in Joseph Barber's name.

The estimated taxes of the total sum is $88,410.00. After taxes are removed from your portion, you will be left with approximately $76,100.00. To collect this check, please sign the enclosed forms and return them to my office in the enclosed self addressed, stamped envelope.

If you have any questions feel free to call, write, or e-mail my office.

Sincerely,

Albert Baker

Attorney at Law

Gasping for air, Jill pinched her arm. Oh God. Jesus, oh… *my word*. Jill's eyes scanned the letter again, just to confirm that what she was reading was right. Why didn't Beth ever tell her the pennies were found? she wondered. And why would Beth give her seventy-six thousand dollars? A faint, muffled noise reached her ears. Chagrined, Jill realized she forgot the phone.

"Mary?" Jill said, as she stood from her chair. "Are you still there?"

"Can you believe it?" Mary's voice was thick with emotion.

"Oh, Mary. I can't take this money!" Jill exclaimed, beginning to pace.

"That's just what I told Beth, Jill. My niece is determined, and just as stubborn as her grandfather, let me tell you," Mary sighed into the phone. "Tom and I have had longer to take this in, since we got our letter yesterday, but I talked to Beth for a long while. She isn't giving us the money to bring Joe back, because nothing will." Mary's voice cracked a bit, but she pushed forward. "And she's not giving us the money to buy Richard's forgiveness. She's giving us the money because she wants us to have it. She told me that it would be a deep insult to her, if we turned it down." Mary frowned audibly. "I didn't know what to do. Neither did Tom. We stewed and prayed and paced, until it finally occurred to me that we can help others. We're going to match Beth's contribution to the scholarship fund, and we're going to help Alice and Jesse with their school loans. With any luck, my girls can start their lives debt free."

Jill smiled, tears springing in her eyes. "That sounds wonderful, Mary. But…I just, I can't accept this. Beth doesn't owe me anything. I'd like you to take my third."

Mary inhaled sharply at the offer. "Absolutely, not. Furthermore, if you don't accept yours, Tom and I aren't going to take ours."

"Mary," Jill argued, "there's no reason for me to even be a part of this."

"Jill, dear…" Mary sighed. "Joe would want you to have it. I know he didn't know you long, honey, but he loved you. Please, Jill. Take the money. If Beth didn't want you to have it, she wouldn't have given it to you. Honor her wishes, Jill."

Jill sank down into her old couch, the phone clutched to her ear. Her tears blended with laughter. "How can I not accept this, when you put it that way?"

"Good. Then you'll take it?"

"I guess I will," Jill agreed. "I can't help feeling badly about it."

Mary hesitated, unsure of whether or not to say what was on her mind. "I believe in God, Jill. I believe in a plan, and I think there's a reason for all of this. There's a reason why you're supposed to have this money, just like there's a reason Tom and I are supposed to have a portion. I worried about how it would look, how I would feel… but I feel… like I've been given a wonderful gift, and in some small way, I can help my girls, and I can help people remember my son because of it."

Stunned, Jill leaned back, quiet for a moment, nerves tingling along her spine. "I want to be a part of the scholarship fund too. I'll give the same amount of money. If you want to give three smaller scholarships each year, or one big one... it doesn't matter. I'm in."

"Oh, Jill. That's so kind of you. You're such a dear girl."

Jill's voice strained with her emotions, "Thank you, Mary."

"It's Tom and I that should be thanking you. You brought my son peace, and purpose. I'll never forget you for it."

Jill struggled to find something to say, but Mary beat her to it.

"Jill, I need to go. Tom has a doctor's appointment and I need to hurry him up. Take care, dear. I'll see you 'round. Bye-bye."

Jill listened to Mary set the phone down, absently clicking hers off. Sixty-five thousand dollars, she thought, overwhelmed. The six sided photo gallery and library she'd wanted desperately could now be hers. Her home could finally be finished. Smiling to herself, she stood up, walked back outside, viewing the grounds. Almost mindlessly, she returned to the house, signed the forms and walked them to her mail box.

Turning the red flag up, she smiled, knowing where she needed to go. She hopped into her Tracker, and drove toward town, turning left at the blinker. When she reached the cemetery, she parked her car along the U-drive, and set out for Joe's gravesite.

JOSEPH THOMAS BARBER

1981-2004

Our Beloved Son

Folding her legs beneath her, she sat next to Joe's granite headstone and talked to him. She told him about what they were building at work, her friend Carly's visit, the bank robberies and murders. She told him about her first island barbecue, and her new garage. Finally, she talked to him about Beth's gift, and what she was going to do with it. Joe couldn't talk to her. Of course, she knew that, but it made her feel better to relinquish her fears and concerns, somehow knowing that he could hear her, wherever he was. When she was finally done talking about everything else, she talked about Quinn. She questioned whether she was making the right choice with him, if Joe would have given his blessing had he been able to.

When she was all talked out, she sat in comfortable silence. She smiled at the area, perfectly groomed and festooned with flowers. Joe was laid to rest under a large Maple tree, offering shade and shelter. Searching for answers, she curled her arms around her crooked legs and waited, knowing not what she waited for.

Resting her head against her arm, she allowed her eyes to close as she listened to the rustling leaves and birdsong. Opening her eyes, her vision filled with the bright red, puffy cardinal that perched on the edge of Joe's tombstone. With tears filling her eyes, Jill gave herself over to the emotions swelling within her and cried tears of joy, as well as grief. The bird looked at her expectantly, crooking its small head from side to side, settling down and singing its song, before spreading its wings and disappearing in to the evening sky.

Standing on her feet, Jill dusted herself off, kissed her fingertips and touched the face of his stone. On a whisper, carried with the breeze, she said, *"Goodbye, Joe."*

SIXTY-SEVEN

SATURDAY MORNING

Waking up well after the sun rose, Jill spent the first couple hours of her day charged with energy and taking it out on her house. She cleaned with gusto, scrubbing her spare bedroom, with every ounce of energy she could muster. When she finished cleaning, she spent hours in her dark room processing the pictures, that Dean was sure to be getting edgy about. Jill loved spending time alone, enjoyed the solitude of her work, and spending time with her pictures. Organizing her office, was just what she needed. As she sorted pictures into drawers, her mind was able to sort ideas together.

Her thoughts kept returning to one conclusion: it seemed *too easy*. Four people were dead, and who knows how much money stolen (although Jill guessed Gary's approximation of $640,000 was probably very accurate), and the case was pretty neatly tied up, with all the suspects killed. Tower was obviously involved, if not the brain behind the operation. Something unknown nagged at Jill's mind.

With a prolonged sigh, Jill allowed the worries brewing in her stomach to settle for the moment, as she consulted her wish list. With the major exception of the six-sided addition of her dreams, everything Jill wanted/needed could be purchased with her $2500 cover fee easily, with some leftover. After developing her pictures, she knew she had the right shots.

Doodling, she penned in $64,000.00. It was a difficult
decision for her to spend the money, her parents willed her on
her house. She could replace the nest egg and sleep easier at
night, or she could spend it. Tapping her pen rhythmically
against her desktop, Jill shelved that notion for the moment
too. Choices seemed to divide themselves into the "smart,"
and "not so smart" piles, with her grandparents voices, mixed
into the works from beyond. Grandma would say, save, save,
save. Grandpa would say, life is an adventure.

Missing her grandparents, Jill stood from her desk, tidying
the area behind her. Quinn would be looking for her to come
over this afternoon, but she wasn't ready yet.

Traipsing over her gravel driveway, Jill walked next door,
not bothering to knock on the screen, before she entered.
Nearly groaning, the scent of baking apples and cinnamon
filled Jill, as she leaned back against the doorframe, letting her
eyes wander over her second home of sorts. Antiques were
crammed into every conceivable space, with old copper pots
hanging from the ceiling above an island in the kitchen. Terra
cotta pots bursted with vibrant greenery everywhere. Fresh
flowers from Arlene's garden almost wrestled for freedom, in
their tight-squeeze vase hold. Thick hand-loomed rugs of
various colors, covered the age-old wooden floor. Every step
Jill took, squeaked with life, but no one ever minded.
"Arlene?!" She called.

"Hi, Jill. I'm back here!" Grinning, Jill found Arlene in the
spare room/store room which housed Clark's collectibles.

Arlene's wrinkled face sprang upwards with a smile when
she laid eyes on her favorite neighbor, and pseudo-
granddaughter. Her short, bright-white hair was wrapped
around curlers, peeking out from under a paint splattered
scarf. "Can you believe this mess?" she asked, by way of
greeting. "If I'd known what I was getting into fifty-three
years ago, when I married the pack-rat, I'd have marched
other way, Jill. I'd have turned around in my good Sunday

dress, and walked right away. I would have," Arlene grumbled, emphasizing her points with a firm nod. Her eyes lingered on Jill's face for a moment. "Don't believe me, do ya?"

"Not for a second," Jill smiled.

Arlene chuckled. "Ya, I s'ppose yer right. But I'm not dealin' with this mess anymore. My grandson wants to come stay a week or two before school starts, and where am I gonna put him?"

"Is Wes coming? Or Jacob?"

"Tommy," Arlene responded, smiling so much she nearly glowed. "So, I'm throwing this stuff out, by God, Jill. It's leaving this house. I won't have my grandson taking one look around and leaving, not to return for another year or so. He'll be comfortable. I'll see to it, even if I have to kill his granddad."

"Arlene, that's wonderful," Jill enthused.

"A good boy," Arlene nodded. Her eyes sparkled. "You know, Jill. We've got some of your grandpa's stuff in here, and out in the garage. If I could get you to take it, Clark might be pushed along a bit, y'know? Would you be willing to do me the favor? It's about time you took this stuff along with ya, anyway. Don't you think?"

Trapped, Jill had no choice but to agree. Sorting through antiques her grandfather cherished, was the last thing she wanted to do today. "I'd be happy to take them. Are they out in the garage, or in here? Up in the attic, maybe?" Jill winced, hoping they weren't there.

"I know I've got a couple boxes right in here… somewhere," Arlene trailed, as she dug through the piles. "Ah…here we go. You could be a sweet girl and take these right over to your house. Come back for another load, and we'll have a rest with a piece of pie and coffee. I made two pies, actually. I was gonna have Clark run one over for ya. Since you're here, you can just take it with you, soon as it cools down. Speaking of which, I better check the oven," Arlene continued, edging around the piles.

With no real choice, Jill heaved the boxes into her arms and carried them back to her garage. While she was there, it occurred to her that she hadn't called Cole about the dirt in her shower yet. Setting the boxes on the floor of her office, she made her way back through the house, making a mental note to put a phone out in the garage as soon as possible.

Cole answered on the first ring, "Cole."

"Hey, it's Jill."

"Listen, I forgot to tell you that I think Tower showered in my garage. There looks to be some dirt. I'm guessing it will match the dirt on the shovels."

"Well, the way this is looking, Jill. We're not going to need it, but I'll let Bishop know and get back to you. Carly's been released, and the case is damned near closed at this point. Since there's evidence of the money burning, the Treasury's probably going to reprint, and shut down the search for those bills."

Jill was silent for a moment, as she considered this. "Do you think that's smart?"

"Do you know something you're not telling me?" Cole asked, his voice weary.

"No, no," Jill rushed. "It just seems... too easy, doesn't it?"

"Sometimes, Jill, cases fall right into your lap. Let's not look the gift-horse in the mouth, eh? Bishop's organizing the effort to search Tower's residence. Maybe they'll find something, maybe they won't, but there's no doubt in my mind who killed those people, Jill."

"Right," Jill agreed, as she walked aimlessly through her house. "What about the bones?"

"They're going to try and find relatives of Hamilton's, see

if they can do a DNA comparison. We'll be contacting your friend there, to have her fill us in on what was said. Honestly, it's not a real high priority at the moment. I mean, there's pressure to get this robbery/murder case cleared up, so we're focusing on that. At this point, I'm pretty much out of it, Jill."

"I'll just leave my shower as is, for the moment then, and you'll call me if it's okay to clean up?"

"Yep, I'll check it out, and keep in touch," Cole replied.

"Great, well…"

"Wait, ah… thanks, Jill. I appreciate your help. So does Bishop."

"You don't need to thank me, Cole. It was my responsibility to tell you what I learned, as it landed on my doorstep," Jill explained.

"Well, all the same, I appreciate it," Cole said. "Bye, now."

The phone clicked off in her ear. Jill locked her house up, and drove the few short feet to Arlene's.

"Oh, dear. You're not staying, are you?" Arlene questioned, spying the Tracker in the driveway.

"No, I need to go talk to Quinn. Are you going to be around tomorrow? Can I come visit then?"

"Sure, thing, dear. I'll get some more of your granddad's stuff together for ya, then. Here, now. Don't run off, without yer pie."

"Oh, you don't have to…"

"Nonsense," Arlene huffed. "Take it on over to your man, if you want. Best way to a man's heart is through his stomach, Jill."

Jill smiled, knowing what was going to come next.

"That's how I hooked Clark. I invited him to my family's house for dinner and helped my ma cook him a real fine meal. The man took one bite of my rhubarb pie, and knew he'd just have to marry me." Arlene sniffed, her eyes glittering, as she wrapped the pie in tinfoil, and carefully handed it over between two potholders. "You run along, and bring back my potholders."

"Thanks, Arlene."

"Shoo. Just tell that lad you cooked it. I won't tell a soul," Arlene encouraged.

Laughing, Jill made her way back to her vehicle, and drove out to Quinn's.

SIXTY-EIGHT

Before Jill could say a word, Chase pulled the pie right out of her hands, ripping the foil from the surface, intending to stab into it with a fork. Quinn shoved his younger brother aside. "For a man who can finesse almost any dish he touches into tasting like gold, you have absolutely no concept of etiquette," Quinn laughed, taking the pie from his brother.

"Dude, it's pie. It smells to-die-for. You didn't cook it," Chase accused, pointing at Jill.

Jill chortled, at the glint in his eye. "Arlene made it."

Chase howled. "I'd marry that woman if she wasn't already taken."

Quinn sliced the pie into eight exact pieces, carefully removing them from the dish onto plates. "She's got grandkids older than you."

"Doesn't matter," Chase insisted. "With my natural born abilities and her sorcery in the kitchen, can you imagine the offspring?" His eyes took on a dreamy quality, as he twirled the fork like a baton in his fingers.

"She's well past the child-bearing years, so I think you can relax," Jill teased. "But you're right, Arlene's gifted."

Quinn set the three plates on the table. "Does anyone want some ice cream with it? I think we've got some."

Chase shook his head quickly. "No, who in their right

mind would cover up this flavor with ice cream? Uh-uh."

"You ate it already, didn't you?" Quinn countered.

Chase looked away guiltily, but Quinn and Jill just laughed. The kid quickly changed the subject. "Jill, I'm so glad you're here. I've been bursting to tell Quinn, whose sorry ass has been gone all day till just now, but it's awesome that you're here. I wanted you to hear it too. I have the absolute best news."

Jill and Quinn shared a look before they each took a bite of their pie slices, waiting. Chase's enthusiasm was contagious.

"I talked to Mom, and she's letting me use my money to help Quinn."

Quinn's eyes became saucers sparkling with a thousand shooting stars before they clouded over again. "No, Chase. You can't just give me your money…"

"I'm not going to," Chase countered. "I want to buy in."

"That's really nice of you but we still don't have enough…" Quinn began. "I need $280,000. You've got… how much?"

Chase pulled a crumpled piece of paper from his pocket. "I've got $57,832.74 in that account, with interest and everything."

"How on earth did you come by such money at your age?" Jill questioned.

"Social security checks. They're supposed to go for raising me, but Mom put a portion of them aside. She did the same thing for Quinn. And on that note, I have a bone to pick with you, big brother." Chase waited till he had Quinn's full attention. "Mom said you refused to take any money for housing me? She offered you the security checks, and you told her to roll them into the account. Hell, Quinn, you didn't have to do that."

Quinn waved his hand. "There's no way I'm taking money to feed you. You're my brother, and besides you buy just as many damned groceries as I do. If you weren't here, I'd be paying the same bills I pay now to live here anyway. Forget it."

Chase considered pressing it, but he decided to let it go. "I also have another $13,261.42."

If possible, Jill's mouth opened even further. Sputtering, she gestured for Chase to explain himself.

Chase grinned. "I'm not a spender. I bought that old Bronco for change, practically. Mom pays the insurance still, even. I've been working construction and whatnot this summer. I saved money from my job last summer too. There's no sense in spending money, when you don't need too." Chase shrugged happily. "Anyway, altogether, I've got about $71,000.00."

"I'm still $210,000 short, but I want you to know that…"

"Actually, I think we might have enough," Jill said, cutting him off. "I've come into a bit of money, myself. With this boat show job, and the next couple pay checks, I can chip in for about $70,000.00. I want in." She smiled.

Flabbergasted, Quinn just shook his head. "Jill, you spent your inheritance on your garage. Didn't you? How can you possibly have that much money?"

"It's still not enough," Chase said, deflated.

"Wait," Jill patted Chase's arm. "I had my house appraised this spring when I was contemplating building another addition."

"The six sided photo gallery and library," Quinn filled in.

Jill smiled. She'd been dreaming about it almost since she moved to Drummond, but practicality won out for the time being, and the garage/dark room needed to come first. "At the time the Credit Union was willing to loan me more than enough to cover the balance. I can take a lien on my house for the $140,000 left over. I want in, too." She held up her hand, effectively silencing him. She studied Quinn's face. She could tell their kids this story, she thought mischievously. *I love him*, she thought, as the emotion poured through her body like sparkling water flows from an ice cold pitcher, into a glass.

Floored by their generosity, Quinn couldn't think clearly enough to form coherent sentences. Tears gathered in his eyes, but he didn't care. Jill and Chase were allowing his dreams to come true, but how could he let them make such sacrifices? "Jill, Chase..." he stammered. "I can't let you..."

"You don't have a choice, Quinn. Jill and I want in," Chase stated it, squeezing Jill's hand in his own. "We're family, and we're taking care of each other. Right, Jill?"

"That's right," Jill agreed.

"But where did you get the money, Jill?" Quinn asked.

"Beth gave me the money." She paused, allowing Quinn's face to twist up in puzzlement before she continued. "She found the pennies. Real ones."

Floored, Quinn dropped his fork, leaning back into his chair, as if the wind had been knocked out of him. Jill filled him in with details from the letter, her conversation with Mary, and finally her late night conversation with Beth.

"You're telling me that a couple plumbers found the real pennies in the drain pipe in Beth's dad's house? And she gave you the finder's fee?"

"She split it three ways, yes. My share, after the scholarship for Joe, will net about $65,000.00. Quinn, we can do this. Chase can kick in about 70, I've got about 70, and we'll borrow 140k on my house. Is that going to be enough? Do you have bids on the building? What about overrun?"

Chase dug into his pie, going back for seconds while Quinn explained his plans. Excavation, metal work construction, electricity, plumbing, and another healthy chunk besides, were divided into the bigger figure of $658,000, which Quinn originally budgeted for the project. Of course, he would hire Dombrowski Construction for the two story section, finishing the most important rooms first, and continuing as funding became available, and other rooms were needed. After he finished explaining his plans, he began shaking his head.

"What?" Chase asked.

"I cannot let you guys do this. I really can't. Jill, you've wanted a damned gallery since you got here. And Chase, you need to go to school. Your money can really help your life. It's not like selling is the end of the world," Quinn insisted.

Jill laid a hand on Quinn's, intent to refute him, but Chase beat her to the punch.

"Quinn, if it's going to be such a burr in your ass, we'll make a deal. I've already got this worked out in my mind, anyway. The only college I want to go to after I finish up high school, is culinary school. I'll work for free, as much as I can during the next year, as long as you support me. Eventually, when money is no longer in such demand, the company can pay for my tuition. How does that sound? You're on crack if you think I'm letting this opportunity pass me by."

Jill nodded her head in full support of Chase's argument. "I'm not going to give up my job in construction anytime soon, but I know that it's not something I'm going to be doing for the rest of my life. This is a chance to invest in my own future, as well as yours." A soft smile touched her lips. "I'll have the addition on my house soon enough, Quinn. I'm not worried about it, because *I have faith in you.* I believe in your talent and your vision. Don't turn our offer down, Quinn."

"Well…" Quinn cleared his throat, struggling with his emotions. What kind of an argument would stand up to that? "We'll pay your loan off first, Jill, so your house will be free and clear."

"That sounds like a yes," Chase whispered, his eyes darting between his brother and Jill.

"It is a yes," Jill finished.

"We'll do it legally, have papers drawn up and everything. We'll split it down the middle." Quinn stated.

"The hell we will," Jill argued. "You're putting more money into this than either Chase or me. You're the one who built this thing, and you have all the creative capital kicking. No way, I'm not taking a third."

"Me either," Chase agreed.

Quinn considered this. "Let's not worry about the last few years of building it. It was a hobby. Let's just think about the money now. How about we split it into halves? You two can control one half of the stock jointly, and I'll control fifty percent?" He suggested.

Jill rolled the figures over in her mind, for a moment. "You take 52%, and Chase and I will each have 24%," Jill countered. "Does that work for you, Chase? It makes more sense mathematically, even though we're not taking into consideration the land, and the effort Quinn put in and…"

"I've been collecting checks from this thing, so let's call it services rendered." Quinn interrupted.

"Works for me!" Chase agreed.

"Are you guys really sure?" Quinn asked, not surprised to find his hands slightly shaky. This might just be the best day of my life, he thought.

"Shut the hell up. It's decided. Call Brenda and tell her to kiss off. We're not selling!" Chase yelled.

"Wow… it's so much to take in. I've been preparing myself for the reality, that I'd have to sell the damned business for weeks."

"Now, you won't. Well, you'll have Chase and I to deal

with now, but that's not so bad. How do you feel?" Jill asked, studying his face.

"Like I'm in a dream," Quinn admitted. "Thank you." His eyes met Jill's connecting with her, before he looked to Chase. "Thank you both so much."

"You're more than welcome," Jill replied.

"It's going to be tight. I have no idea how hard this is going to become at times, but don't think this is an easy course of action," Quinn warned.

"Who ever said we wanted it to be easy?" Chase countered.

"I mean, we're going to cut every cost corner in our personal lives that we can, Chase."

"No more chocolate milk?" Chase asked, pouting.

Quinn and Jill laughed heartily.

"I've still got social security checks coming in for eight more months. Those will help," Chase added.

Quinn nodded. "We might need those to live."

"Whatever it takes, we'll get through it."

"There is something I'd like to buy though. An indulgence, if you guys are okay with it."

Jill's eyes sparkled. "You want that safe, don't you?"

"Yeah," Quinn breathed.

"What safe?" Chase asked.

"It's just a really old, big safe," Quinn said, by way of explanation.

"It's yours," Jill agreed.

SIXTY-NINE

Sam Sparrow smiled warmly at the couple walking into her shop, excusing herself when the phone rang. Inside the Wayfarer's Mart, Doreen Helsberger picked an old looking, aluminum canister off the top of a safe marked "sold." "Honey, what do you make of this?"

Her husband, Terry, turned toward her, studying the canister in his wife's hands. "Let me see," he suggested.

She handed it to him, curiously looking over his shoulder. "221163? What does that mean?"

Terry dug his reading glasses out of his pocket, contemplating the number. "Well, it's not a phone number. It's not a social security number, but why would anyone scratch that into a canister anyway," he muttered. His face flooded with an idea as if a light bulb flickered in his mind. "It's a date."

"Oh, Terry. There's no month, 22." She said, thinking her husband was teasing her.

"It's written military style. When I was in the military, everything was written day, month, then year." Terry supplied.

"Why on God's earth do they do that?" Doreen asked.

Terry scratched his chin as he considered it. "I know some of the European countries write dates that way. When I was stationed in Germany, that's how they did it there too. I think the military does it that way, because of NATO or something like that." He shrugged, sitting the canister back down.

"So this date is November 22nd, 1963." She looked to her husband for confirmation. When he nodded, she contemplated this new information for a moment, before she asked, "Why does that date ring a bell?"

Terry's brow furrowed. "Wasn't that the day Kennedy was shot?"

"Oh, Terry, you're right. That's exactly what day it was." Doreen smiled, pleased to have figured it out.

"Odd coincidence, isn't it? A film of some Drummond Island family doing God knows what on the day Kennedy was killed?" Terry rubbed the whiskers at his chin, chuckling. "Bizarre."

"We should buy this." Doreen suggested.

"For heaven's sake, why?" Terry questioned, obviously thinking the notion was quite ridiculous.

"Because it's neat," Doreen argued.

"That's what you always say." Terry shook his head. "It'll just be another piece of junk for the attic. Set it down, Doreen. There's some books over there we should look at." Terry said, dragging his wife along behind him.

"Actually, Terry," Doreen started, glancing at her watch. "We need to get going. We'll miss the ferry if we don't leave right now."

"Alright then," Terry muttered following his wife out the door.

On the couple's way out, they passed a blue workshirt clothed man, on his way in, who didn't stop moving until he found Sam hanging up the antique, rotary dial phone handle.

"That's some phone," the man whistled.

Sam grinned. "It's going to be the death of me, but I love

it." She looked up at him, smiling. "Are you all done with the safe then?" Sam asked.

"Yep. It's good to go. I just wanted to tell you that it was empty, except for an old aluminum canister I pulled from it."

"A canister?" Sam questioned, following the man to the safe.

"Looks like an old film canister to me," the man shrugged.

"I don't even own a reel to reel machine. It's an 8mm, isn't it?" Sam asked.

"I think it's 16mm," the man suggested. "I'm no expert, but I think that's what professionals would have used back in the day."

Thinking she'd do something with it later, she set it on one of the long shelves behind her. When she turned around, she noticed the man hiding his chuckle. "What?"

The man didn't say anything, as he eyed up the impossibly long shelves, filled to capacity with a great variety of…stuff. "Don't mind me, ma'am. I'm leaving. Take care."

"You too," Sam called out, glancing at her wall clock. In less than an hour she had a party of twelve coming for dinner, and much to do. Canister forgotten, she closed the door behind the man, as he left, flipped the sign, and headed back to the kitchen.

SEVENTY

THREE WEEKS LATER

Quinn maneuvered the fry pan over the stove, carefully shaking it a bit to ensure heat was evenly dispersed to all popcorn kernels possible. The last three weeks had passed... comfortably. Officially, the robbery/murders case was closed. No new evidence came forth to suggest anyone else's involvement. The combined effort between city and local authorities revealed no new indicators within Tower's apartment, to point fingers in any other directions. Gossip about the cases died down a bit with the passing of Labor Day, as tourists went home in groves, returning the bar scene to weekenders and Drummond Island locals. Quinn, of course, seemed just as busy, but in a *good* way.

With a phone call to his lawyer, Quinn started the ball rolling for the business papers to be drawn up, selling 24% each to both his younger brother and Jill. The loan was as easily procured as Jill expected, so the trio only needed to wait for Jill's share of the finders fee to arrive, to make it official. The concrete forms were ready to be poured, and in mere days he'd be able to walk on his factory's floor.

Of course, the news of Quinn's ownership of Three Bobbers Over Land products, as well as the new development on M-134, spread like wildfire. Bottles of barbecue sauce were being passed from coffee cup to coffee cup in gossip circles, and Quinn was cornered with questions everywhere he went. Some of the locals didn't believe he'd kept the business quiet for so long, while others skipped through the chatter to ask for jobs, or samples.

All in all, Quinn considered, lowering the heat as the popcorn finished popping, things were going well. He didn't think Drummond locals would ever understand why he'd kept his business venture to himself, but that was okay with Quinn.

The ringing phone pulled him back to the present, as Jill picked it up from her perch on the stool near Quinn's counter. Quinn shook his head at Jill, indicating that he didn't want to talk to anyone at the moment.

"McCord Residence," she greeted, winking broadly.

"Hi. Is Quinn there?"

"No, he's not. Can I take a message?"

"Sure. This is Sam Sparrow, over at Wayfarer's…"

"Hi, Sam. It's Jill Traynor."

"Oh, Jill. Hello. I was just calling to tell Quinn, that the safe locksmith, or whatever he's called, unlocked and reset the safe. The man told me he's going to call Quinn himself, since he's is paying for it, but I just wanted to let Quinn know that he can pick it up anytime."

"Very good, I'll tell him. Thanks for calling, Sam."

"Take care, Jill. Just have him let me know when he plans to come get it, so I can be here." Sam chuckled. "And tell him to bring lots of strong backs."

"I'll tell him. Bye." Jill waited for the echoing goodbye before she hung up the phone. "Your safe is ready."

Quinn's face lit up like a little boy discovering a candy store. "Yes!" He hissed, tossing a kernel into his mouth.

Jill scooted off the stool, wrapping her arms around Quinn from behind. "Smells good."

"Is it ever!" He teased, squeezing her hands lightly in his.

"What movie did you pick?" Jill asked.

"Raiders of the Lost Ark. The DVD is in the machine and waiting for us."

"Mmmm," Jill pressed her nose in the arch between his shoulder blades and inhaled. "I bet you're really excited about your new kitchen, hey?"

He frowned. "I am, but I shouldn't be thinking about it. If there are more overruns than I'm expecting, it'll have to be cut or postponed."

"You'll have it, babe. I know you will. You smell like… some really delicious spice or something… are you working on a new blend?"

"I botched my efforts a bit, but yeah. I'm working on a chicken seasoning." Quinn responded. "Nothing I did in the kitchen today seemed to work… but I always have a bad day before I have a brilliant one."

Jill moved her head back, grinning mischievously. "So tomorrow's going to be brilliant? Should I plan on coming by after work for a sample?"

Quinn chortled. He turned around, taking her with him as he gathered the popcorn and beers into his arms. "Come on, hon. Indy is waiting for us." He turned the lights off, pulling Jill onto the couch next to him.

Jill's eyes twinkled, as she snuggled close. She pulled the gigantic bowl of popcorn into her lap and relieved Quinn of one of the long necks. She widened her eyes, looking up at him expectantly. "Where's yours?"

Quinn laughed, taking a sip of his beer, before he hit the play button. "Now, I'm ready," he said, when his arms were snuggly around her. Cozy, in the dark living room, with the love of his life nestled against him, Quinn grinned, settling to watch the classic he had seen a dozen times before.

SEVENTY-ONE

CLEVELAND, OHIO

Beth clanked the heavy porcelain cup, filled with tea, onto the glass coffee table in Lisa's apartment. It was so good to be near her friend again, even if it was just for a day, sharing the stories of the last several weeks in person. Like their phone conversations of late, Beth and Lisa continued to revisit Frank's tale. With Hamilton's remains finally being identified conclusively by the FBI, as actually being Hamilton's remains, the women were left with no choice but to believe Frank's story. Over and over again, they'd dissected Lisa's memories of Frank's statements, attempting to unbury possible clues on where the film Frank mentioned could be hidden.

Lisa propped her feet up on the table, as she leaned back against the couch. "This growing up thing kind of sucks, doesn't it?"

Beth laughed. "Tell me about it," she agreed.

"Don't you just wish we were both back in New York, going to college? I never would have dreamed I'd end up in Cleveland. And who would have ever guessed that you would end up in Northern Michigan?" Lisa asked, swallowing a large sip of the still too hot tea. She wrinkled her nose. "I don't know why I let you talk me into drinking this stuff."

Beth ignored the complaint about the tea, considering their paths. "I know. If Richard hadn't… eh, it's too much to think about. I'm going to believe in fate, I guess."

"How is Richard doing?" Lisa asked. It wasn't something they liked to discuss on the phone, as it often depressed Beth.

Beth frowned, thinking past the quick answers she usually gave to family members and acquaintances who asked to be polite, rather than because they really wanted to know. "He's better than he could be. He's taking some classes online, and he's in a work program that will reduce his twenty to life sentence by a third, if it goes according to plan. So far, he hasn't caused or gotten himself into any trouble, which is why they moved him. And he says that Kinross is a paradise compared to Jackson, so the move has helped." Beth's voice hitched, before she continued. "But he's different, Li. He's so much harder, so much more bitter than he ever was before. He's learned things inside that I can't even comprehend, and I don't want to." Beth shuddered.

"Do you visit him quite a bit?"

Beth nodded. "Yes, as much as I can. The prison's about fifteen miles, maybe a little more than that, from where I'm living now."

"And how is that going? Beyond of course the great pain in the ass of moving," Lisa muttered. "I bet it's quite different, hey?"

"You know, though Li... I like it. I really like the Soo." She turned to her friend. "Do you like it here, Lisa? I mean, really?"

Lisa shrugged, considering. "I like it well enough. I love my job, but the hours are so long. I miss Mom and Dad something fierce. The work is just what I imagined it would be, helping people. I love my patients... but then you get close to one, like Frank, and he passes." Lisa's mind returned to her charge, and she shook her head sadly. "I didn't know him very long, but he affected me."

"That must be tough," Beth said, supportively.

"Nancy, another nurse at Green Meadows, says I need to find a way to deal with it, so it doesn't bother me so much."

Beth nodded agreement. "Emergency is a bit different, but I know what you mean. I don't have the long-term bonds that you might share with your patients, but I still care so much about them. In the Soo, at least there aren't inner city crime victims that we would see, if we were somewhere bigger, you know? I'm not sure I would do well with that, but I like the pace, and they've got a nice group there. Good people to work with."

"Boy, it'd help me a great deal if some of the women I worked with would carry their share. I still can't believe Nancy forgot to call me when Frank passed." Lisa shook her head angrily. "I still can't believe he was a priest."

"Are you sure he was telling the truth?" Beth questioned, gently.

"His story about Hamilton checked out. Jill called me and explained everything that happened. They confirmed that the body was Hamilton's, but they didn't find any treasure. Of course, since that bank robber fellow dug up the area beforehand, it's possible that he relocated the treasure, or maybe it could have been destroyed in the fire." Lisa conjectured. "Anyway, with that kind of evidence, and the fact that he was a priest… yes, I believe him."

"That's just bizarre. He never mentioned to you that he was a priest, and he never mentioned to his priest friends that he was… what was he called? Some sort of a bad guy?" Beth asked.

"He was an enforcer, but that part of it isn't so big of a deal to me. I mean, if I had lived a really shitty life, and needed to turn it around, I certainly wouldn't tell anyone from my new life, about the dark deeds of my old life." Lisa commented.

"Then why say anything at all? Why not just die as a

priest, and let the rest of it go? I mean, if he spent years and years, as one thing, being secretive about the past, why would he bring it up at all?" Beth challenged.

"Guilt," Lisa responded. "I bet he needed to sort of perform a full confession. Allow some possibility for the truth to go free. He must want me to find it."

Beth leaned forward, removing the tea cozy from the kettle, to refill her cup. "I guess that makes sense, but I don't think you'll find it now."

Lisa raised an eyebrow. "You don't think so?"

Beth leaned back, pondering the challenge. "In Frank's lifetime, where would he consider a safe place? When, as you've told me, he lived in destinations scattered from New Orleans, to Drummond Island? It could be anywhere. You don't have nearly enough details to find it."

"I guess you're right." Disgruntled, Lisa touched her forefinger to the end of her tea-burned tongue, glaring at the teacup comically. "You know, I'm almost tempted to think it's on Drummond somewhere," she said, tentative.

"What makes you think that?"

"Well, he buried a body there. Dillinger stole his woman from there, which according to Frank, sent him down the wrong paths. He had a sort of kinship with the place, I think." Lisa shrugged. "It doesn't help us though. Drummond's big, right?"

Beth nodded. "Way too big to search. I mean... a safe place? That's not nearly enough," Beth decided.

"Do you think we should tell the authorities?" Lisa asked.

"They'd never believe you. Even if they did, I'd bet anything that the FBI wouldn't want the truth to get out."

"I'm not so sure of that, Beth. I've been researching it on the internet, and there seem to be a lot of people who believe Hoover was involved in Kennedy's death. If we approached

one of those internet groups, maybe they'd have ideas on how
to find the film," Lisa suggested.

"And then we'd have every weirdo from here to the ends
of the world on our doorsteps, picking our brains and
exploiting this. Can you imagine what this film is worth?
Millions, Lisa. We'd be labeled as freaks, and treasure hunters.
Most people wouldn't believe us, and those that would believe
us… well, they just might be a bit scary." Beth sighed,
considering all the ramifications. "Frankly, I already have
enough problems like that to deal with, with my paranormal
abilities and my brother's being a convicted murderer. In a
small place like the Soo, I really can't afford to add another
wacko label behind my name."

"Isn't it incredible? We can answer one of the world's
most perplexing mysteries, and we can't really tell anyone.
Not without proof, anyway," Lisa acknowledged. "I just wish I
knew where it was."

Beth didn't need to be told that Lisa was thinking about
the canister again. She rolled her shoulders back, tracing her
fingers along the base of her neck, as she considered.

Lisa arched an eyebrow, observing the motion. "You don't
have… you know… a sense of it, do you?" she asked,
lowering her voice.

Beth's voice softened as she shook her head. "No. I've
been concentrating on my feelings, and I'm learning how to
explore them, but without having talked to Frank myself, or
seen the canister, there's just no way. Even if I had talked to
him, I don't think I'd know where it was. Honestly, I know
you want to find this thing, but I'm sort of glad we don't
know where it is."

Lisa studied her friend's face, questioning silently.

Beth knew she owed her friend more explanation, but she
had trouble forming it. "It's the pennies all over again, Li.
Those coins ruined my family. My father spent his lifetime

looking for them, and never really accomplished anything. If you let it, this film has the power to consume you.

"I feel like I've aged a decade in the last year and a half, what with the trial, and Richard being in prison, and a new town and… I'm just so tired, Lisa. I would give almost anything to go back. I miss my Dad. I regret not spending more time with him, you know?" Beth leaned back into the couch. "God, I'm such a drag aren't I? I'm sorry, Lisa. I don't mean to rain on your parade or anything. If you want to go looking for this thing, I'll support you. Just don't ask me to be a part of it, okay?"

Lisa understood, and made the decision. If Beth didn't think they should pursue this, than Lisa would trust her judgment. "I'm not going to look for it. But…should we tell your friend, Jill? If it is on Drummond, she could at least keep her eyes open?"

Beth contemplated this for a long moment, before she shook her head again. "No, I don't think so. Jill has been through so much lately, with the situation up there."

Lisa nodded. "Isn't that something? Did I tell you that a police officer from there called me and questioned me about Frank's story?"

Beth nodded. "Yes, you did."

"He seemed like a nice guy." Lisa sipped her tea, lost in thought. "Jill's really nice, too," Lisa added. "She told me the cop was going to call, and explained what happened up there. Pretty crazy, hey? That would be like you showing up here with a criminal boyfriend. Can you imagine?" Lisa asked.

"Except in my case, it's a criminal brother," Beth countered.

Taken aback, Lisa coughed, spitting out her tea in the process. "I'm so sorry, Beth. I wasn't thinking at all," Lisa apologized, absently wiping the area with a towel.

"Don't be silly, Lisa. You shouldn't have to tiptoe around me. You're right, it would be a shock. I've talked to Jill a couple times over the last few weeks. Mostly, we've been talking about the penny money, but..." Beth's voice trailed off, as laughter overtook her.

"What's funny?"

"Well, it's really not funny, but she made me talk to her boyfriend on the phone."

"Oh?" Lisa asked.

"Yeah. There was a misunderstanding about who picked up her phone once, but we've figured that it must have been the murderer." Beth explained.

"Oh, yes. You mentioned that to me. You got a bad feeling from the phone. So your conversation with her boyfriend went alright?"

Beth nodded. "Yeah, Quinn's a good guy."

"Hey, that reminds me. How's your grandpa?" Lisa asked.

"Really good. He was quite proud of me, about the decision to give the finders fee from the pennies, away." Beth smiled.

"Well, duh. I'm proud of you too. But, do you realize how much money you gave them? I can't believe you're not keeping any of it for yourself."

"Well, I am using part of it for that scholarship fund," Beth pointed out.

"Precisely. The only money you're not giving away or holding for Richard, you're putting in a scholarship fund." Lisa rolled her eyes. "Way too generous, as far as I'm concerned. And after all the trouble your great-grandfather went to, yikes."

"Those pennies destroyed my brother's life," Beth countered. "I didn't want any part of them. I feel badly enough that we're using nearly a third of the money for Richard, but I'm glad about the scholarship."

"It's really great that the Barbers and Jill are all chipping in too." Lisa commented. "It was such a good idea, Beth. This way, Joe will be remembered and you'll be able to help so many kids."

A full smile graced Beth's face. "Yes, I'm very pleased myself."

A few moments passed in comfortable silence before Lisa spoke again.

"You know what I miss about New York?"

"What?" Beth asked.

"Really good pizza."

Beth laughed. "There must be something in Cleveland that's comparable? Should we order some in?"

"Yes! And some Coke! I'm not drinking any more of this hot tea shit." Lisa joked, picking up the phone.

Beth's sparkling eyes gave Lisa pause for a moment. "It's so good to be here, Li. We can't lose touch, just because we're in two different states, okay? You have to promise to come see me."

Lisa grinned. "I promise," she agreed, and dialed the pizza place's number from memory.

SEVENTY-TWO

"Dew-To-Do-Dew-Do-To-Dew…" Quinn sang the Indiana Jones theme as the credits began rolling over the screen.

Jill laughed softly, leaning back against him on the couch. "Can you imagine?" She asked.

"Imagine what?" He responded gruffly, pausing to nip her neck affectionately, as his arms encircled her, dragging her onto his lap.

She shooed his wandering hands away, laughing. "The Ark of the Covenant hiding in plain sight? It's almost too much to consider."

"I think it's brilliant," Quinn argued.

"Oh, me too. It's just heavy. It's one of, if not, *the* most sought after relics in the world, and when someone finds it, they hide it in an unmarked crate, in a warehouse filled with crates the same size. It's too important to destroy, and yet… in effect, it is destroyed, because no one's going to find it."

"Not true, honeybear."

"Honeybear?" she groaned, laughing. "You are *not* calling me that."

He ignored her, enjoying the new ability to annoy her, with a thousand pet names if he wanted to. "Someone eventually is going to find it. An object of that value… of that power… will find its way into the right hands eventually. It's the way of things."

"You really think so?" Jill tugged her lower lip, looking into Quinn's steel colored eyes. She kissed him quickly before she backed up again, still contemplating the movie.

Quinn growled, but she ignored him. "You think it's lost forever?"

"I think it might be, yes. That's what's so cool about it. If it was guarded or some place more secure, it would attract attention. This way, it'll just disappear as one crate in the masses."

"No way," Quinn stated emphatically. "It's not lost, it's in a warehouse! This way, we can enjoy another great movie on someone tracking it down and the adventure that entails."

"If it was such a great movie idea, wouldn't they have made it already?" Jill laughed, while Quinn hit the power button on the remote.

Quinn narrowed his eyes, playfully. "You've been wrong before, you know."

"Oh? I don't remember ever being wrong," she teased.

"You didn't think the real pennies existed, and now, because they did... and of course, because of Beth's generosity, my dreams are coming true."

Jill's face softened. "I think you would have found a way to make it happen."

"Yeah, but this way it kind of makes us happen too," Quinn ventured.

Jill's eyes widened.

"You're my partner, now," he explained. "And Chase, of course. I couldn't have orchestrated this whole thing to happen any more perfectly than it did. You are stuck with me now, Miss Jillian, whether you like it or not," he teased.

Jill's eyes radiated warmth, as she leaned down to him,

placing her mouth near his ear. "I like it," she whispered.

Quinn melted.

"I'd like it better if you had better sense in movies," Jill laughed. "I mean, anyone with a real appreciation for movies would just know that the Ark disappearing again is as brilliant of an ending as is possible."

Quinn growled. "Are you done talking about this now?" Quinn asked, tugging a strand of her hair.

Jill smirked, leaning down to plant a kiss on Quinn's nose. "When did you say Chase was going to get home?" she whispered.

"Late. Really, *really* late," Quinn emphasized, gently tugging on her lower lip with his teeth.

Jill ended the kiss, before she pulled back, arching an eyebrow to torment him. "How do you know that?"

"Football practice."

"It can't last forever," she pointed out.

"I gave him twenty bucks to get lost for a long while," Quinn admitted, incorrigible.

Jill laughed. "Now, why on earth would you do that?" she drawled, batting her eyelashes innocently.

"Why do you think?" He snarled affectionately, pulling her face back to his.

And this time, she went with him, vaguely aware of the crackling fire in the background as Quinn nuzzled her hair, losing his fingers in the lustrous brown strands that surrounded him.

SEVENTY-THREE

Holding the freshly bathed, and pajama clad baby in her arms, Katherine Lorraine Dombrowski pushed back gently on the balls of her feet, rocking backward in the white wicker rocking chair. She studied her son's sweet cherub-like face. His large dark eyes watched hers. His tiny fingers closed around her own. As his eyelids began to droop, Kate stood up, careful not to wake him. She laid him in the wooden crib, placed the colorful bunny blanket over him, and watched him fall asleep.

She studied the room, taking in the white wooden molding above the wall paper border, and mint painted walls. Pete was beginning to apply a bit of pressure to buy land and build a new home from the ground up. It made sense, she knew, as she collected soiled laundry into her arms. A contractor like Pete should be able to showcase his home as something he built. They lived in this house since they married, and although Pete added on rooms to accommodate their needs as their family grew, it wasn't an ideal home. She dearly loved it, almost as much as she loved Drummond.

Drummond was more than a part of her heritage, she thought as she quietly picked up strewn toys, placing them on the shelves where they belonged. She couldn't quite define what it was, but Kate knew she was destined to live here. Her mother never appreciated it the same way she had. Kate's mother had always planned to move off Drummond when she became an adult, but found herself caught when she fell in love with someone who would never leave. Eventually, she grew to accept it. Especially, she thought, when Kate and Megan grew up in their father's footsteps, completely in love with the place.

Of course, Kate's path reached further back than her destiny, to merely follow her father's footsteps. Her mother wouldn't have recognized that, since she herself didn't know the truth. Her mother was raised with two parents, never the wiser that the man she called "daddy," wasn't in fact, her father. When Kate became a teenager, her grandmother, Lorraine confided the truth: Kate was John Dillinger's granddaughter. If Dillinger had returned, the way he'd planned to, their lives would have irrevocably changed.

After Dillinger died, Kate's grandmother thought her family might just be better off. John hadn't known Lorraine was pregnant at all, but she believed he would have come back for her. The only reason she told Kate the truth was because she saw the sparkle in Kate's eyes that could have only come from one place, John.

Glancing down at her baby boy, Kate contemplated his name, *John Joseph Dombrowski*. Baby Joey was named after two men: one that would never be acknowledged publicly, or privately, for that matter. Kate didn't believe she would ever tell any of her children about their true heritage. And she would never tell a soul why she'd become the mastermind criminal, Red.

Red, Kate thought, smiling softly. Naming herself after the original *Lady in Red*, the Madame from a Chicago brothel, that sold out her grandfather, was nothing short of genius. Of course, the woman who'd given up John Dillinger's whereabouts to Hoover's G-Men actually wore orange and tan that fatal day, but few people realized that. Her grandmother had really known very little about Dillinger at the time, but what she did know, swept her off her feet. A charismatic man,

Lorraine told her, with the ability to steal anything, *including a woman's heart.*

Smiling at the thought of her grandmother being romanced by a celebrity, Kate's thoughts returned to the same question that always plagued her: what came first, she wondered, the chicken or the egg? If Lorraine remained silent, would she have followed her grandfather's footsteps? Would she have been able to quiet her lifelong dark ambition to plan something meticulously? To do something completely unexpected and carry it through, just to see if she could? Haunted for years before she attempted anything of the sort, Kate contemplated the path she'd chosen.

She loved her husband, and her three beautiful children with her whole heart. Becoming Red didn't have anything to do with the rest of her life. She enjoyed helping her husband with the business, and loved being a part of Drummond's social circles. If the community knew the truth about her, they'd most likely believe she was a monster, she realized. Her friends would wonder if they'd ever known her at all. Kate was not a careful composite of lies—she was in fact, a loving mother and wife, devoted to her family and friends.

Her grandmother tried to warn her not to follow her grandfather's footsteps. Dillinger's run led to his demise, Lorraine told her, and bad choices would lead to Kate's as well. This time, she thought sadly, she'd made mistakes, terrible mistakes. She never wanted to hurt anyone, and was sickened that three people were killed. Recruiting Tower was a terrible error in judgment, resulting in murders that never should have taken place. Thankfully, Kate was smart enough to cover her own trail, but she wouldn't have been able to counteract Tower's statement, if he'd been arrested, and chose to implicate her.

With Tower out of the picture, Kate knew that his apartment didn't have so much as an envelope with a postmark to indicate her involvement. Everything she mailed him was shipped from post offices below the bridge. Even *the plan* was typed in a public library in Traverse City, while on a mini-vacation with her family. No one would find a stitch of evidence, like a fingerprint, to implicate her anywhere, since she wore gloves every step of the way.

The only evidence she held was her half of the cash, $336,640.00. Thanks to her Sunday morning coffee visits with Jill, she knew that the case was now closed. Cooper, Junior and Officer Cloudfoot, were Tower's victims, not hers. The distinction didn't ease her conscience. Three people were killed because of Kate's decision to recruit Tower. Haunted, Kate's lower lip trembled as she tried to clear her mind of it.

She was sure her grandfather had lapses in judgment too. Glancing down at the hem of her summer dress, she realized a piece of lint was stuck to her. She took a moment to brush it off, thinking that maybe the motion held a hint for her future course of action. If she could simply brush the error off, she could go on. The smarter choice, Kate knew, was to use this experience as a lesson. If she walked away from the 'Red' persona, that she carefully constructed, she wouldn't be responsible, by accident or otherwise, for anyone else's suffering. Whether or not Tower's decision to murder was premeditated, it wouldn't have been on Kate's shoulders, if she hadn't involved him in her bank robberies.

Next time, she wouldn't trust someone she barely knew to carry out her perfectly laid plans. If a *next time* even presented itself, she corrected. Maybe, next time the payoff wouldn't be worth the risk.

Then again, maybe it would.

Kate bent down to pick up a fluffy white rabbit, comforted by the canvas bag tucked safely under the crib, out of sight. Just like she planned, she removed her bag of money from Tower's Jeep at Jill's barbecue. If Tower had simply followed my instructions, no one would've been killed... she allowed the thought to trail off. There was nothing she could do about it now.

When she was satisfied that the room was neat and tidy once again, she leaned over the edge of the crib and caressed her baby's cheek. "Good night, baby Joey. Mumma loves you." Kate left the room, softly closing her son's bedroom door behind her. She glanced at her wristwatch, thinking, *six more minutes before I have to pull the cookies out of the oven.*

Epilogue

Mike Marinello stepped off the mahogany and gold trimmed elevator into the mosaic tiled foyer. The majestic tiered fountain splashed crystal clear water into great onyx basins in an elaborate structure, only the rich would deem worthwhile. Granite sculptures guided the way through the genteel design of frosted doors and tapestry hung walls. Potted trees and plants, both exotic and domestic, were cared for by professional gardeners. The entire floor of the skyscraper, towering amidst the Chicago horizon, was designed to lead those who walked through it, toward the room with the very best view of Lake Michigan. The office Mike sought was flanked by secretaries who resembled debutantes in physique, but shared personality traits with pit bulls.

Mike leaned against the tall, sweeping barricade and flashed his 100-watt smile. The man inside the office was a merciless, greedy son-of-a-bitch, who intimidated lesser men, with a wall of ice in his nearly black eyes that bordered the glacial. Although Mike drove nearly ten hours with intent to see him, he wasn't happy about it.

The secretary returned the smirk. "Hello, Mr. Marinello. Would you like to schedule an appointment?"

"No. I'm going in. I just thought you might want to announce me first."

"You can't. He's…"

Mike hurried around the desk, yanking one of the mahogany doors open. The leather chair swiveled around until Mike was face to face with his father.

"I'm sorry, Sir. He just barged in…"

Anthony Marinello waved the woman off with a flick of his wrist. "Hello, Michael."

"Dad." Mike greeted, struggling not to gulp air nervously.

"What brings you here? I thought you were summering in Michigan?" Anthony questioned. "Need money? You could have made a phone call, rather than come down. Not that you're not welcome *at home*." Mike's father emphasized, needlessly reminding his son of the distinction. Family and business were *separate* in the Marinello household. Anthony lowered his eyes, sorting through some documents on his desk. "Your mother will be delighted to see you."

"I'm not here for a visit," Mike responded, attempting to keep the irritation from his voice. "I have something you'll want to hear. Are you sitting down?" Michael asked, amused.

It was obvious to both men that Anthony was in fact, sitting down. "Well then?"

Mike's mouth quirked upward. He waited until his father's eyes met his own. "I found another piece."

If Mike hadn't been staring into his father's eyes, he would have missed the bright flicker that passed through them, the slight opening of Anthony's mouth in shock.

"I found the locket," Mike clarified.

"Are you sure?"

"Yes."

Anthony dropped his papers, work forgotten and stared his son down. "Do you have it?"

"No." Mike settled into a trim leather chair. "When I discovered it, I wasn't in the position to take it. I found it around a woman's neck at a party."

"Where, exactly?"

"Northern Michigan. A place called Drummond Island. I was living on my new boat up there, doing some diving. Have you heard of it?"

Anthony smiled. "I've yachted there, yes. Does this woman have any idea what she has?"

Mike shook his head. "No. To her, it's merely a family heirloom."

"Who is she?"

"Nobody, really. Her name is Jill Traynor. She's a local. Her grandmother, a woman named Edna Kinney gave it to her."

"Edna Kinney?"

"Yes. Is the name familiar to you? I didn't remember ever hearing it."

Anthony removed the thin wire framed glasses from his face, as he concentrated in thought. "No, not at all."

"I thought it best to come directly to you. I would have called but… I thought you'd want to hear it from me in person."

"Thirty years of searching… and you just happen across it at a party. I believed it was gone forever. Unbelievable," Anthony muttered, dumbstruck. "How hard will it be to obtain it?"

Mike paused, considering. "She doesn't wear it too often. I'd guess she keeps it in a jewelry box or something. I think I even glimpsed a jewelry box on her night stand. I'm not sure, it was a quick glance, but it should be easy enough for a snatch and grab. Hell, I might even be able to do it."

"But we have to consider that she might know what it is. She might be able to shed some light on some of the other pieces. If she has one, it's possible that she has more," Anthony said, thinking out loud.

"If she knows what it is, why would she be wearing it?" Mike asked.

Anthony shrugged, toying with a pencil. "Maybe to keep it close?"

Michael nodded, but the idea didn't play for him. She couldn't have known.

"This means we're closer than we've ever been," Anthony said.

Anthony wasn't talking about their relationship, but for the first time in years, Michael felt somewhat at ease with his father. Perhaps, this was going to become a bonding experience after all. *Not likely,* Mike reconsidered when his father started yelling out orders.

"Paula!" Pressing down on the intercom button, Anthony barked his secretary's name. "Get in here! Bring Ellen with you!"

Seconds later, the petite woman followed by another of Anthony's secretaries, walked through the door. "Yes, Sir?"

"Find out everything you can on Jill Traynor, and Edna Kinney. I want to know about school records, financial records, known associates and acquaintances, marriages, relatives, as deep and as broad as you can. My son will tell you everything he knows to get you started." With orders given, Anthony waved his hand dismissing them. When the women had left the room, he pressed a button hidden on a console at the backside of a sculpture replica of Da Vinci's Vitruvian Man.

A mechanized whirring noise from the adjacent wall sounded as a painting slid back to reveal a safe. Anthony pressed his combination to the keypad, accessed the secondary measure of security with his thumb pressed firmly to the plate, and waited for the steel door to unlatch. Reverent, Anthony reached past special documents and other items to pull out an old tattered, fabric covered box.

Michael's quietly drawn breath quickened as his father opened the box, revealing a nearly identical age old golden locket. And so, Michael thought, *it begins again.*

Authors' Notes

If you've read Lighthouse Paradox, and now Legacy, you'll realize that we've continued our book writing adventures with a present day story that intertwines elements from the past. In this novel, like in our first, we've mixed truthful historical figures and events with fiction for the purposes of multi-generational story-telling.

Although the story we have told is a work of fiction, we found our inspiration for this story based on historical events/figures. In 1934, John Dillinger and John Hamilton visited Sault Ste. Marie, Michigan. The people mentioned in the Dillinger/Soo chapters are real people. Growing up, the story was passed down about Dillinger's visit to Drummond, DeTour, and the Hessel Woods. Did he really, or is this merely folklore? There is no proof that they visited the area, and those who claimed to have seen him have all passed away. Of course, there are no bodies or treasure from Dillinger (to our knowledge) buried anywhere on Drummond.

If you're familiar with forensics, you'll realize that it would take much longer than three weeks to get a match to John Hamilton's DNA. We also state Foye Hamilton was in jail at the time John Hamilton arrived at his sister's on April 17th, 1934. In truth, he did not go to court, or jail for that matter, until after his older brother had passed away.

J. Edgar Hoover was the director of the FBI (or Bureau of
Investigation, as it was called in Dillinger's time) in both 1934
and 1963, when Kennedy was assassinated. In 1963, John F.
Kennedy was the President of the United States. There have
been many books, movies, and evidence collected to suggest
Hoover's involvement. More information on the historical
elements that inspired this book can be found in the books and
newspaper articles referenced.

If the artwork on the cover looks familiar, it's because it is
from the 28th Annual Les Cheneaux Islands Antique Wooden
Boat Show and Festival of Arts 2005 poster. On the poster, the
boat depicted is titled "Boat Show," where as on our book
cover, it lists the name of our novel, Legacy. Both the poster
and artwork were completed by John and Diana Grenier of Up
North Studios.

In Chapter 35, a fictitious newspaper article discusses the
State of Michigan's intent to brand Michigan as the "Great
Lakes Maritime Heritage Destination," which is true. Working
with other groups, museums, and private companies we claim
they want to begin an Upper Peninsula Circle Tour, with
Cedarville (or Clark Township) bequeathed with a museum of
national merit and learning center on antique wooden boats.
The organizations, and cabinet posts listed exist, but the circle
tour concept and museum are fictional.

References

Cromie, Robert. <u>Dillinger: A Short and Violent Life</u>. Chicago Historical Bookworks, Evanston, 1962.

Gentry, Curt. <u>J. Edgar Hoover: The Man and the Secrets</u>. W.W. Norton & Company, New York, 1991.

Matera, Dary. <u>John Dillinger</u>. Carrol & Graff, New York, 2004.

North, Mark. <u>Act of Treason: The Role of J. Edgar Hoover in the Assasination of President Kennedy</u>. Carol & Graff, New York.

Potter, Claire. <u>War On Crime</u>. Rutgers University Press, New Brunswick, 1958.

Stewart, Tony. <u>Dillinger: The Hidden Truth</u>. Xlibris Corporation, 2002.

Toland, John. <u>The Dillinger Days</u>. Da Capo Press, New York, 1963.

Newspaper articles from the Sault Evening News, April 1934

Manhunt Continues In Northern Country

Dillinger Before Long, That is Pledge of Department of Justice Men hunting Outlaw.

Hamilton Brazenly Visits Soo

Department of Justice officers Seek to Pick Up Mobsters Trail Here.

Sault Woman Arraigned for Aiding Outlaw

Several Knew Dillinger was in Soo Tuesday

Conversation between Indiana Outlaws and Sault Women

100 Crack U.S. Marksmen on Bandit's Trail

Interviews:

Marti Hart, Chairman: Les Cheneaux Islands Antique
  Boat Show & Festival of Arts

Linda Hudson, Supervisor: Clark Township

Willard LaJoie, President & CEO: Central Savings Bank

Jim Howie, Grandson of Sheriff Willard Walsh

Shirley *(Welsh)* Howie, Daughter of Sheriff Willard Walsh

Josh Husted, Birmingham Police Department

ABOUT THE AUTHORS

D. Ann Kelley

D. Ann currently lives in Mount Pleasant, Michigan, where she studies in the MFA program at Central Michigan University. She is a member of the National Writers Association. She spends as much time on Drummond Island as possible. In her spare time, she enjoys reading and traveling.

James G. Kelley

From great grandparents who homesteaded on Drummond Island in the 1800's, James has always called Drummond home except for one year in 1976/77 when he helped build the Alaskan Pipeline. He has traveled extensively in the National Park system, visiting 117 National Parks, Monuments, and Historic Sites. For over 10 years, James worked as a professional photographer. Today, he and his wife own multiple businesses in Northern Michigan. In his spare time, he writes novels with his daughter, D. Ann. James is a member of the DeTour Reef Light Preservation Society, Great Lakes Shipwreck Historical Society, and National Writers Association.